REYN

VOLUME 1

WARDEN OF FATE

WRITTEN by KEL SYMONS
ART by NATE STOCKMAN
COLORS by PAUL LITTLE
LETTERING AND DESIGN by PAT BROSSEAU
LOGO DESIGNER TIM DANIEL

FOLLOW US ON TWITTER: @KELSYMONS @STOCKMANNATE @DROOG811
LIKE US ON WWW.FACEBOOK.COM/REYNWARDENOFFATE
EMAIL QUESTIONS AND COMMENTS TO REYNCOMIC@GMAIL.COM
OR WRITE TO: REYN C/O KEL SYMONS
P.O. BOX 481301 LOS ANGELES, CA 90048
SEND A SASE AND WE'LL SEND YOU BACK A REYN STICKER

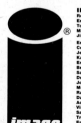

IMAGE COMICS, INC.
Robert Kirkman – Chief Operating Officer
Erik Larsen – Chief Financial Officer
Todd McFarlane – President
Marc Silvestri – Chief Executive Officer
Jim Valentino – Vice-President

Eric Stephenson – Publisher
Corey Murphy – Director of Sales
Jeremy Sullivan – Director of Digital Sales
Kat Salazar – Director of PR & Marketing
Emily Miller – Director of Operations
Branwyn Bigglestone – Senior Accounts Manager
Sarah Mello – Accounts Manager
Drew Gill – Art Director
Jonathan Chan – Production Manager
Meredith Wallace – Print Manager
Randy Okamura – Marketing Production Designer
David Brothers – Content Manager
Addison Duke – Production Artist
Vincent Kukua – Production Artist
Sasha Head – Production Artist
Tricia Ramos – Production Artist
Emilio Bautista – Sales Assistant
Jessica Ambriz – Administrative Assistant
IMAGECOMICS.COM

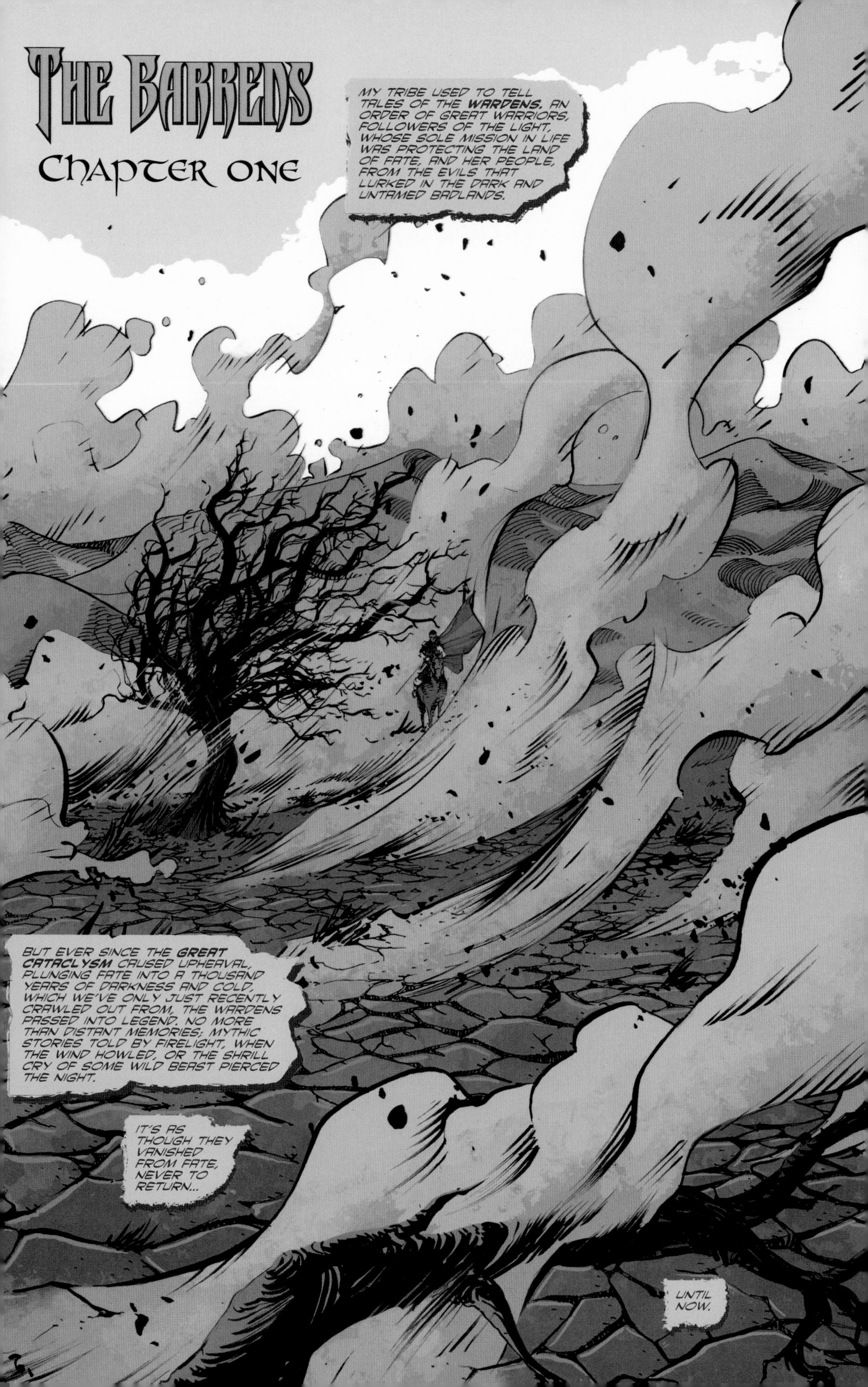
THE BARRENS
CHAPTER ONE
MY TRIBE USED TO TELL TALES OF THE WARDENS. AN ORDER OF GREAT WARRIORS, FOLLOWERS OF THE LIGHT, WHOSE SOLE MISSION IN LIFE WAS PROTECTING THE LAND OF FATE, AND HER PEOPLE, FROM THE EVILS THAT LURKED IN THE DARK AND UNTAMED BADLANDS.
BUT EVER SINCE THE GREAT CATACLYSM CAUSED UPHEAVAL, PLUNGING FATE INTO A THOUSAND YEARS OF DARKNESS AND COLD, WHICH WE'VE ONLY JUST RECENTLY CRAWLED OUT FROM, THE WARDENS PASSED INTO LEGEND. NO MORE THAN DISTANT MEMORIES; MYTHIC STORIES TOLD BY FIRELIGHT, WHEN THE WIND HOWLED, OR THE SHRILL CRY OF SOME WILD BEAST PIERCED THE NIGHT.
IT'S AS THOUGH THEY VANISHED FROM FATE, NEVER TO RETURN...
UNTIL NOW.

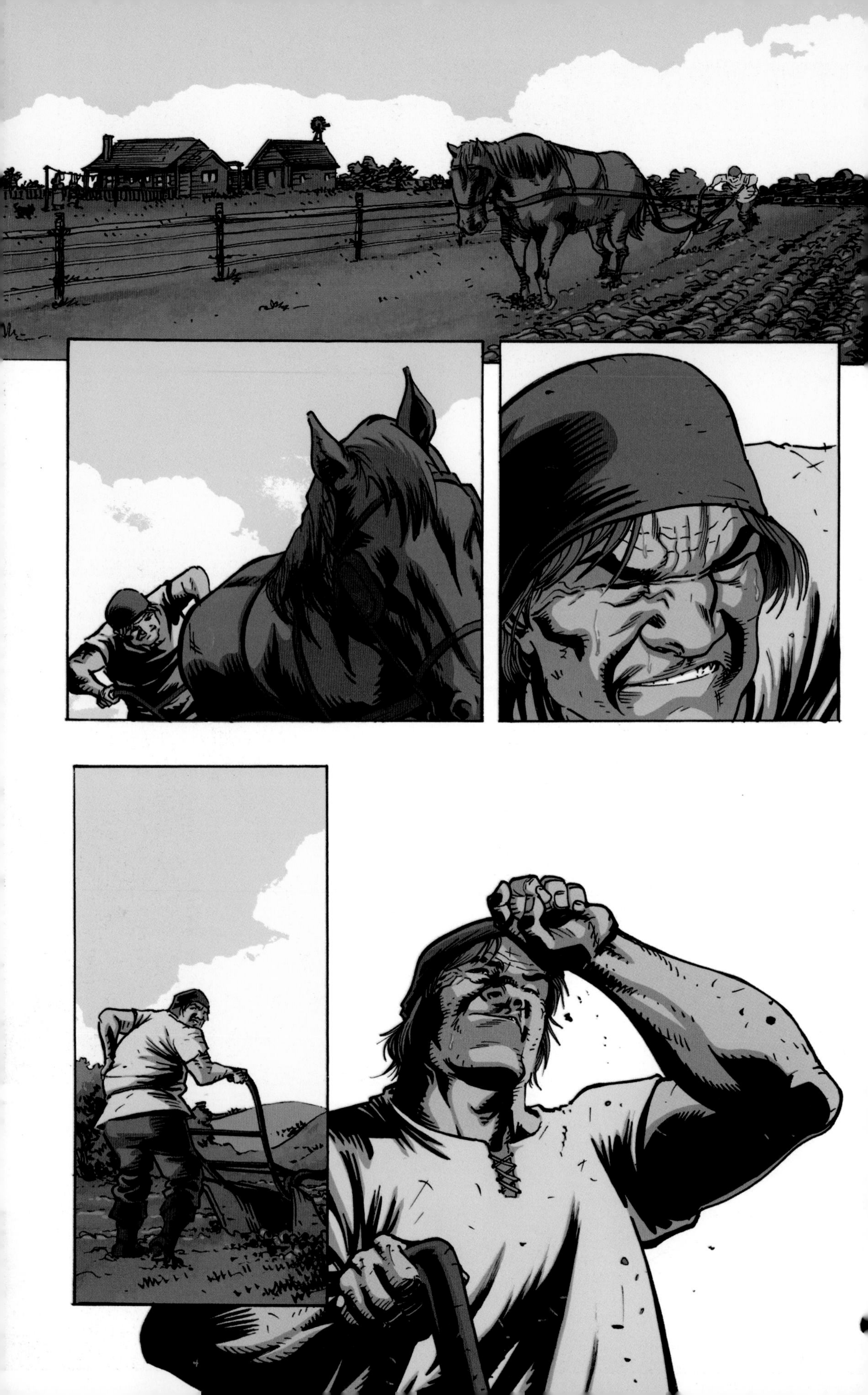

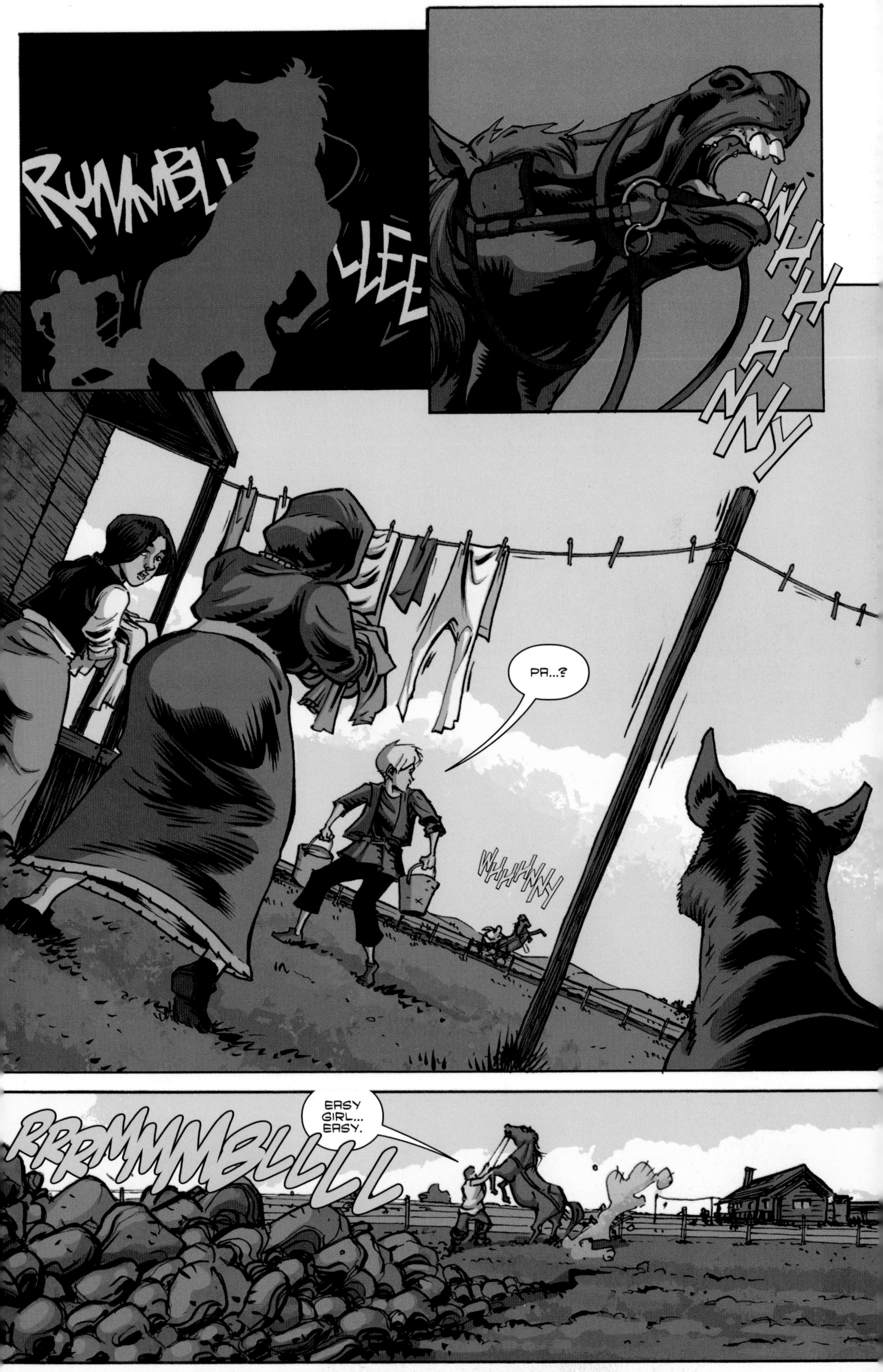
RUMMBLLLEE
WHHHHNNNY
PA...?
WHHHHNNNY
RRRMMMBLLLLL
EASY GIRL... EASY.

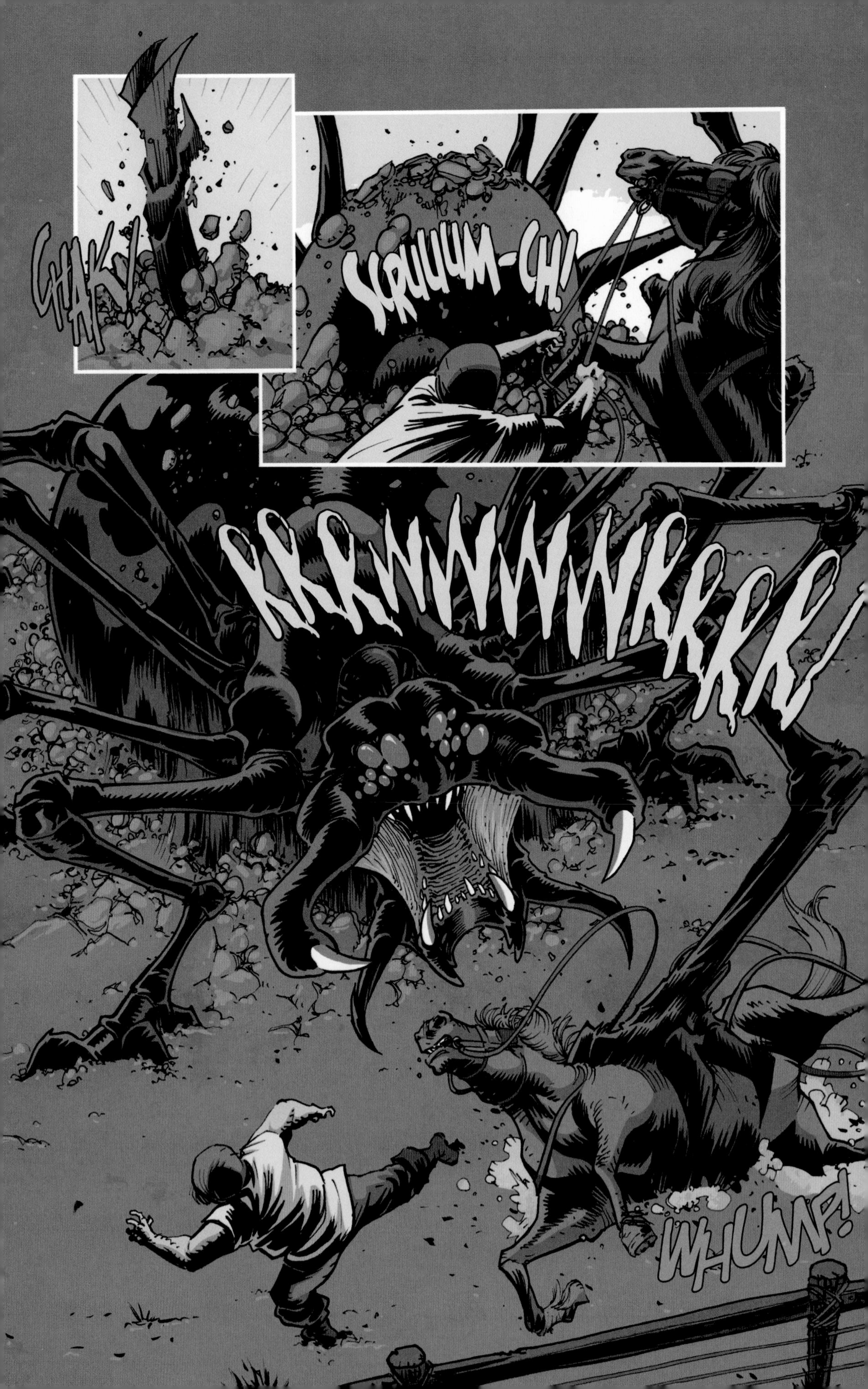
CHAK!
SCRUUUM-CH!
RRRWWWWWRRRR!
WHUMP!

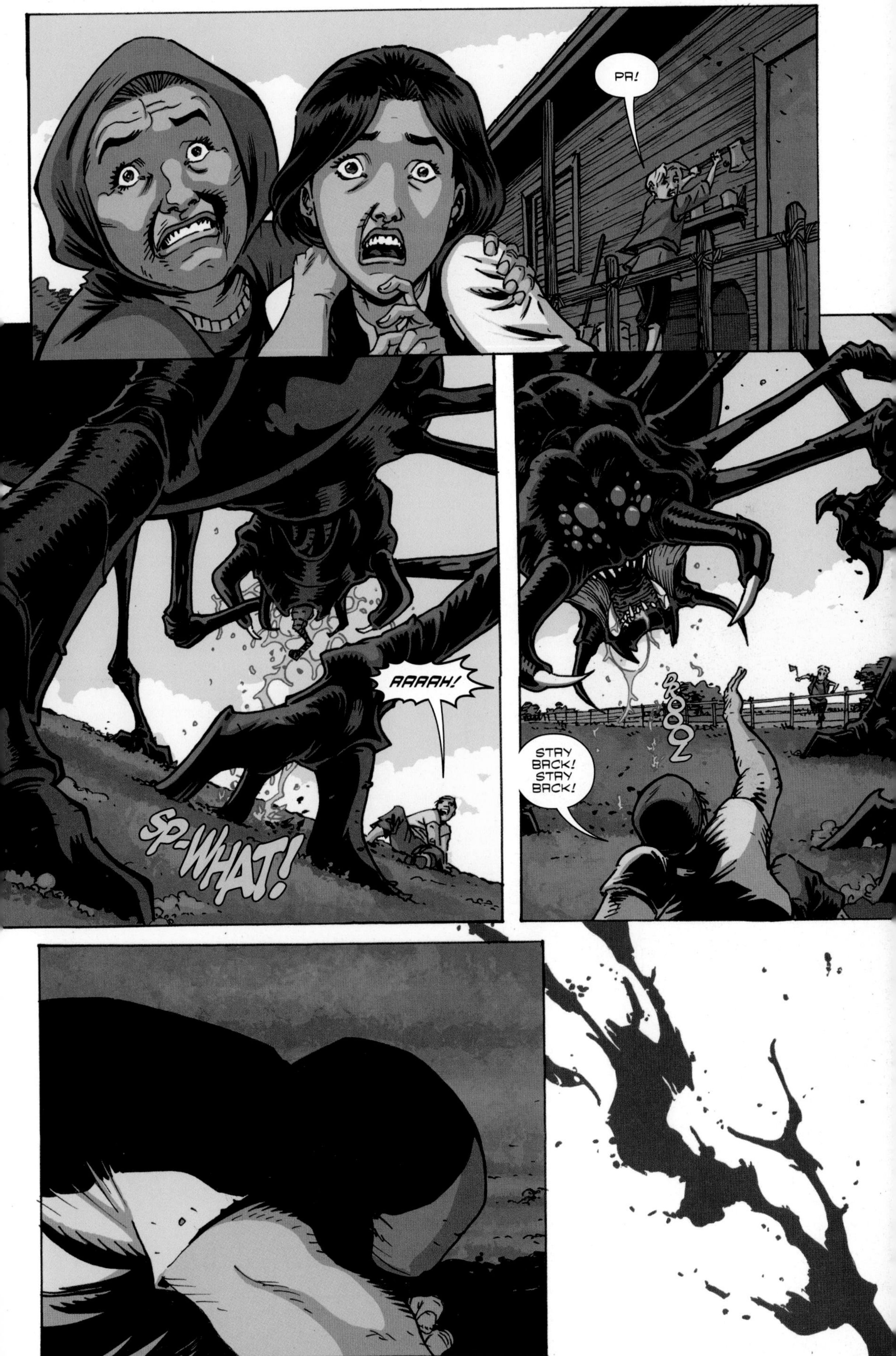
PA!
SP-WHAT!
AAAAH!
BROOOZ
STAY BACK! STAY BACK!

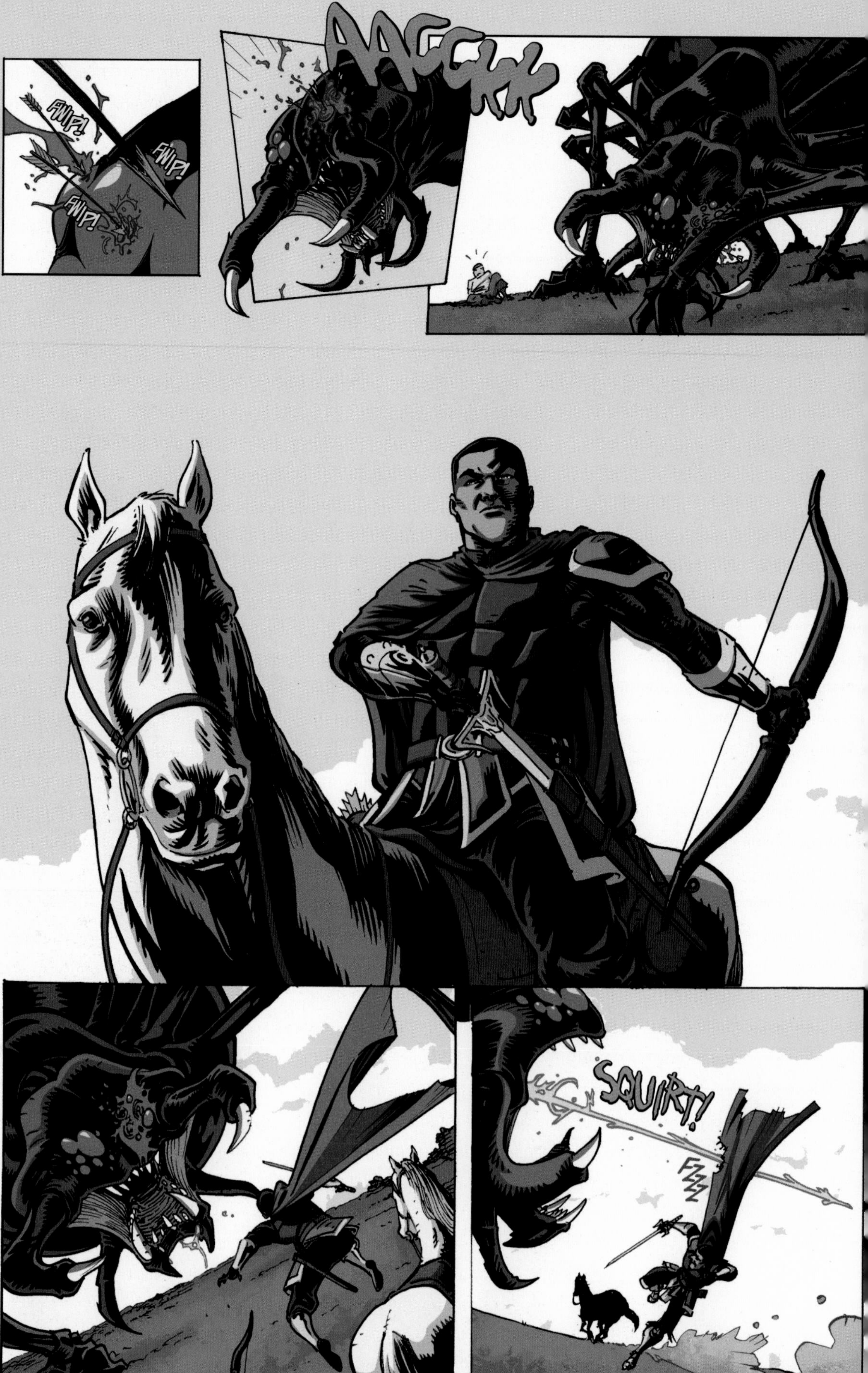
FWIP!
FWIP!
FWIP!
AACGKK
SQUIRT!
FZZZ

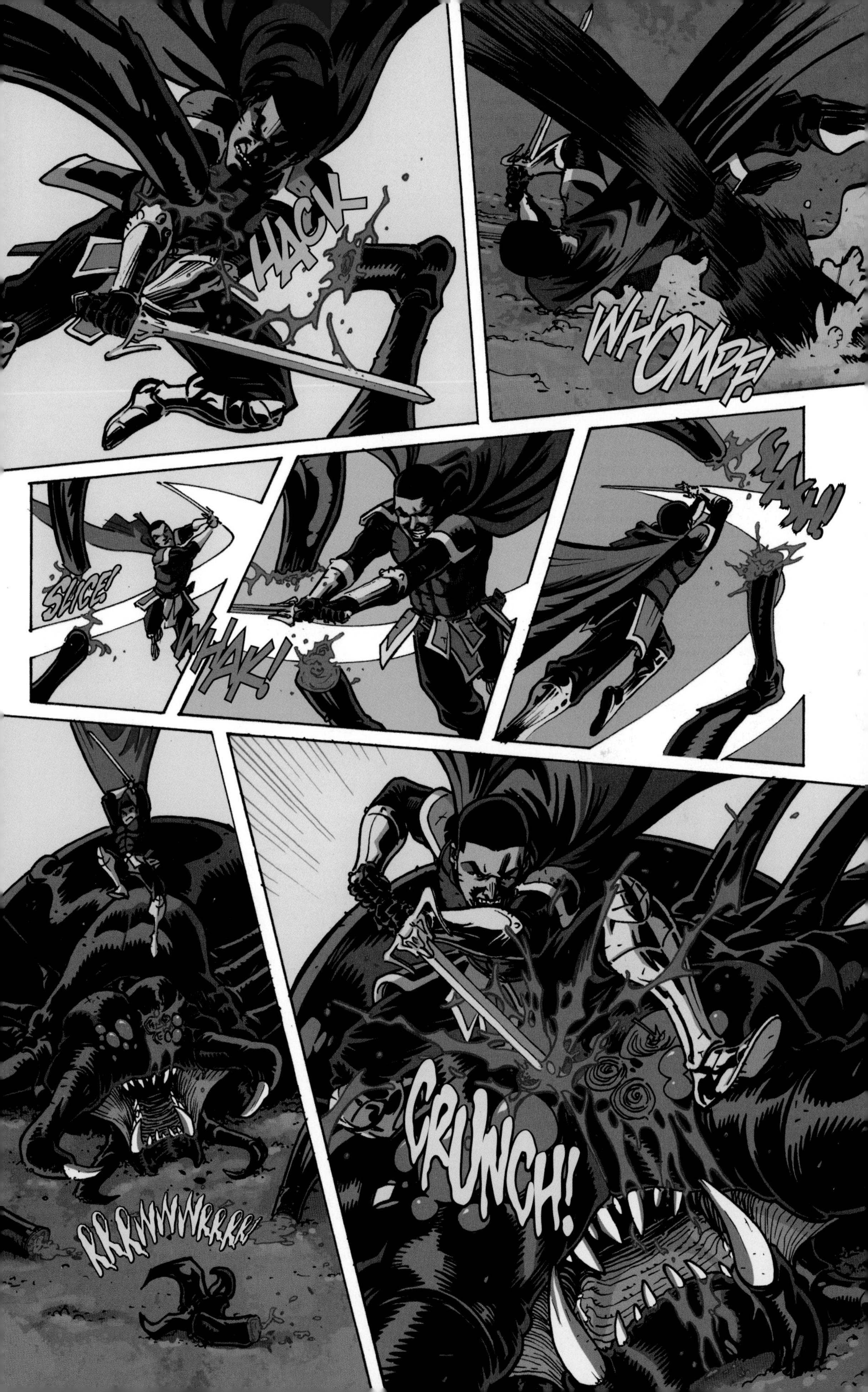
HACK
WHOMPF!
SLICE!
WHAK!
SLASH!
RRRNNNWRRRR
CRUNCH!

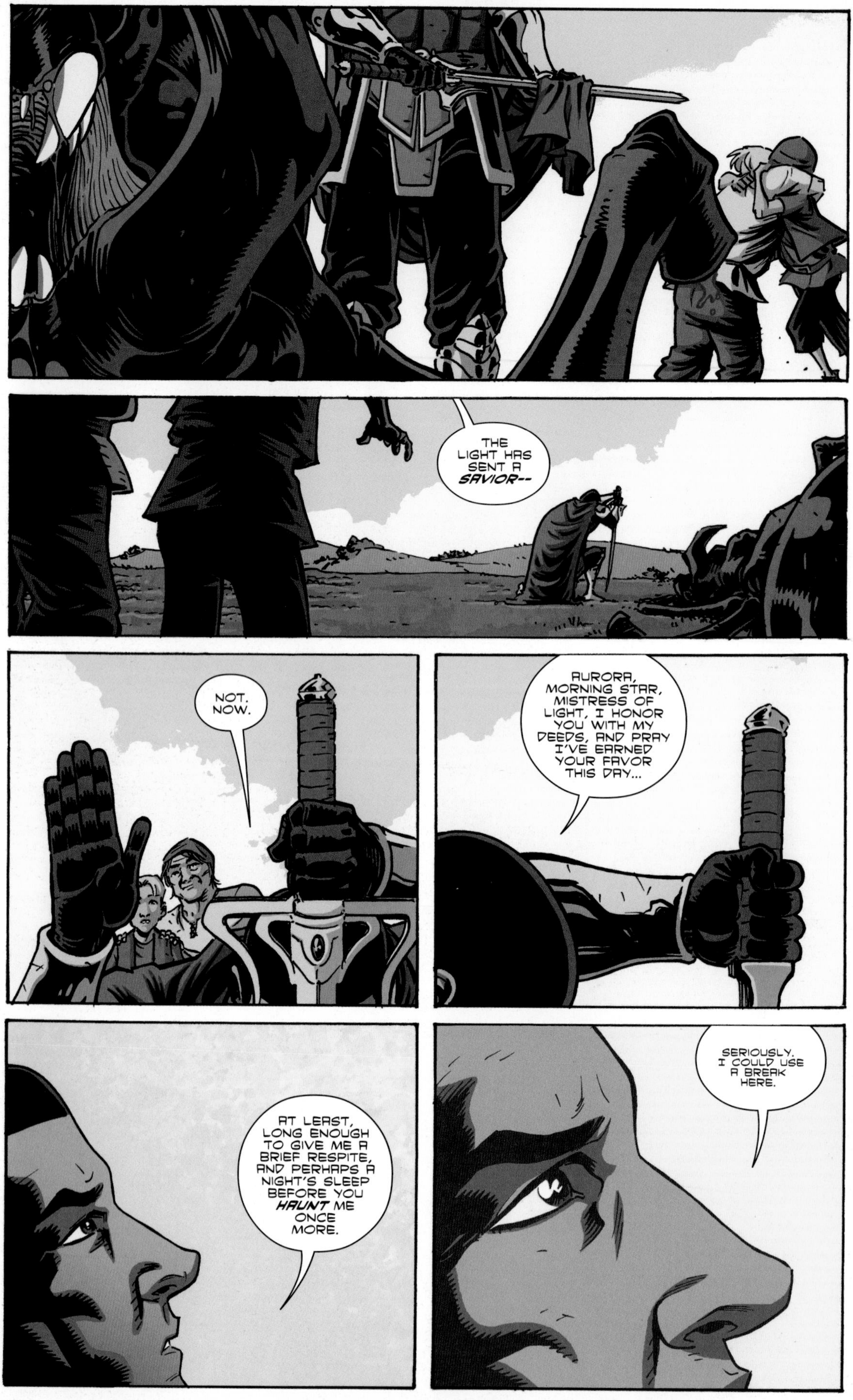
THE LIGHT HAS SENT A *SAVIOR--*
NOT. NOW.
AURORA, MORNING STAR, MISTRESS OF LIGHT, I HONOR YOU WITH MY DEEDS, AND PRAY I'VE EARNED YOUR FAVOR THIS DAY...
AT LEAST, LONG ENOUGH TO GIVE ME A BRIEF RESPITE, AND PERHAPS A NIGHT'S SLEEP BEFORE YOU *HAUNT* ME ONCE MORE.
SERIOUSLY. I COULD USE A BREAK HERE.

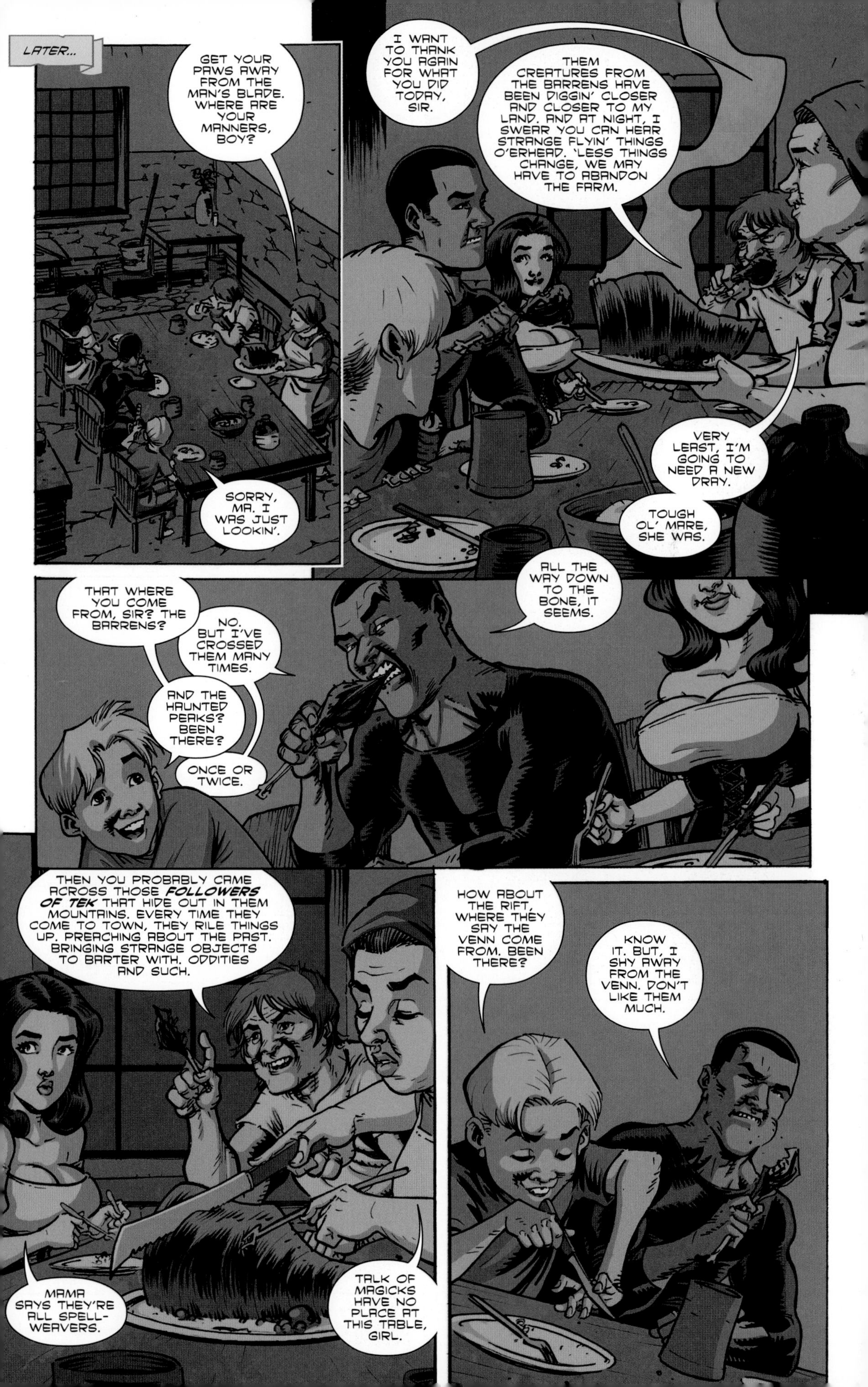
LATER...
GET YOUR PAWS AWAY FROM THE MAN'S BLADE. WHERE ARE YOUR MANNERS, BOY?
SORRY, MA. I WAS JUST LOOKIN'.
I WANT TO THANK YOU AGAIN FOR WHAT YOU DID TODAY, SIR.
THEM CREATURES FROM THE BARRENS HAVE BEEN DIGGIN' CLOSER AND CLOSER TO MY LAND. AND AT NIGHT, I SWEAR YOU CAN HEAR STRANGE FLYIN' THINGS O'ERHEAD. 'LESS THINGS CHANGE, WE MAY HAVE TO ABANDON THE FARM.
VERY LEAST, I'M GOING TO NEED A NEW DRAY.
TOUGH OL' MARE, SHE WAS.
ALL THE WAY DOWN TO THE BONE, IT SEEMS.
THAT WHERE YOU COME FROM, SIR? THE BARRENS?
NO. BUT I'VE CROSSED THEM MANY TIMES.
AND THE HAUNTED PEAKS? BEEN THERE?
ONCE OR TWICE.
THEN YOU PROBABLY CAME ACROSS THOSE FOLLOWERS OF TEK THAT HIDE OUT IN THEM MOUNTAINS. EVERY TIME THEY COME TO TOWN, THEY RILE THINGS UP. PREACHING ABOUT THE PAST. BRINGING STRANGE OBJECTS TO BARTER WITH. ODDITIES AND SUCH.
MAMA SAYS THEY'RE ALL SPELL-WEAVERS.
TALK OF MAGICKS HAVE NO PLACE AT THIS TABLE, GIRL.
HOW ABOUT THE RIFT, WHERE THEY SAY THE VENN COME FROM. BEEN THERE?
KNOW IT. BUT, I SHY AWAY FROM THE VENN. DON'T LIKE THEM MUCH.

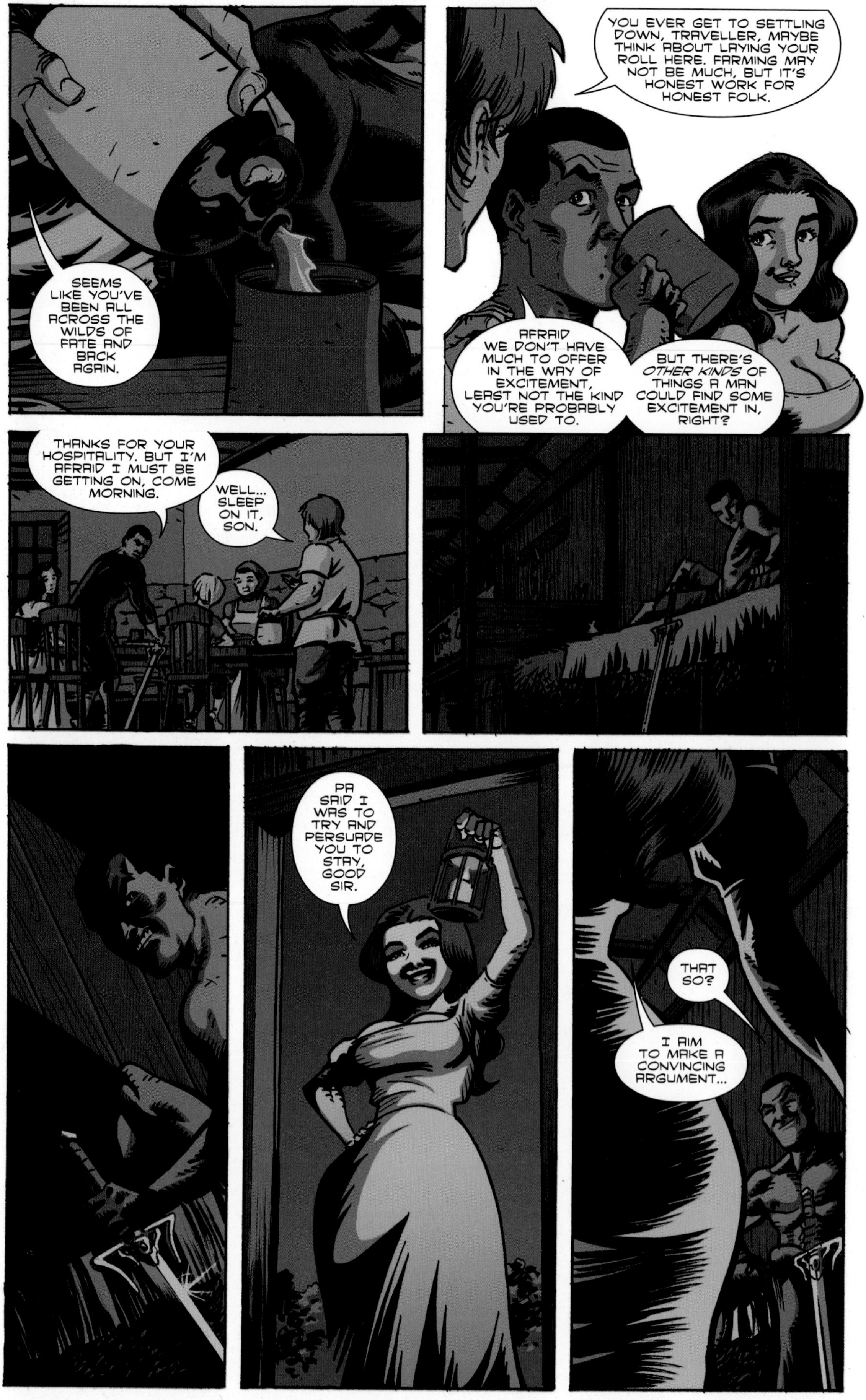
SEEMS LIKE YOU'VE BEEN ALL ACROSS THE WILDS OF FATE AND BACK AGAIN.
YOU EVER GET TO SETTLING DOWN, TRAVELLER, MAYBE THINK ABOUT LAYING YOUR ROLL HERE. FARMING MAY NOT BE MUCH, BUT IT'S HONEST WORK FOR HONEST FOLK.
AFRAID WE DON'T HAVE MUCH TO OFFER IN THE WAY OF EXCITEMENT, LEAST NOT THE KIND YOU'RE PROBABLY USED TO.
BUT THERE'S *OTHER KINDS* OF THINGS A MAN COULD FIND SOME EXCITEMENT IN, RIGHT?
THANKS FOR YOUR HOSPITALITY. BUT I'M AFRAID I MUST BE GETTING ON, COME MORNING.
WELL... SLEEP ON IT, SON.
PA SAID I WAS TO TRY AND PERSUADE YOU TO STAY, GOOD SIR.
THAT SO?
I AIM TO MAKE A CONVINCING ARGUMENT...

THE LAND OF FATE

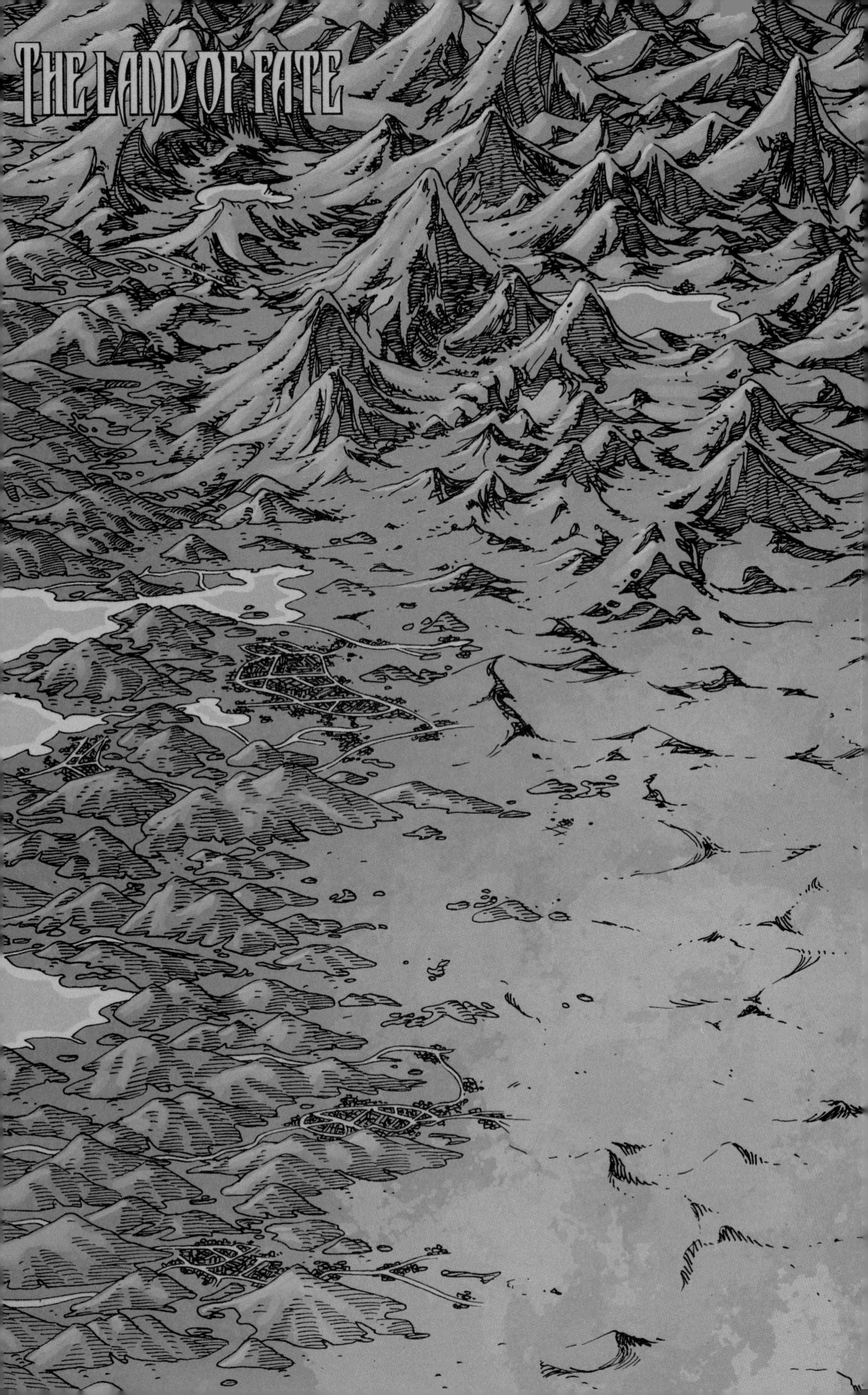

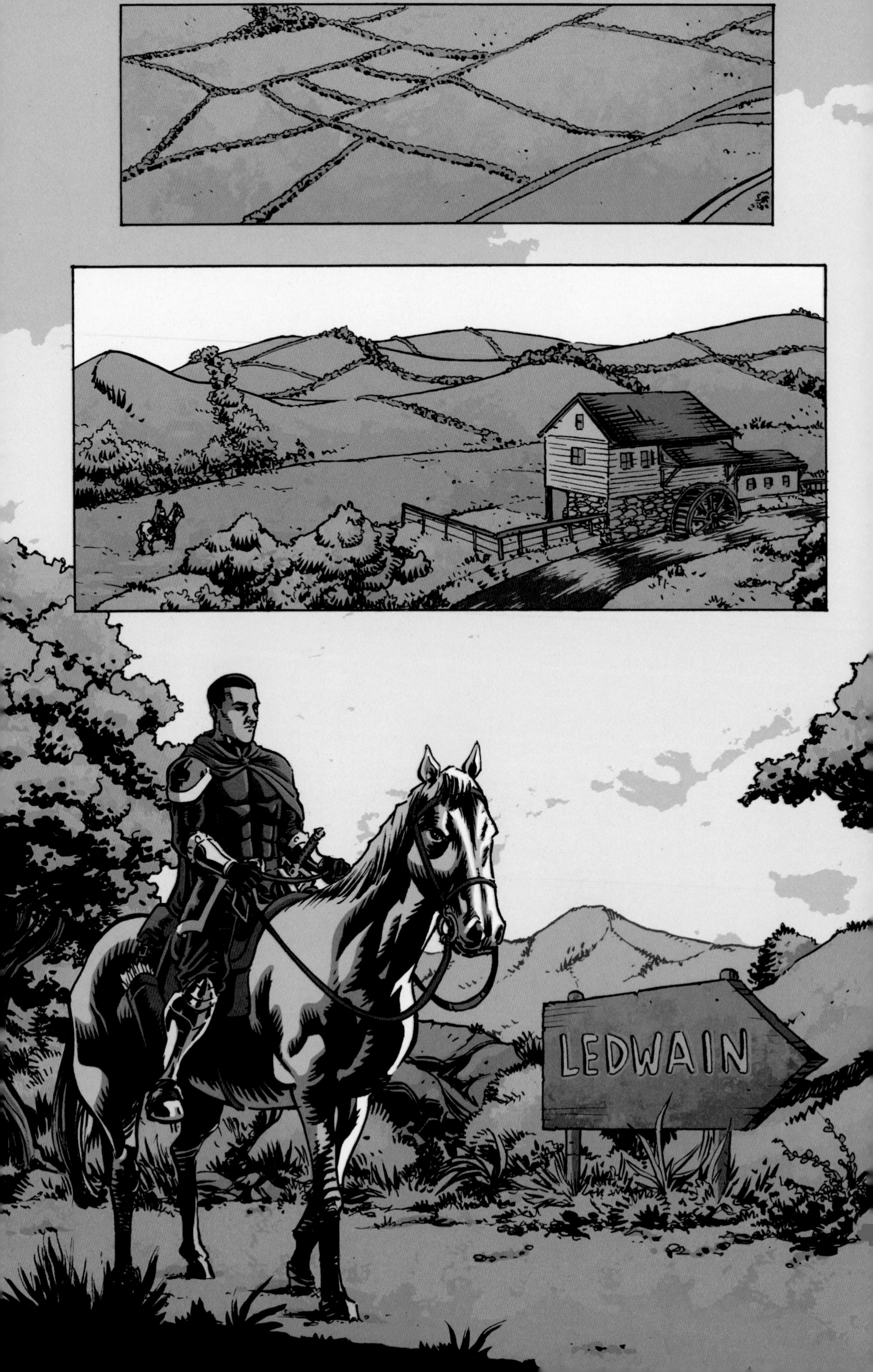
LEDWAIN

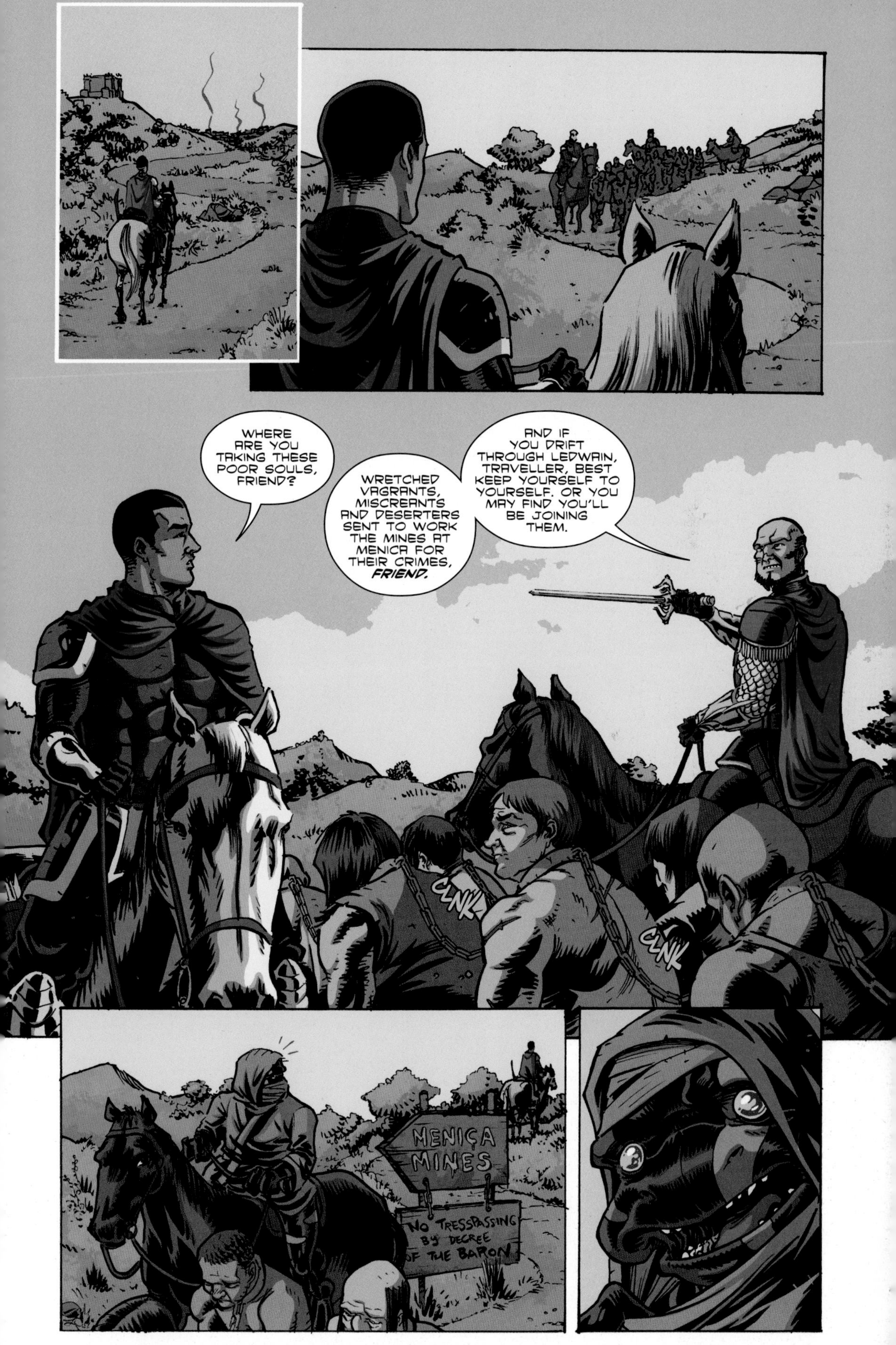
WHERE ARE YOU TAKING THESE POOR SOULS, FRIEND?
WRETCHED VAGRANTS, MISCREANTS AND DESERTERS SENT TO WORK THE MINES AT MENICA FOR THEIR CRIMES, FRIEND.
AND IF YOU DRIFT THROUGH LEDWAIN, TRAVELLER, BEST KEEP YOURSELF TO YOURSELF. OR YOU MAY FIND YOU'LL BE JOINING THEM.
CLNK
CLNK
MENIÇA MINES
NO TRESSPASSING BY DECREE OF THE BARON

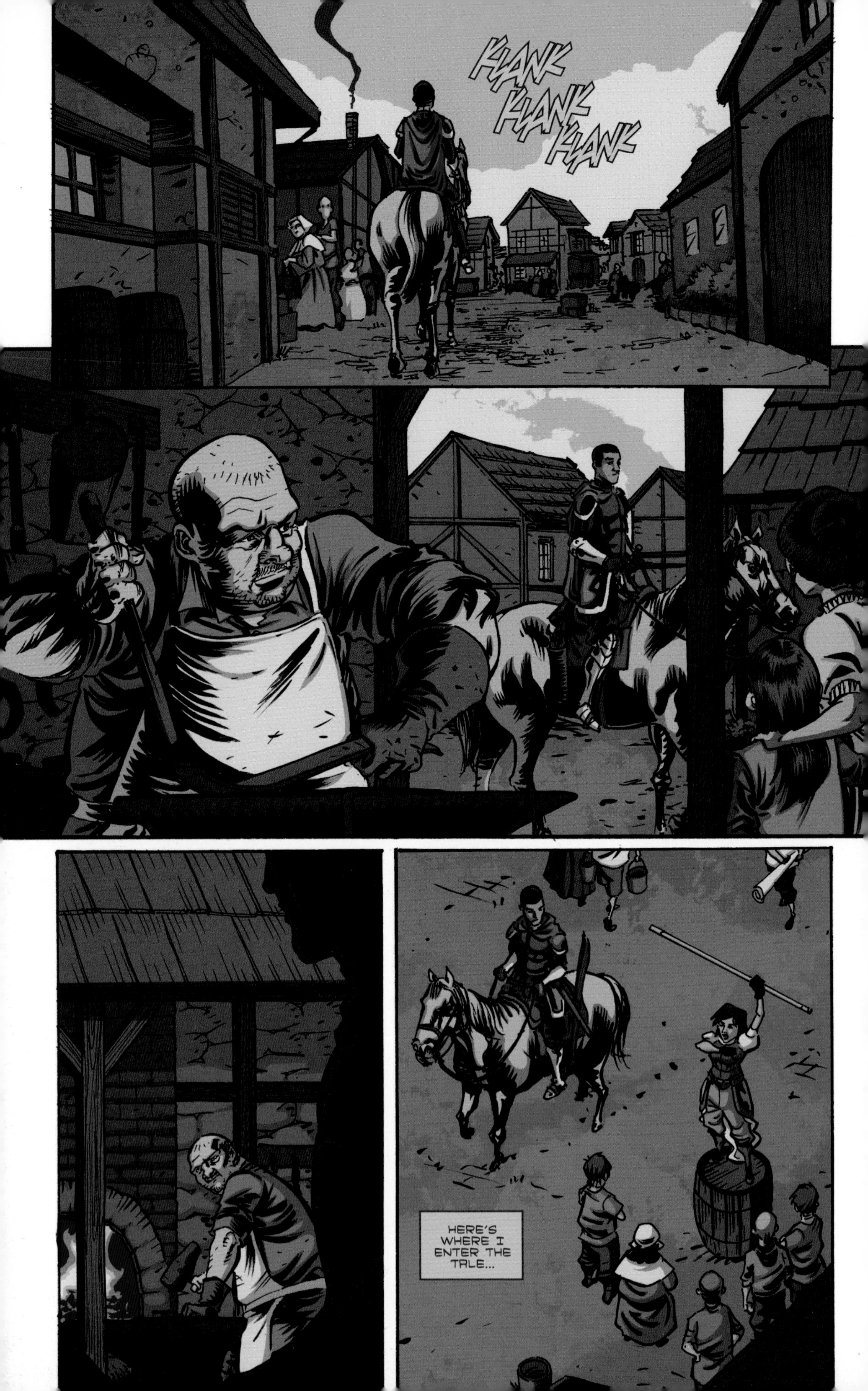
KLANK
KLANK
KLANK
HERE'S WHERE I ENTER THE TALE...

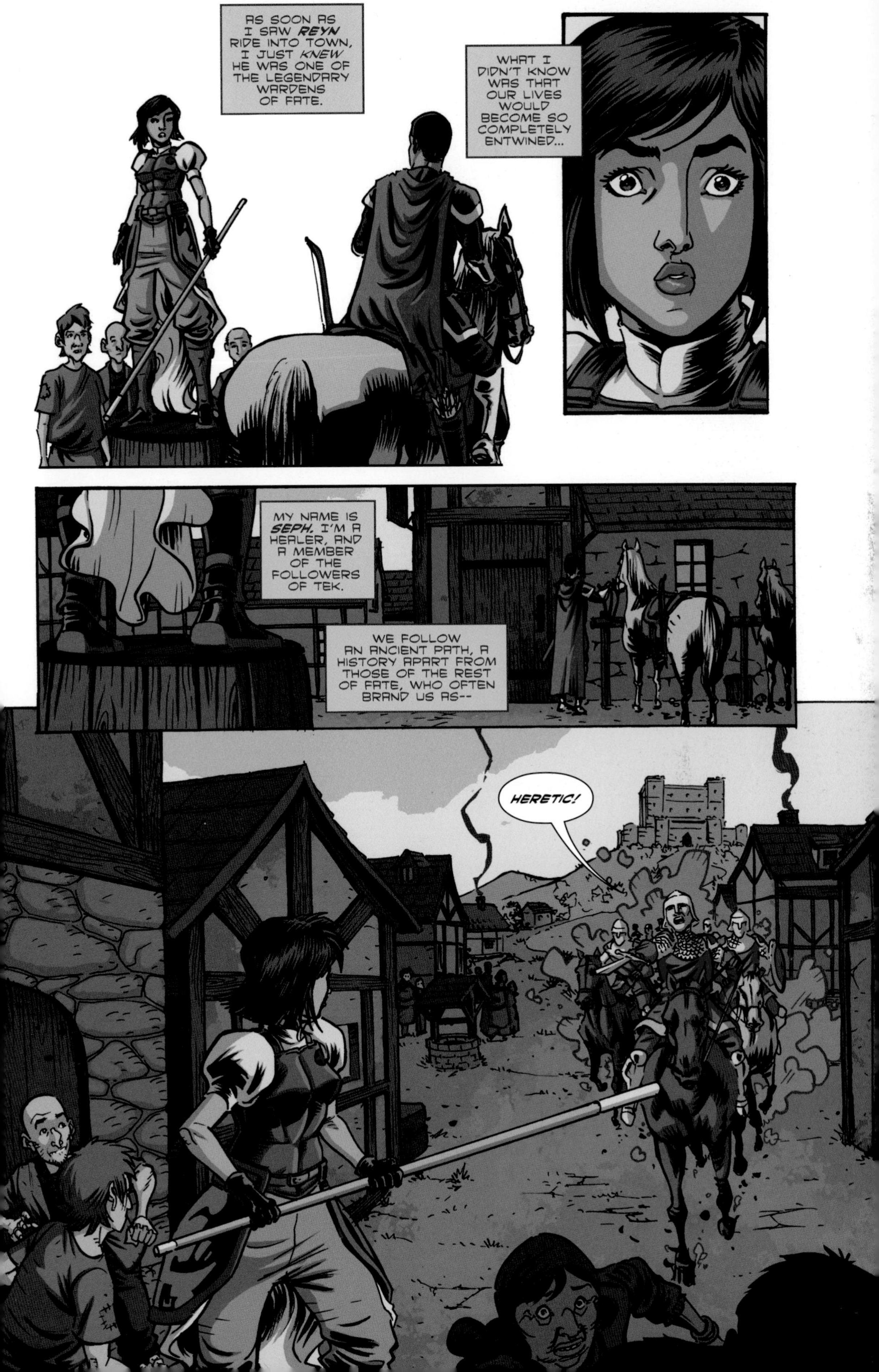
AS SOON AS I SAW REYN RIDE INTO TOWN, I JUST KNEW HE WAS ONE OF THE LEGENDARY WARDENS OF FATE.
WHAT I DIDN'T KNOW WAS THAT OUR LIVES WOULD BECOME SO COMPLETELY ENTWINED...
MY NAME IS SEPH. I'M A HEALER, AND A MEMBER OF THE FOLLOWERS OF TEK.
WE FOLLOW AN ANCIENT PATH, A HISTORY APART FROM THOSE OF THE REST OF FATE, WHO OFTEN BRAND US AS--
HERETIC!

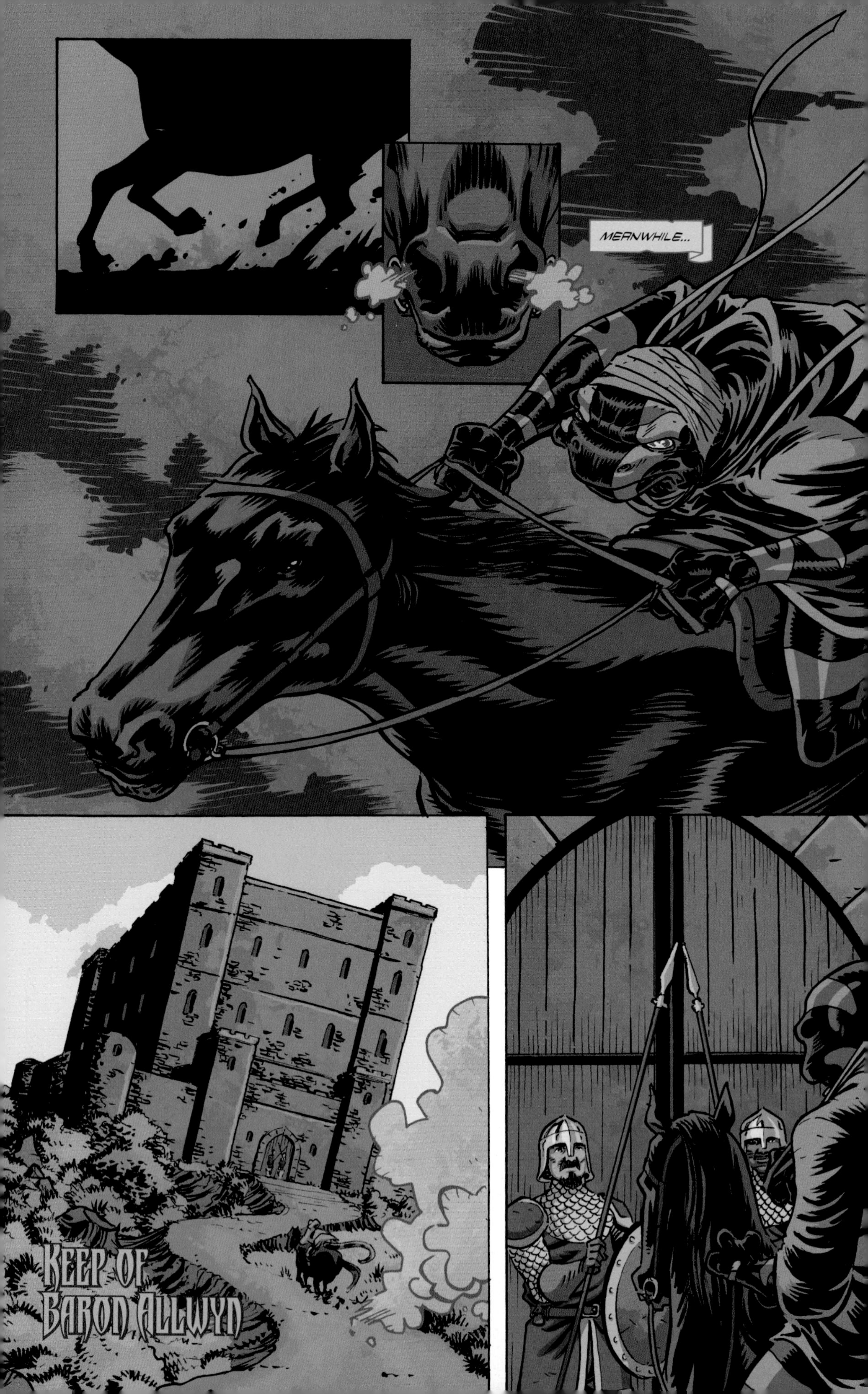
MEANWHILE...
KEEP OF
BARON ALLWYN

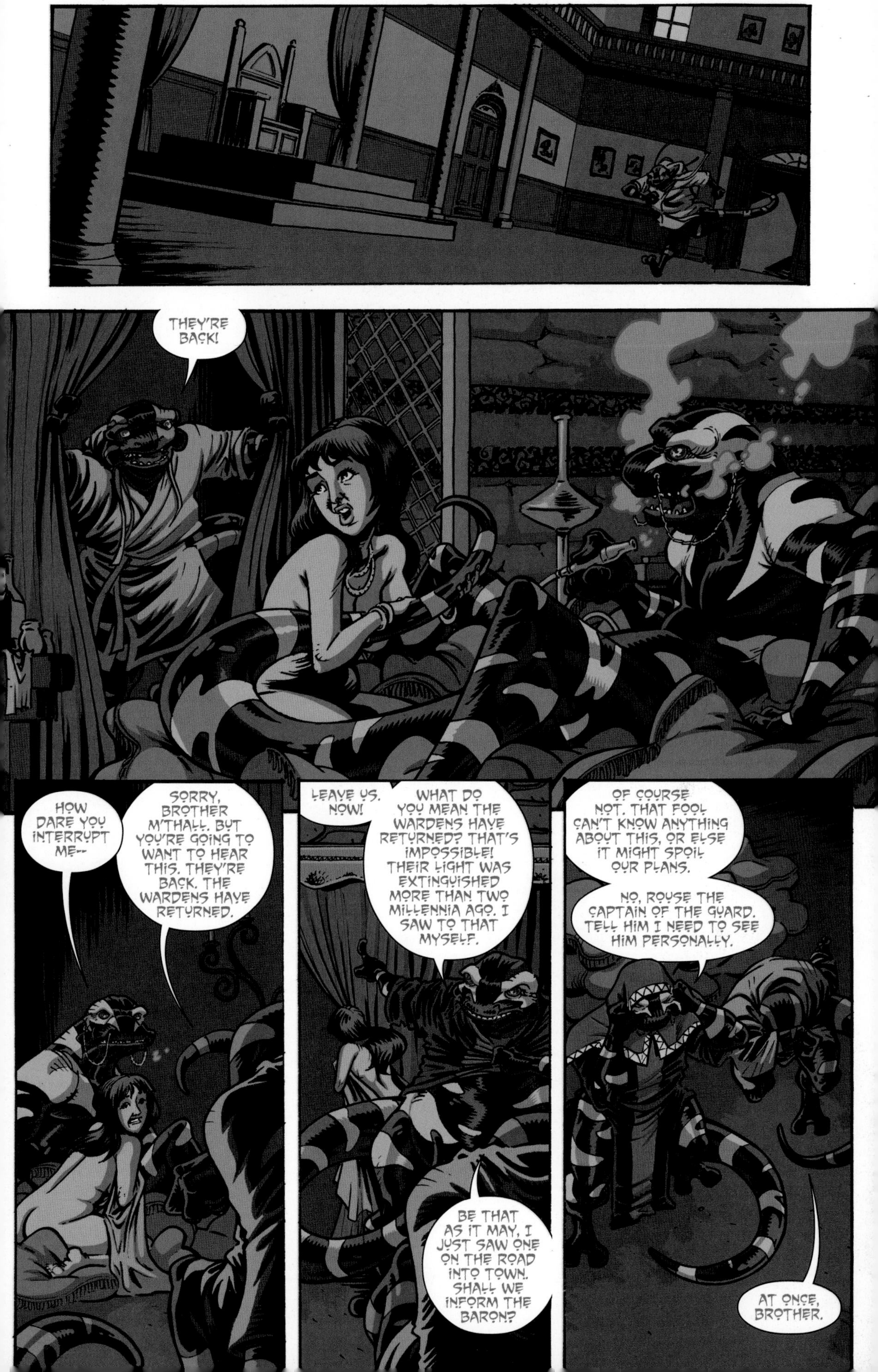
THEY'RE BACK!
HOW DARE YOU INTERRUPT ME--
SORRY, BROTHER M'THALL. BUT YOU'RE GOING TO WANT TO HEAR THIS. THEY'RE BACK. THE WARDENS HAVE RETURNED.
LEAVE US. NOW!
WHAT DO YOU MEAN THE WARDENS HAVE RETURNED? THAT'S IMPOSSIBLE! THEIR LIGHT WAS EXTINGUISHED MORE THAN TWO MILLENNIA AGO. I SAW TO THAT MYSELF.
BE THAT AS IT MAY, I JUST SAW ONE ON THE ROAD INTO TOWN. SHALL WE INFORM THE BARON?
OF COURSE NOT. THAT FOOL CAN'T KNOW ANYTHING ABOUT THIS, OR ELSE IT MIGHT SPOIL OUR PLANS.
NO, ROUSE THE CAPTAIN OF THE GUARD. TELL HIM I NEED TO SEE HIM PERSONALLY.
AT ONCE, BROTHER.

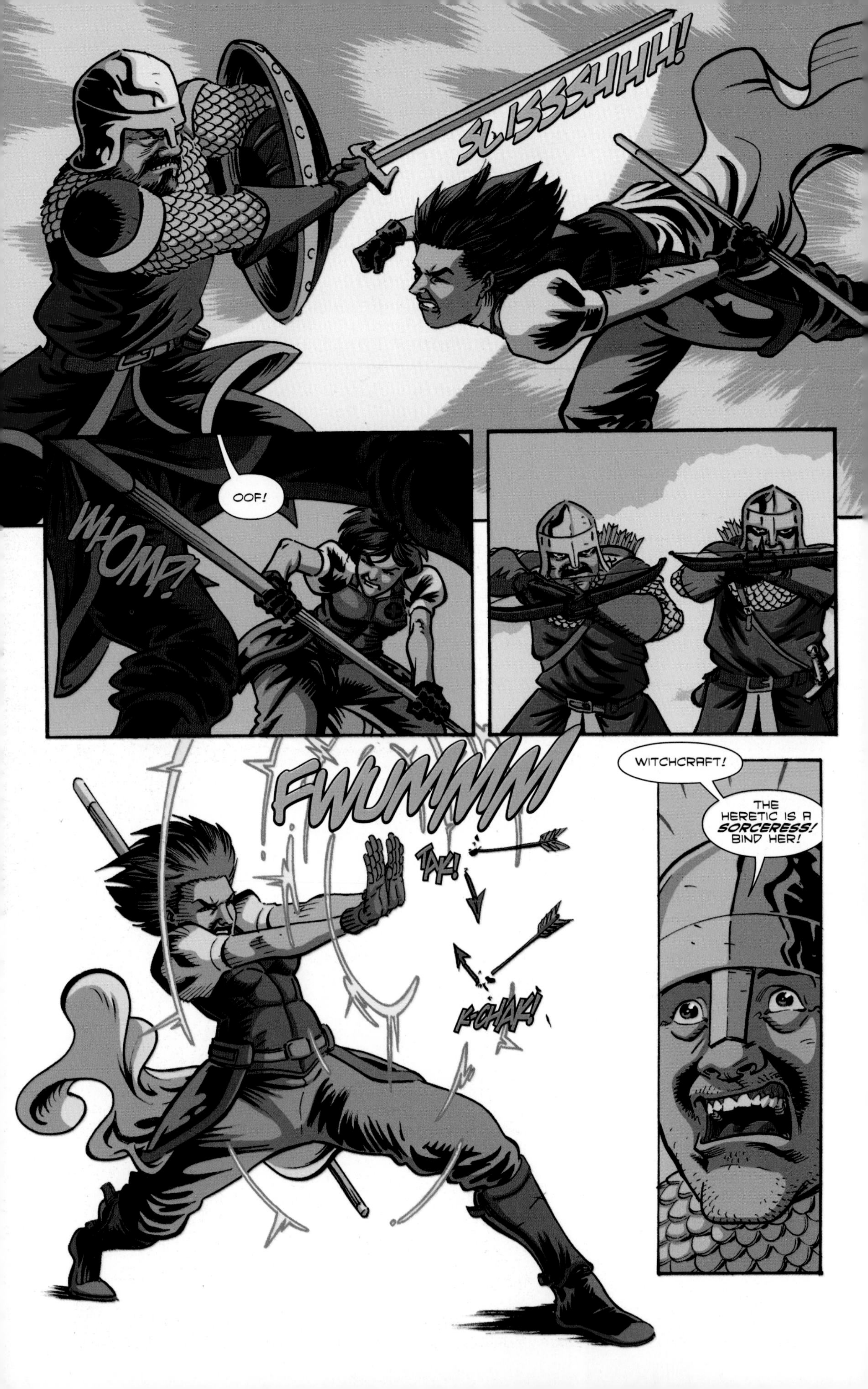
SLISSSHHH!
WHOMP!
OOF!
FWUMMM
TAK!
K-CHAK!
WITCHCRAFT!
THE HERETIC IS A *SORCERESS!* BIND HER!

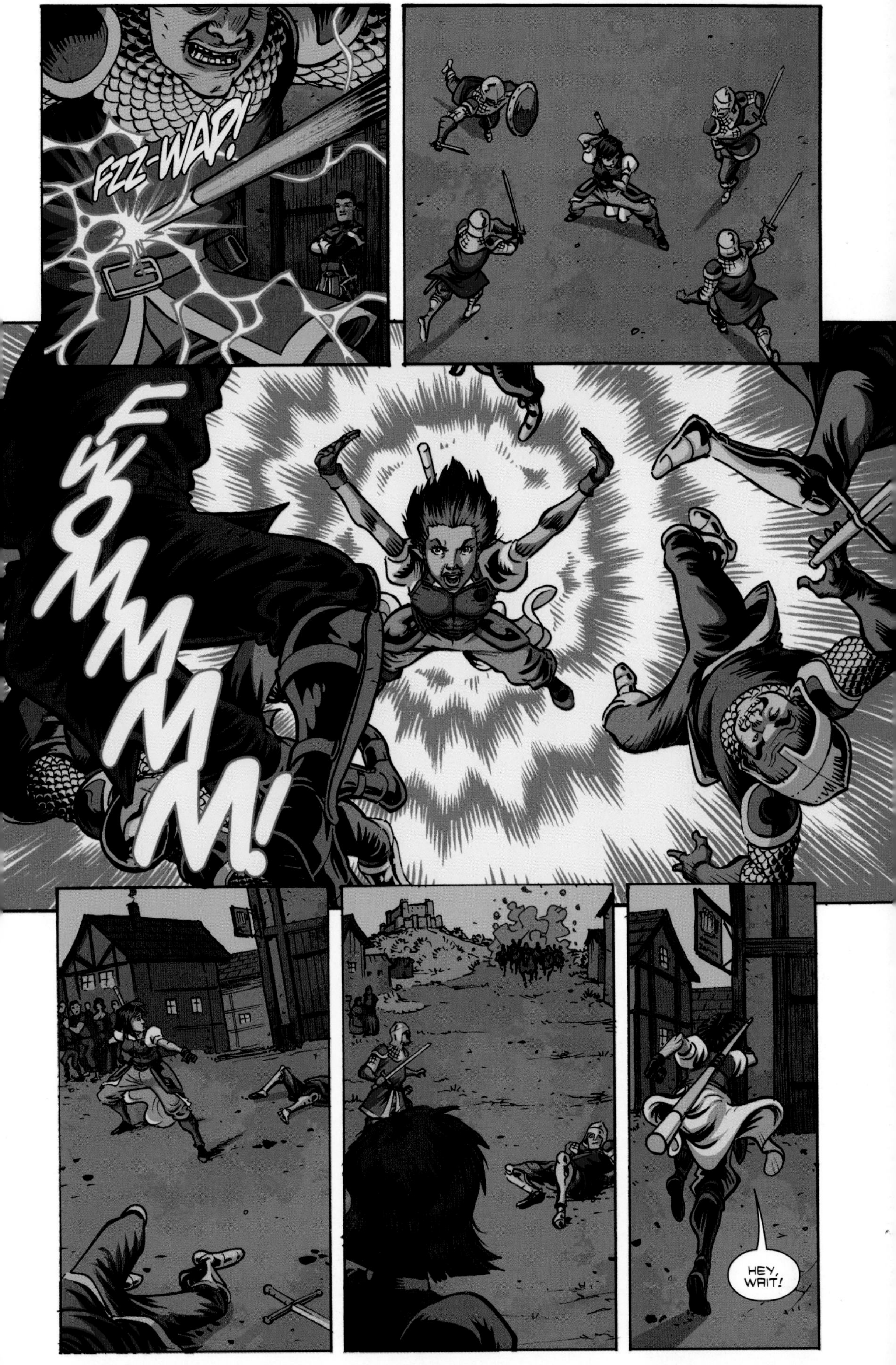
FZZ-WAP!
FWOMMMM!
HEY, WAIT!

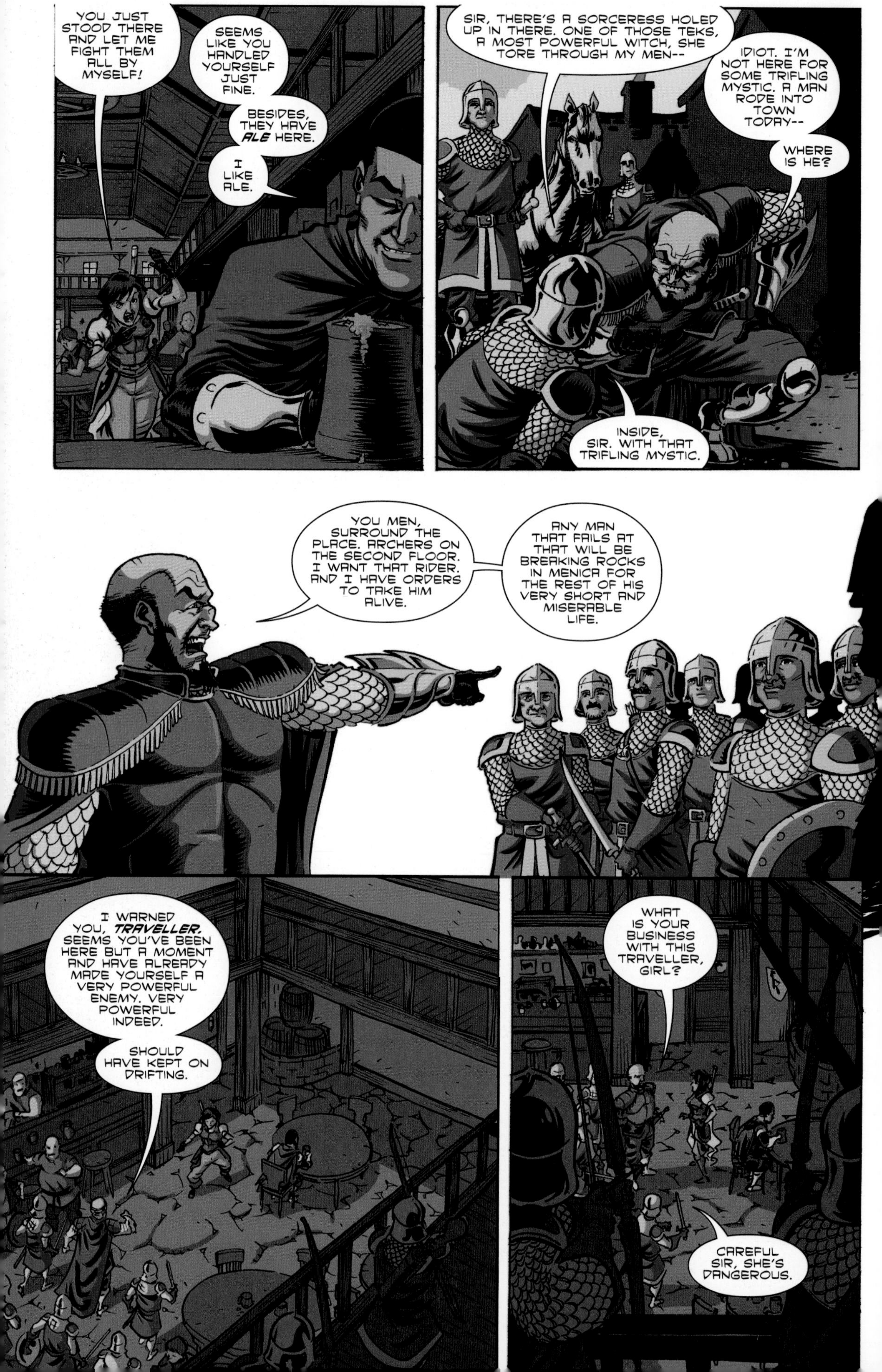
YOU JUST STOOD THERE AND LET ME FIGHT THEM ALL BY MYSELF!
SEEMS LIKE YOU HANDLED YOURSELF JUST FINE.
BESIDES, THEY HAVE *ALE* HERE.
I LIKE ALE.
SIR, THERE'S A SORCERESS HOLED UP IN THERE. ONE OF THOSE TEKS, A MOST POWERFUL WITCH, SHE TORE THROUGH MY MEN--
IDIOT. I'M NOT HERE FOR SOME TRIFLING MYSTIC. A MAN RODE INTO TOWN TODAY--
WHERE IS HE?
INSIDE, SIR. WITH THAT TRIFLING MYSTIC.
YOU MEN, SURROUND THE PLACE. ARCHERS ON THE SECOND FLOOR. I WANT THAT RIDER. AND I HAVE ORDERS TO TAKE HIM ALIVE.
ANY MAN THAT FAILS AT THAT WILL BE BREAKING ROCKS IN MENICA FOR THE REST OF HIS VERY SHORT AND MISERABLE LIFE.
I WARNED YOU, *TRAVELLER.* SEEMS YOU'VE BEEN HERE BUT A MOMENT AND HAVE ALREADY MADE YOURSELF A VERY POWERFUL ENEMY. VERY POWERFUL INDEED.
SHOULD HAVE KEPT ON DRIFTING.
WHAT IS YOUR BUSINESS WITH THIS TRAVELLER, GIRL?
CAREFUL SIR, SHE'S DANGEROUS.

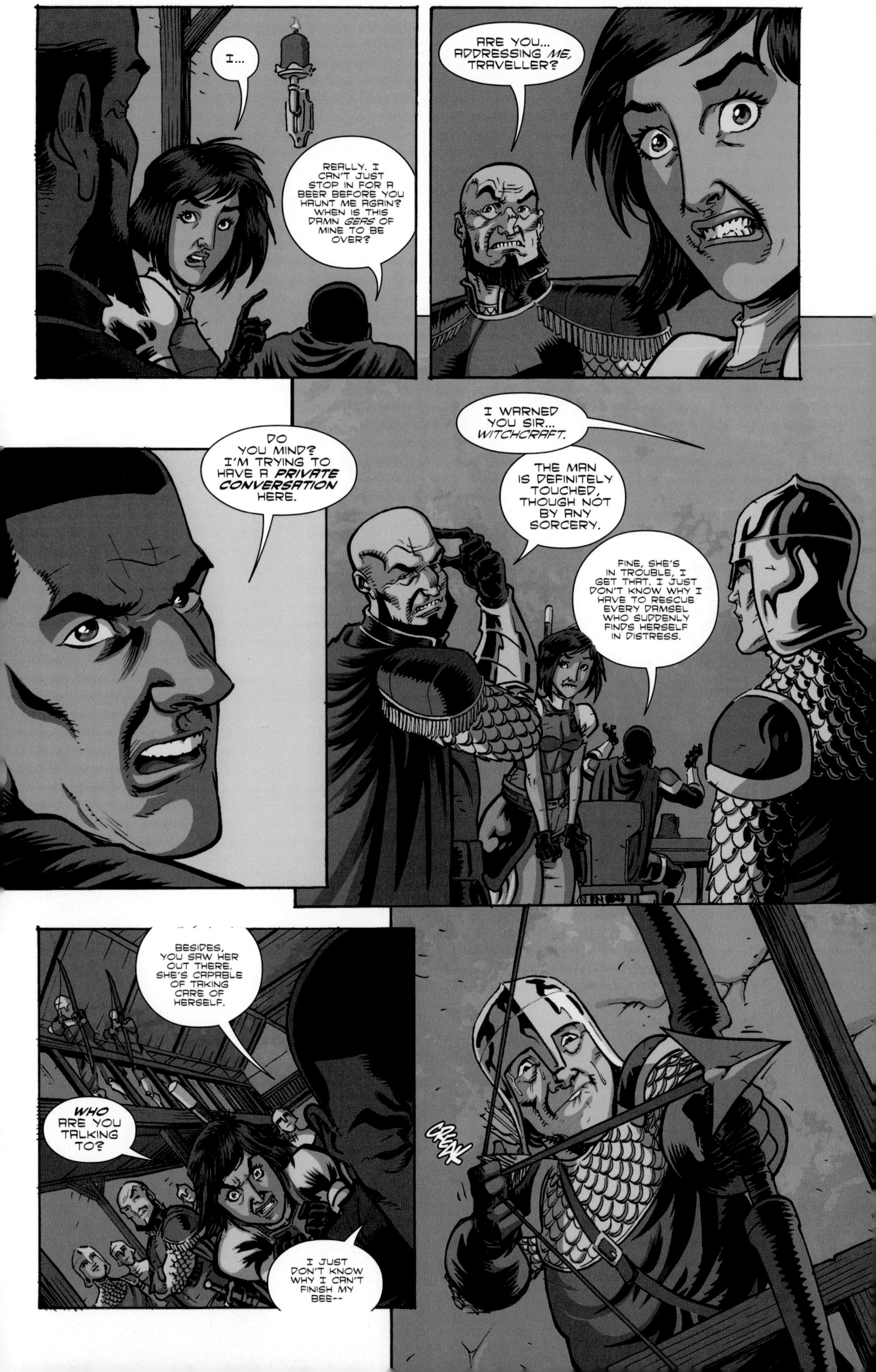
I...
REALLY. I CAN'T JUST STOP IN FOR A BEER BEFORE YOU HAUNT ME AGAIN? WHEN IS THIS DAMN GEAS OF MINE TO BE OVER?
ARE YOU... ADDRESSING ME, TRAVELLER?
DO YOU MIND? I'M TRYING TO HAVE A PRIVATE CONVERSATION HERE.
I WARNED YOU SIR... WITCHCRAFT.
THE MAN IS DEFINITELY TOUCHED, THOUGH NOT BY ANY SORCERY.
FINE, SHE'S IN TROUBLE, I GET THAT. I JUST DON'T KNOW WHY I HAVE TO RESCUE EVERY DAMSEL WHO SUDDENLY FINDS HERSELF IN DISTRESS.
BESIDES, YOU SAW HER OUT THERE. SHE'S CAPABLE OF TAKING CARE OF HERSELF.
WHO ARE YOU TALKING TO?
I JUST DON'T KNOW WHY I CAN'T FINISH MY BEE--
CREAK

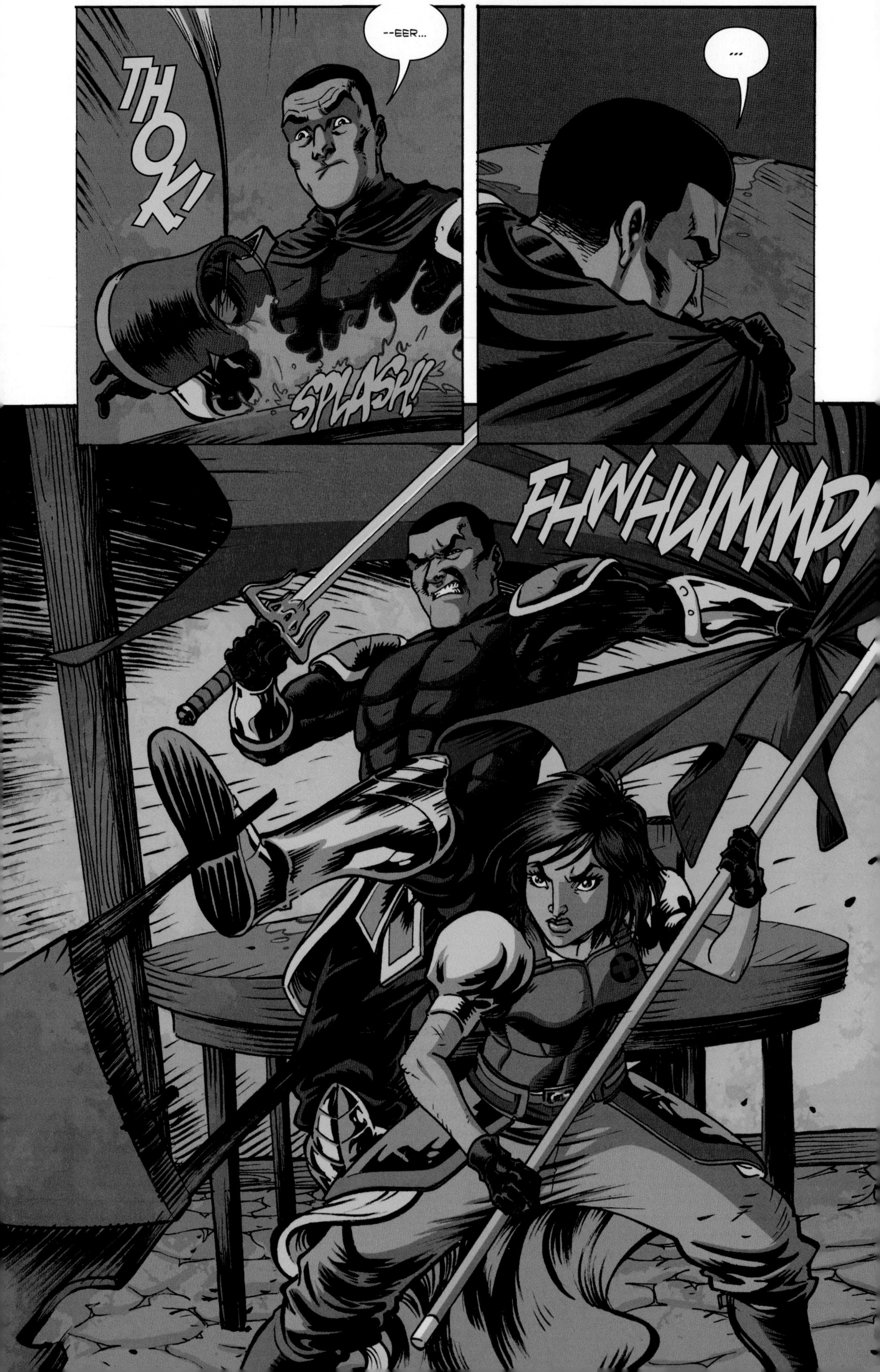
THOK!
--EER...
SPLASH!
...
FHWHUMMP!

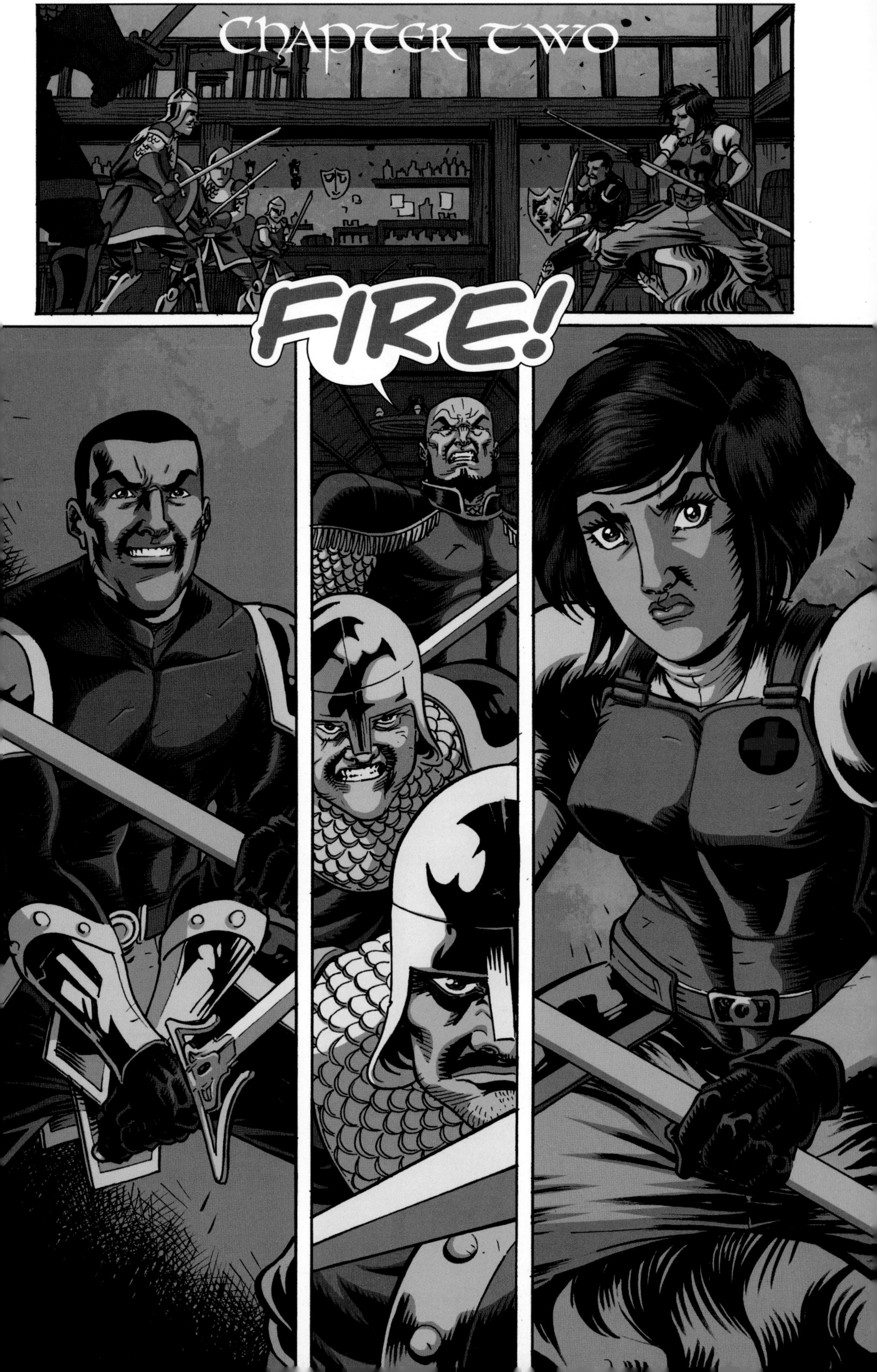
Chapter Two
FIRE!

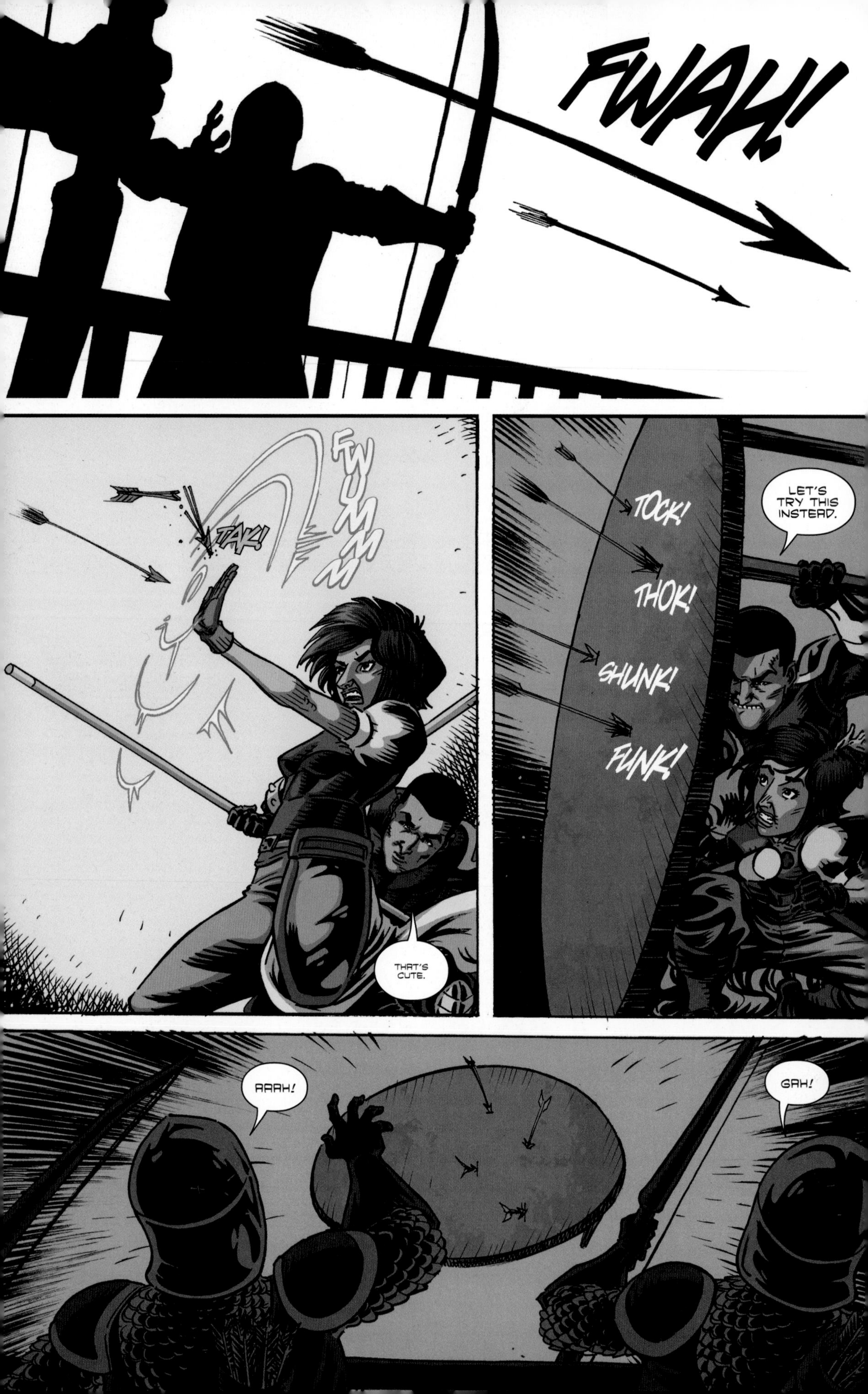
FWAK!
FWUMMM
TAK!
THAT'S CUTE.
TOCK!
THOK!
SHUNK!
FUNK!
LET'S TRY THIS INSTEAD.
AAAH!
GAH!

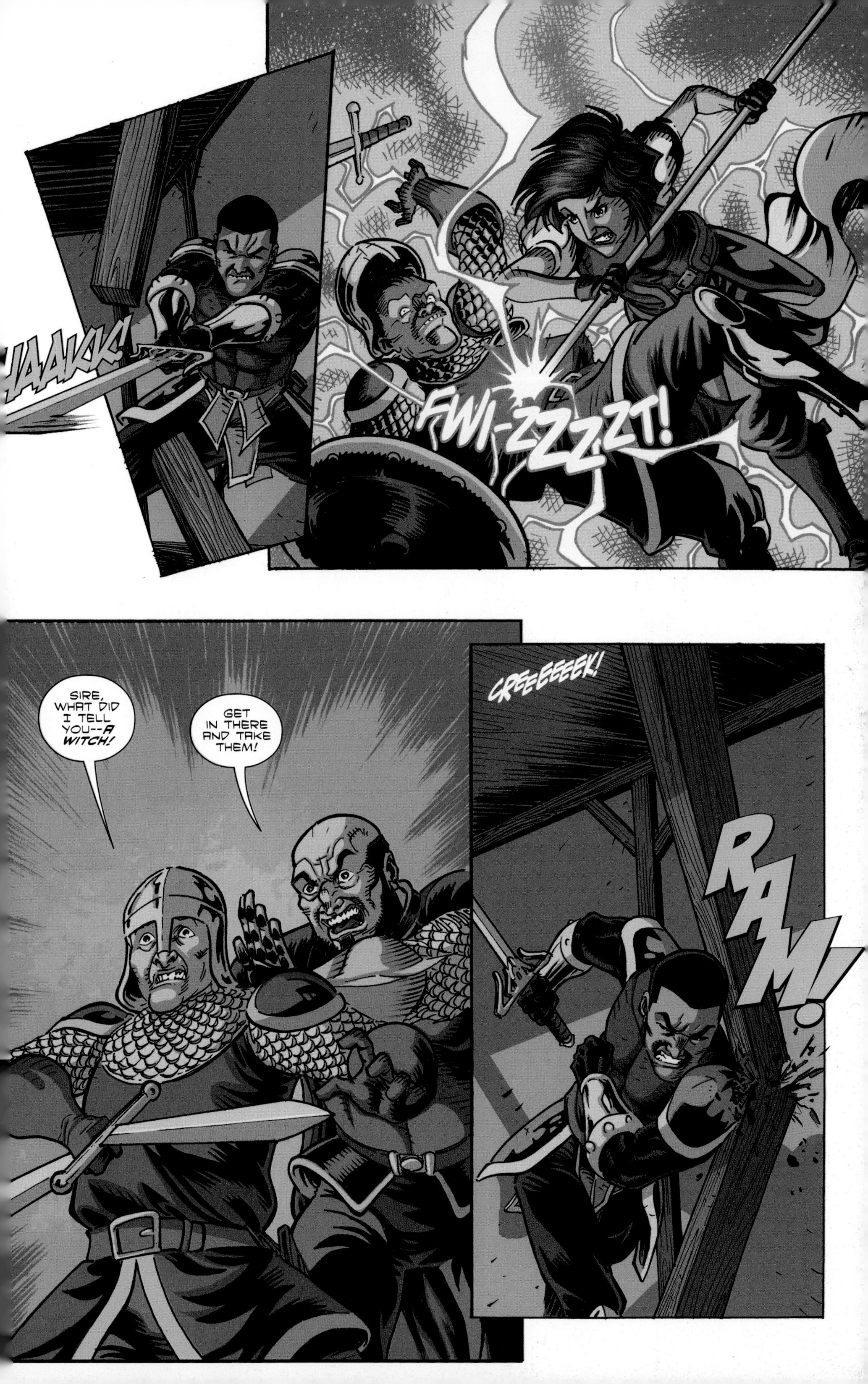
HAAKK!
FWI-ZZZZZT!
SIRE, WHAT DID I TELL YOU--A WITCH!
GET IN THERE AND TAKE THEM!
CREEEEEEK!
RAM!

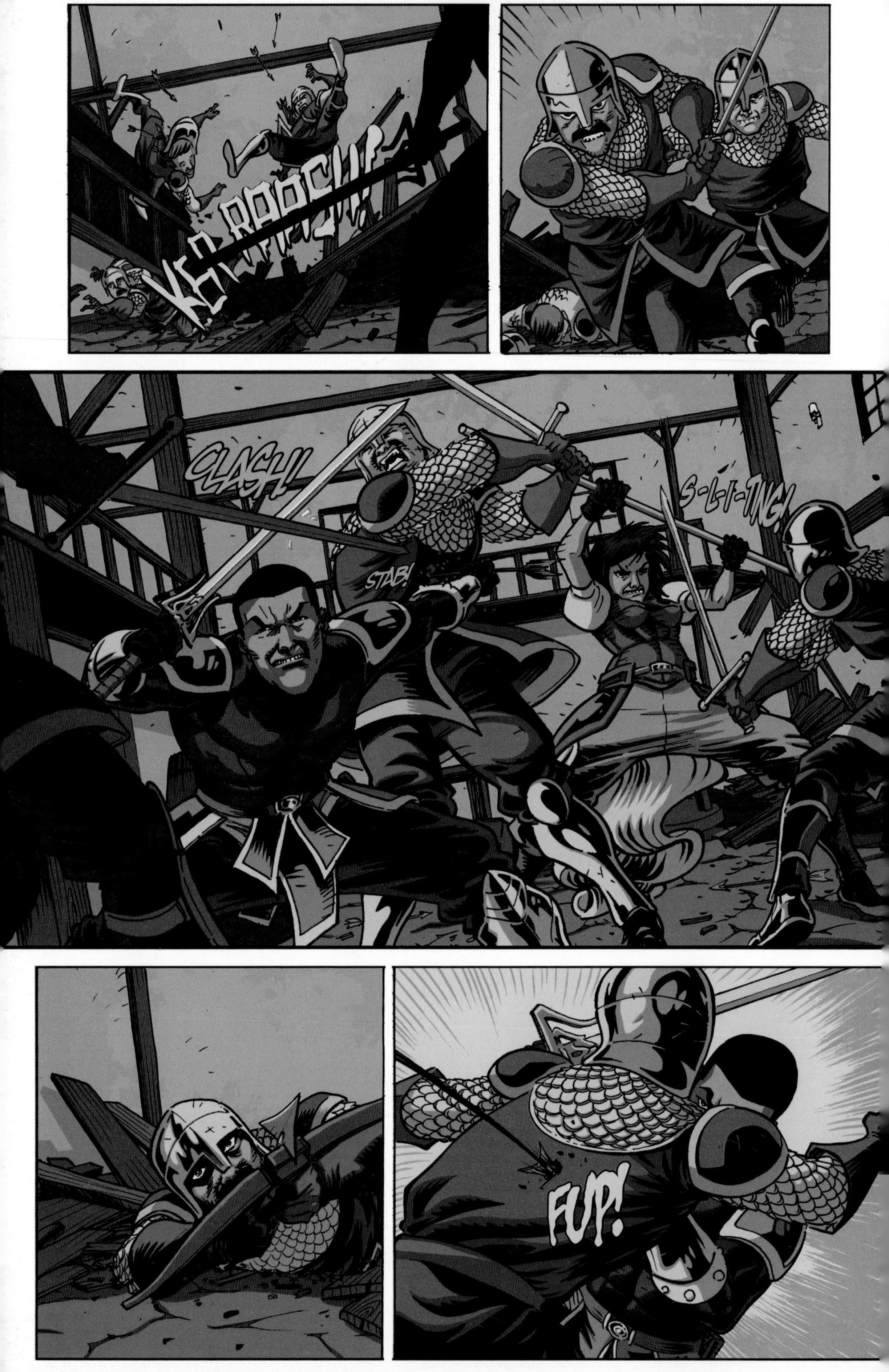
CLASH!
STAB!
S-L-I-TNG!
FUP!

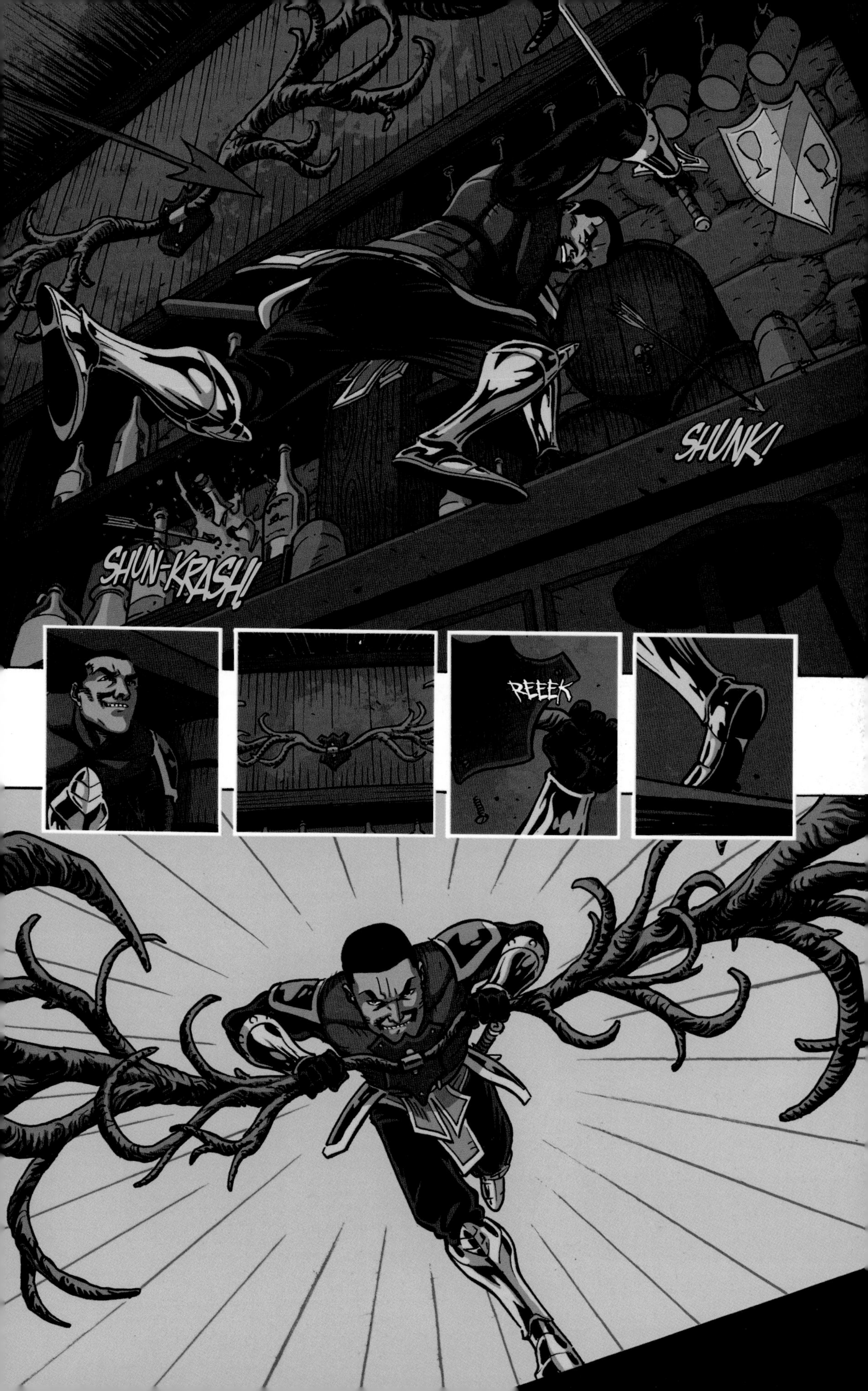
SHUNK!
SHUN-KRASH!
REEEK

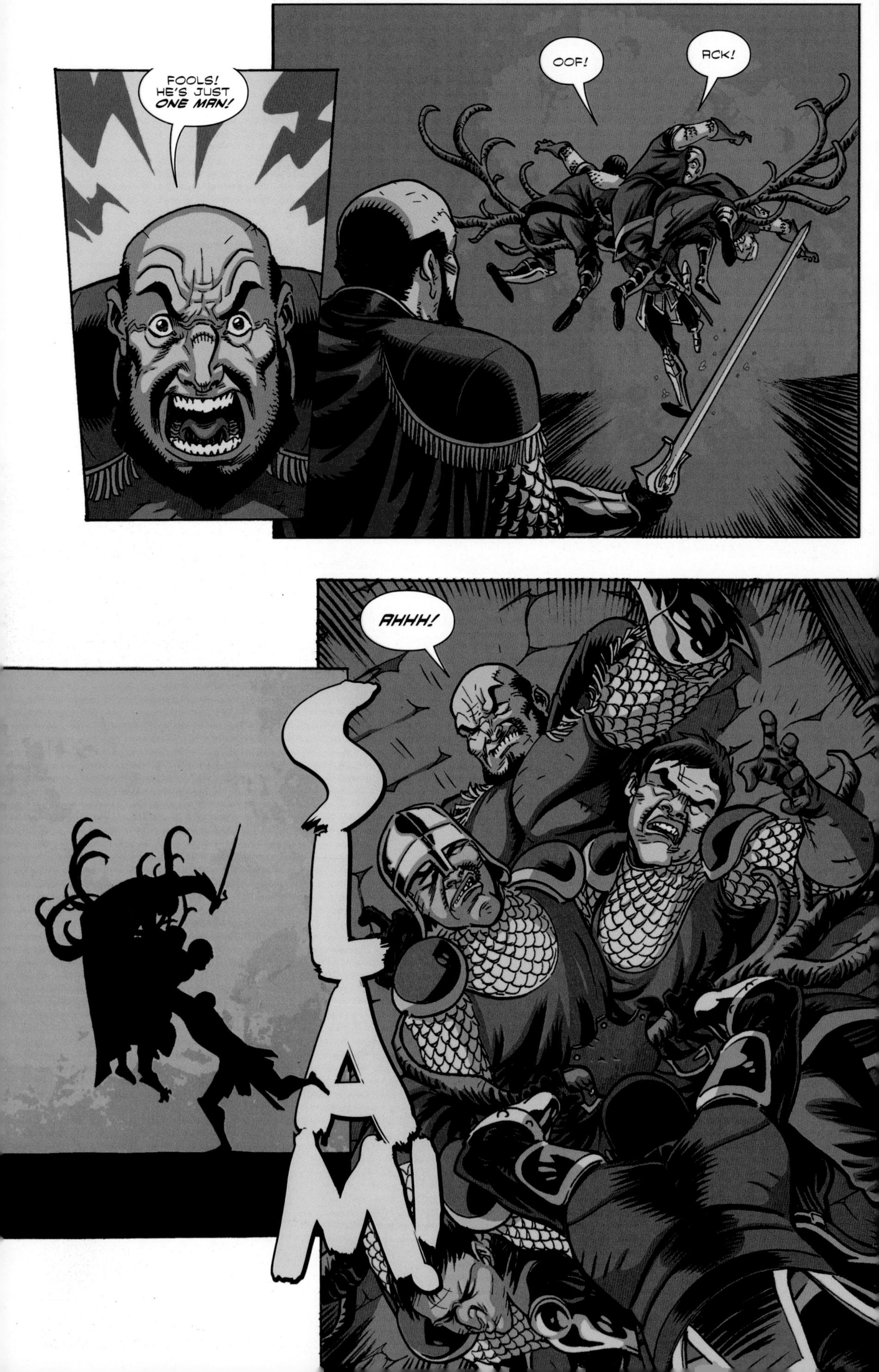
FOOLS! HE'S JUST ONE MAN!
OOF!
ACK!
AHHH!
SLAM

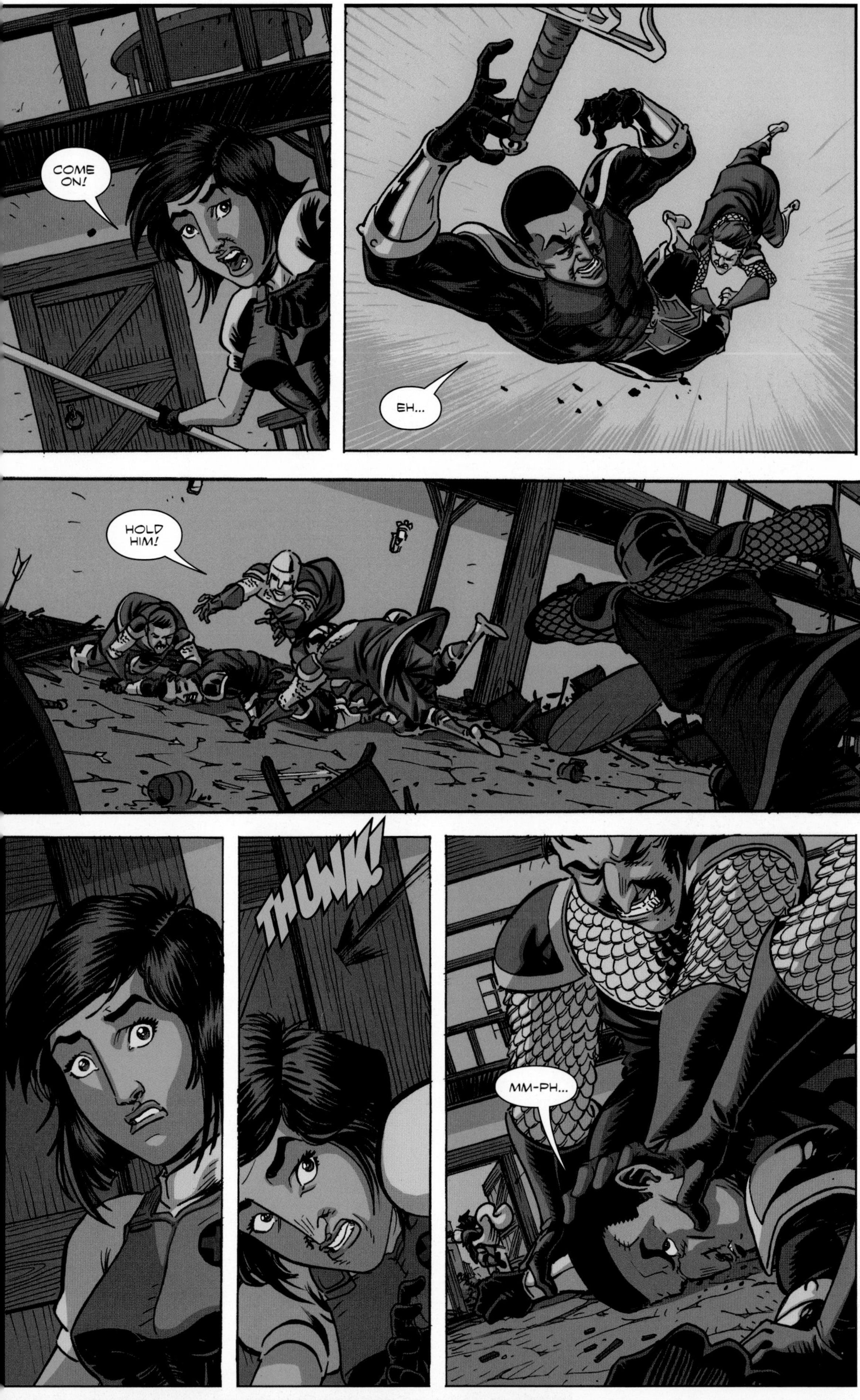
COME ON!
EH...
HOLD HIM!
THUNK!
MM-PH...

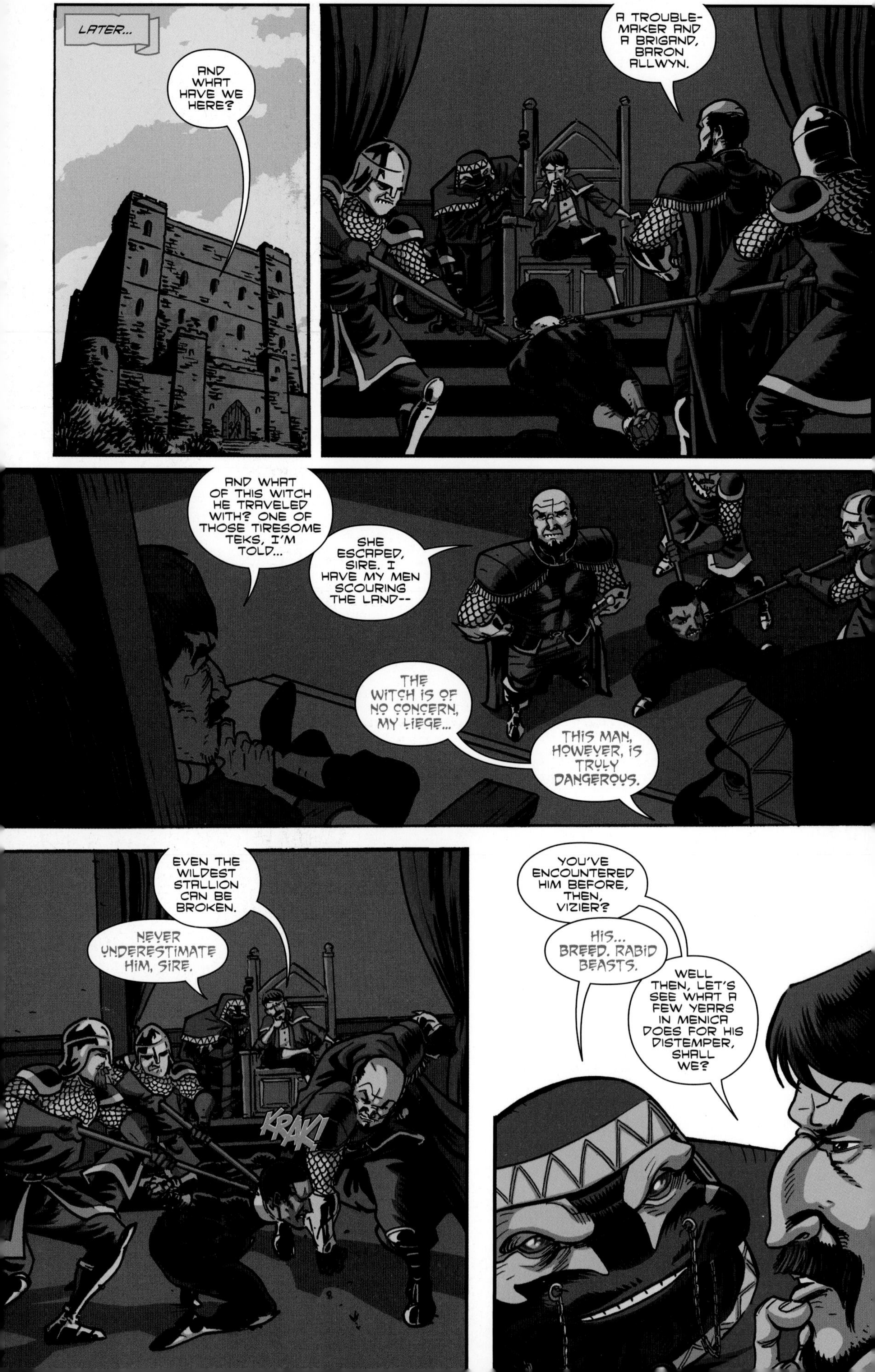
LATER...
AND WHAT HAVE WE HERE?
A TROUBLE-MAKER AND A BRIGAND, BARON ALLWYN.
AND WHAT OF THIS WITCH HE TRAVELED WITH? ONE OF THOSE TIRESOME TEKS, I'M TOLD...
SHE ESCAPED, SIRE. I HAVE MY MEN SCOURING THE LAND--
THE WITCH IS OF NO CONCERN, MY LIEGE...
THIS MAN, HOWEVER, IS TRULY DANGEROUS.
EVEN THE WILDEST STALLION CAN BE BROKEN.
NEVER UNDERESTIMATE HIM, SIRE.
KRAK!
YOU'VE ENCOUNTERED HIM BEFORE, THEN, VIZIER?
HIS... BREED. RABID BEASTS.
WELL THEN, LET'S SEE WHAT A FEW YEARS IN MENICA DOES FOR HIS DISTEMPER, SHALL WE?

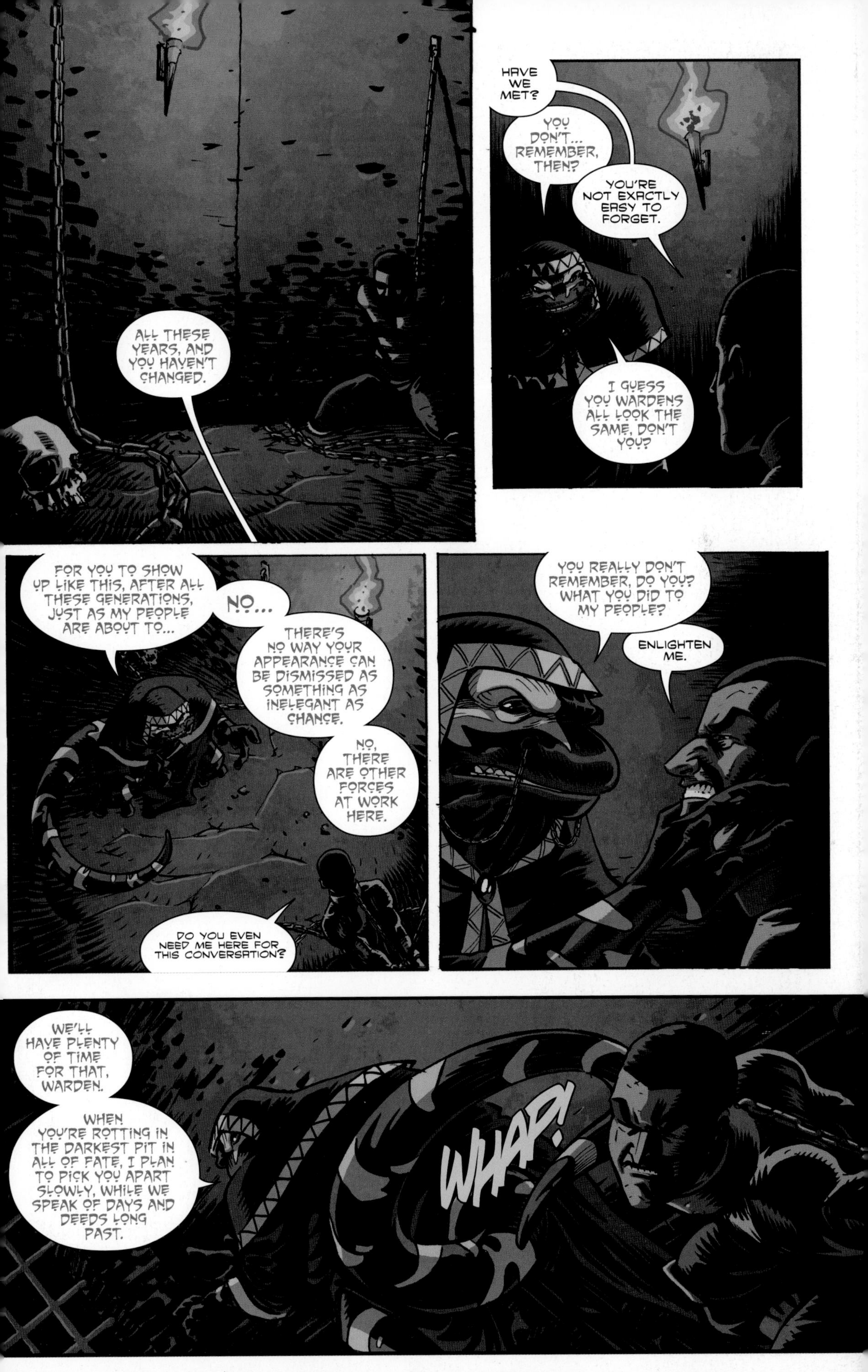
ALL THESE YEARS, AND YOU HAVEN'T CHANGED.
HAVE WE MET?
YOU DON'T... REMEMBER, THEN?
YOU'RE NOT EXACTLY EASY TO FORGET.
I GUESS YOU WARDENS ALL LOOK THE SAME, DON'T YOU?
FOR YOU TO SHOW UP LIKE THIS, AFTER ALL THESE GENERATIONS, JUST AS MY PEOPLE ARE ABOUT TO...
NO...
THERE'S NO WAY YOUR APPEARANCE CAN BE DISMISSED AS SOMETHING AS INELEGANT AS CHANCE.
NO, THERE ARE OTHER FORCES AT WORK HERE.
DO YOU EVEN NEED ME HERE FOR THIS CONVERSATION?
YOU REALLY DON'T REMEMBER, DO YOU? WHAT YOU DID TO MY PEOPLE?
ENLIGHTEN ME.
WE'LL HAVE PLENTY OF TIME FOR THAT, WARDEN.
WHEN YOU'RE ROTTING IN THE DARKEST PIT IN ALL OF FATE, I PLAN TO PICK YOU APART SLOWLY, WHILE WE SPEAK OF DAYS AND DEEDS LONG PAST.
WHAP!

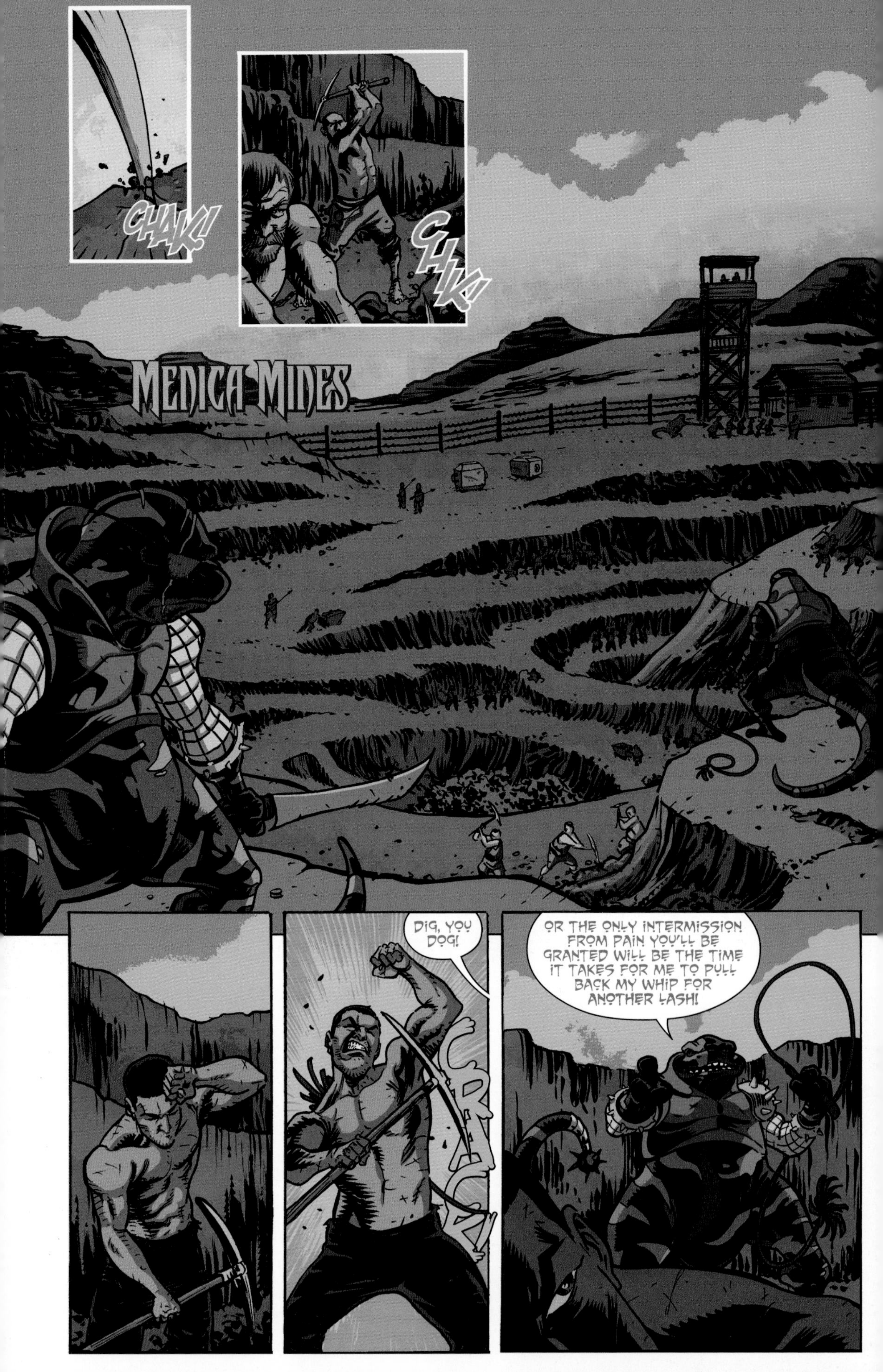
CHAK!
CHIK!
MENICA MINES
DIG, YOU DOG!
CRACK
OR THE ONLY INTERMISSION FROM PAIN YOU'LL BE GRANTED WILL BE THE TIME IT TAKES FOR ME TO PULL BACK MY WHIP FOR ANOTHER LASH!

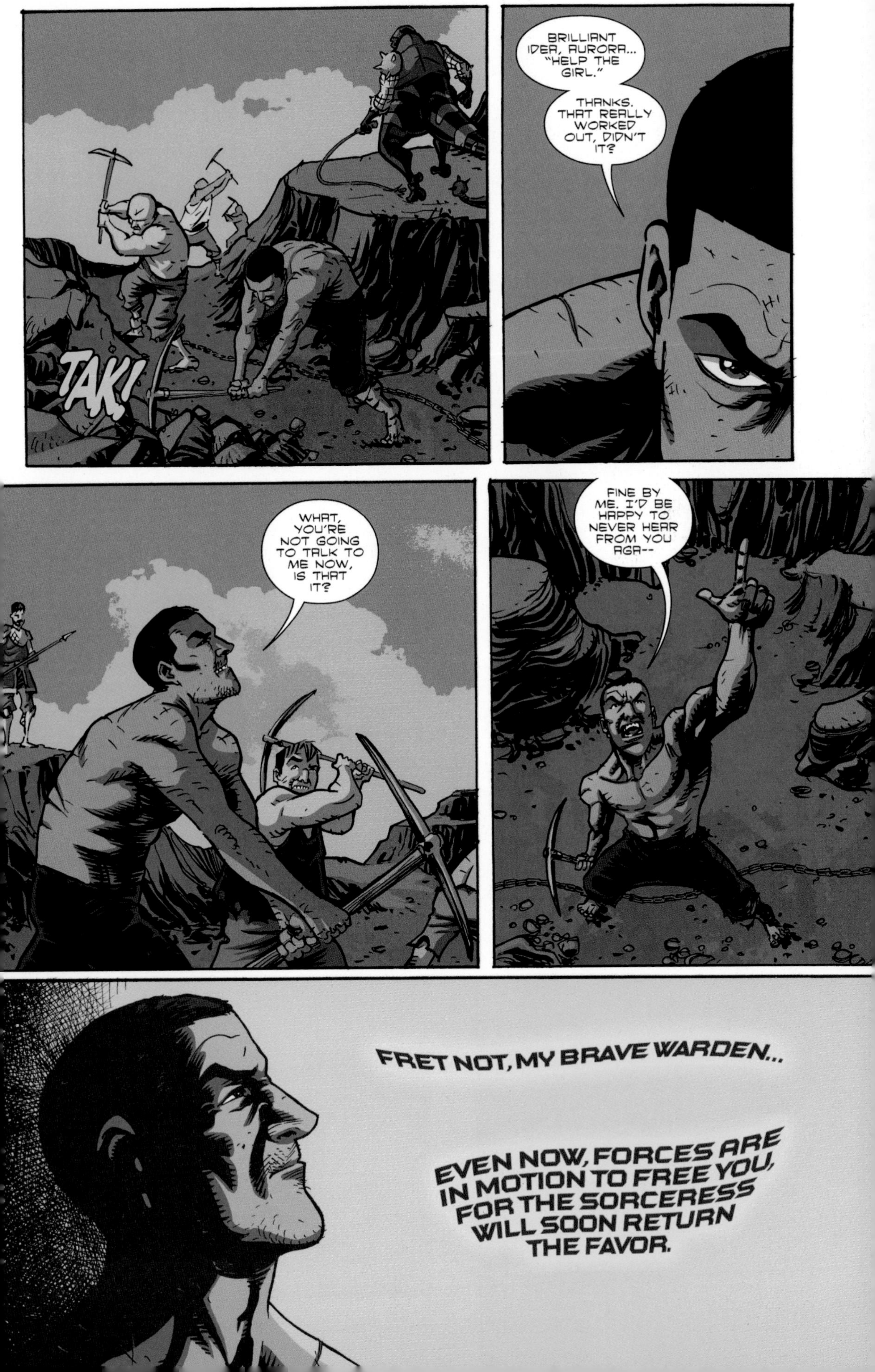
TAK!
BRILLIANT IDEA, AURORA... "HELP THE GIRL."
THANKS. THAT REALLY WORKED OUT, DIDN'T IT?
WHAT, YOU'RE NOT GOING TO TALK TO ME NOW, IS THAT IT?
FINE BY ME. I'D BE HAPPY TO NEVER HEAR FROM YOU AGA--
FRET NOT, MY BRAVE WARDEN...
EVEN NOW, FORCES ARE IN MOTION TO FREE YOU, FOR THE SORCERESS WILL SOON RETURN THE FAVOR.

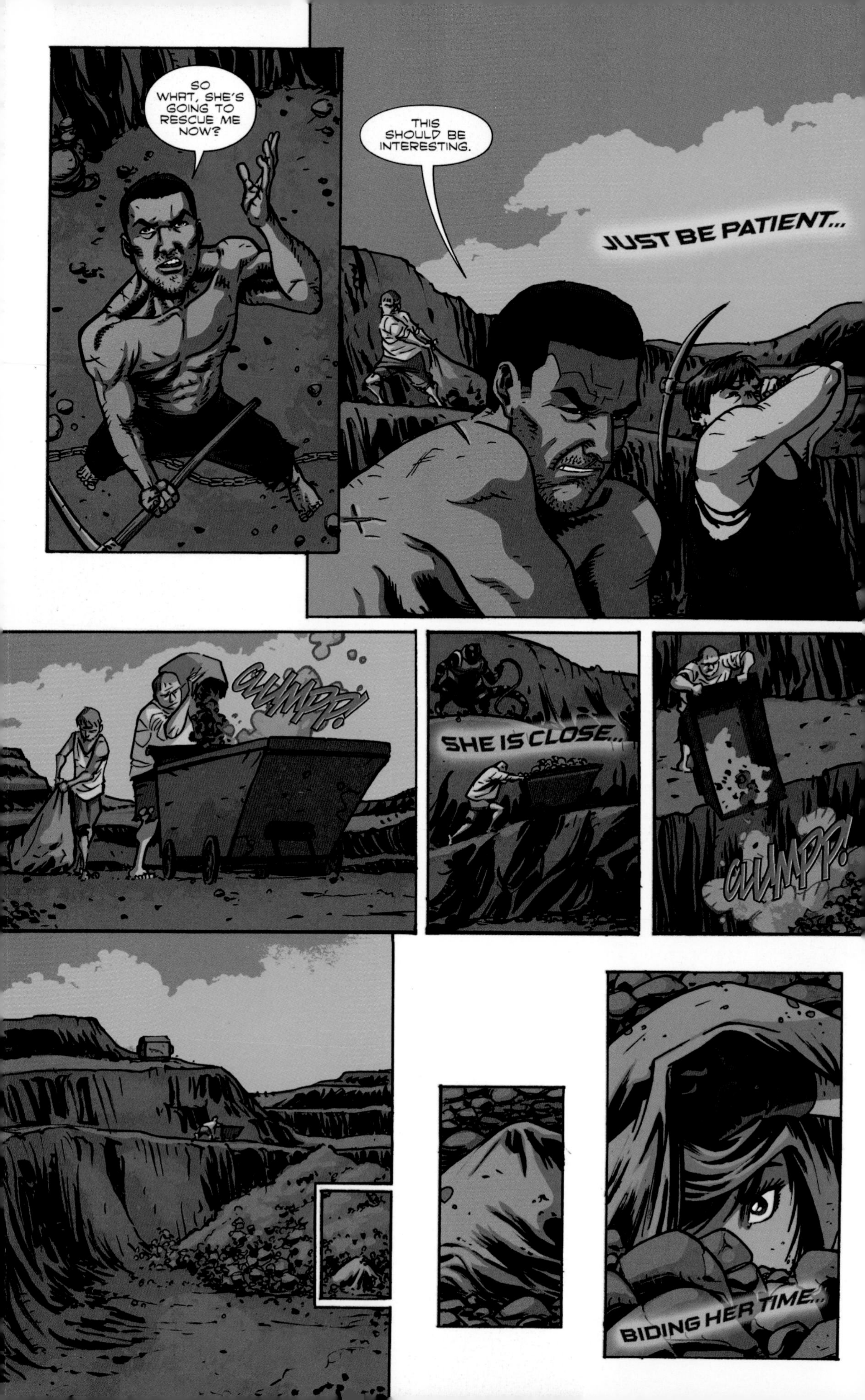
SO WHAT, SHE'S GOING TO RESCUE ME NOW?
THIS SHOULD BE INTERESTING.
JUST BE PATIENT...
CLUMPP!
SHE IS CLOSE...
CLUMPP!
BIDING HER TIME...

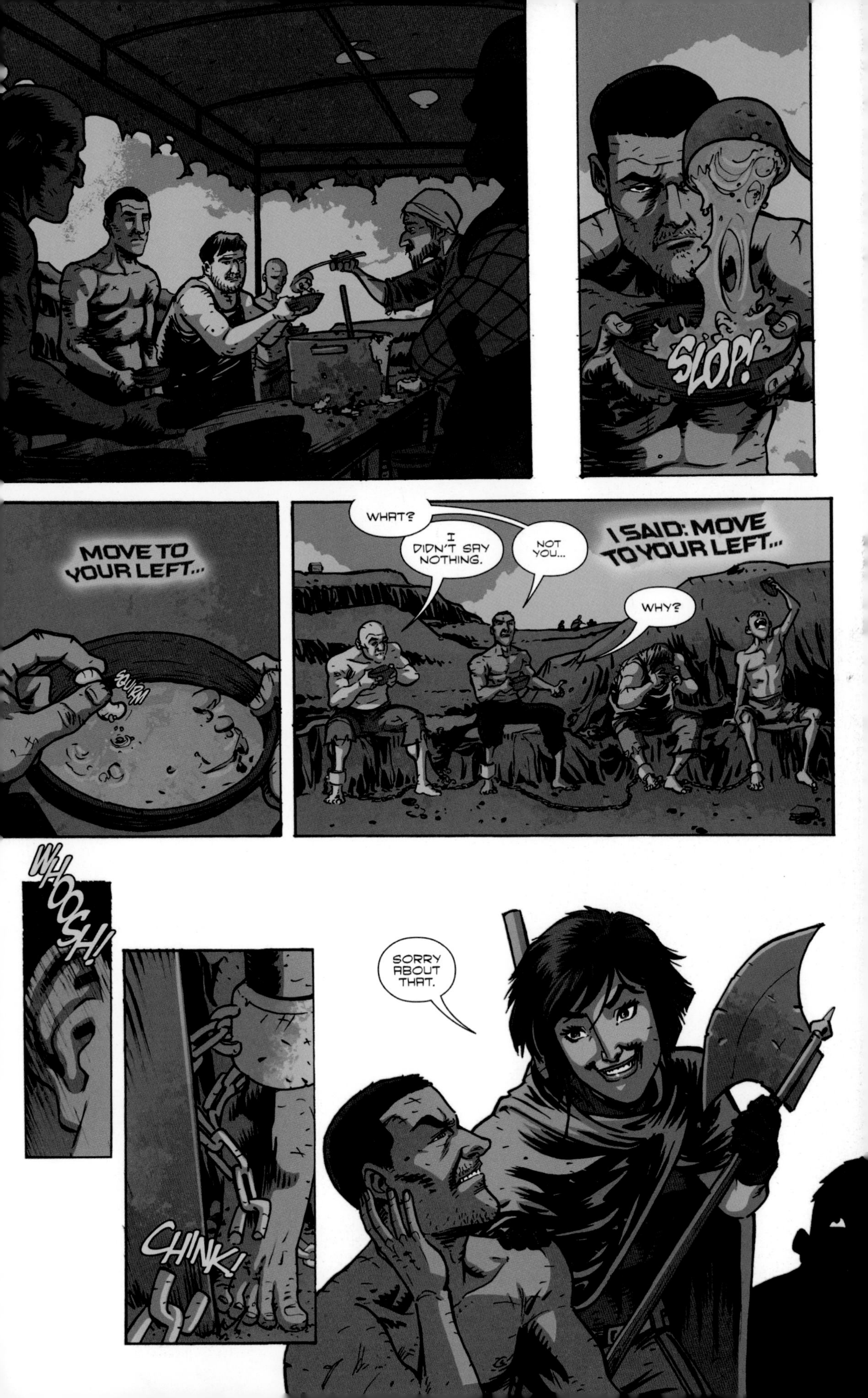
SLOP!
MOVE TO YOUR LEFT...
SQUIRM
WHAT?
I DIDN'T SAY NOTHING.
NOT YOU...
I SAID: MOVE TO YOUR LEFT...
WHY?
WHOOSH!
CHINK!
SORRY ABOUT THAT.

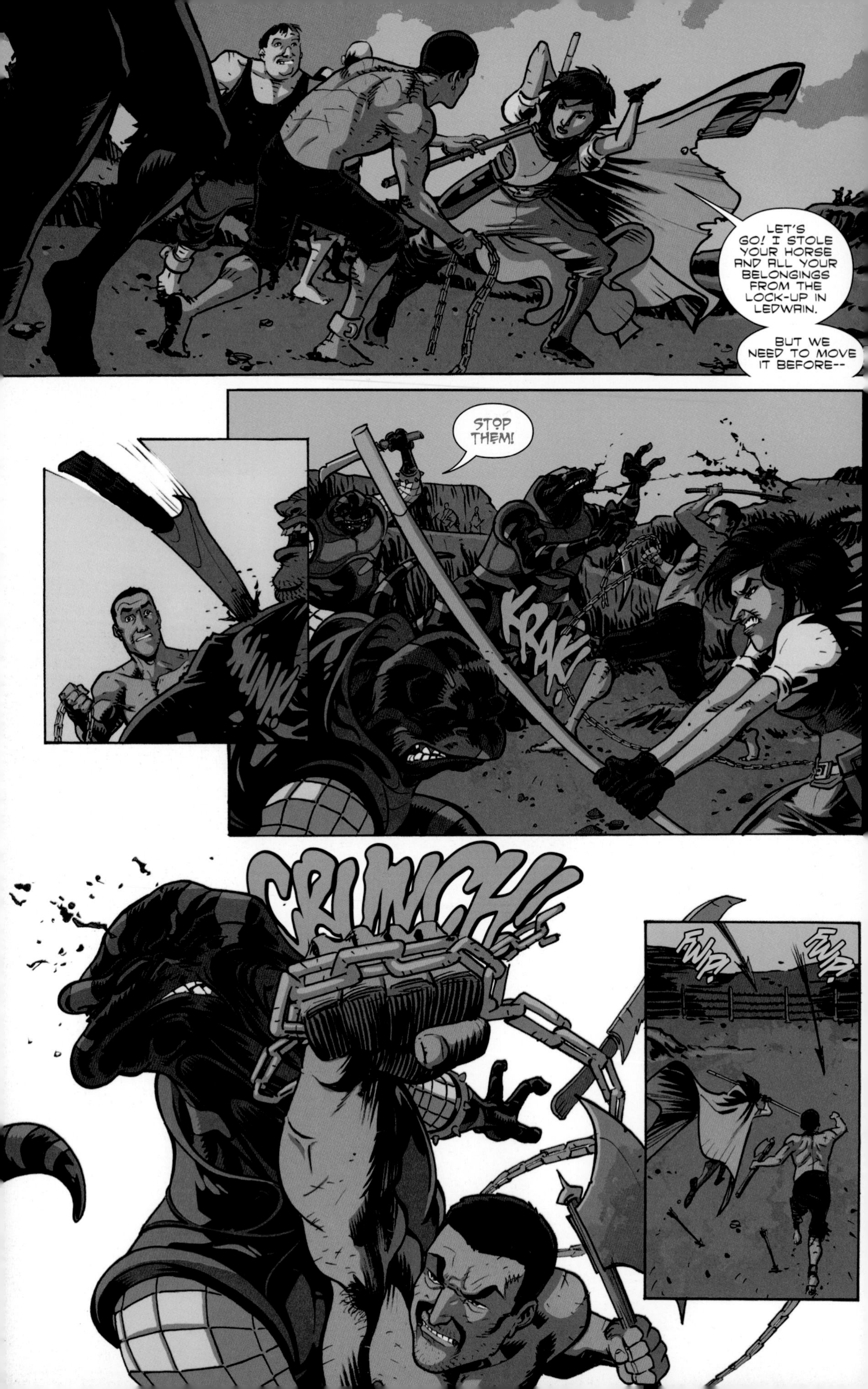
LET'S GO! I STOLE YOUR HORSE AND ALL YOUR BELONGINGS FROM THE LOCK-UP IN LEDWAIN.
BUT WE NEED TO MOVE IT BEFORE--
STOP THEM!
KRAK!
CRUNCH!
FWIP!
FWIP!

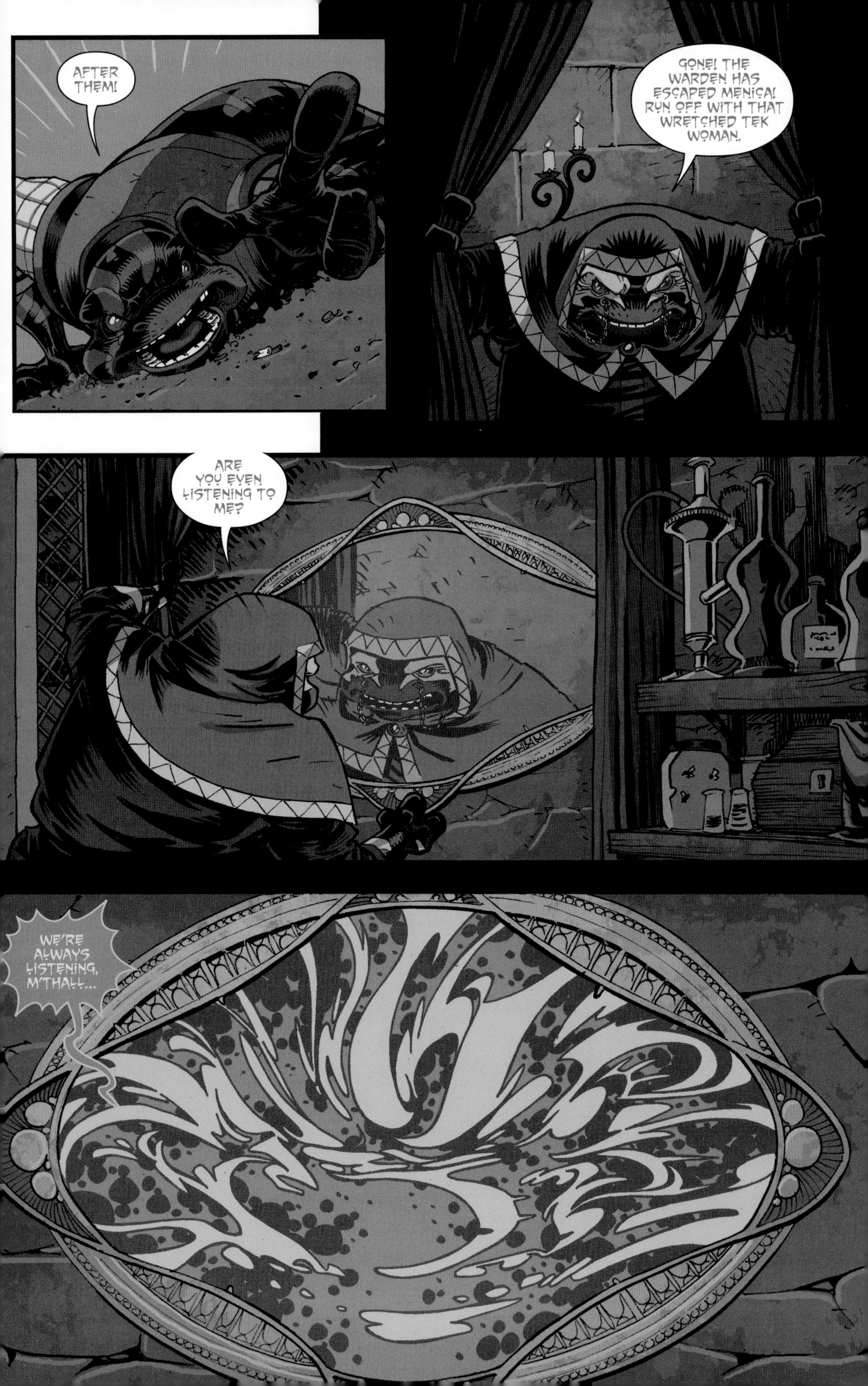
AFTER THEM!
GONE! THE WARDEN HAS ESCAPED MENICA! RUN OFF WITH THAT WRETCHED TEK WOMAN.
ARE YOU EVEN LISTENING TO ME?
WE'RE ALWAYS LISTENING, M'THALL...

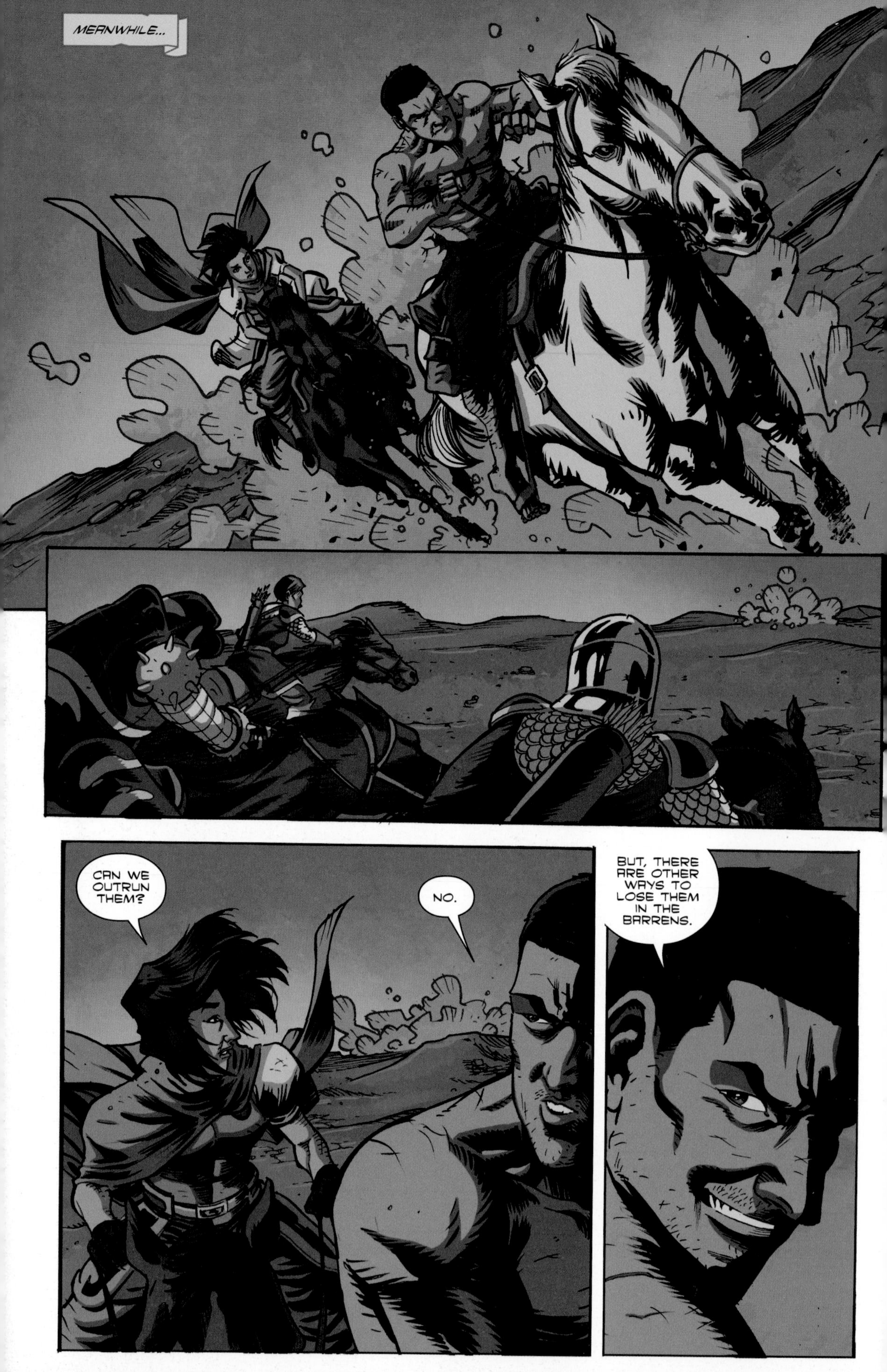
MEANWHILE...
CAN WE OUTRUN THEM?
NO.
BUT, THERE ARE OTHER WAYS TO LOSE THEM IN THE BARRENS.

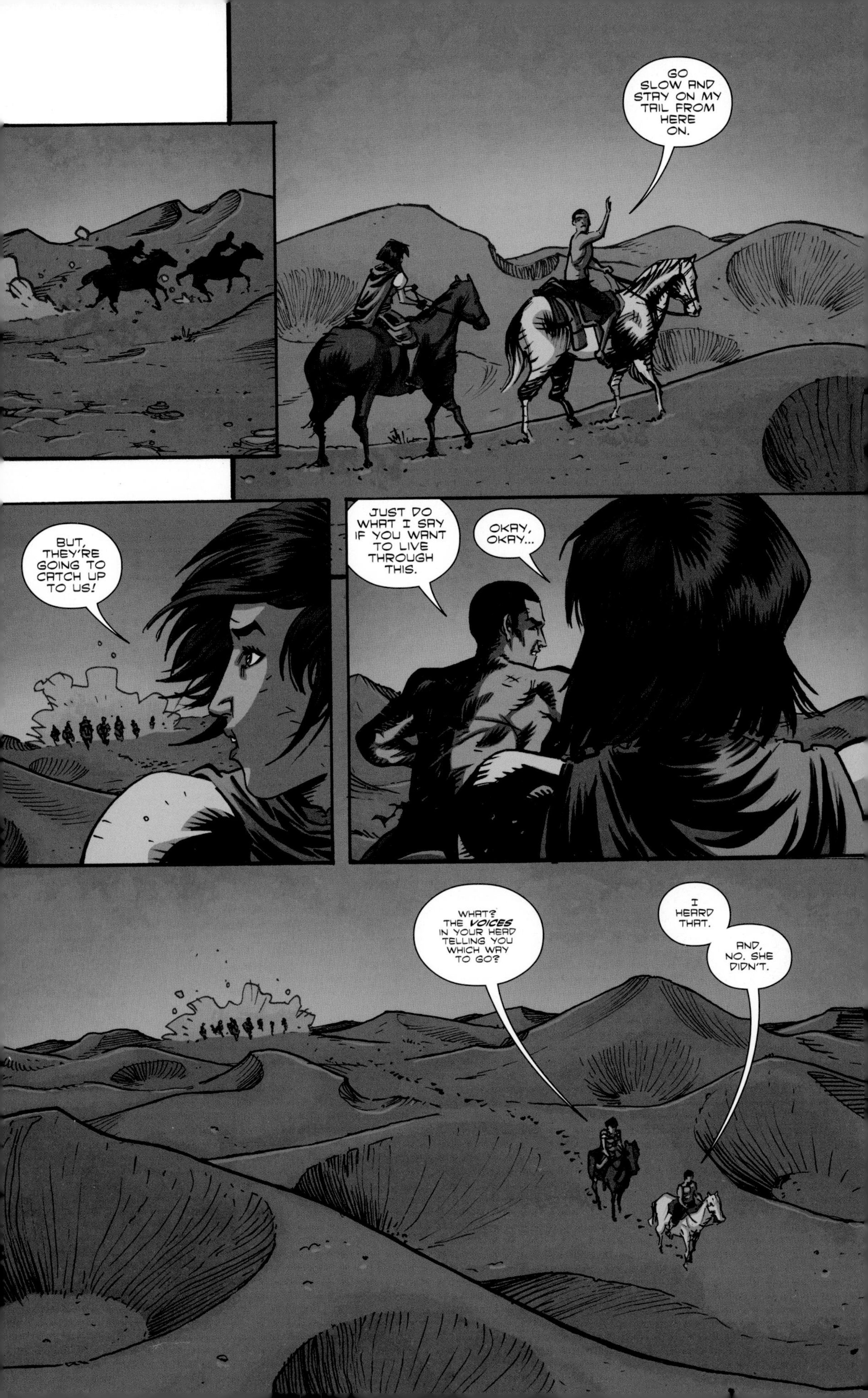
GO SLOW AND STAY ON MY TRAIL FROM HERE ON.
BUT, THEY'RE GOING TO CATCH UP TO US!
JUST DO WHAT I SAY IF YOU WANT TO LIVE THROUGH THIS.
OKAY, OKAY...
WHAT? THE *VOICES* IN YOUR HEAD TELLING YOU WHICH WAY TO GO?
I HEARD THAT.
AND, NO. SHE DIDN'T.

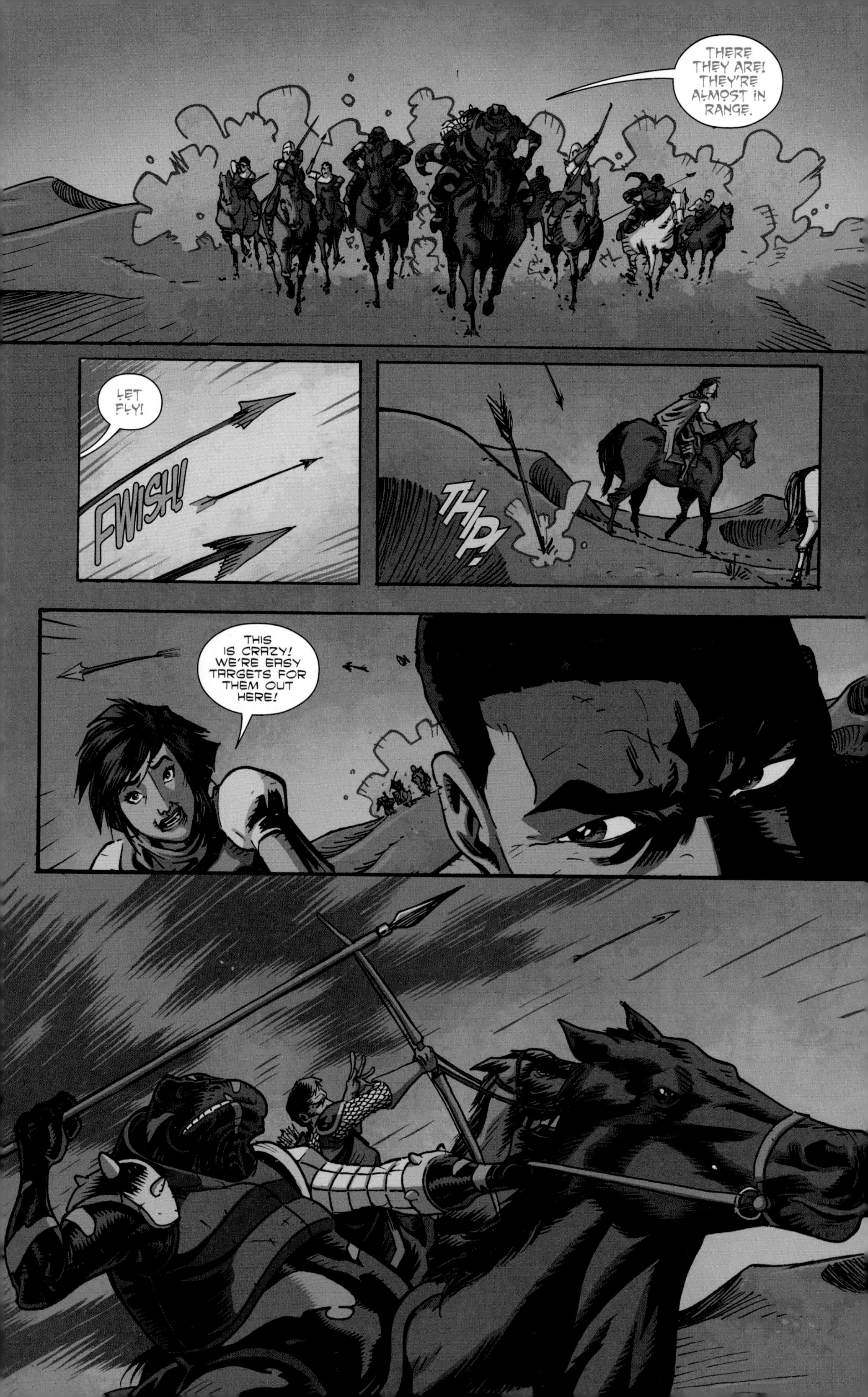
THERE THEY ARE! THEY'RE ALMOST IN RANGE.
LET FLY!
FWISH!
THIP!
THIS IS CRAZY! WE'RE EASY TARGETS FOR THEM OUT HERE!

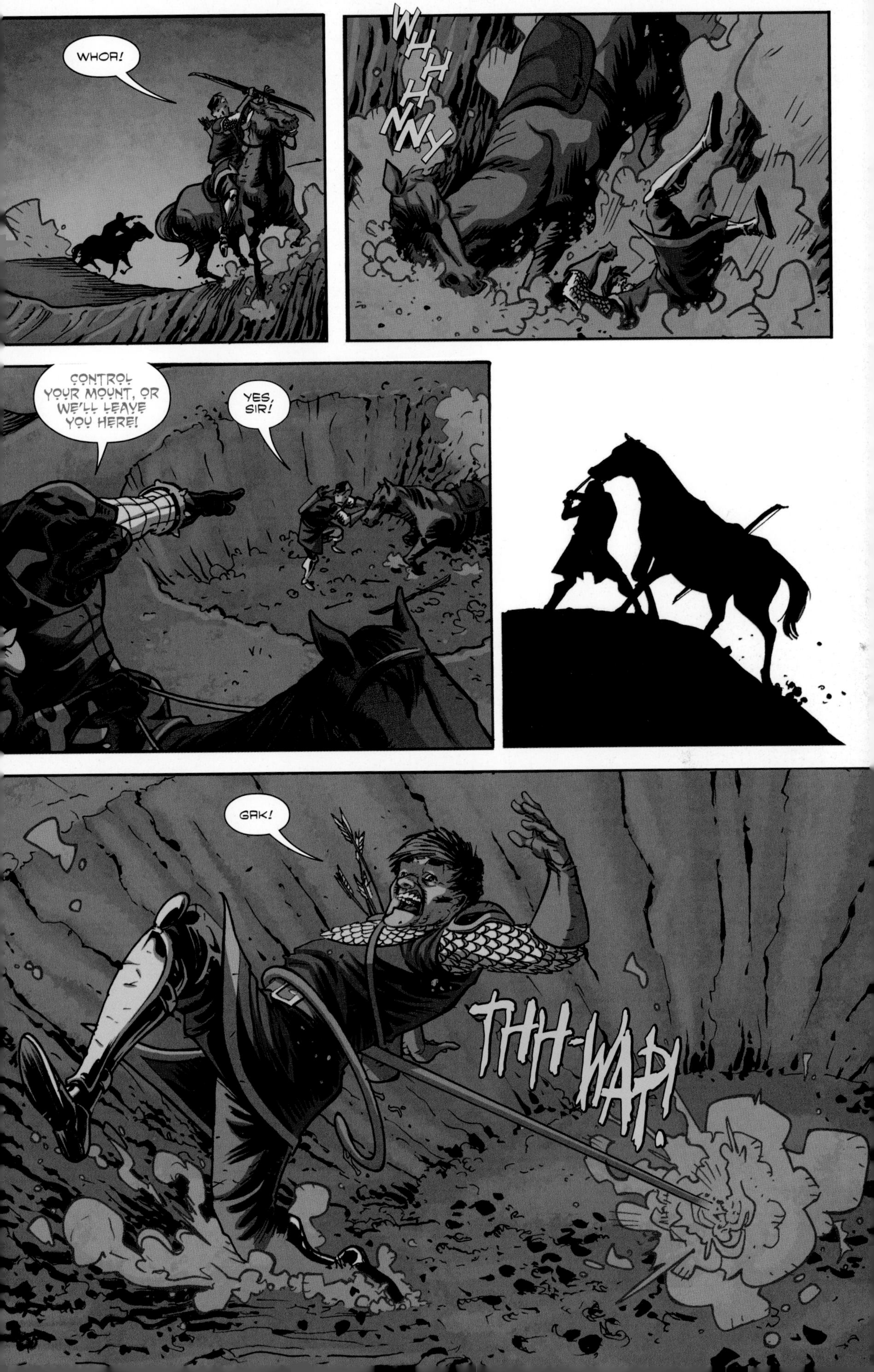
WHOA!
WHHHHNNY
CONTROL YOUR MOUNT, OR WE'LL LEAVE YOU HERE!
YES, SIR!
GAK!
THH-WAP!

SH-I-I-I-F-F-T!

AH!

SKKKT!

HELP!

THWAP!

AAAHHHH!

ACK!

TOLD YOU THERE WERE OTHER WAYS--

REYN--

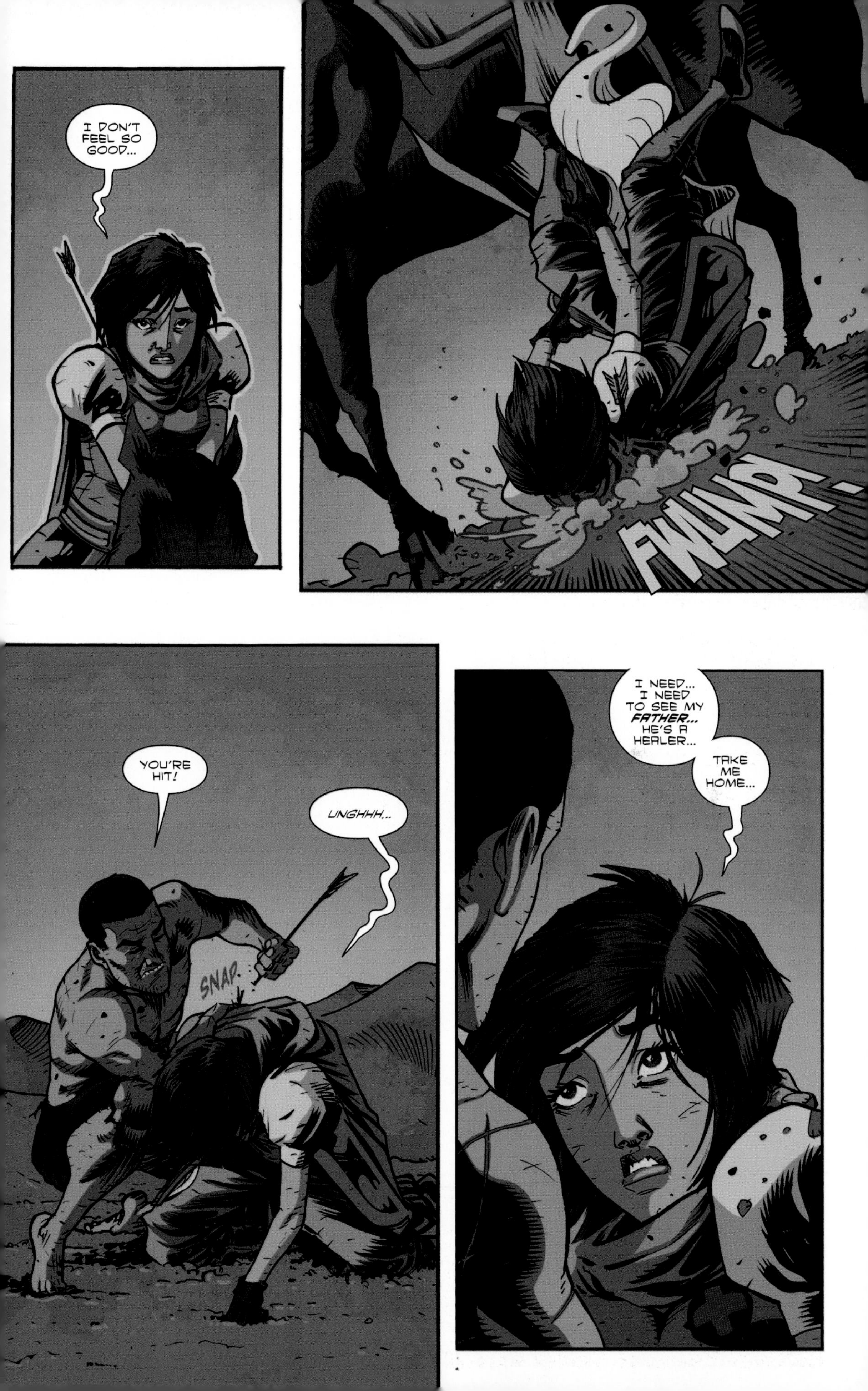
I DON'T FEEL SO GOOD...
FWUMP!
YOU'RE HIT!
UNGHHH...
SNAP
I NEED... I NEED TO SEE MY FATHER... HE'S A HEALER...
TAKE ME HOME...

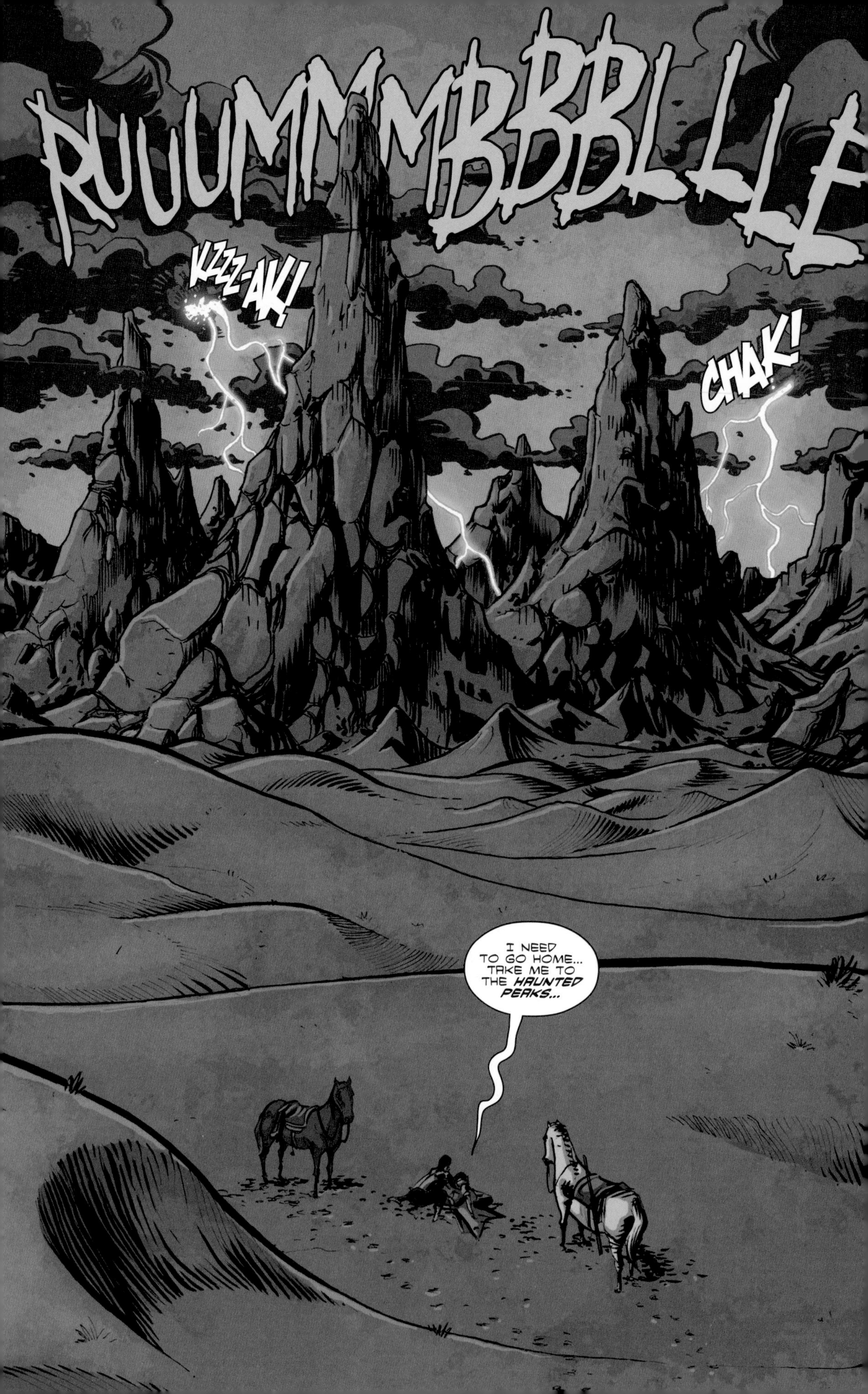
RUUUMMMMBBBLLLE
KZZZ-AK!
CHAK!
I NEED TO GO HOME... TAKE ME TO THE *HAUNTED PEAKS...*

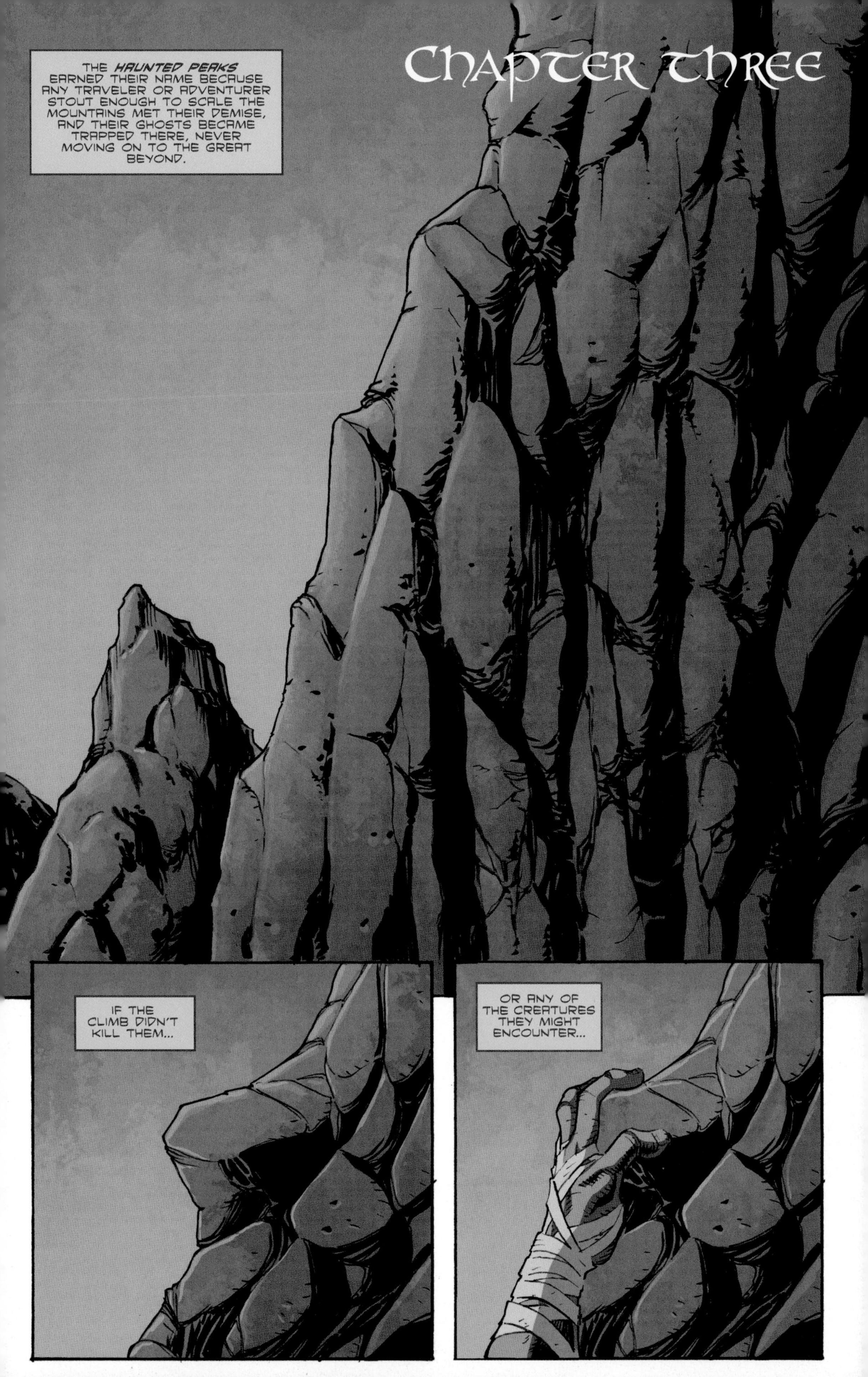
Chapter Three
THE HAUNTED PEAKS EARNED THEIR NAME BECAUSE ANY TRAVELER OR ADVENTURER STOUT ENOUGH TO SCALE THE MOUNTAINS MET THEIR DEMISE, AND THEIR GHOSTS BECAME TRAPPED THERE, NEVER MOVING ON TO THE GREAT BEYOND.
IF THE CLIMB DIDN'T KILL THEM...
OR ANY OF THE CREATURES THEY MIGHT ENCOUNTER...

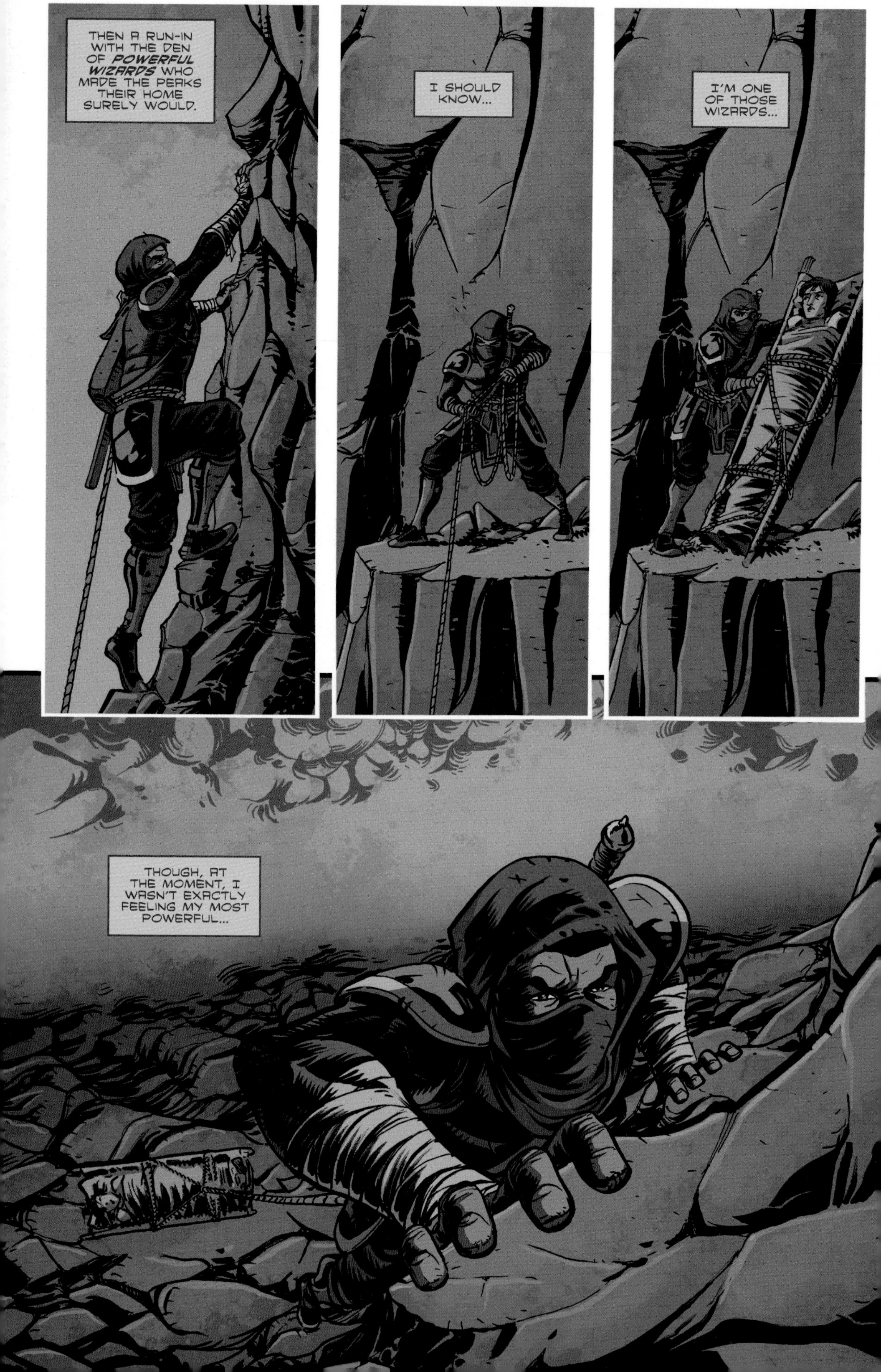
THEN A RUN-IN WITH THE DEN OF **POWERFUL WIZARDS** WHO MADE THE PEAKS THEIR HOME SURELY WOULD.
I SHOULD KNOW...
I'M ONE OF THOSE WIZARDS...
THOUGH, AT THE MOMENT, I WASN'T EXACTLY FEELING MY MOST POWERFUL...

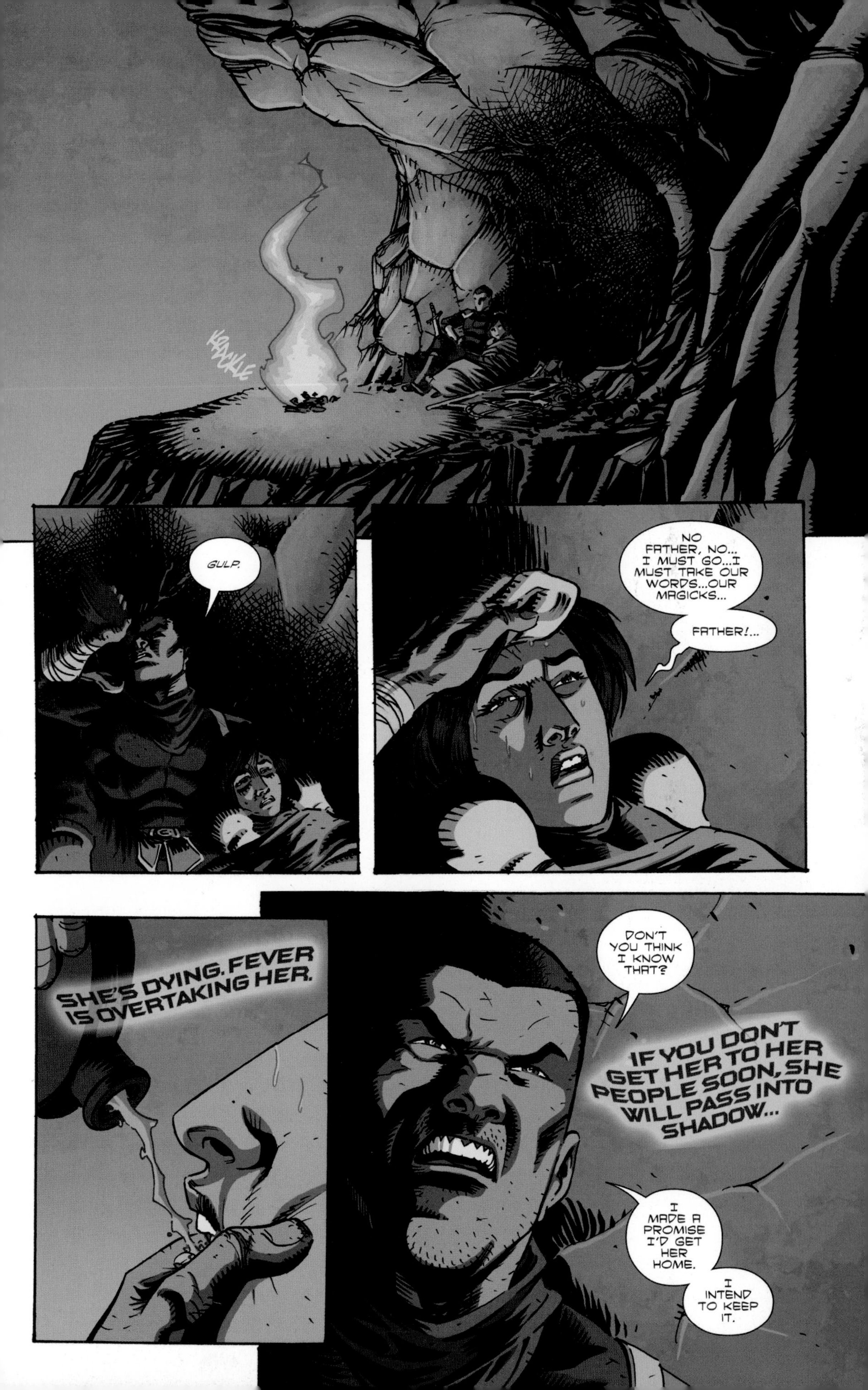
KRACKLE
GULP.
NO FATHER, NO... I MUST GO...I MUST TAKE OUR WORDS...OUR MAGICKS...
FATHER!...
SHE'S DYING. FEVER IS OVERTAKING HER.
DON'T YOU THINK I KNOW THAT?
IF YOU DON'T GET HER TO HER PEOPLE SOON, SHE WILL PASS INTO SHADOW...
I MADE A PROMISE I'D GET HER HOME.
I INTEND TO KEEP IT.

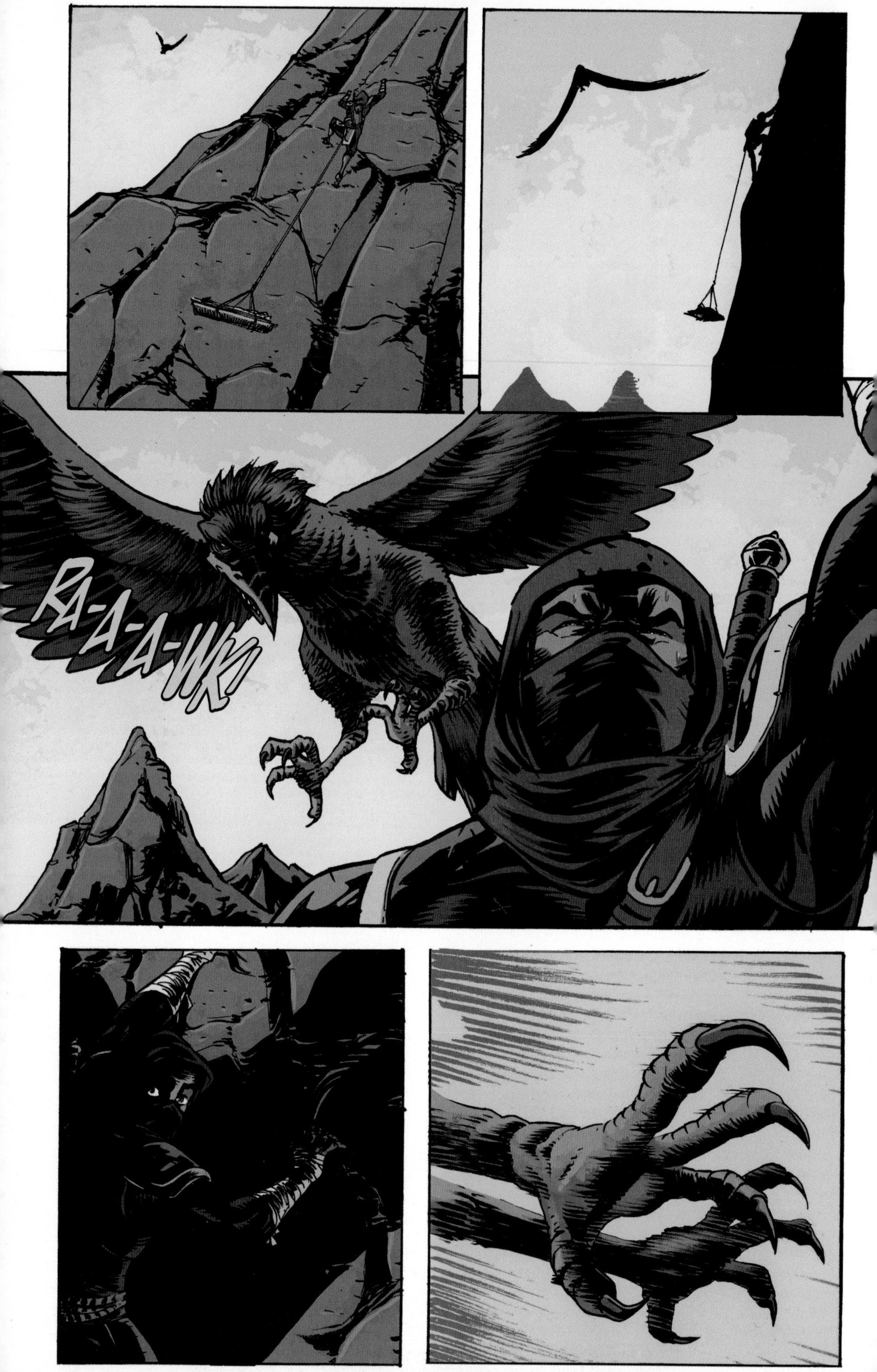
RA-A-A-WK!

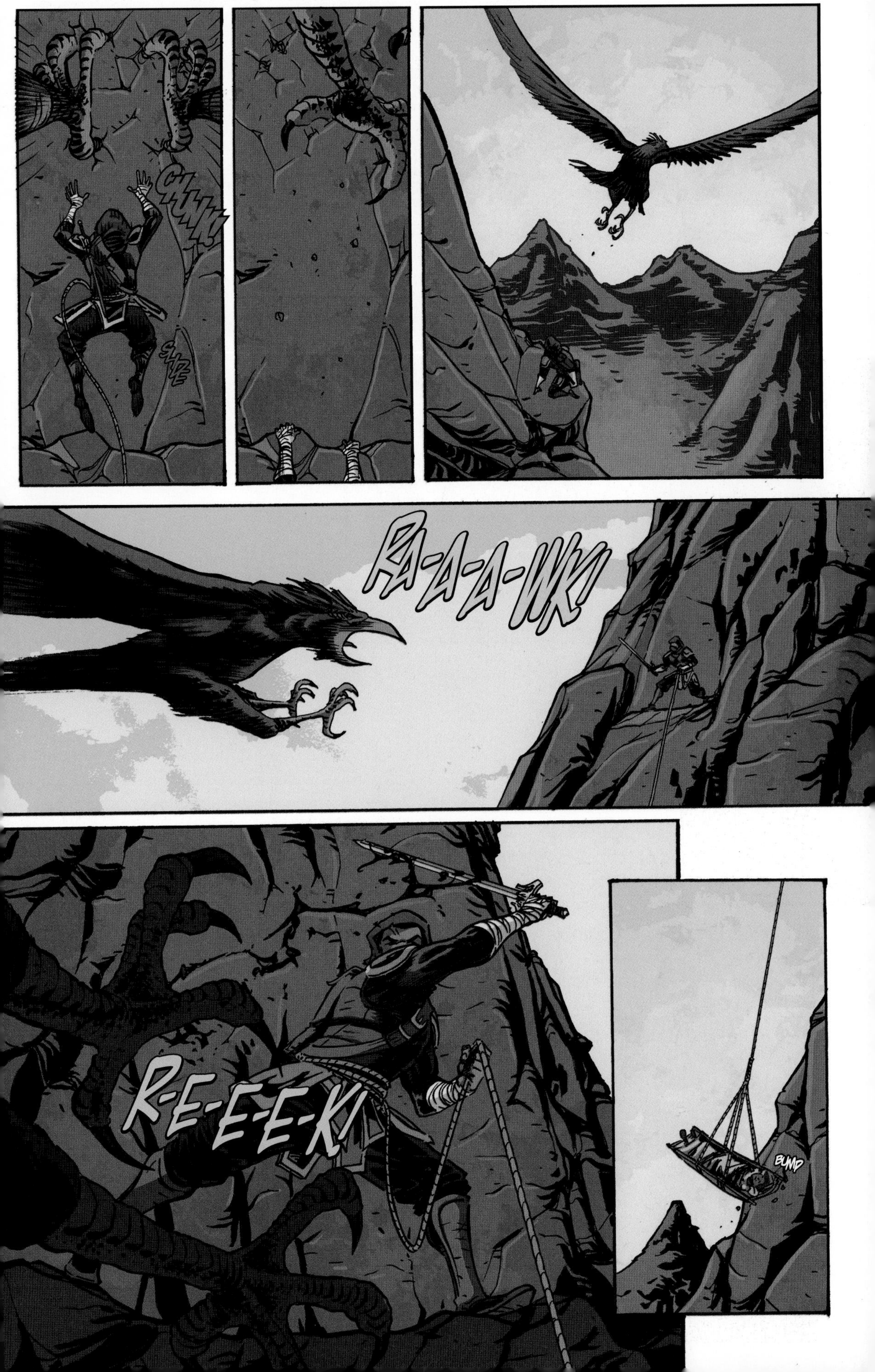
CHUNK!
SLIDE
RA-A-A-WK!
R-E-E-E-K!
BUMP

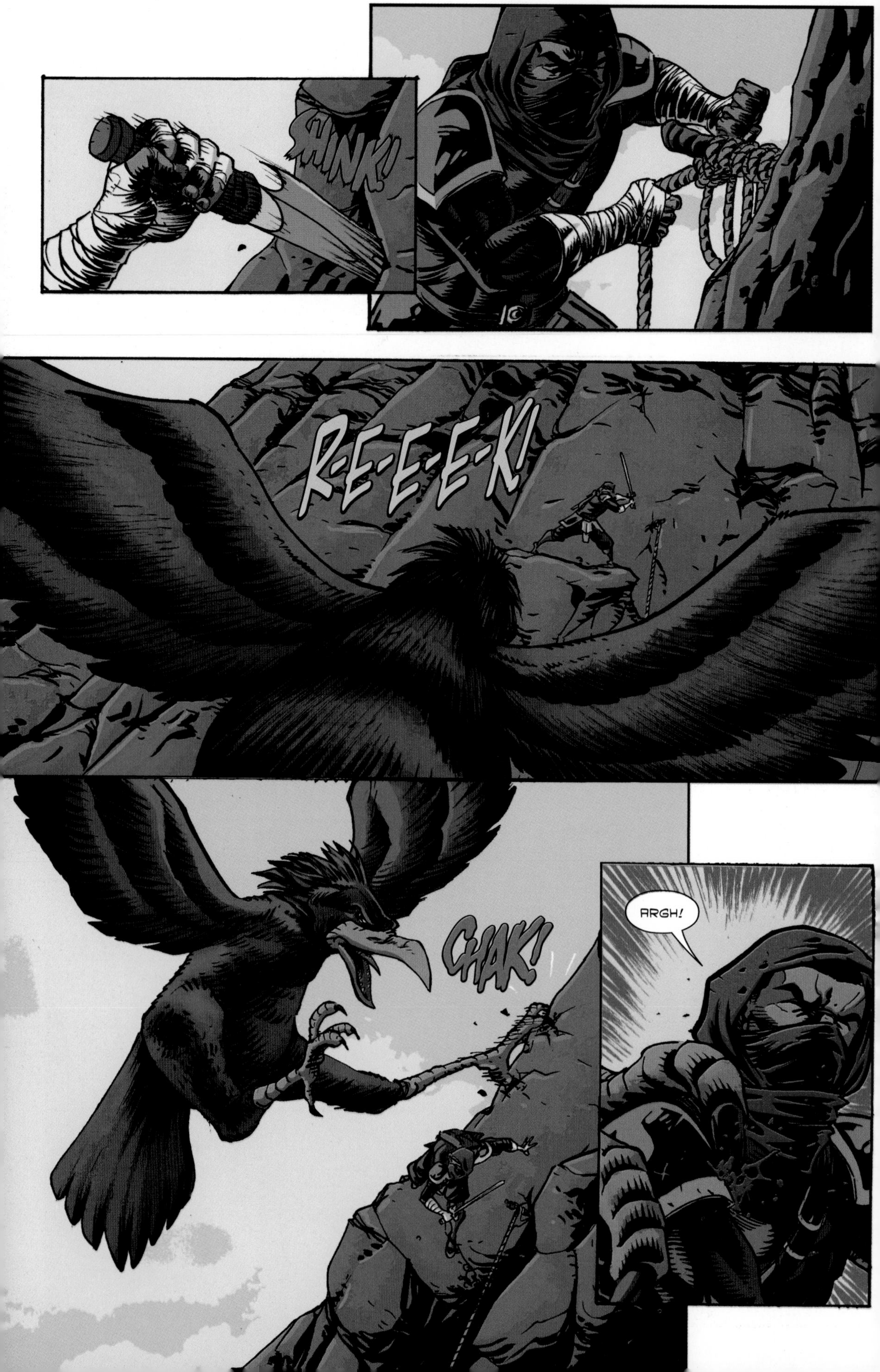
SHINK!
R-E-E-E-K!
CHAK!
ARGH!

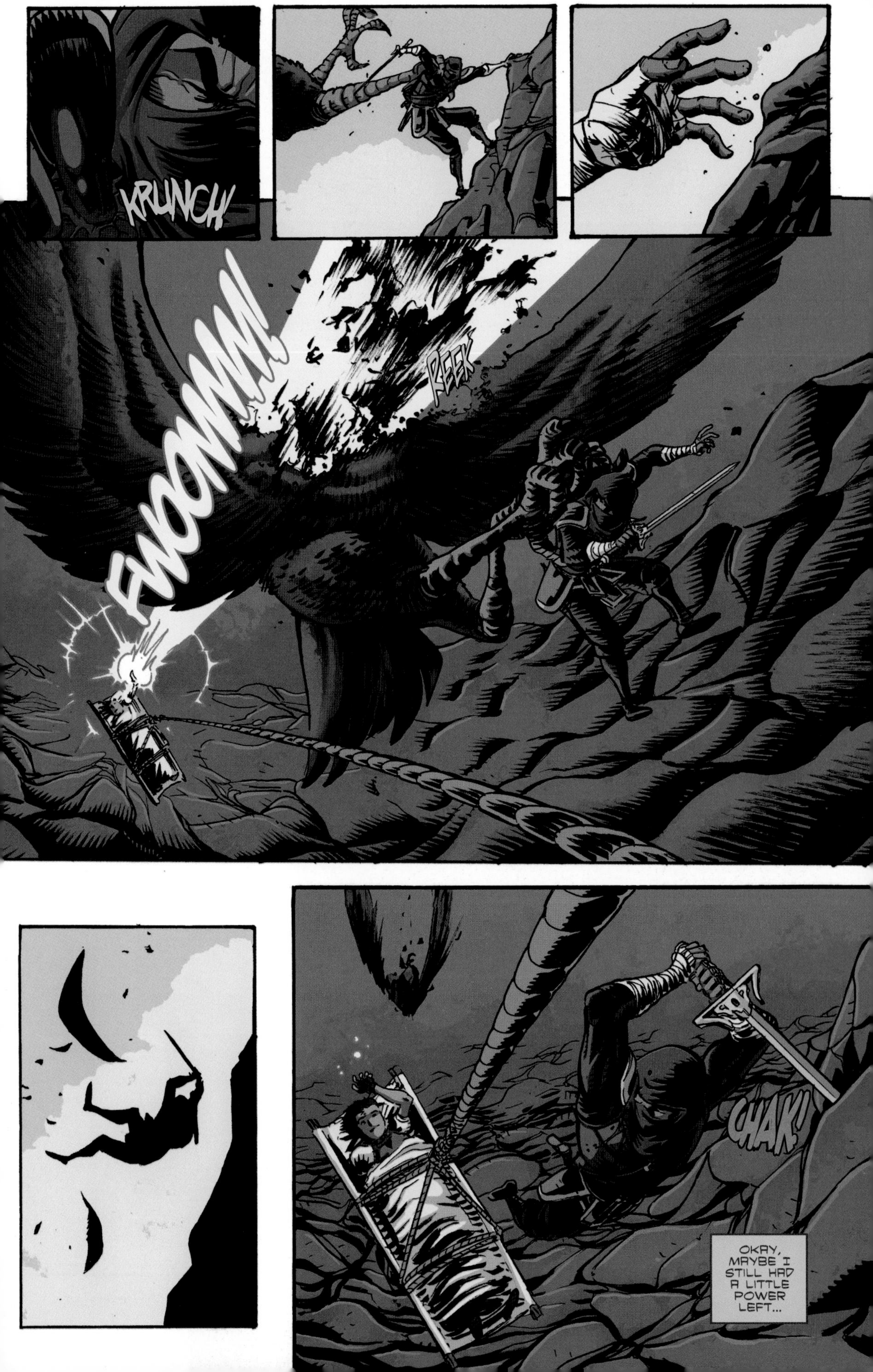
KRUNCH!
FWOOMM!
REEK
CHAK!
OKAY, MAYBE I STILL HAD A LITTLE POWER LEFT...

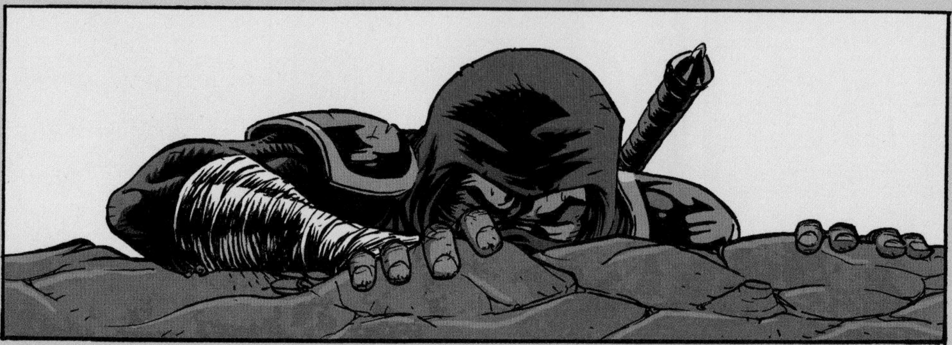

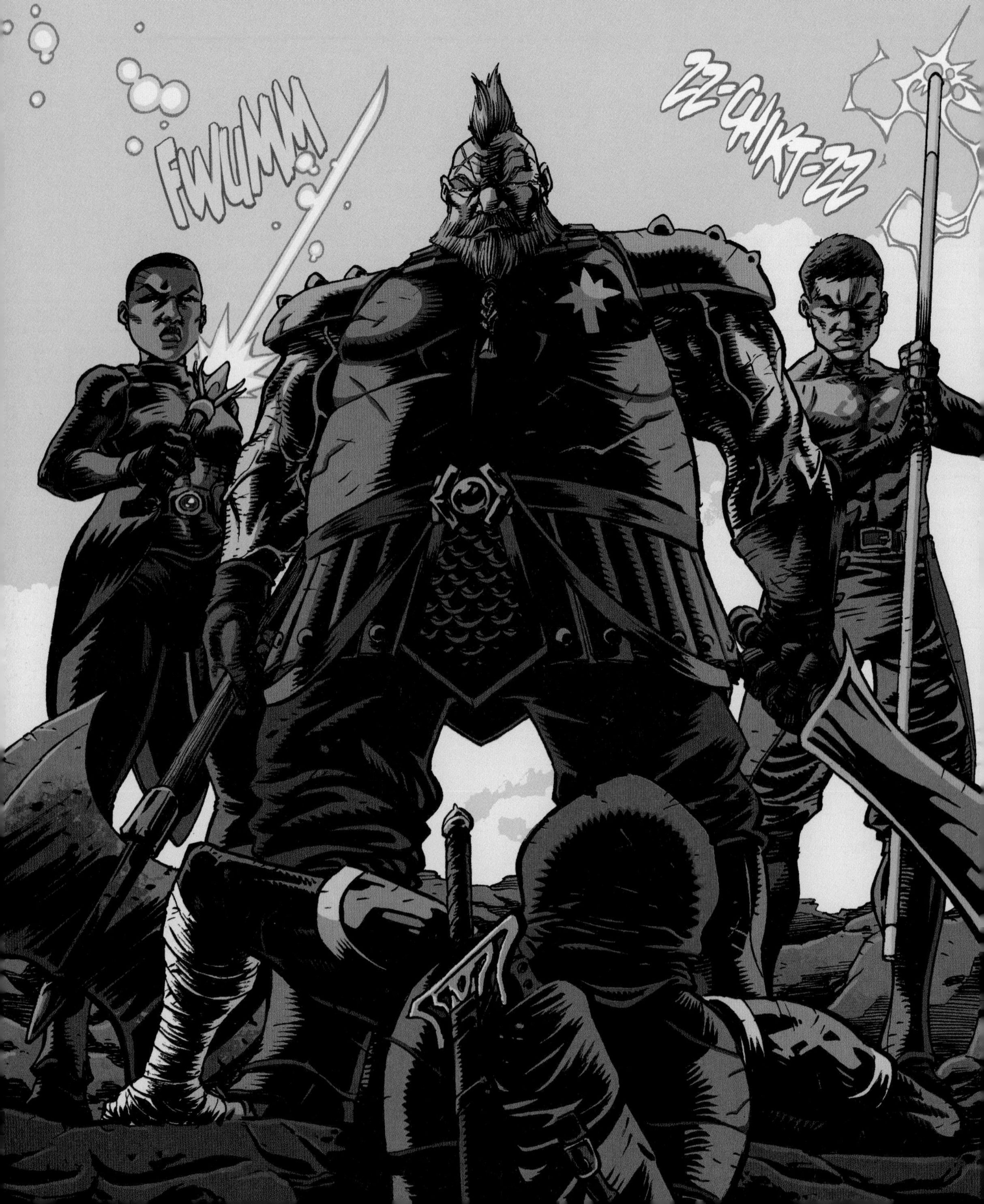
FWUMM
ZZ-CHIKT-ZZ

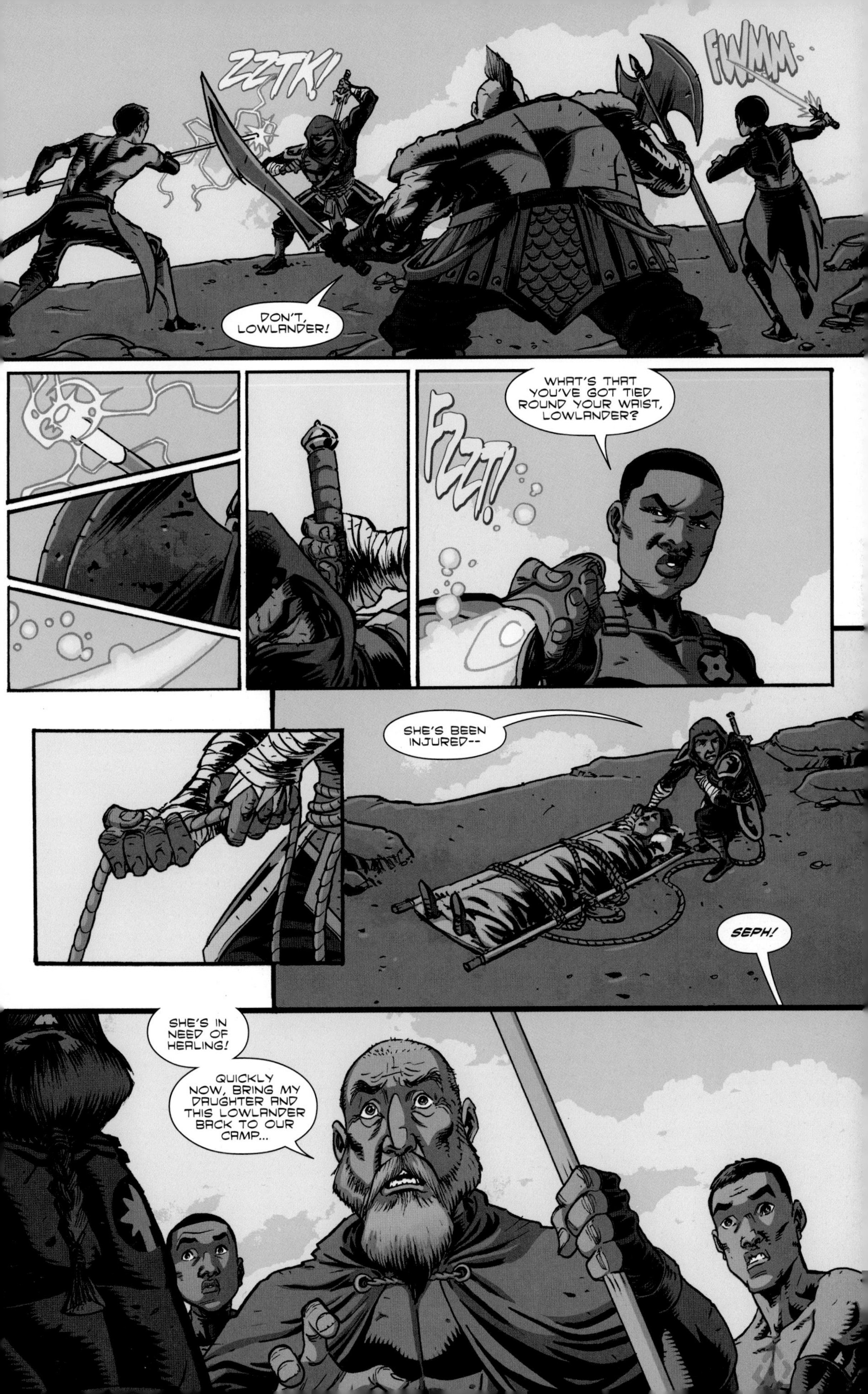
ZZTK!
FWMM
DON'T, LOWLANDER!
WHAT'S THAT YOU'VE GOT TIED ROUND YOUR WRIST, LOWLANDER?
FZZT!
SHE'S BEEN INJURED--
SEPH!
SHE'S IN NEED OF HEALING!
QUICKLY NOW, BRING MY DAUGHTER AND THIS LOWLANDER BACK TO OUR CAMP...

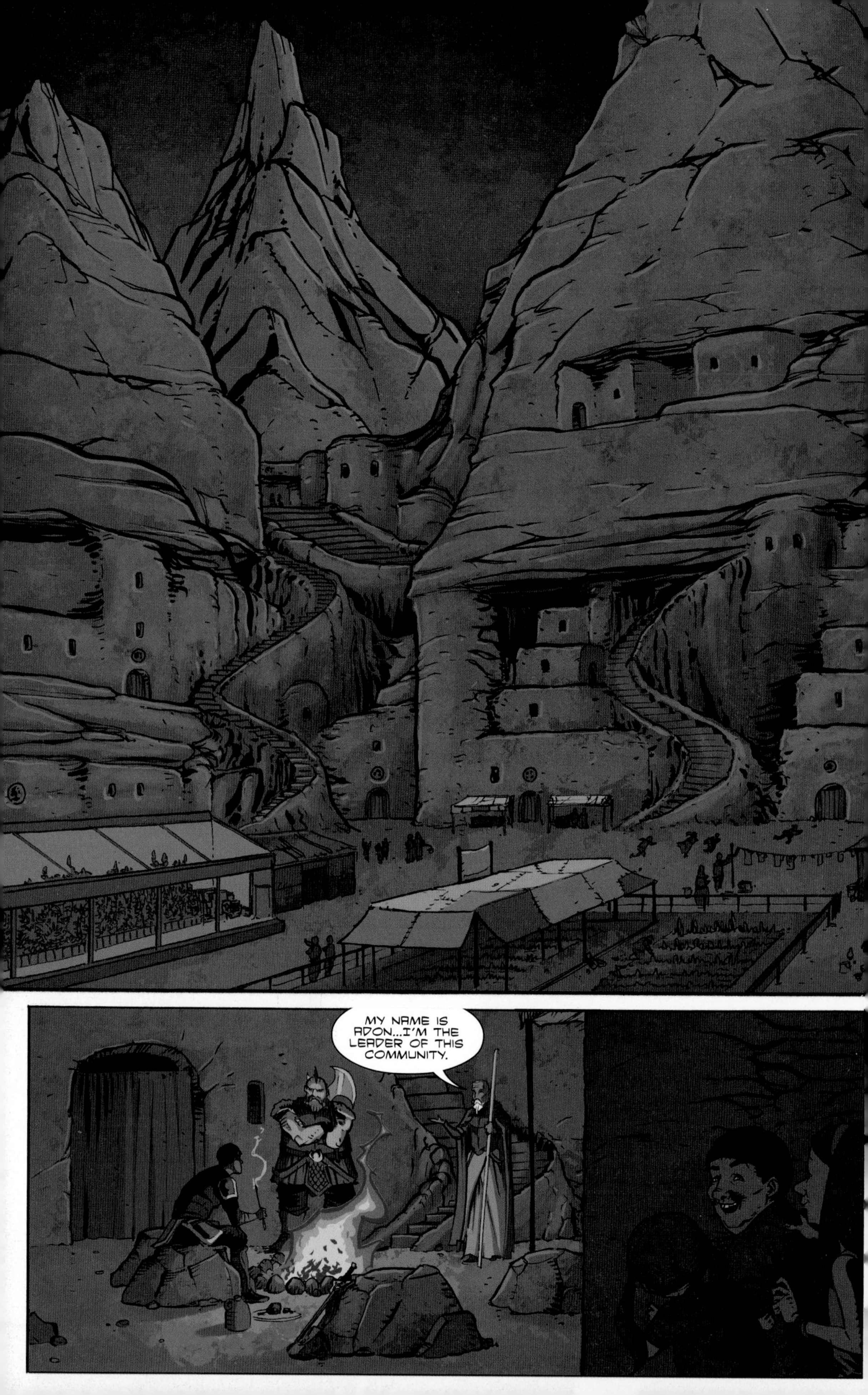
MY NAME IS ADON...I'M THE LEADER OF THIS COMMUNITY.

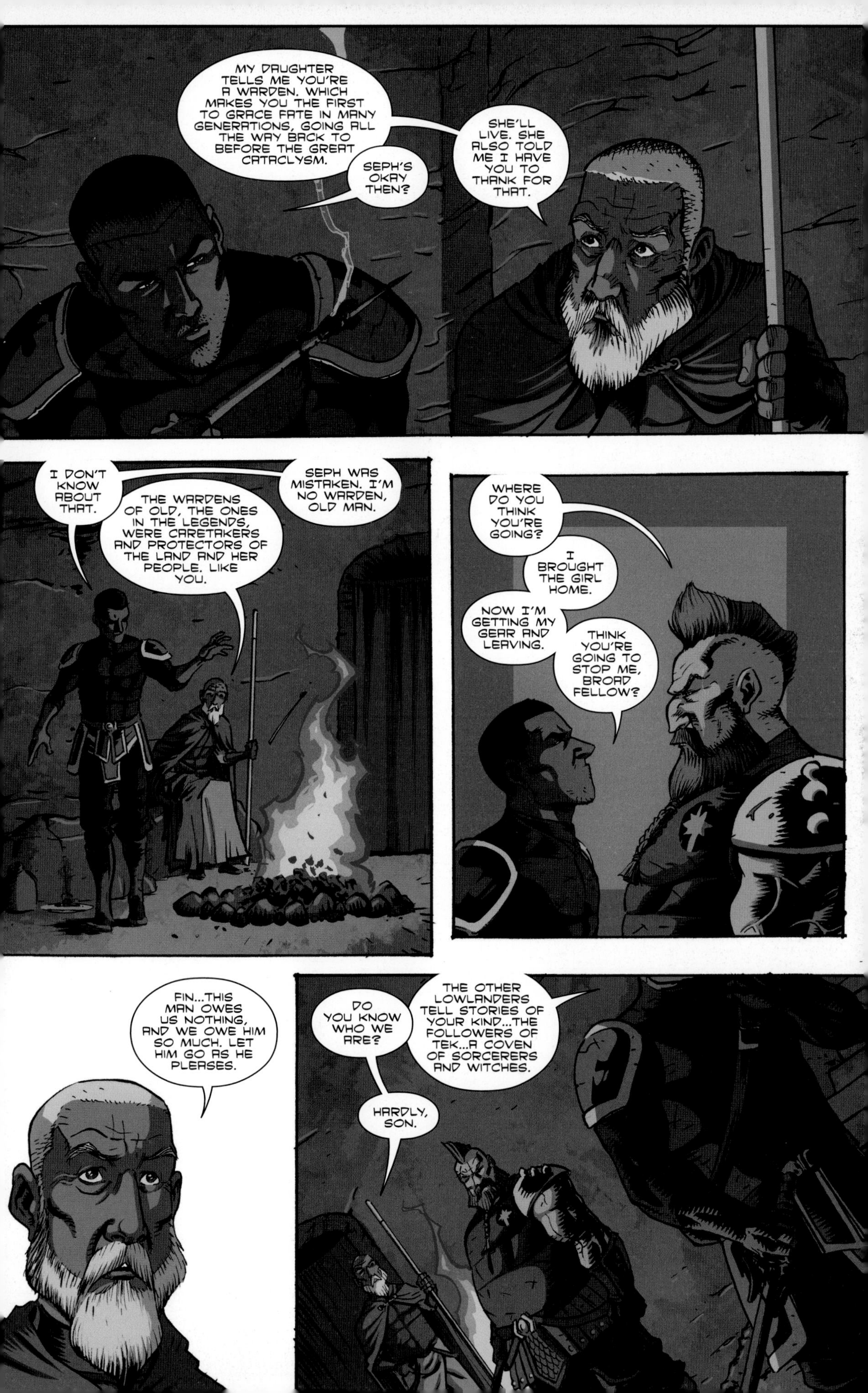
MY DAUGHTER TELLS ME YOU'RE A WARDEN. WHICH MAKES YOU THE FIRST TO GRACE FATE IN MANY GENERATIONS, GOING ALL THE WAY BACK TO BEFORE THE GREAT CATACLYSM.
SEPH'S OKAY THEN?
SHE'LL LIVE. SHE ALSO TOLD ME I HAVE YOU TO THANK FOR THAT.
I DON'T KNOW ABOUT THAT.
SEPH WAS MISTAKEN. I'M NO WARDEN, OLD MAN.
THE WARDENS OF OLD, THE ONES IN THE LEGENDS, WERE CARETAKERS AND PROTECTORS OF THE LAND AND HER PEOPLE. LIKE YOU.
WHERE DO YOU THINK YOU'RE GOING?
I BROUGHT THE GIRL HOME.
NOW I'M GETTING MY GEAR AND LEAVING.
THINK YOU'RE GOING TO STOP ME, BROAD FELLOW?
FIN...THIS MAN OWES US NOTHING, AND WE OWE HIM SO MUCH. LET HIM GO AS HE PLEASES.
DO YOU KNOW WHO WE ARE?
THE OTHER LOWLANDERS TELL STORIES OF YOUR KIND...THE FOLLOWERS OF TEK...A COVEN OF SORCERERS AND WITCHES.
HARDLY, SON.

MOSTLY WE'RE SCHOLARS... ARCHIVISTS OF THINGS LONG PAST.

KEEPERS OF THE LIGHT.

BEFORE THE CATACLYSM THREW THE WORLD INTO CHAOS AND DARKNESS.

I HAVE ONLY KNOWN THE DARKNESS.

AS HAVE I. AND MY FATHER, AND HIS FATHER BEFORE HIM, AND SO ON.

BUT ONCE THERE *WAS* LIGHT. A GREAT LIGHT THAT WARMED NOT JUST THE LAND, BUT OUR MINDS, AND OUR SOULS. A BRIGHT STAR POINTED THE WAY TO INNOVATION... TECHNOLOGY... THE BETTERMENT OF HUMANKIND...

JUST STORIES. FIRESIDE TALES BY OLD MEN IN THEIR CUPS... ALL BUT FORGOTTEN COME THE MORNING.

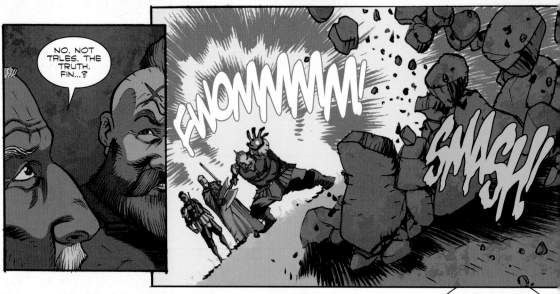

NO. NOT TALES. THE TRUTH. FIN...?

FWOMMMMM!

SMASH!

SORCERY!

IT'S NOT SPELLCRAFT, WARRIOR...

IT'S *TECHNOLOGY.* WE ALL WEAR THEM...THEY ARE MACHINES...TOOLS... BUILT LONG AGO.

THAT'S WHAT WE DO HERE, WARDEN...WE KEEP THE FIRES OF INNOVATION LIT FOR THE DAY THAT THE MEN OF FATE CAN WARM THEMSELVES ONCE MORE IN THEIR GLOW.

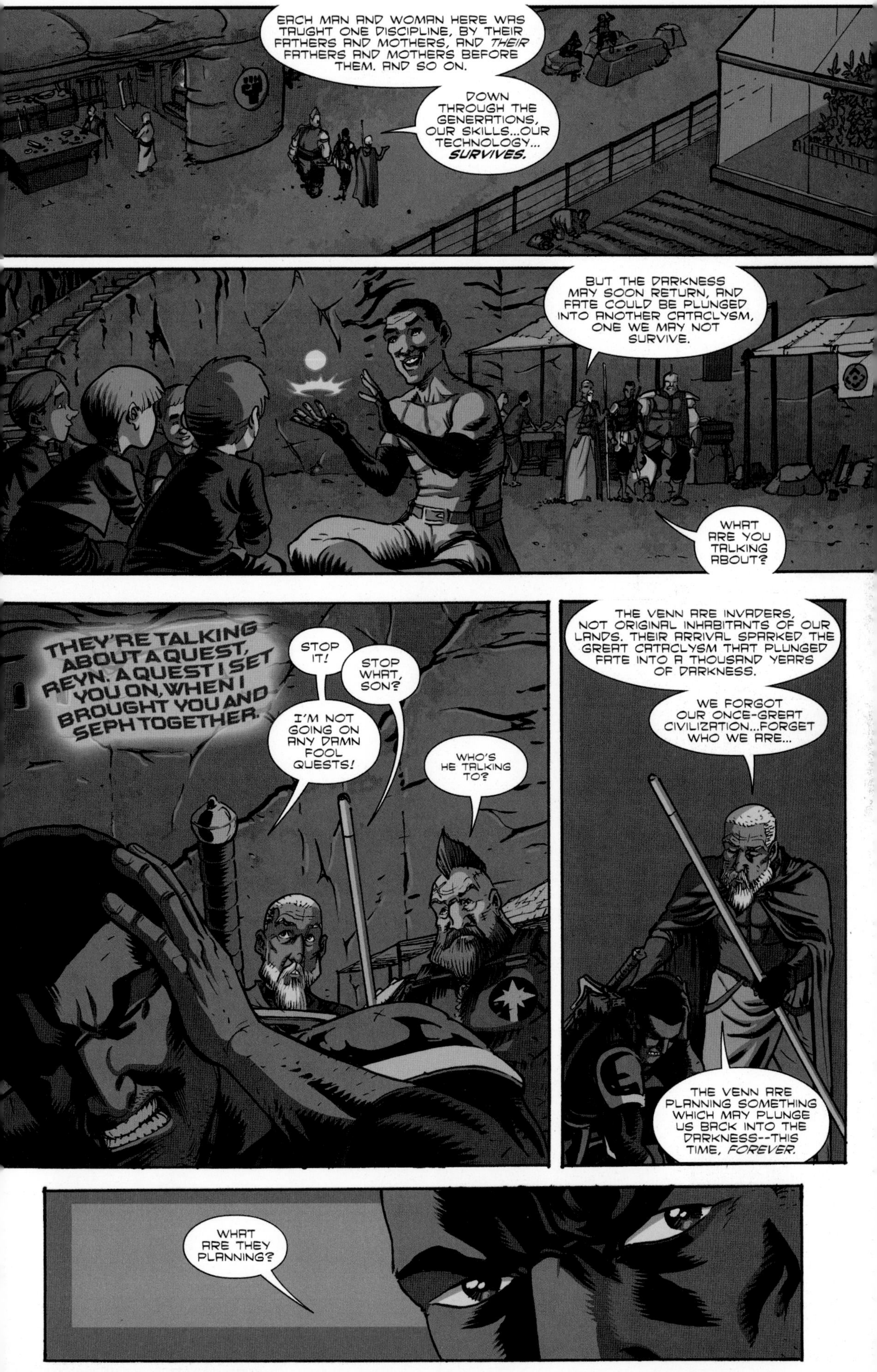
EACH MAN AND WOMAN HERE WAS TAUGHT ONE DISCIPLINE, BY THEIR FATHERS AND MOTHERS, AND *THEIR* FATHERS AND MOTHERS BEFORE THEM. AND SO ON.
DOWN THROUGH THE GENERATIONS, OUR SKILLS...OUR TECHNOLOGY... **SURVIVES.**
BUT THE DARKNESS MAY SOON RETURN, AND FATE COULD BE PLUNGED INTO ANOTHER CATACLYSM, ONE WE MAY NOT SURVIVE.
WHAT ARE YOU TALKING ABOUT?
THEY'RE TALKING ABOUT A QUEST, REYN. A QUEST I SET YOU ON, WHEN I BROUGHT YOU AND SEPH TOGETHER.
STOP IT!
I'M NOT GOING ON ANY DAMN FOOL QUESTS!
STOP WHAT, SON?
WHO'S HE TALKING TO?
THE VENN ARE INVADERS, NOT ORIGINAL INHABITANTS OF OUR LANDS. THEIR ARRIVAL SPARKED THE GREAT CATACLYSM THAT PLUNGED FATE INTO A THOUSAND YEARS OF DARKNESS.
WE FORGOT OUR ONCE-GREAT CIVILIZATION...FORGET WHO WE ARE...
THE VENN ARE PLANNING SOMETHING WHICH MAY PLUNGE US BACK INTO THE DARKNESS--THIS TIME, *FOREVER.*
WHAT ARE THEY PLANNING?

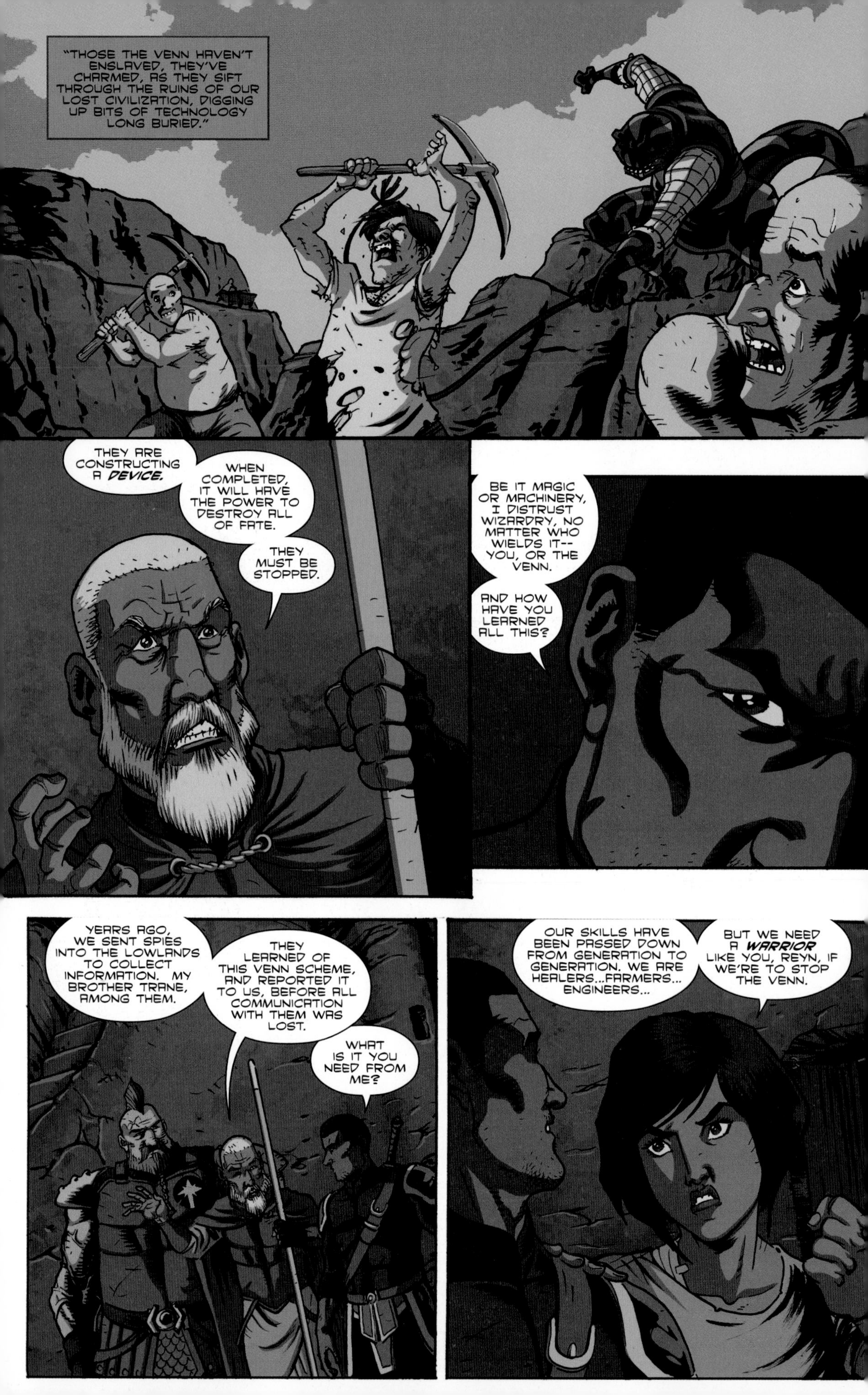
"THOSE THE VENN HAVEN'T ENSLAVED, THEY'VE CHARMED, AS THEY SIFT THROUGH THE RUINS OF OUR LOST CIVILIZATION, DIGGING UP BITS OF TECHNOLOGY LONG BURIED."
THEY ARE CONSTRUCTING A *DEVICE.*
WHEN COMPLETED, IT WILL HAVE THE POWER TO DESTROY ALL OF FATE.
THEY MUST BE STOPPED.
BE IT MAGIC OR MACHINERY, I DISTRUST WIZARDRY, NO MATTER WHO WIELDS IT-- YOU, OR THE VENN.
AND HOW HAVE YOU LEARNED ALL THIS?
YEARS AGO, WE SENT SPIES INTO THE LOWLANDS TO COLLECT INFORMATION. MY BROTHER TRANE, AMONG THEM.
THEY LEARNED OF THIS VENN SCHEME, AND REPORTED IT TO US, BEFORE ALL COMMUNICATION WITH THEM WAS LOST.
WHAT IS IT YOU NEED FROM ME?
OUR SKILLS HAVE BEEN PASSED DOWN FROM GENERATION TO GENERATION. WE ARE HEALERS...FARMERS... ENGINEERS...
BUT WE NEED A ***WARRIOR*** LIKE YOU, REYN, IF WE'RE TO STOP THE VENN.

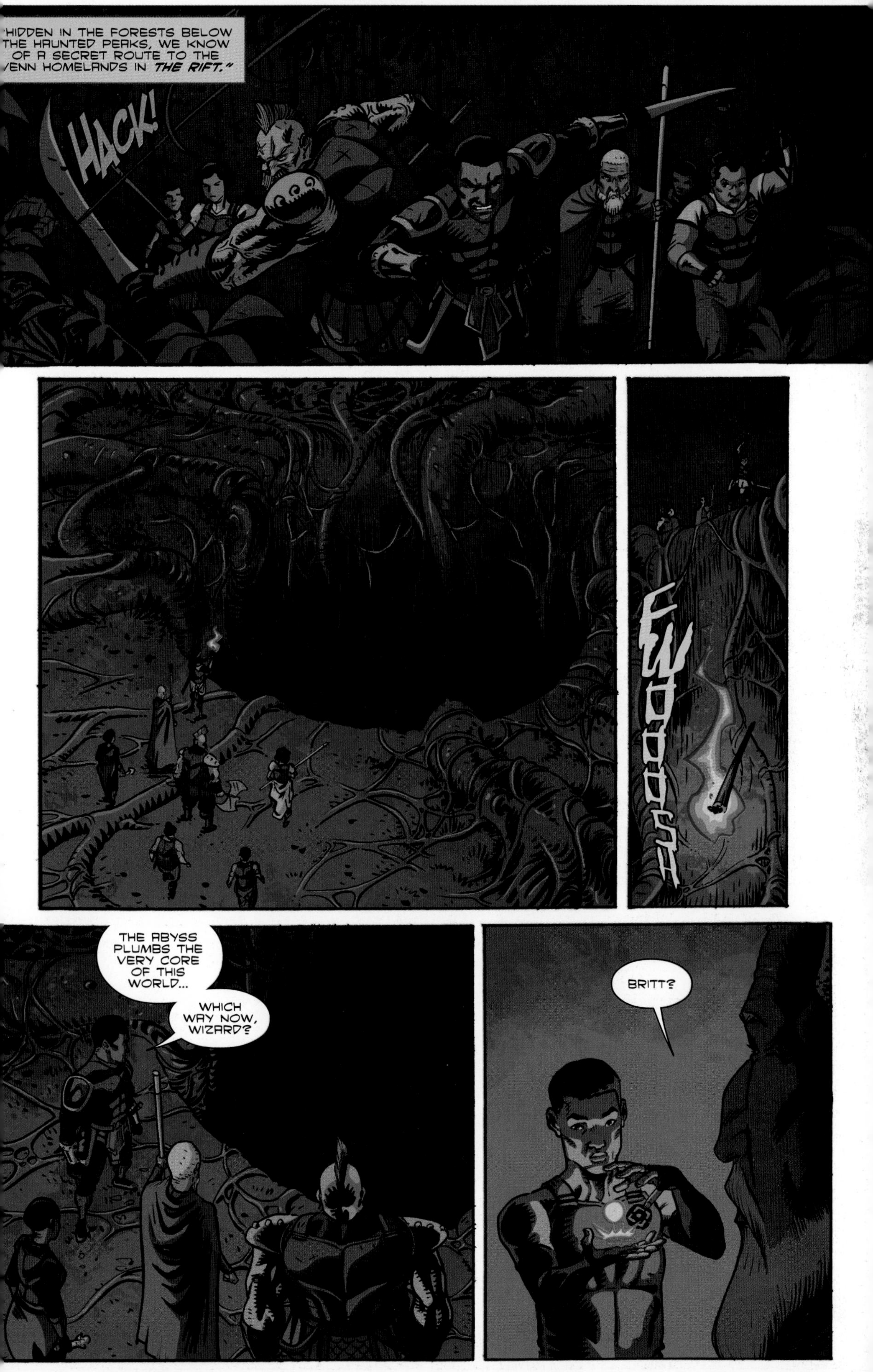
"HIDDEN IN THE FORESTS BELOW THE HAUNTED PEAKS, WE KNOW OF A SECRET ROUTE TO THE VENN HOMELANDS IN *THE RIFT.*"
HACK!
THE ABYSS PLUMBS THE VERY CORE OF THIS WORLD...
WHICH WAY NOW, WIZARD?
BRITT?

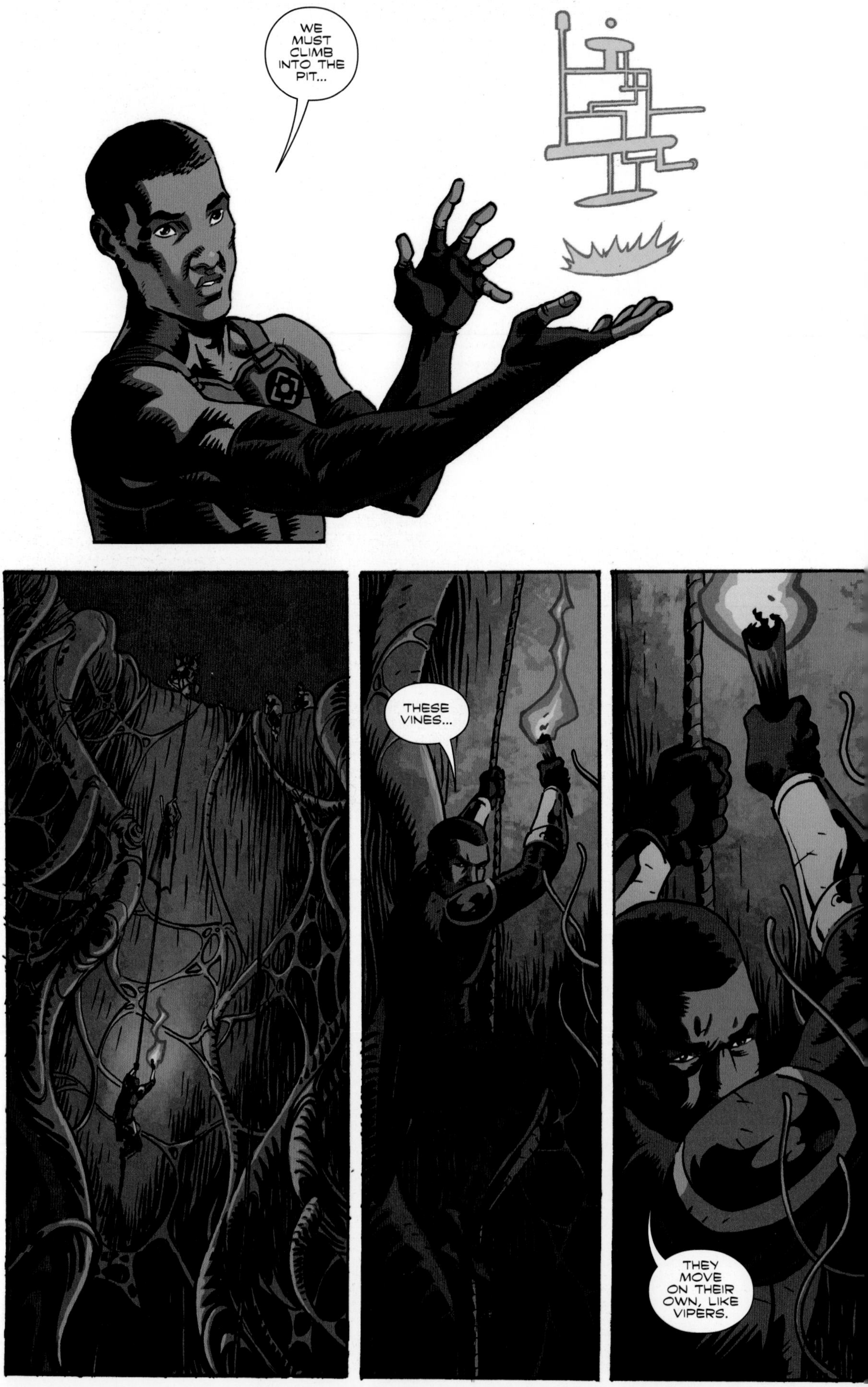
WE MUST CLIMB INTO THE PIT...
THESE VINES...
THEY MOVE ON THEIR OWN, LIKE VIPERS.

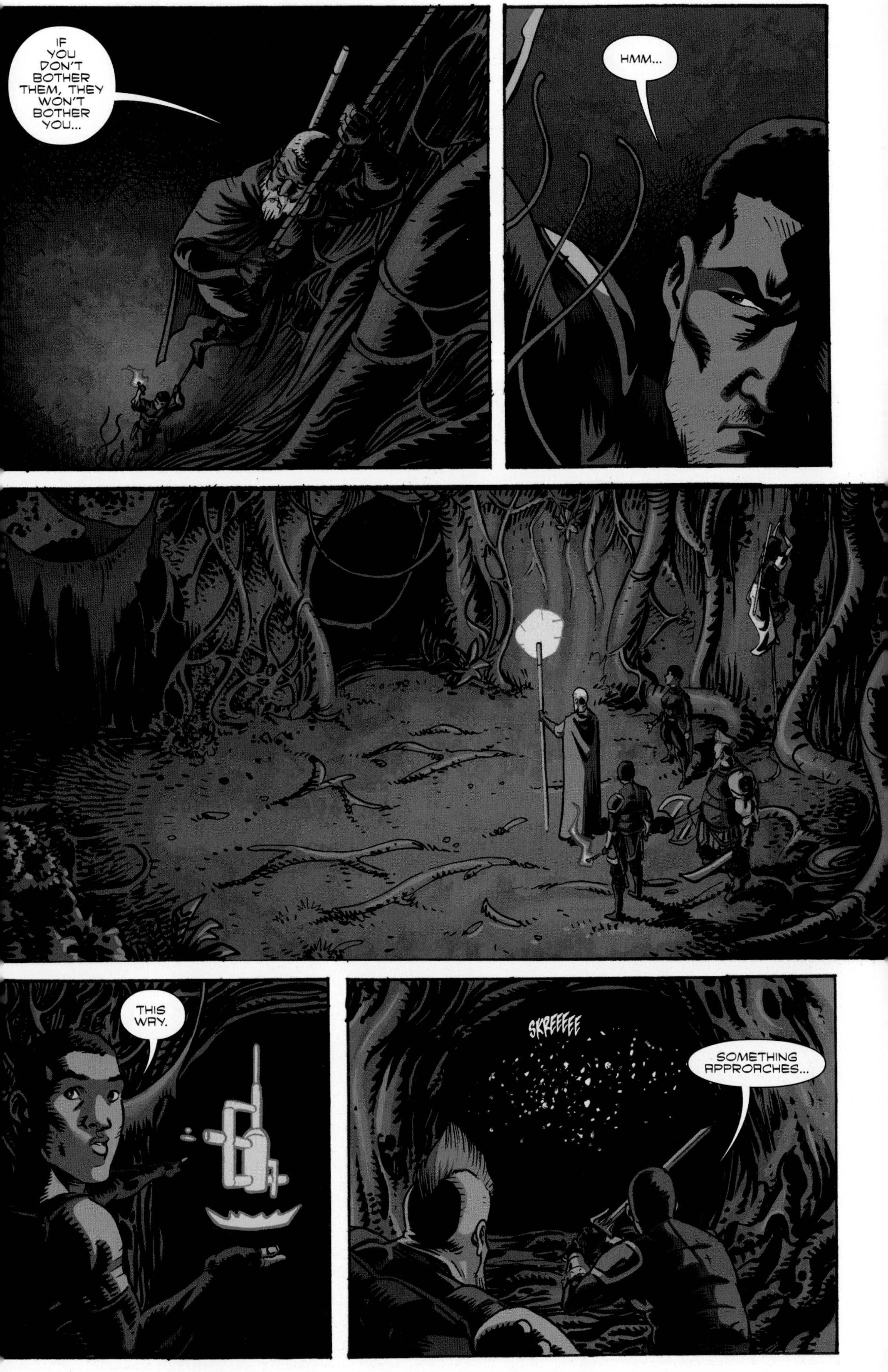
IF YOU DON'T BOTHER THEM, THEY WON'T BOTHER YOU...
HMM...
THIS WAY.
SKREEEEE
SOMETHING APPROACHES...

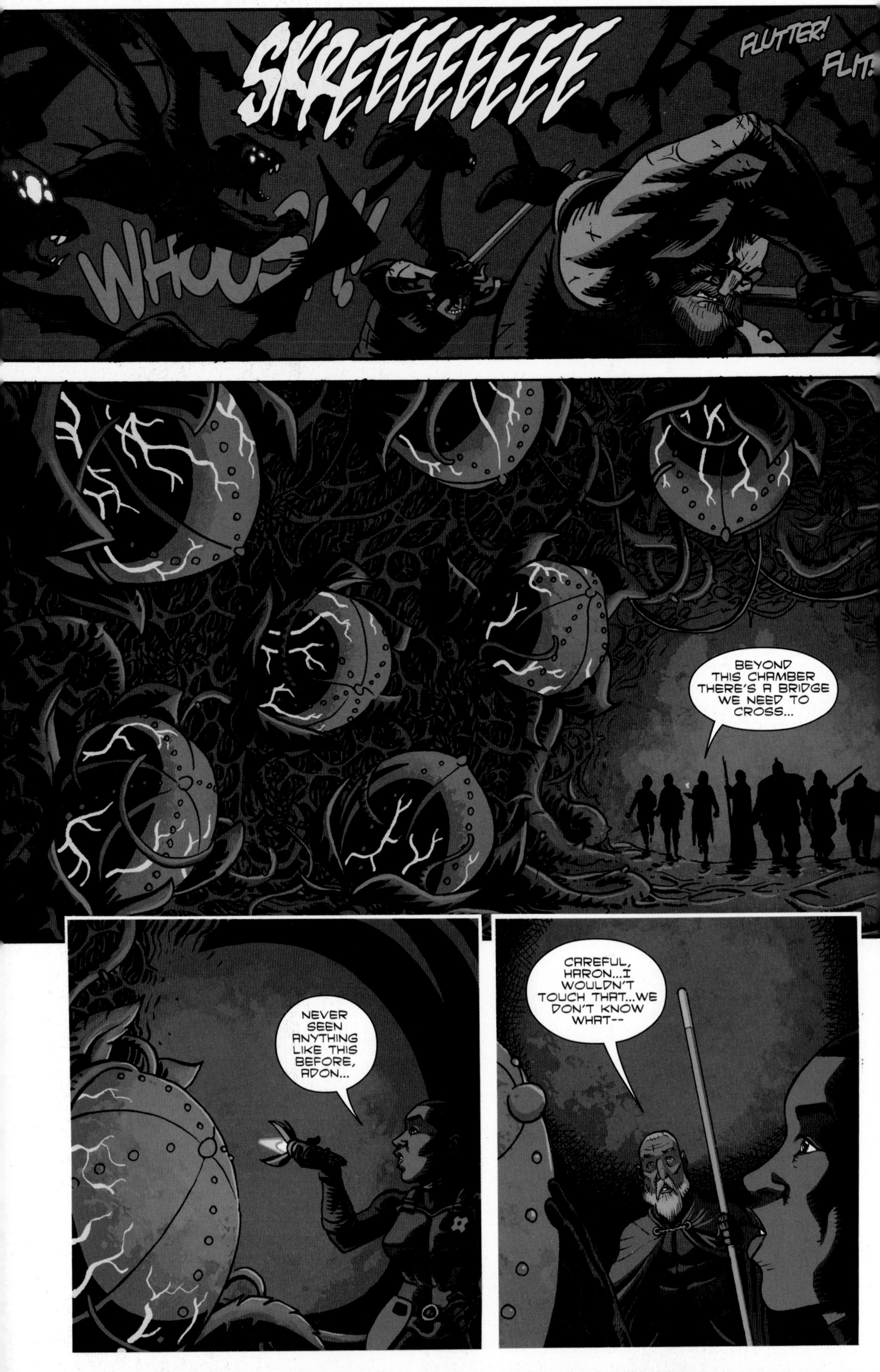
SKREEEEEEEEE
FLUTTER!
FLIT!
WHOOSH!!
BEYOND THIS CHAMBER THERE'S A BRIDGE WE NEED TO CROSS...
NEVER SEEN ANYTHING LIKE THIS BEFORE, ADON...
CAREFUL, HARON...I WOULDN'T TOUCH THAT...WE DON'T KNOW WHAT--

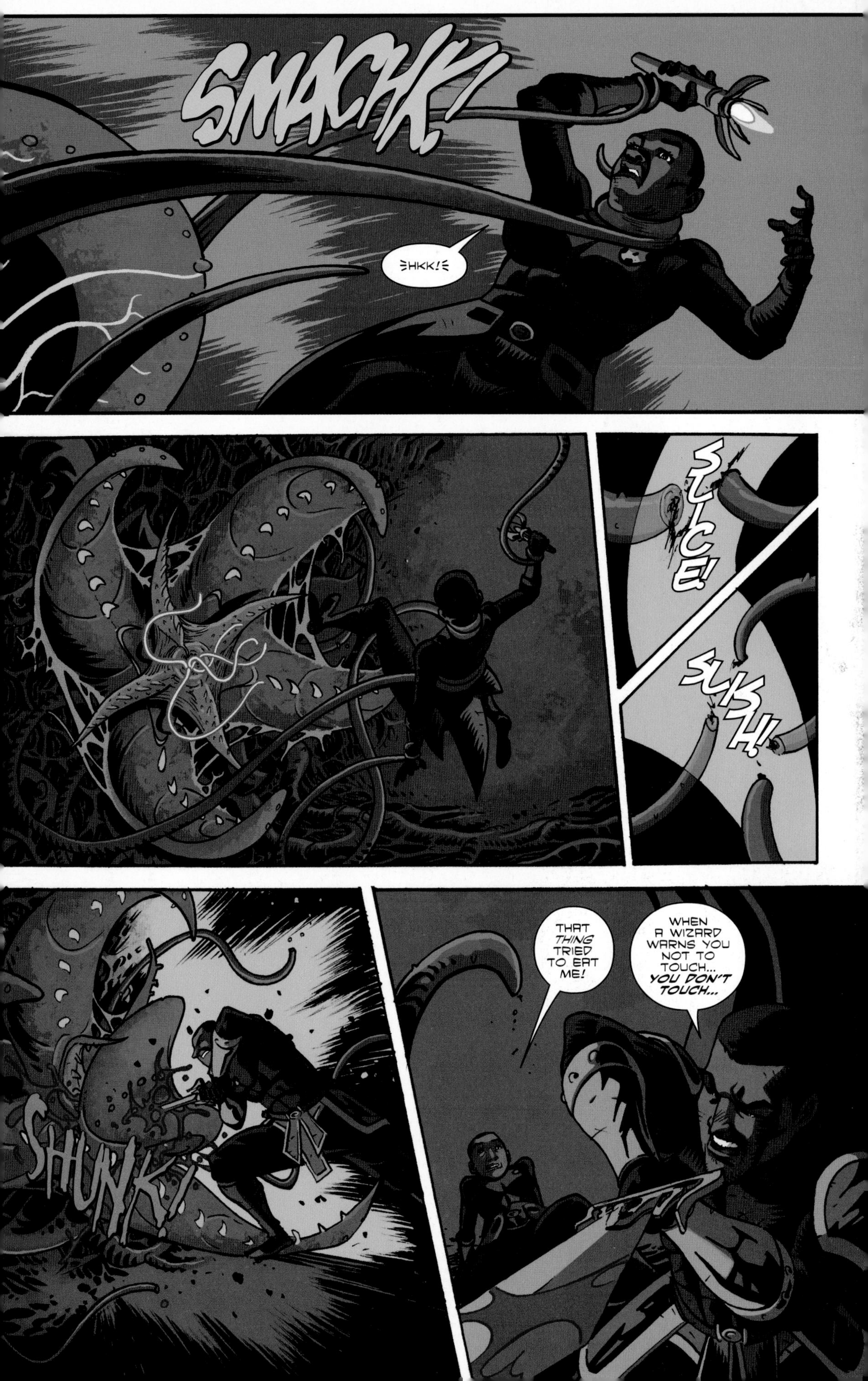
SMACK!
HKK!
SLICE!
SLISH!
SHUNK!
THAT *THING* TRIED TO EAT ME!
WHEN A WIZARD WARNS YOU NOT TO TOUCH... ***YOU DON'T TOUCH...***

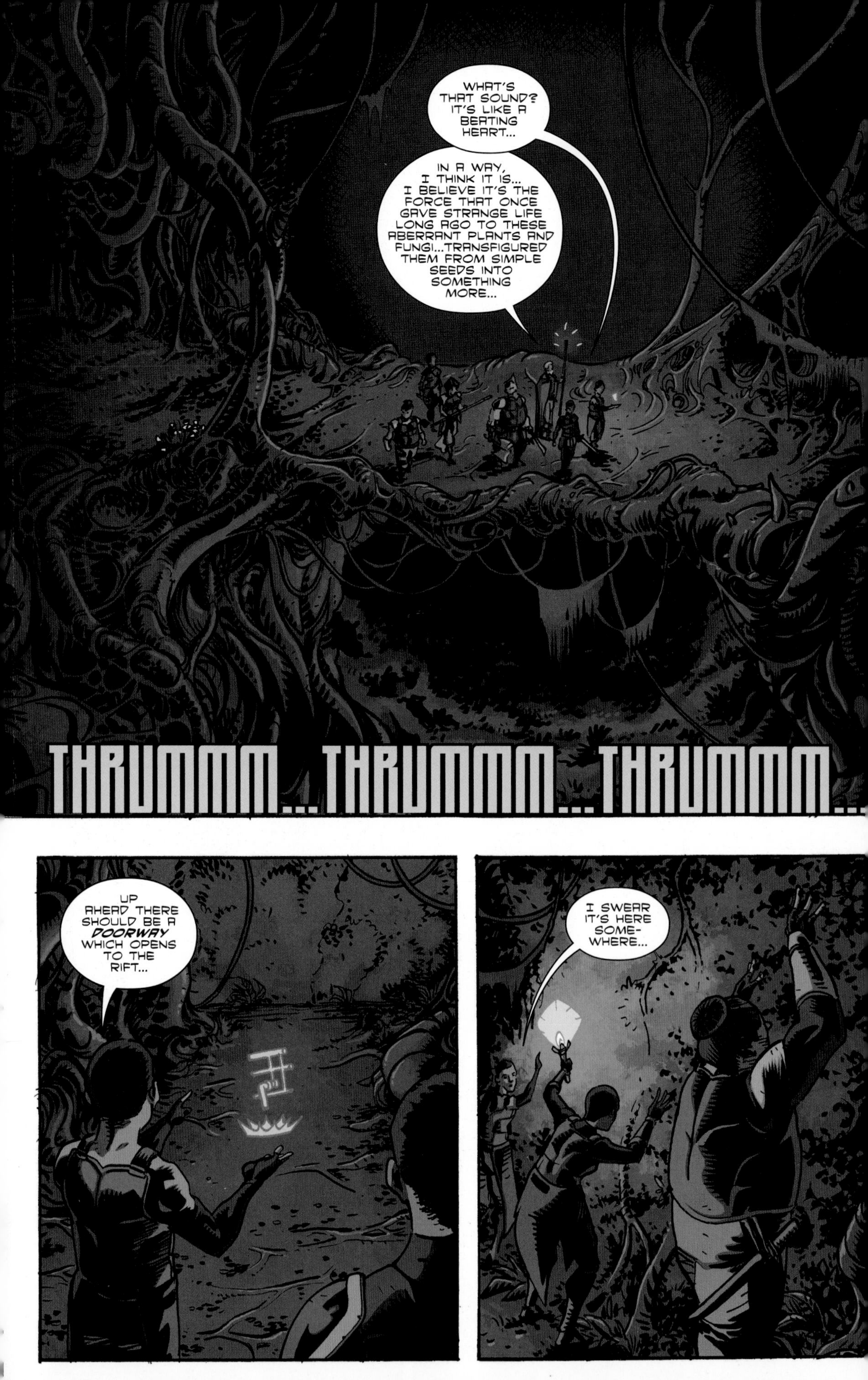
WHAT'S THAT SOUND? IT'S LIKE A BEATING HEART...
IN A WAY, I THINK IT IS... I BELIEVE IT'S THE FORCE THAT ONCE GAVE STRANGE LIFE LONG AGO TO THESE ABERRANT PLANTS AND FUNGI...TRANSFIGURED THEM FROM SIMPLE SEEDS INTO SOMETHING MORE...
THRUMMM... THRUMMM... THRUMMM...
UP AHEAD THERE SHOULD BE A *DOORWAY* WHICH OPENS TO THE RIFT...
I SWEAR IT'S HERE SOME-WHERE...

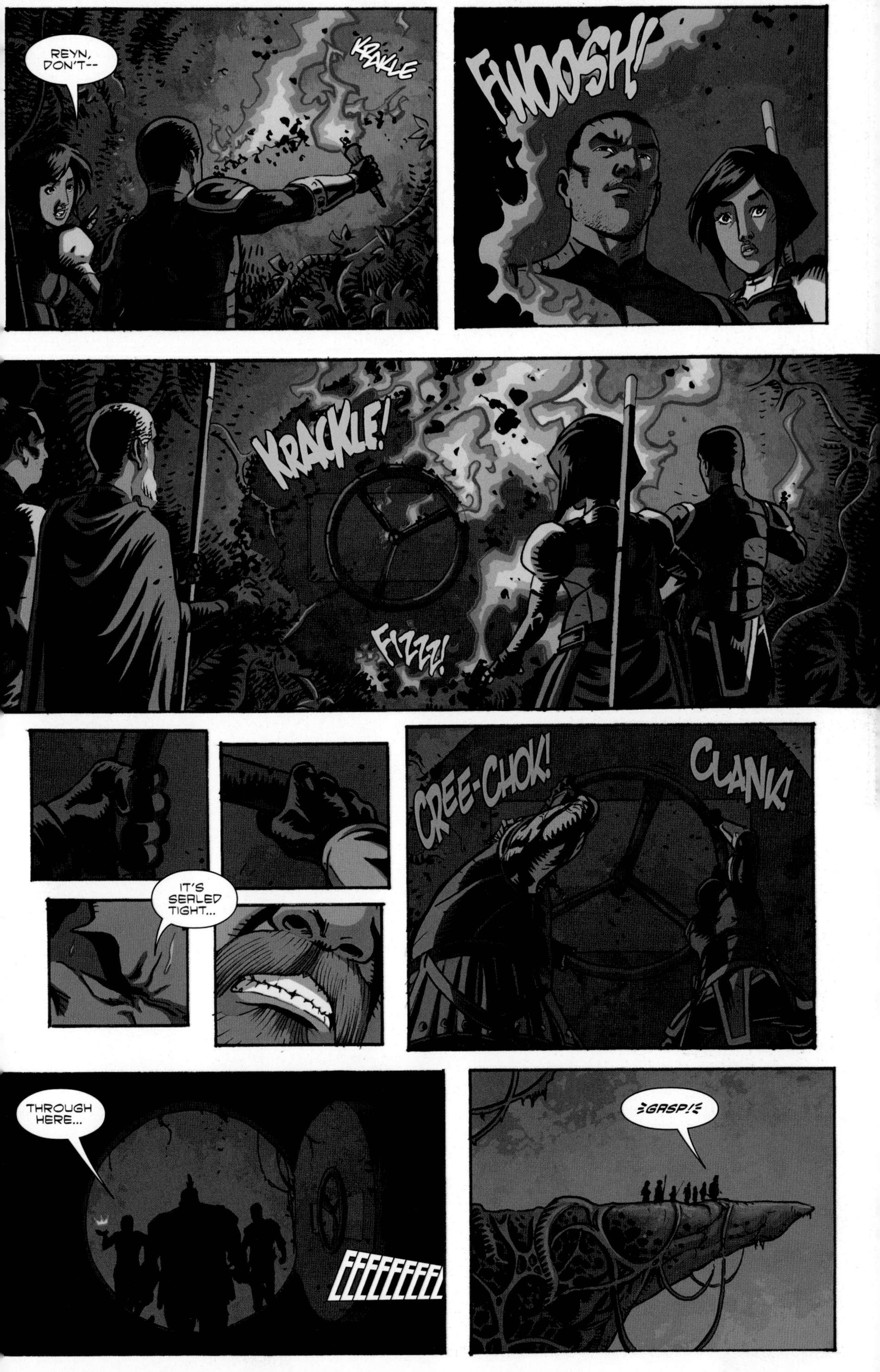
REYN, DON'T--
KRAKLE
FWOOSH!
KRACKLE!
FIZZZ!
IT'S SEALED TIGHT...
CREE-CHOK!
CLANK!
THROUGH HERE...
EEEEEEEEL
GASP!

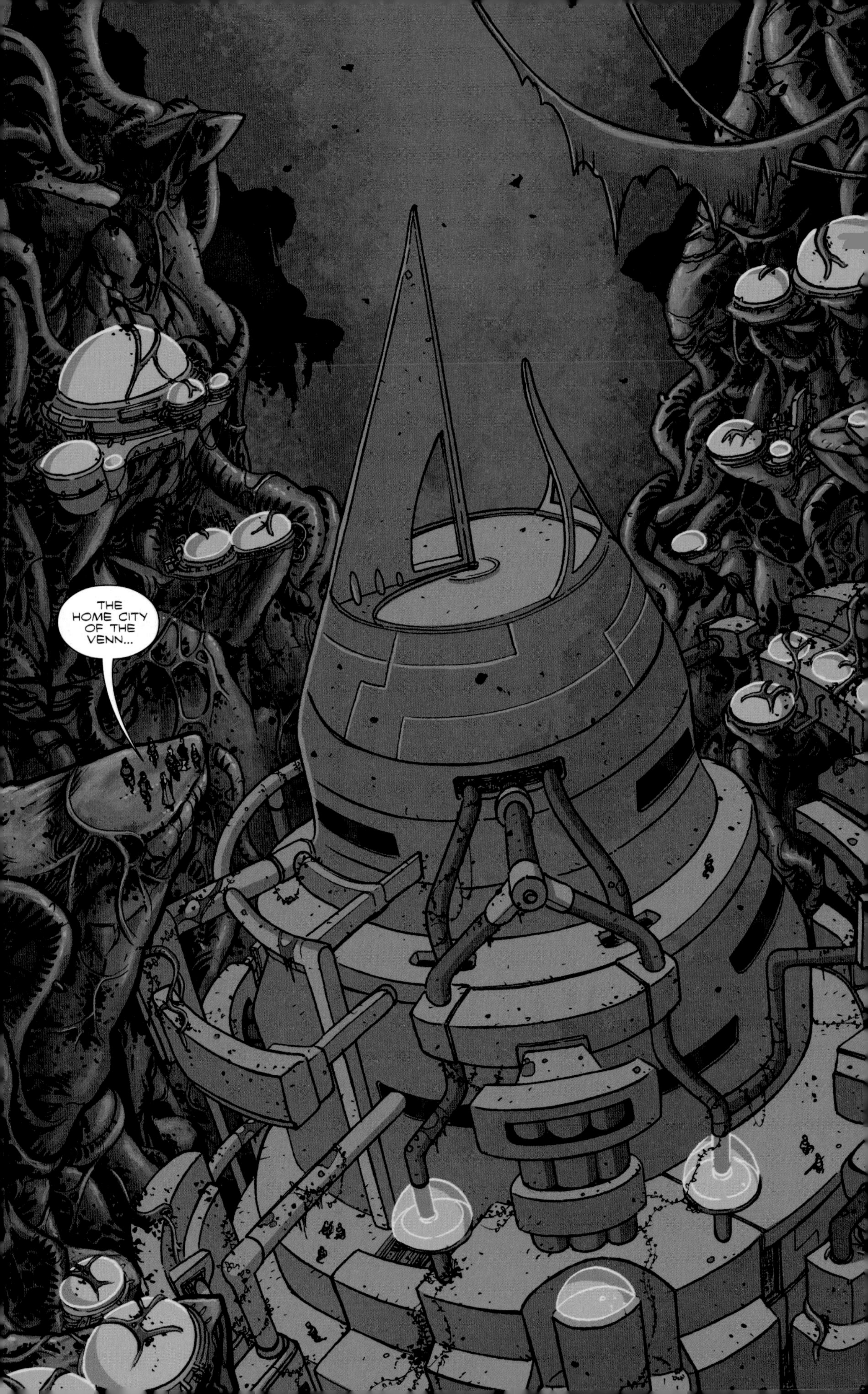
THE HOME CITY OF THE VENN...

Chapter Four

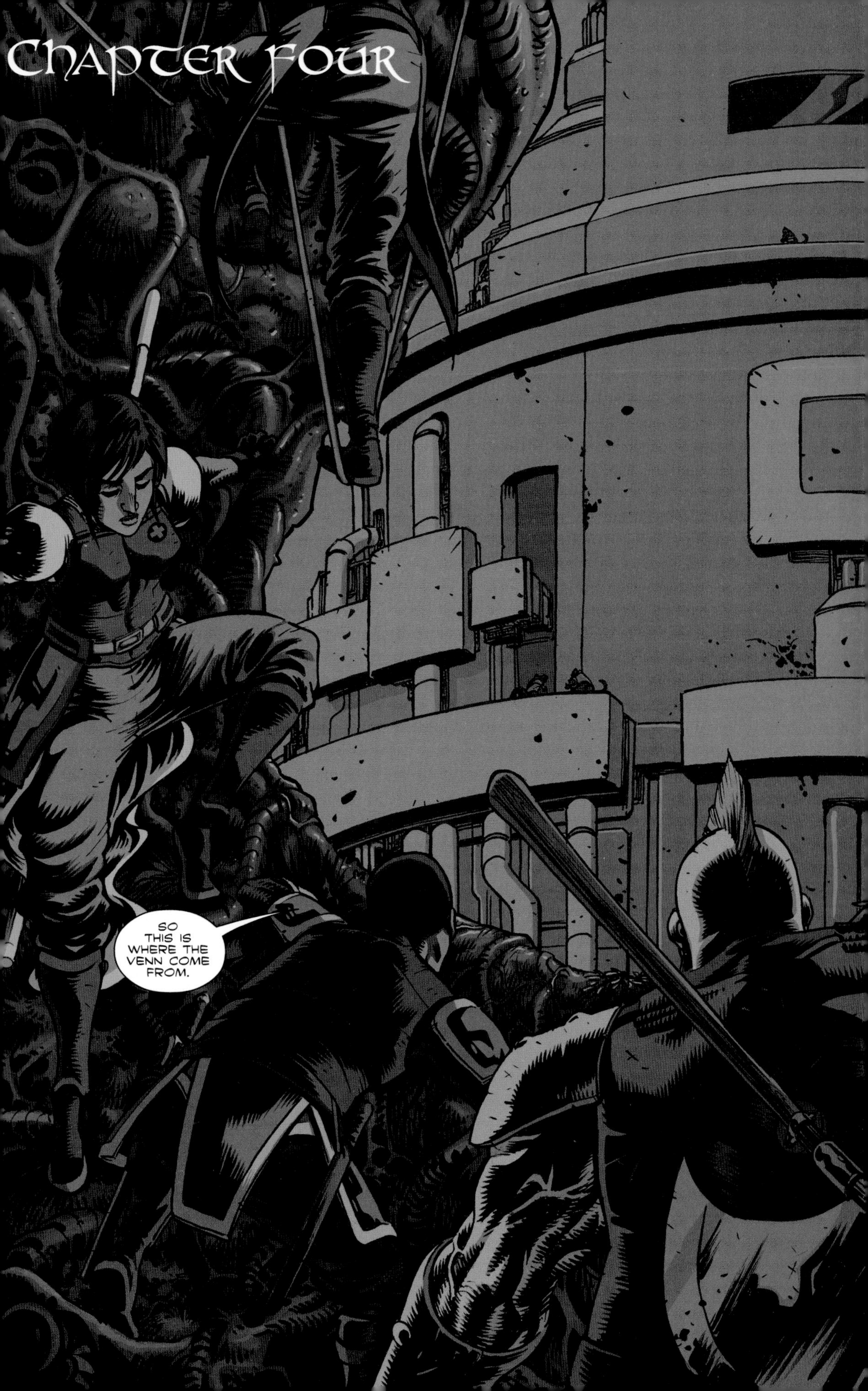
SO THIS IS WHERE THE VENN COME FROM.

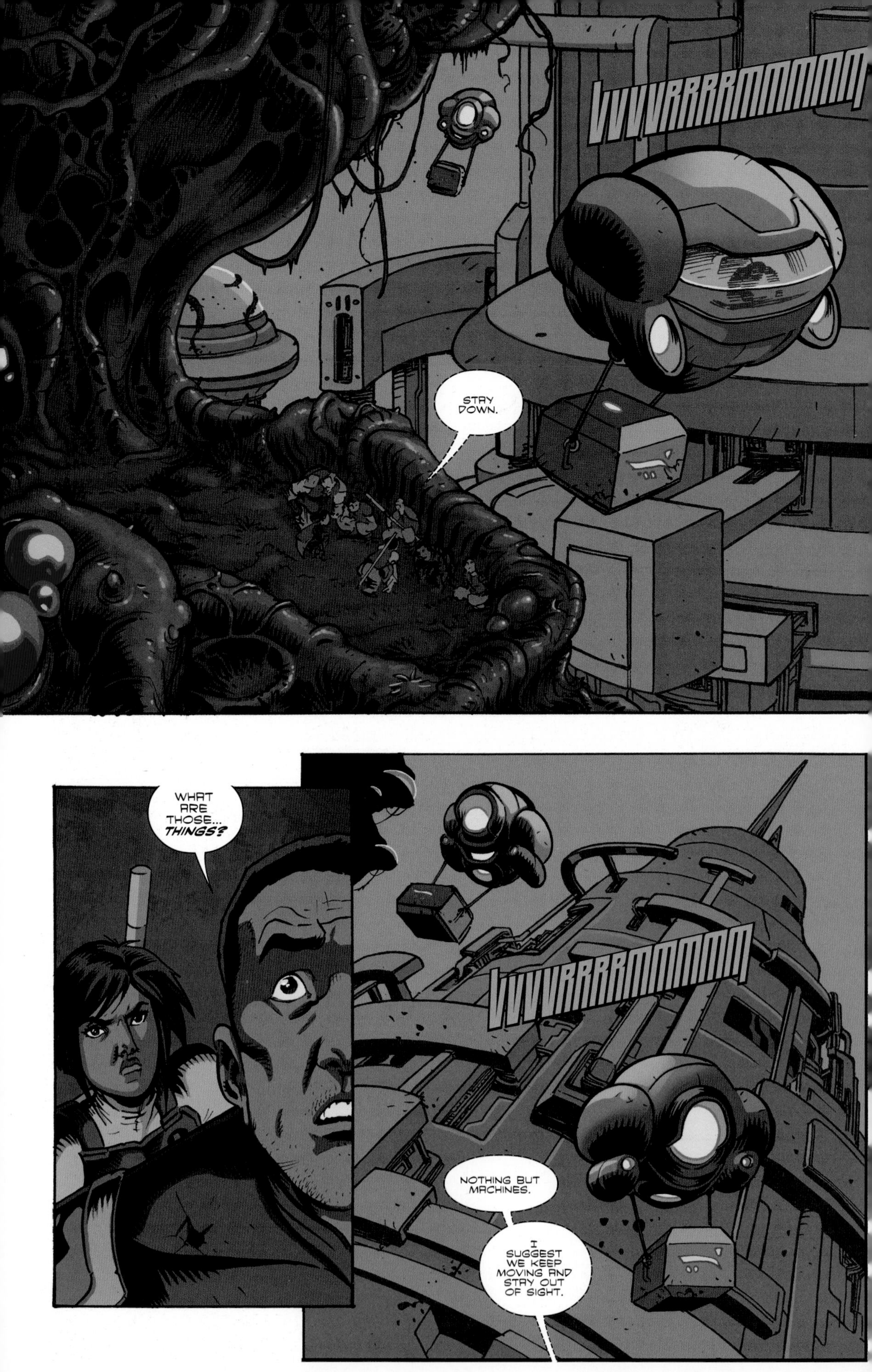
VVVVRRRRMMMMMM
STAY DOWN.
WHAT ARE THOSE... *THINGS?*
VVVVRRRRMMMMMM
NOTHING BUT MACHINES.
I SUGGEST WE KEEP MOVING AND STAY OUT OF SIGHT.

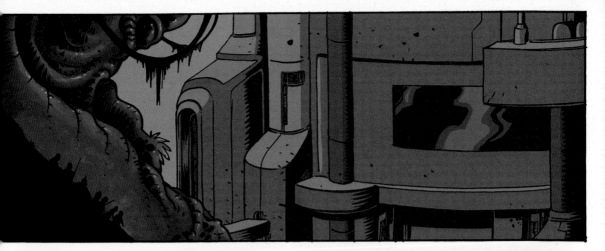

THAT TOWER THEY'RE WORKING ON...

WOULDN'T MIND A CLOSER LOOK.

CAREFUL, HARON...

THWIT-THWIT-THWIT-THWIT

LET'S SEE WHAT WE'VE GOT HERE...

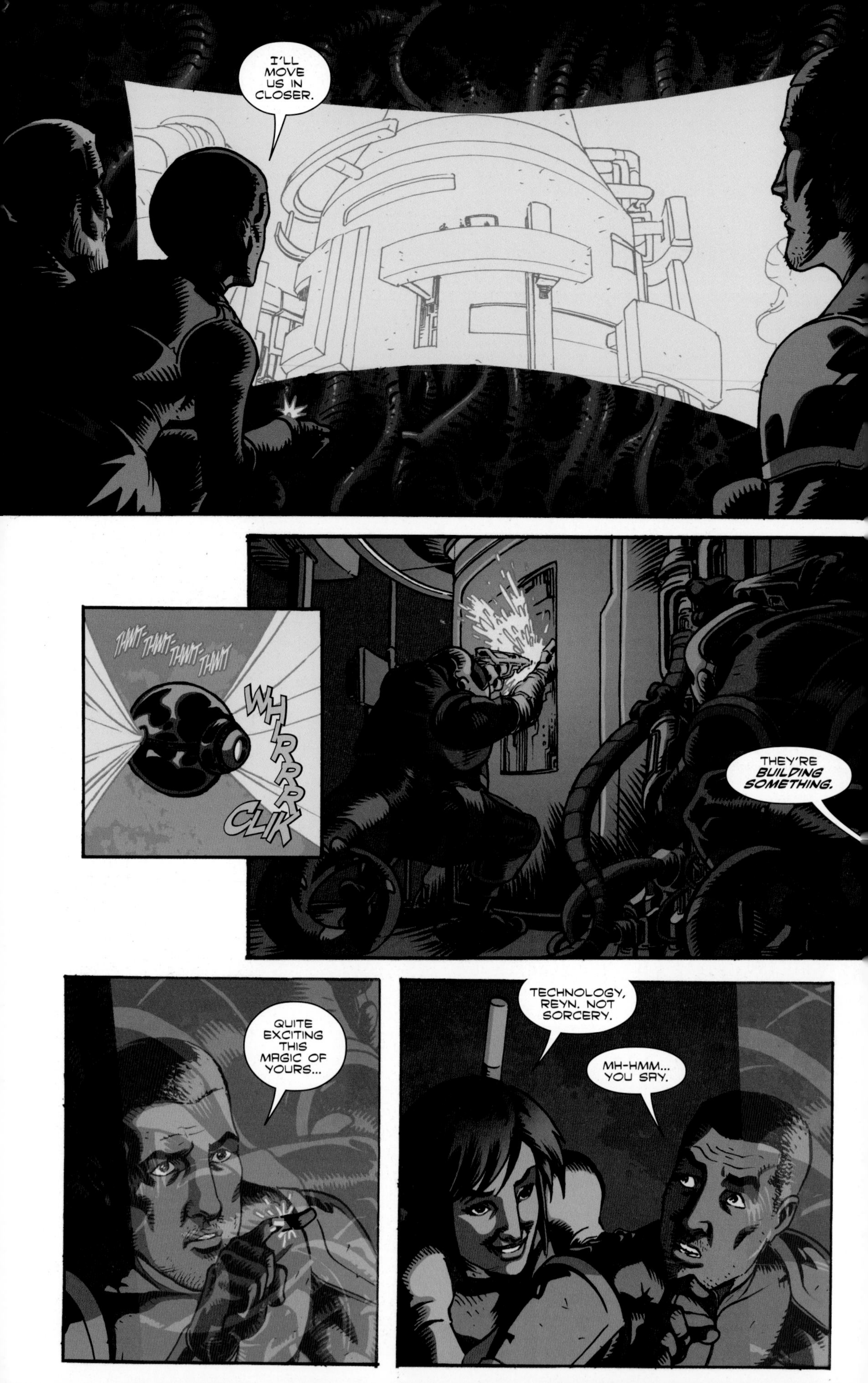
I'LL MOVE US IN CLOSER.
THWT-THWT-THWT-THWT
WHIRRR
CLIK
THEY'RE *BUILDING SOMETHING.*
QUITE EXCITING THIS MAGIC OF YOURS...
TECHNOLOGY, REYN. NOT SORCERY.
MH-HMM... YOU SAY.

THESE LOOK LIKE REINFORCED STRUCTURES...

LIKE THEY'RE DESIGNED TO AMPLIFY OR DIRECT SOME SORT OF ENERGY. HEAT, MAYBE. OR SOME OTHER FORCE.

PERHAPS.

A *WEAPON*, THEN?

WE NEED TO KNOW. FIND US A WAY IN, BRITT.

I THINK I SEE AN ACCESS WAY WE CAN USE.

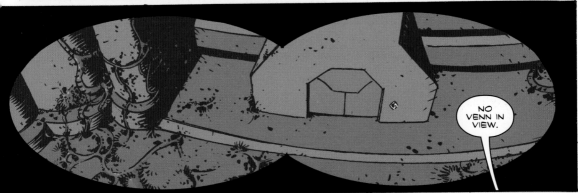

NO VENN IN VIEW.

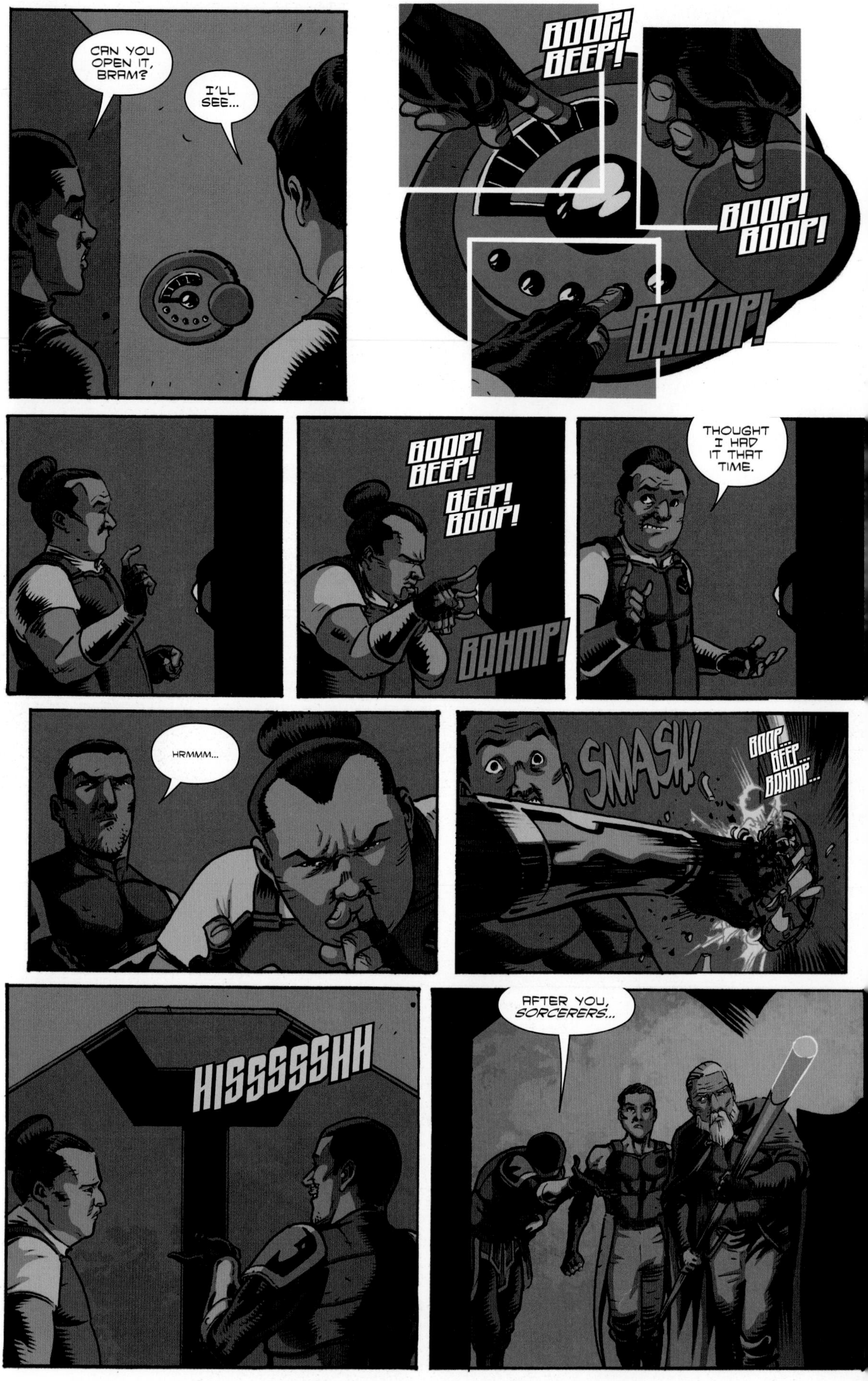
CAN YOU OPEN IT, BRAM?
I'LL SEE...
BOOP! BEEP!
BOOP! BOOP!
BAHMP!
BOOP! BEEP!
BEEP! BOOP!
BAHMP!
THOUGHT I HAD IT THAT TIME.
HRMMM...
SMASH!
BOOP... BEEP... BAHMP...
HISSSSSHH
AFTER YOU, *SORCERERS*...

ANYTHING, BRITT?
I'M SORRY--I DON'T HAVE ANY MAPS THAT COVER THIS PLACE.
THESE VENN MARKINGS POINT THE WAY TO SOMETHING...
BEST GUESS, SON.
THIS WAY, THEN, I GUESS.

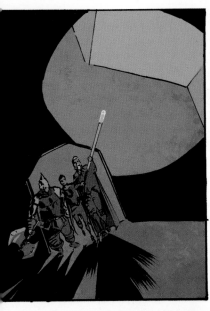

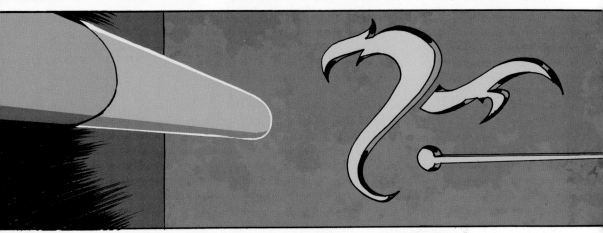

VRRRRRR

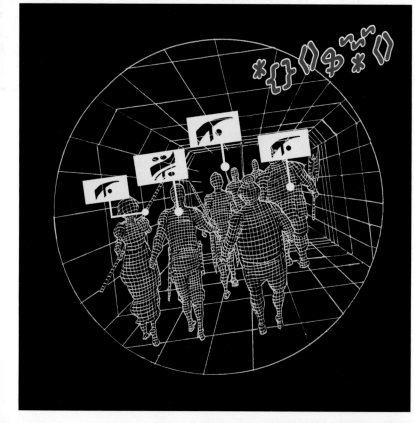

KLIK
TAK

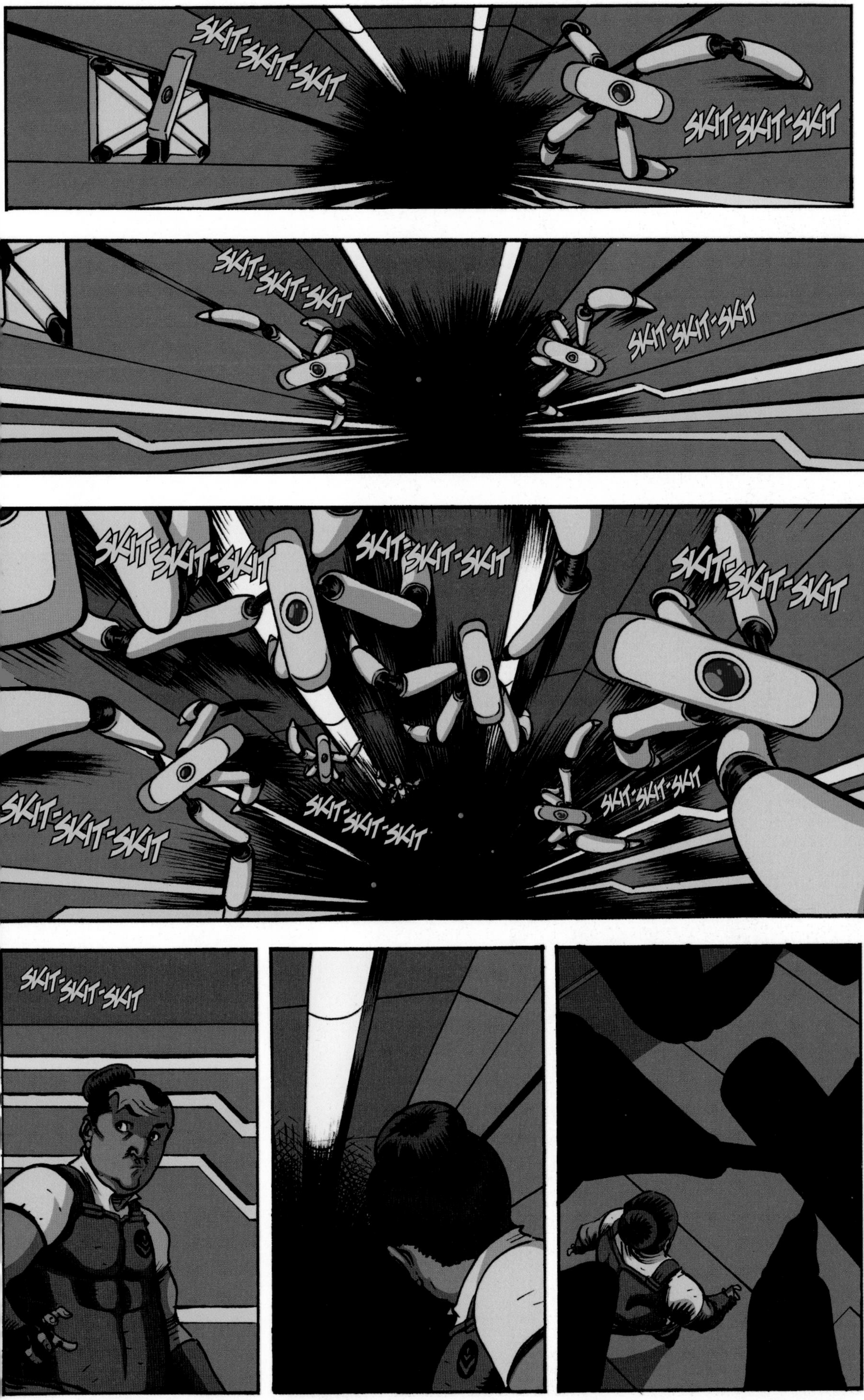
SKIT-SKIT-SKIT
SKIT-SKIT-SKIT
SKIT-SKIT-SKIT
SKIT-SKIT-SKIT
SKIT-SKIT-SKIT
SKIT-SKIT-SKIT
SKIT-SKIT-SKIT
SKIT-SKIT-SKIT
SKIT-SKIT-SKIT
SKIT-SKIT-SKIT
SKIT-SKIT-SKIT

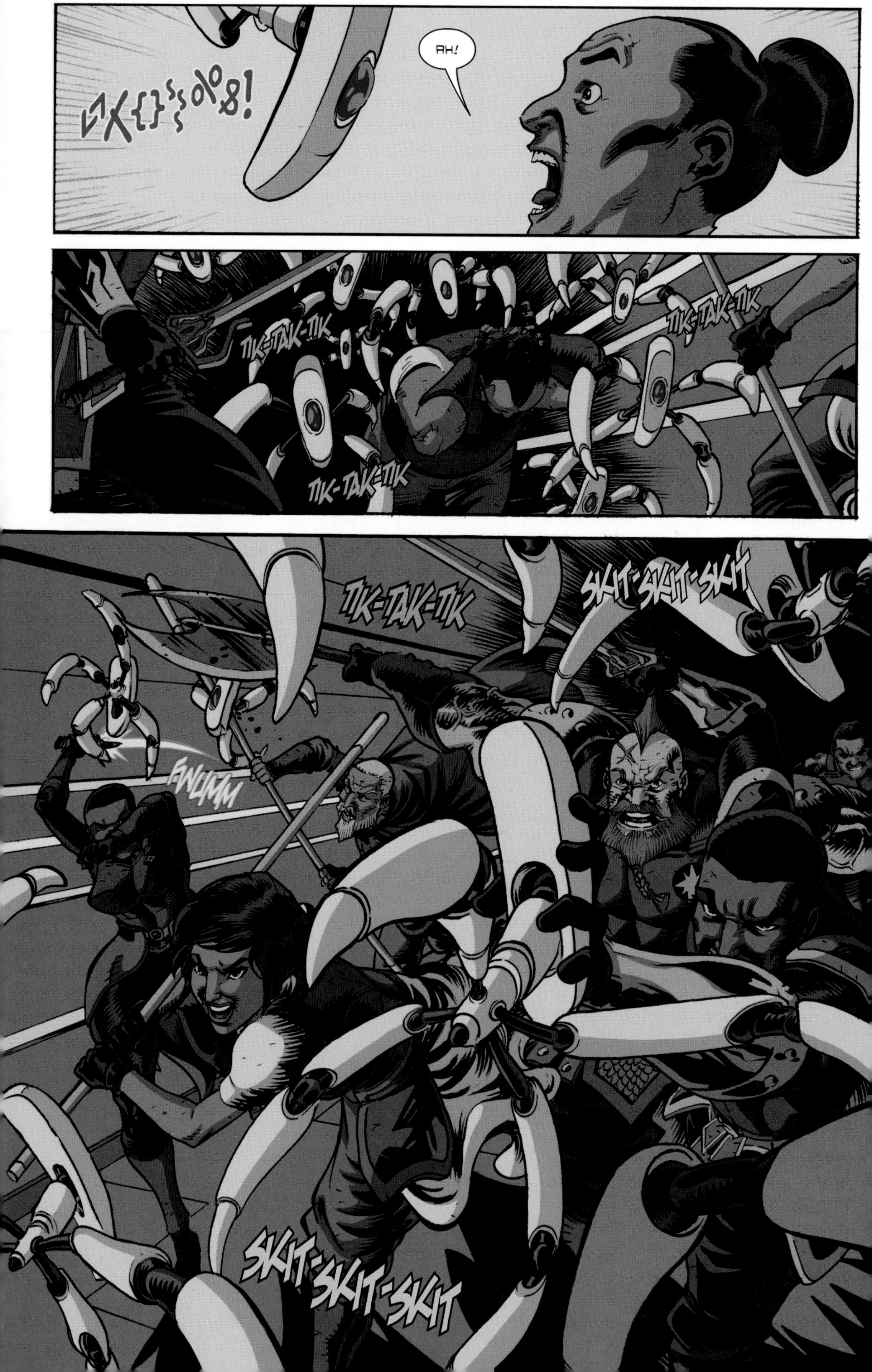
AH!
TIK-TAK-TIK
TIK-TAK-TIK
TIK-TAK-TIK
TIK-TAK-TIK
SKIT-SKIT-SKIT
FWUMM
SKIT-SKIT-SKIT

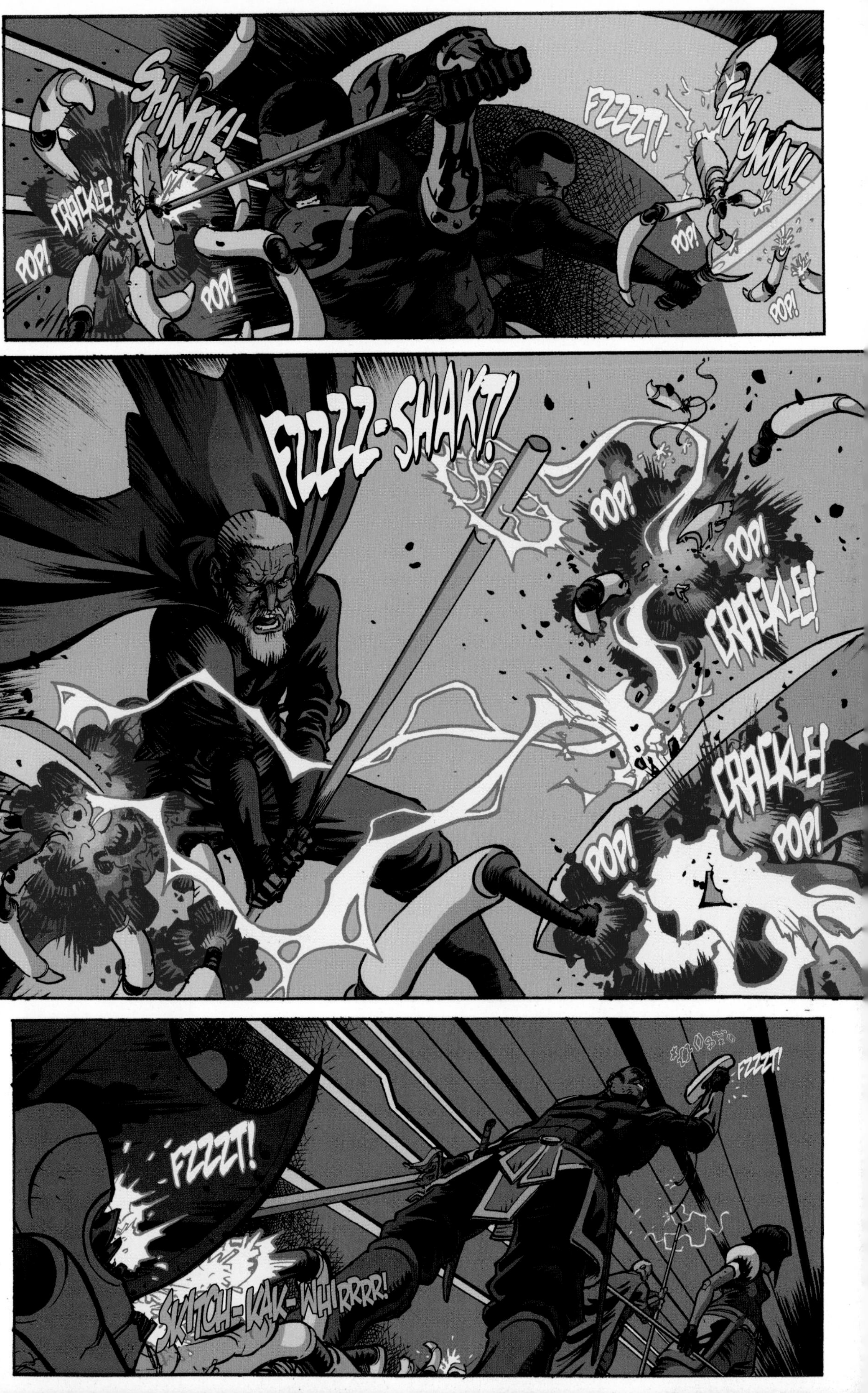
SHINTK!
CRACKLE!
POP!
POP!
FZZZT!
FWUMM!
POP!
POP!
FZZZZ-SHAKT!
POP!
POP!
CRACKLE!
CRACKLE!
POP!
POP!
FZZZT!
FZZZT!
SKITCH-KAK-WHIRRRR!

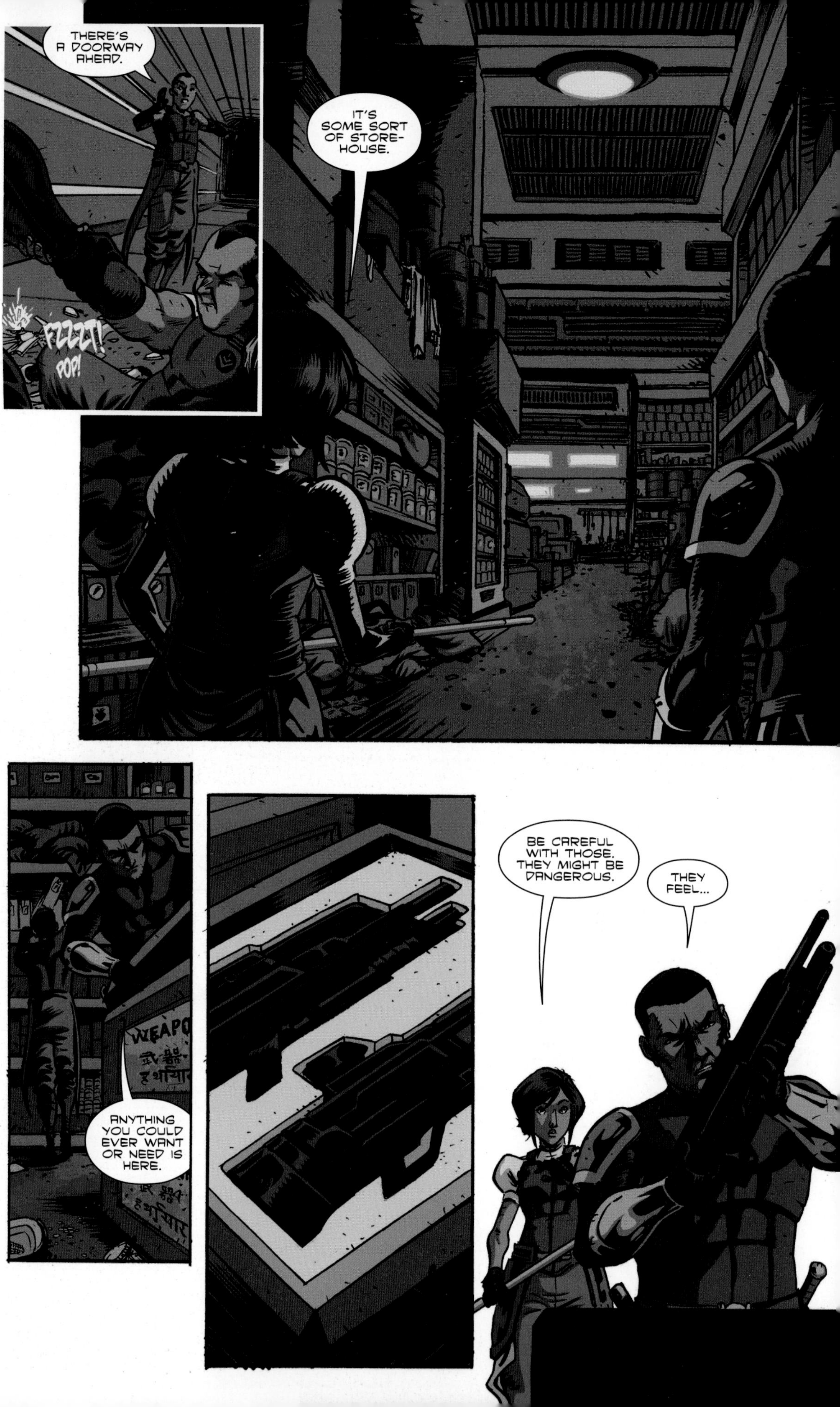
THERE'S A DOORWAY AHEAD.
FZZZT!
POP!
IT'S SOME SORT OF STORE-HOUSE.
ANYTHING YOU COULD EVER WANT OR NEED IS HERE.
BE CAREFUL WITH THOSE. THEY MIGHT BE DANGEROUS.
THEY FEEL...

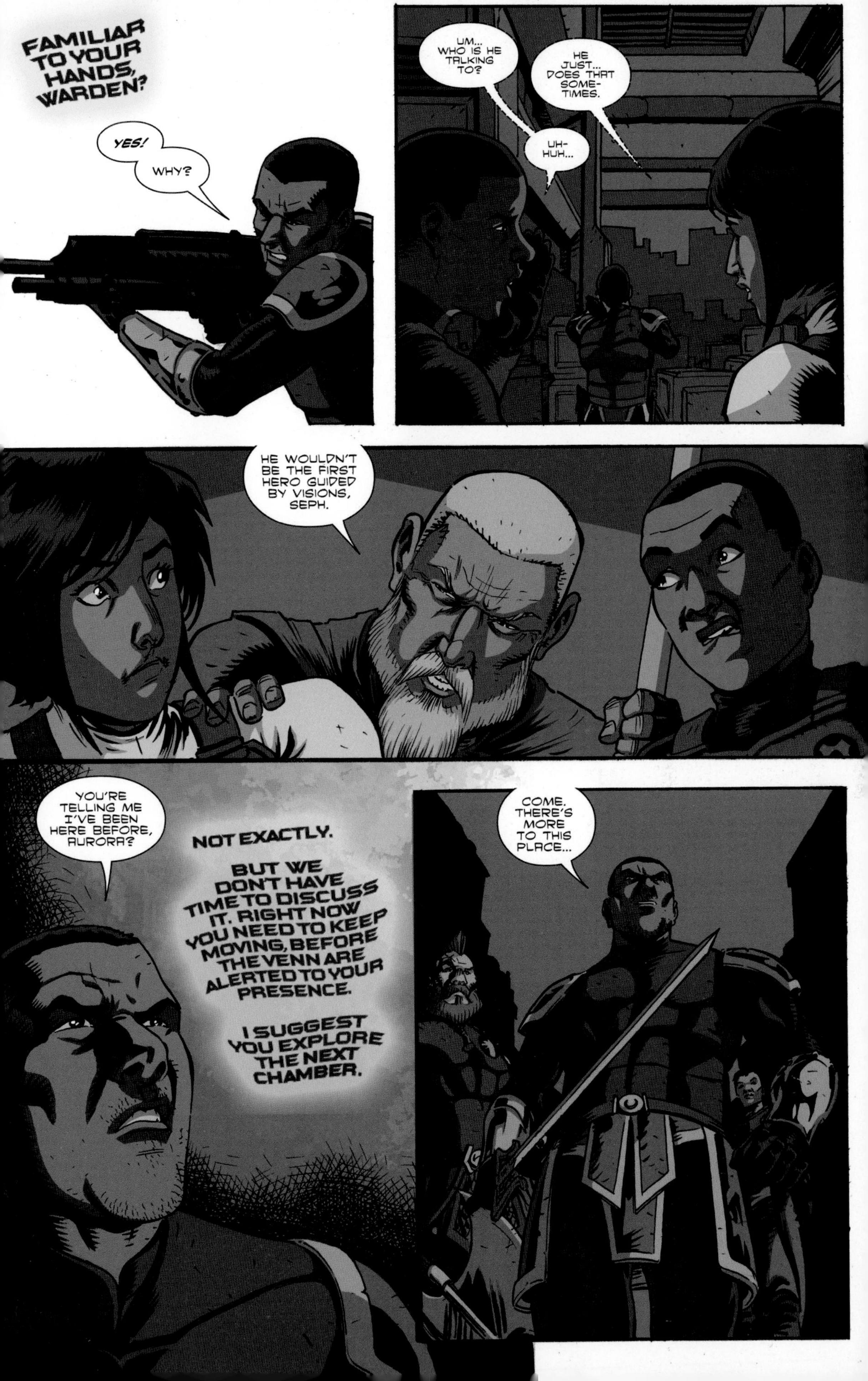

FAMILIAR TO YOUR HANDS, WARDEN?
YES!
WHY?
UM... WHO IS HE TALKING TO?
HE JUST... DOES THAT SOME-TIMES.
UH-HUH...
HE WOULDN'T BE THE FIRST HERO GUIDED BY VISIONS, SEPH.
YOU'RE TELLING ME I'VE BEEN HERE BEFORE, AURORA?
NOT EXACTLY.
BUT WE DON'T HAVE TIME TO DISCUSS IT. RIGHT NOW YOU NEED TO KEEP MOVING, BEFORE THE VENN ARE ALERTED TO YOUR PRESENCE.
I SUGGEST YOU EXPLORE THE NEXT CHAMBER.
COME. THERE'S MORE TO THIS PLACE...

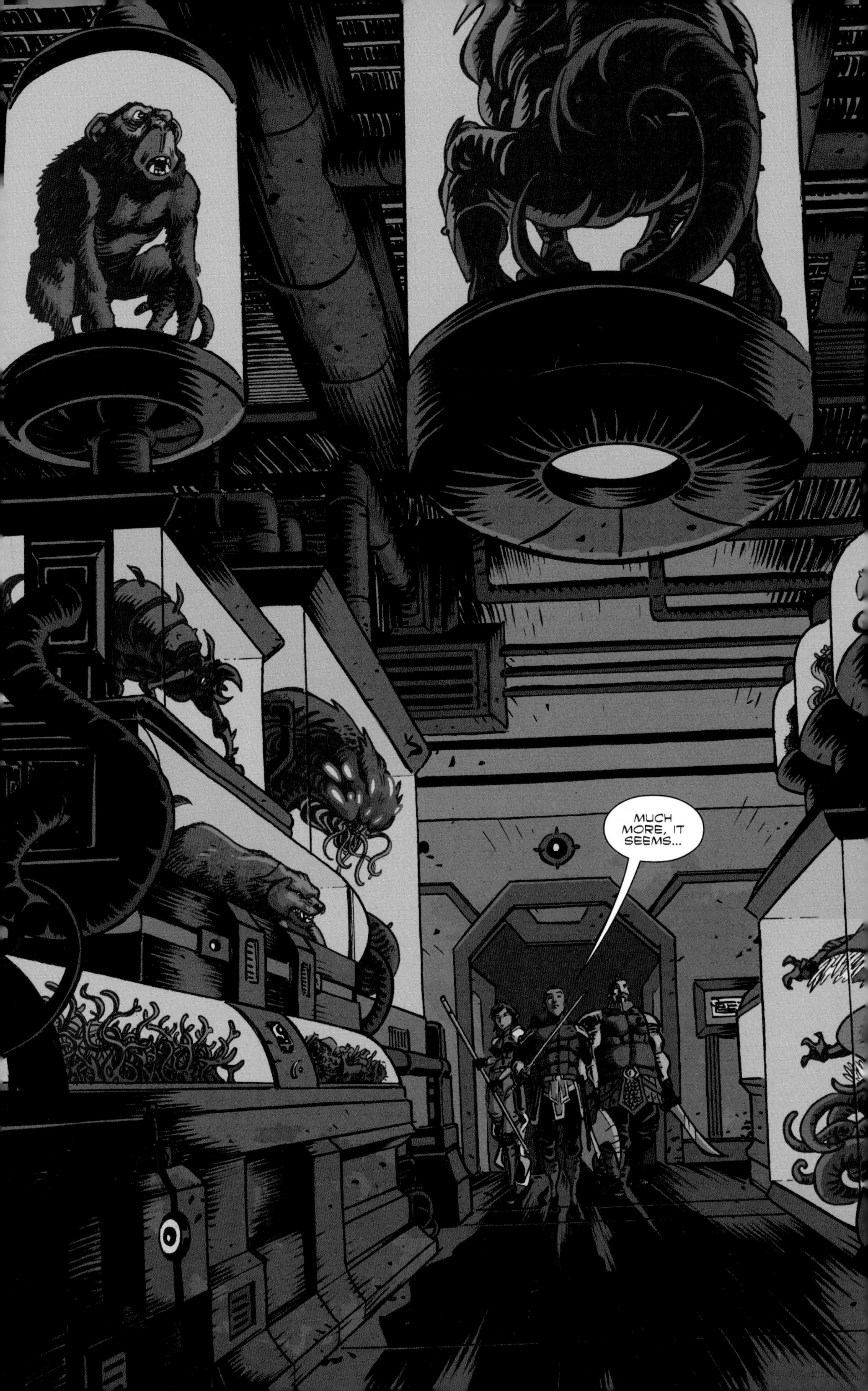
MUCH MORE, IT SEEMS...

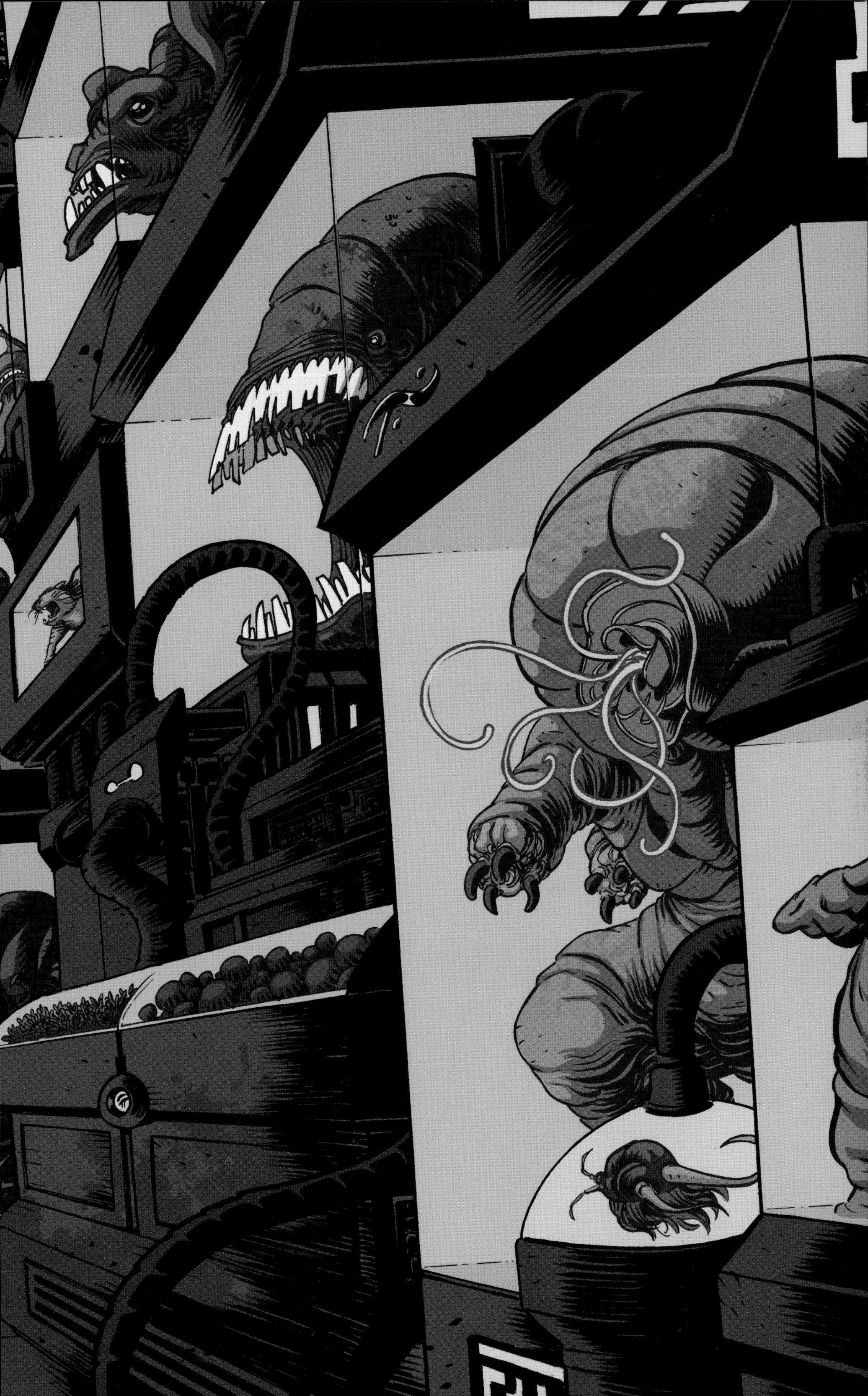

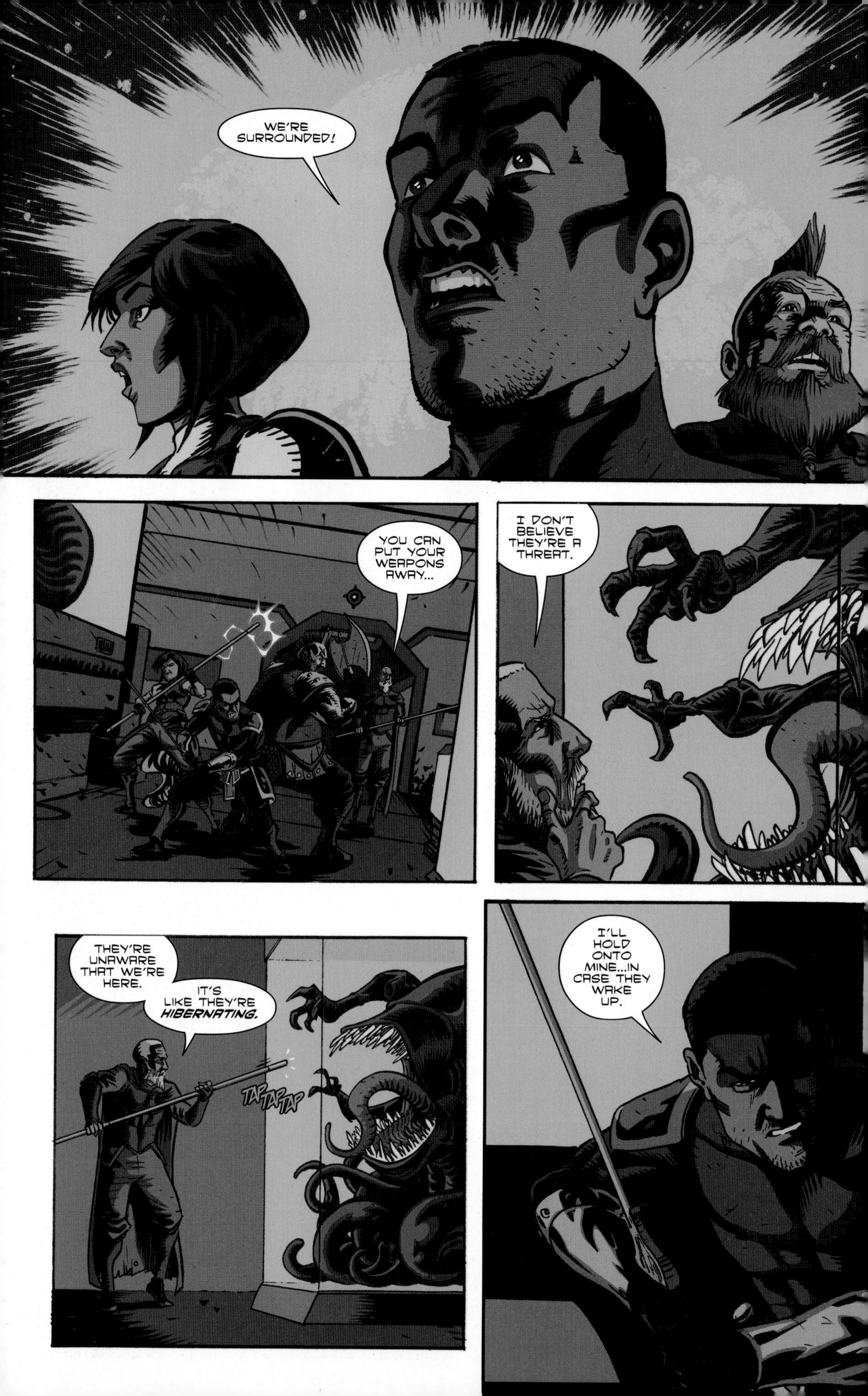
WE'RE SURROUNDED!
YOU CAN PUT YOUR WEAPONS AWAY...
I DON'T BELIEVE THEY'RE A THREAT.
THEY'RE UNAWARE THAT WE'RE HERE.
IT'S LIKE THEY'RE *HIBERNATING.*
TAP TAP TAP
I'LL HOLD ONTO MINE...IN CASE THEY WAKE UP.

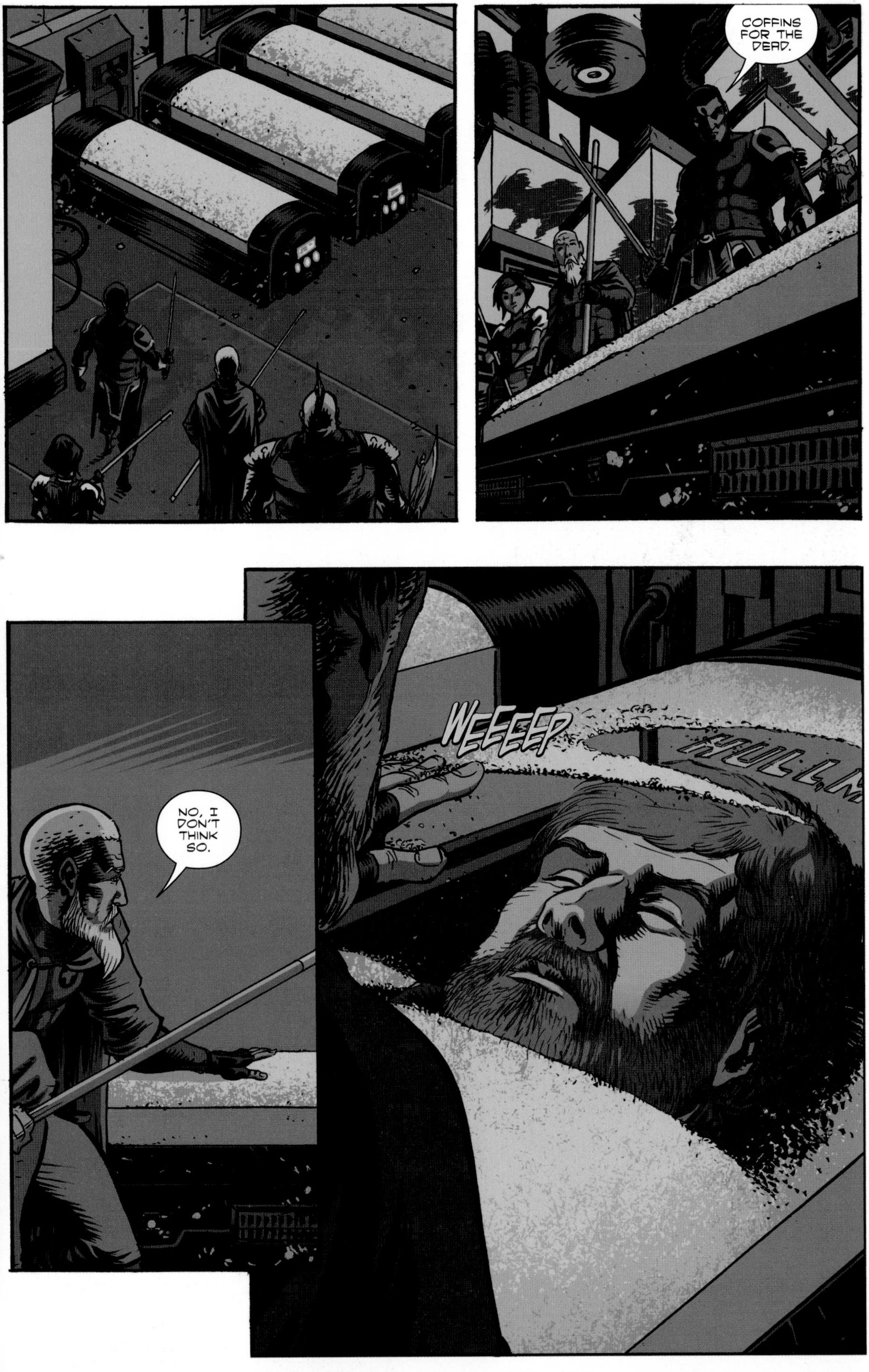
COFFINS FOR THE DEAD.
NO, I DON'T THINK SO.
WEEEEP

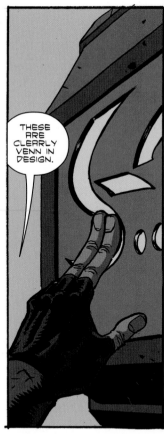

THESE ARE CLEARLY VENN IN DESIGN.

BUT THESE... THESE ARE SOMETHING ELSE...

使用冷凍柜

करायो ताबूत रिहाई के निर्देश

CRYO-COFFIN RELEASE INSTRUCTI

使用冷凍柜

करायो ताबूत रिहाई के निर्देश

CRYO-COFFIN RELEASE INSTRUCTIONS

1 2 3

CLICK!

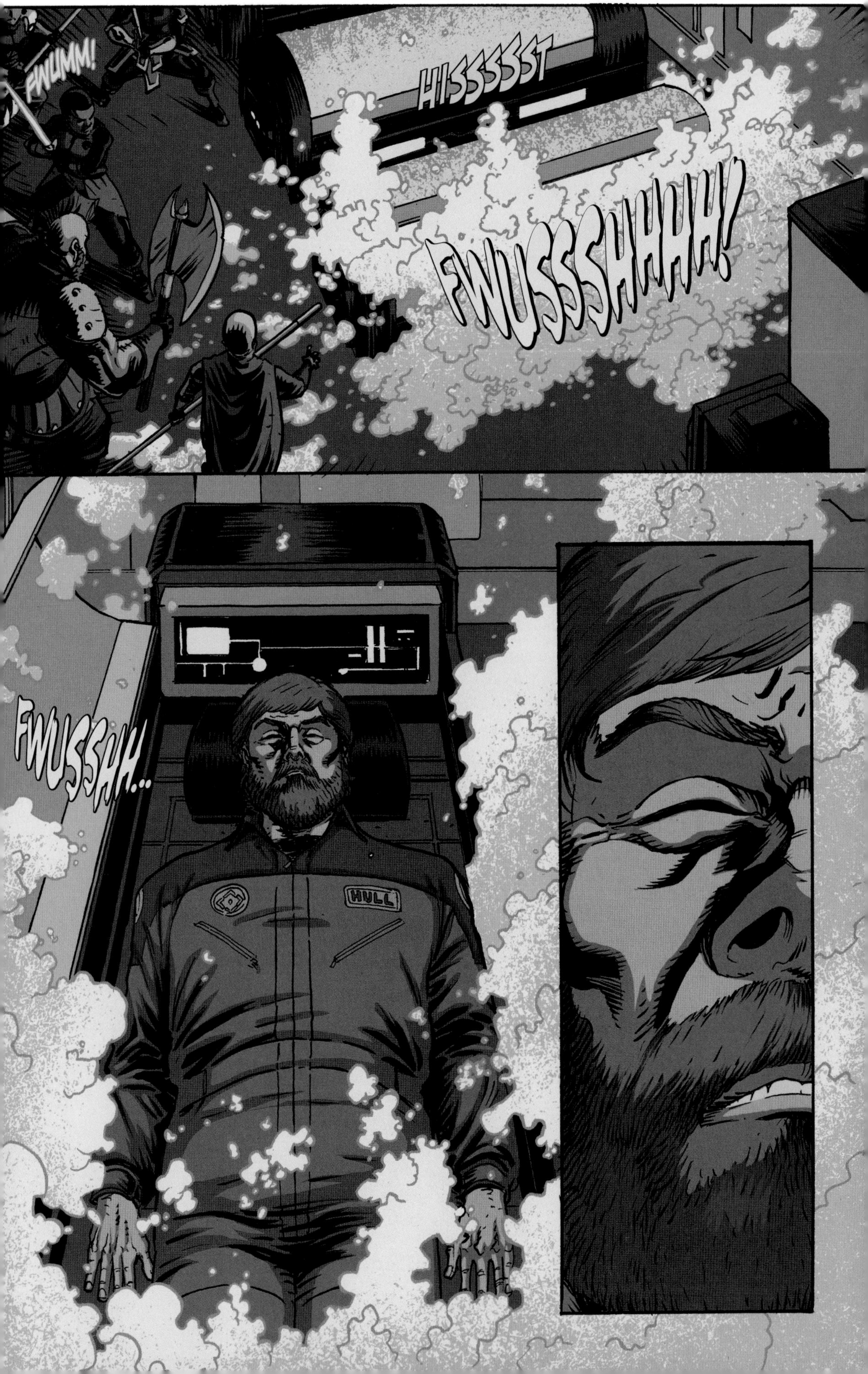
FWUMM!
HISSSSST
FWUSSSHHHH!
FWUSSHH...
HULL

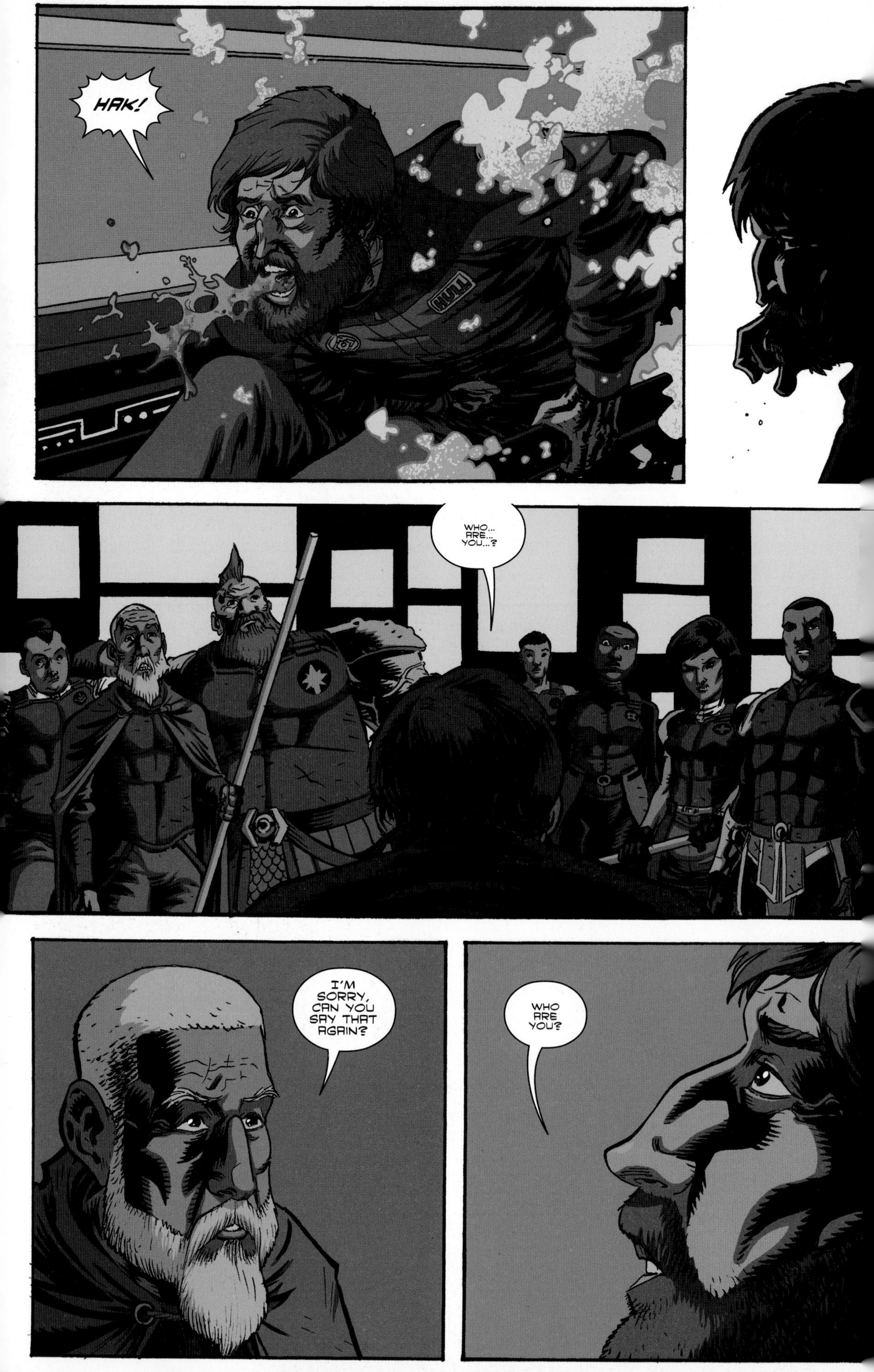
HAK!
WHO... ARE... YOU...?
I'M SORRY, CAN YOU SAY THAT AGAIN?
WHO ARE YOU?

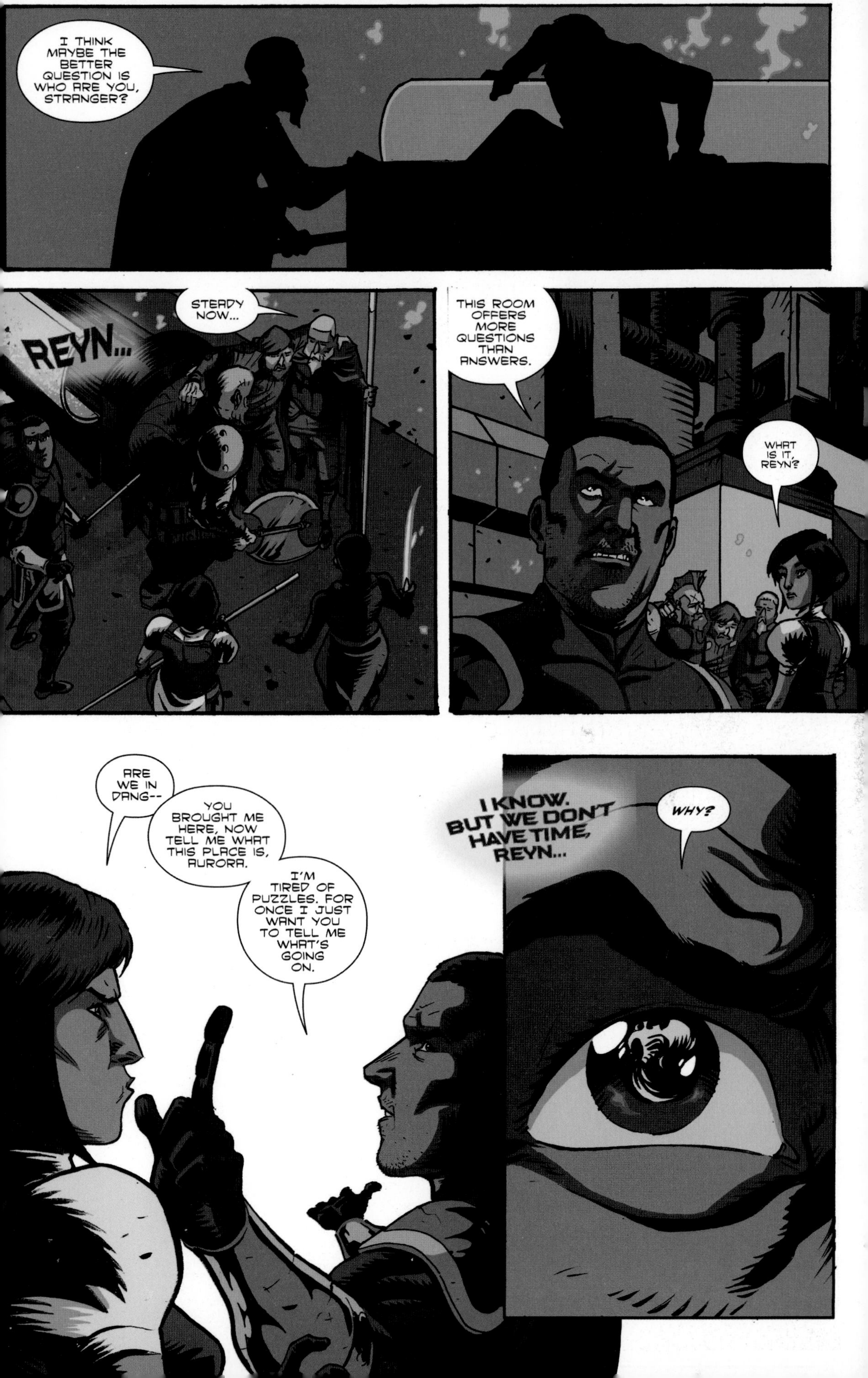
I THINK MAYBE THE BETTER QUESTION IS WHO ARE YOU, STRANGER?
REYN...
STEADY NOW...
THIS ROOM OFFERS MORE QUESTIONS THAN ANSWERS.
WHAT IS IT, REYN?
ARE WE IN DANG--
YOU BROUGHT ME HERE, NOW TELL ME WHAT THIS PLACE IS, AURORA.
I'M TIRED OF PUZZLES. FOR ONCE I JUST WANT YOU TO TELL ME WHAT'S GOING ON.
I KNOW. BUT WE DON'T HAVE TIME, REYN...
WHY?

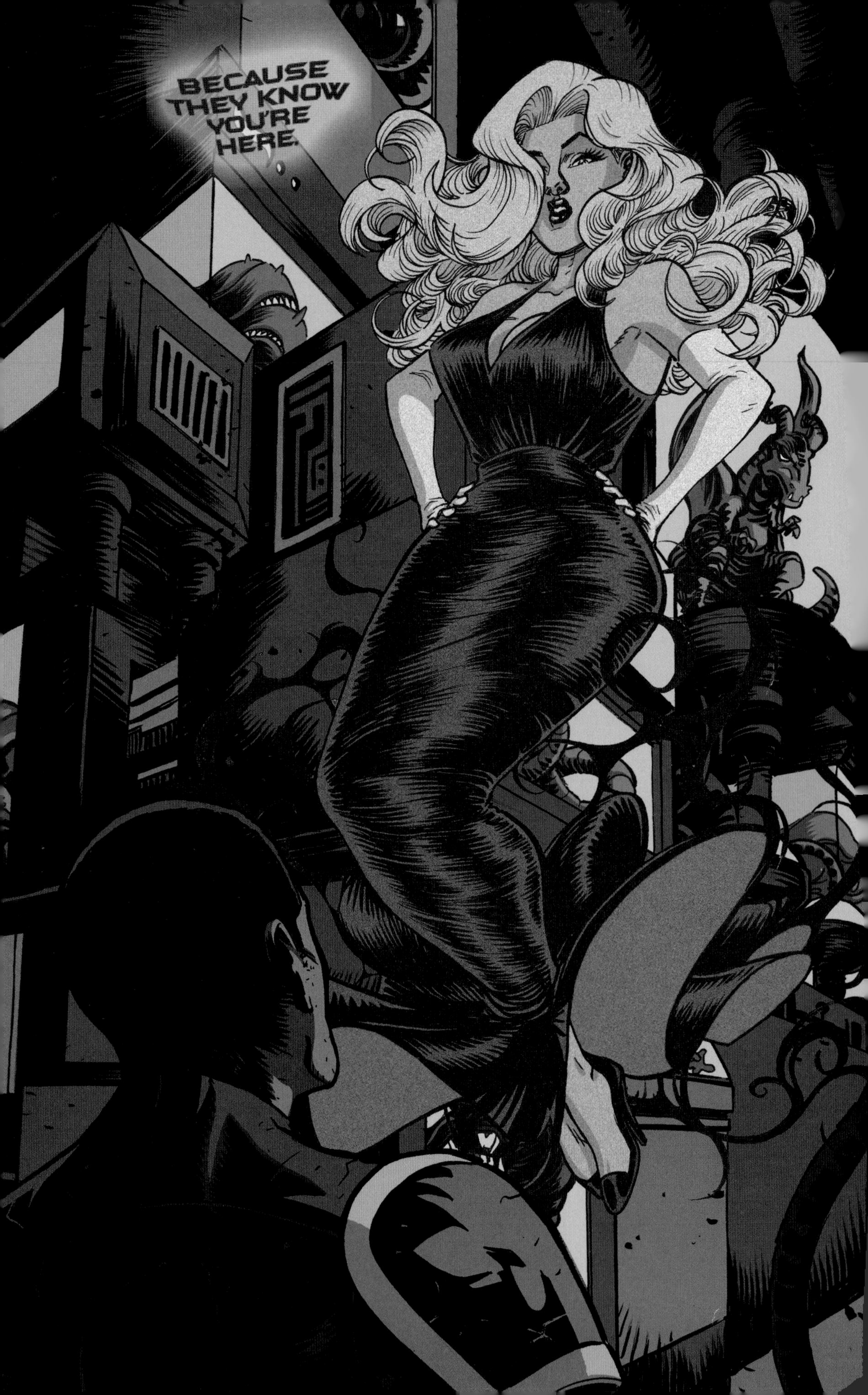
BECAUSE THEY KNOW YOU'RE HERE.

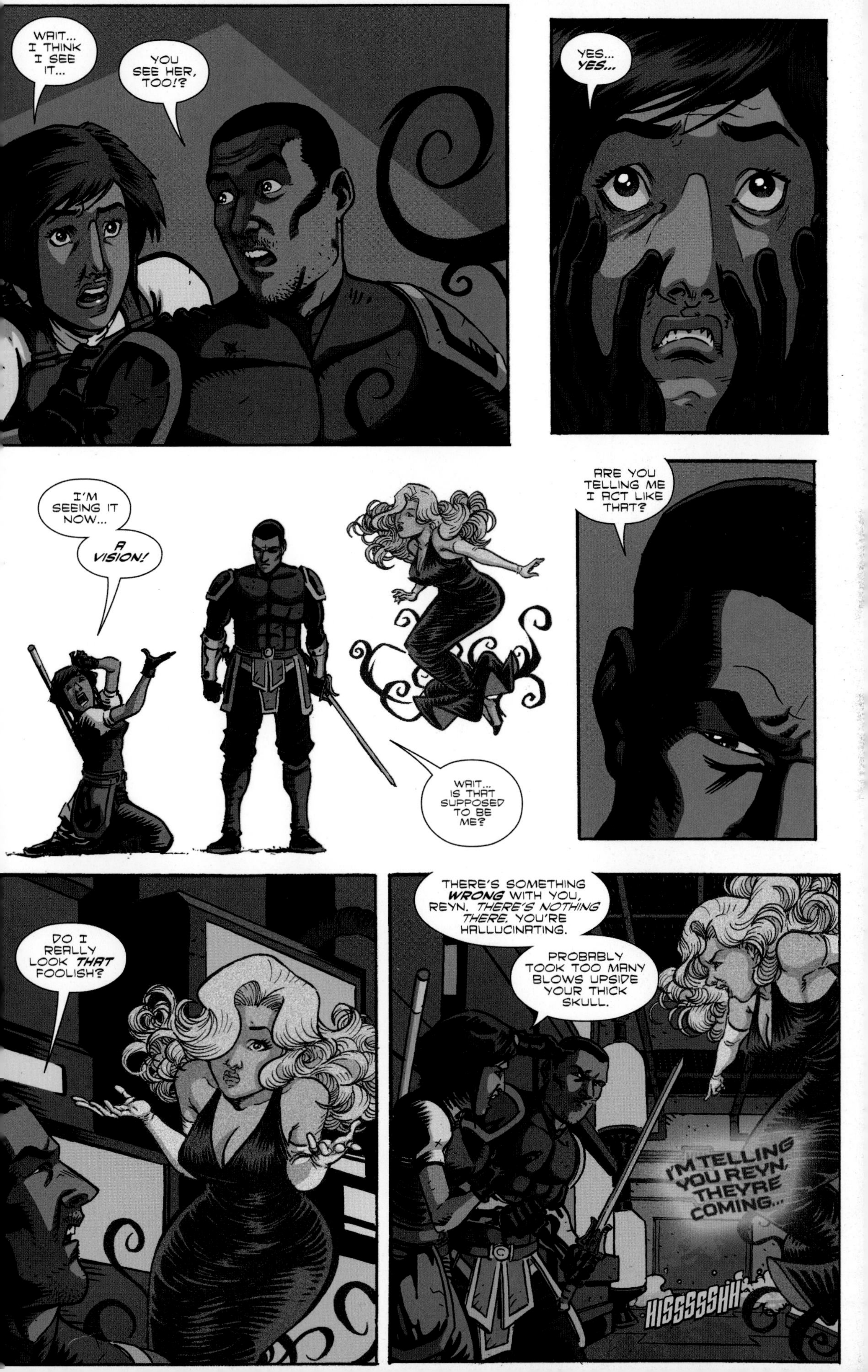
WAIT... I THINK I SEE IT...
YOU SEE HER, TOO!?
YES... YES...
I'M SEEING IT NOW... A VISION!
WAIT... IS THAT SUPPOSED TO BE ME?
ARE YOU TELLING ME I ACT LIKE THAT?
DO I REALLY LOOK THAT FOOLISH?
THERE'S SOMETHING WRONG WITH YOU, REYN. THERE'S NOTHING THERE. YOU'RE HALLUCINATING.
PROBABLY TOOK TOO MANY BLOWS UPSIDE YOUR THICK SKULL.
I'M TELLING YOU REYN, THEYRE COMING...
HISSSSSHH

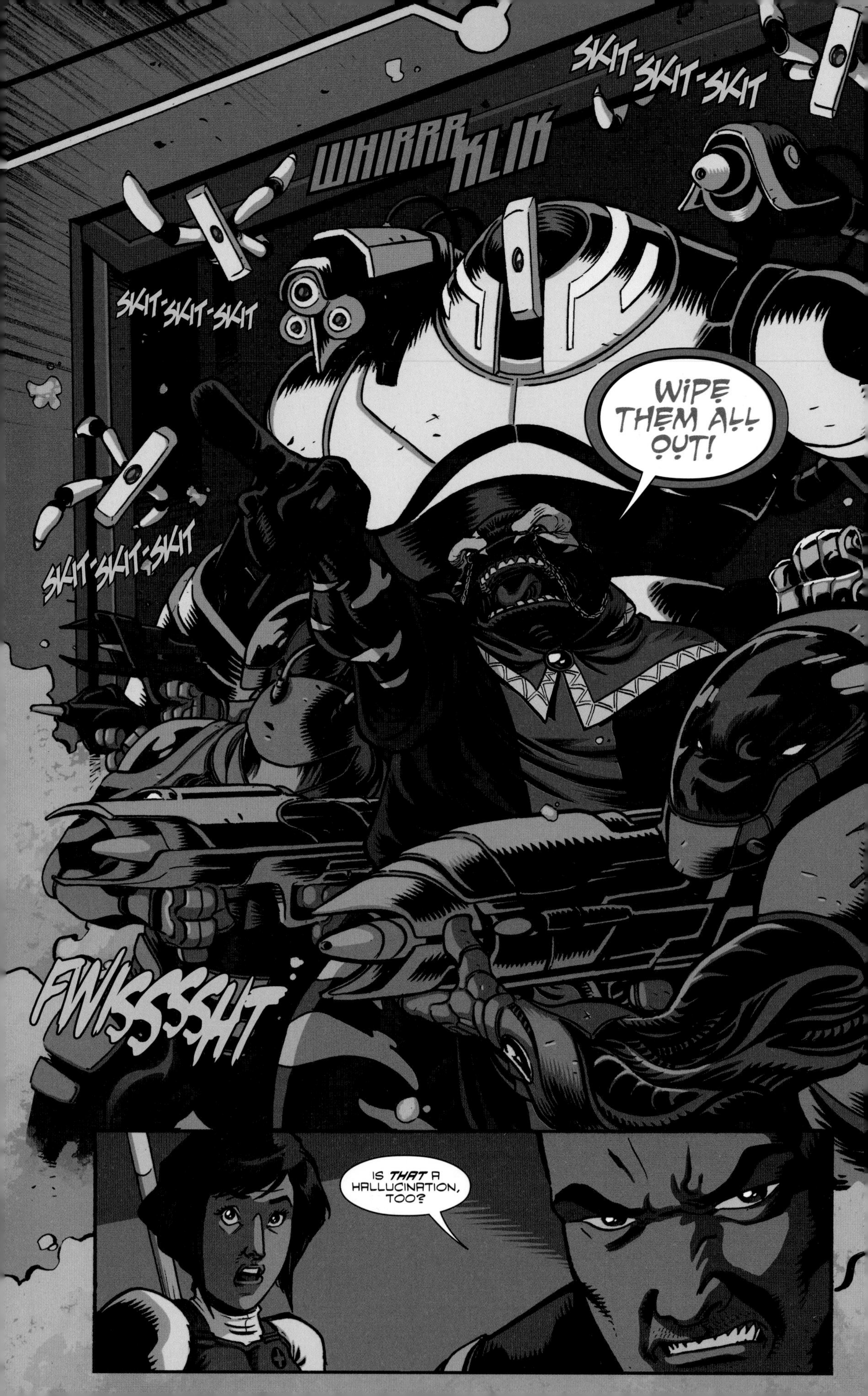
SKIT-SKIT-SKIT
WHIRRR KLIK
SKIT-SKIT-SKIT
WIPE THEM ALL OUT!
SKIT-SKIT-SKIT
FWISSSSHT
IS *THAT* A HALLUCINATION, TOO?

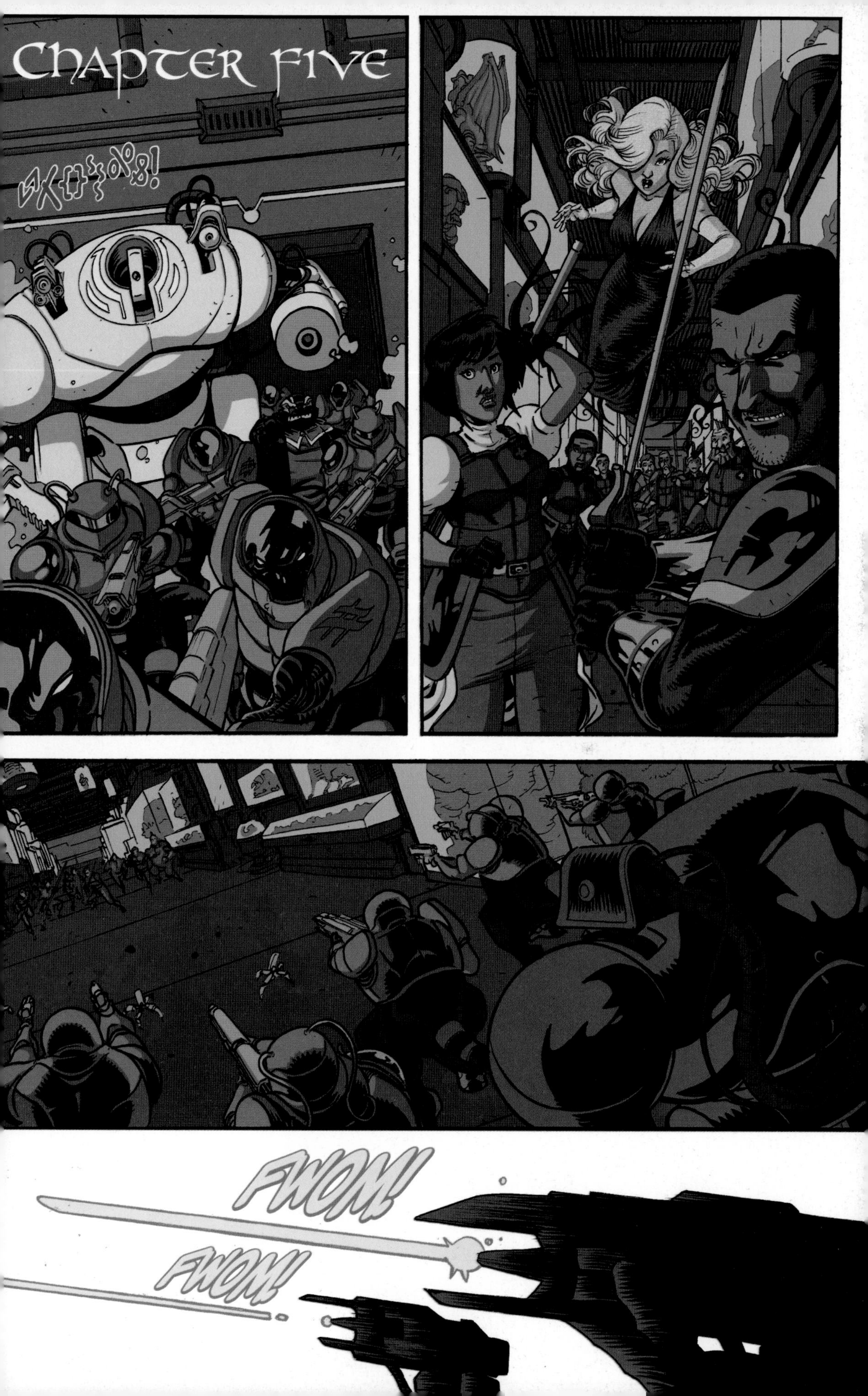
CHAPTER FIVE
FWOM!
FWOM!

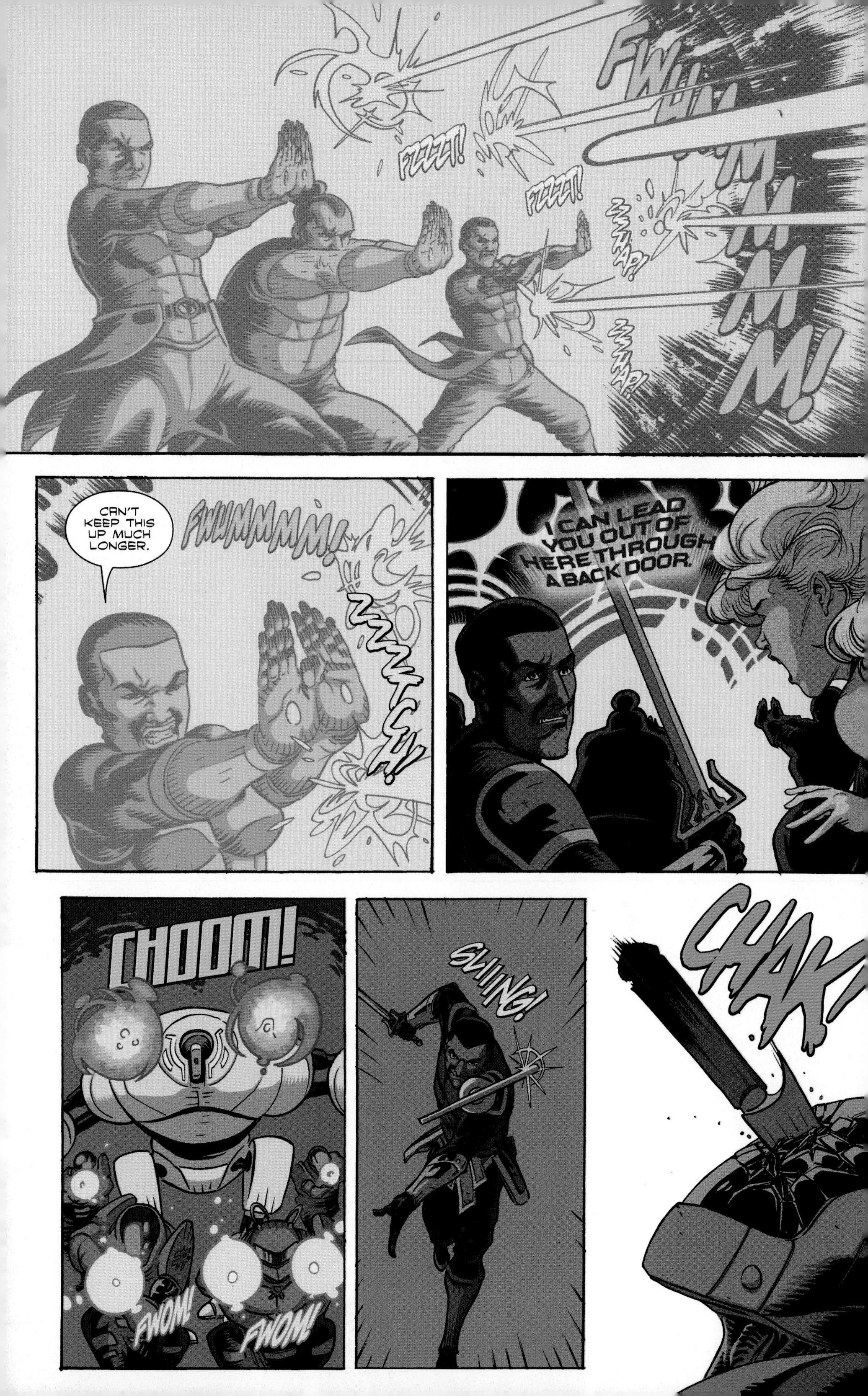

FZZZZT!
FZZZZT!
FWUMMMMM!
ZZZZAP!
ZZZZAP!
CAN'T KEEP THIS UP MUCH LONGER.
FWUMMMMM!
ZZZZZATCH!
I CAN LEAD YOU OUT OF HERE THROUGH A BACK DOOR.
CHOOM!
FWOM!
FWOM!
SWIIING!
CHAK!

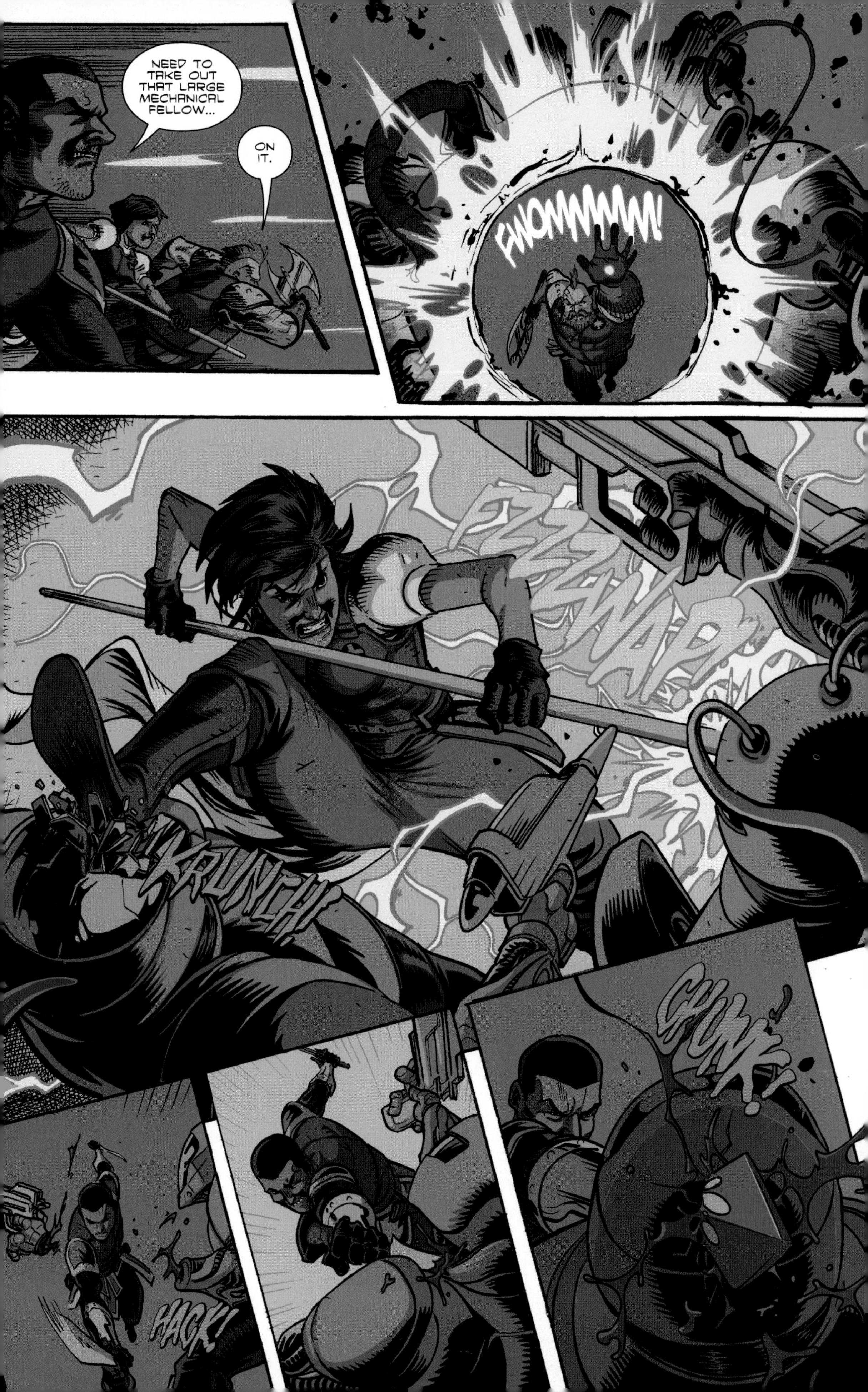
NEED TO TAKE OUT THAT LARGE MECHANICAL FELLOW...
ON IT.
FWOMMMMM!
FZZZWAP!
KRUNCH!
CHUNK!
HACK!

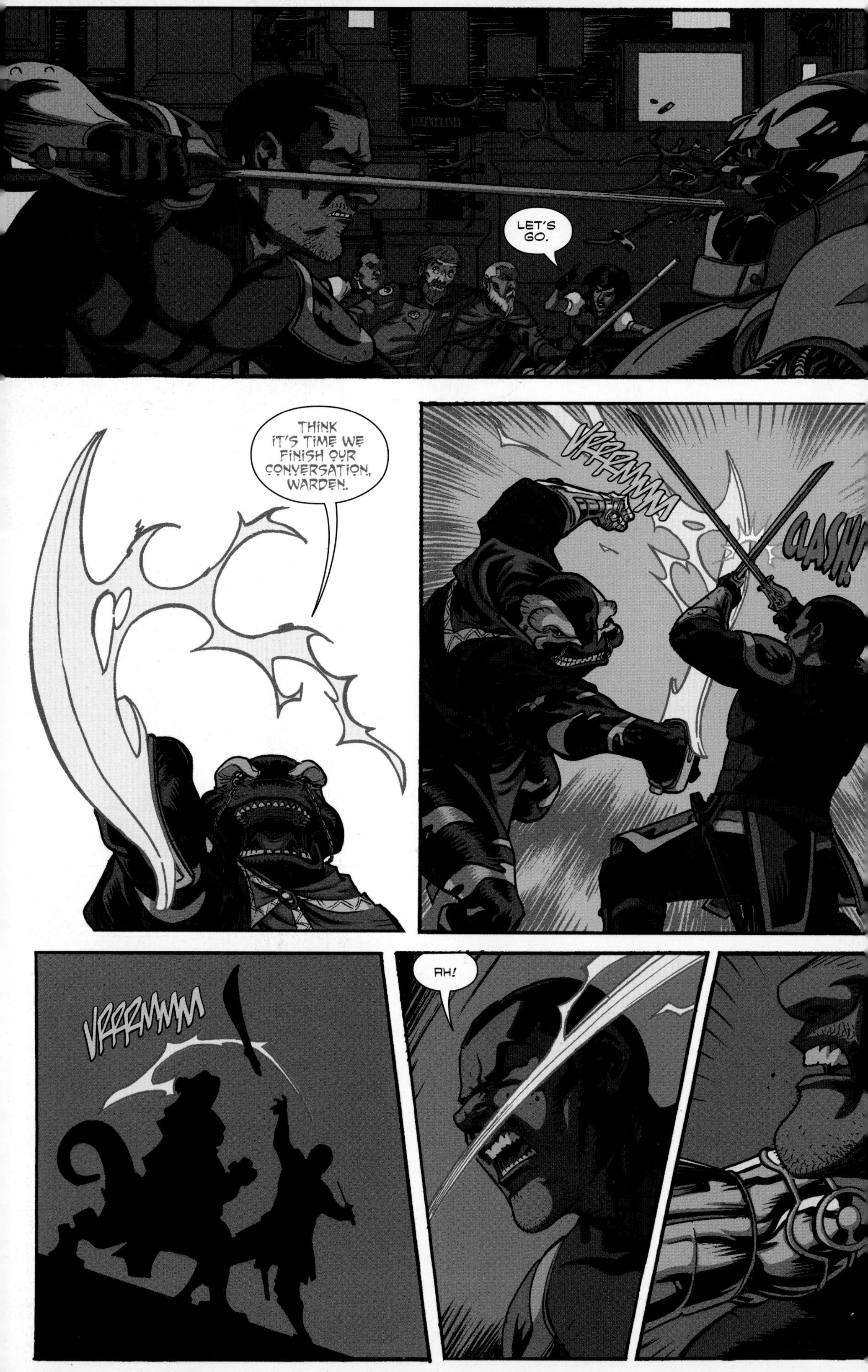
LET'S GO.
THINK IT'S TIME WE FINISH OUR CONVERSATION, WARDEN.
VRRRMMMM
CLASH!
VRRRMMMM
AH!

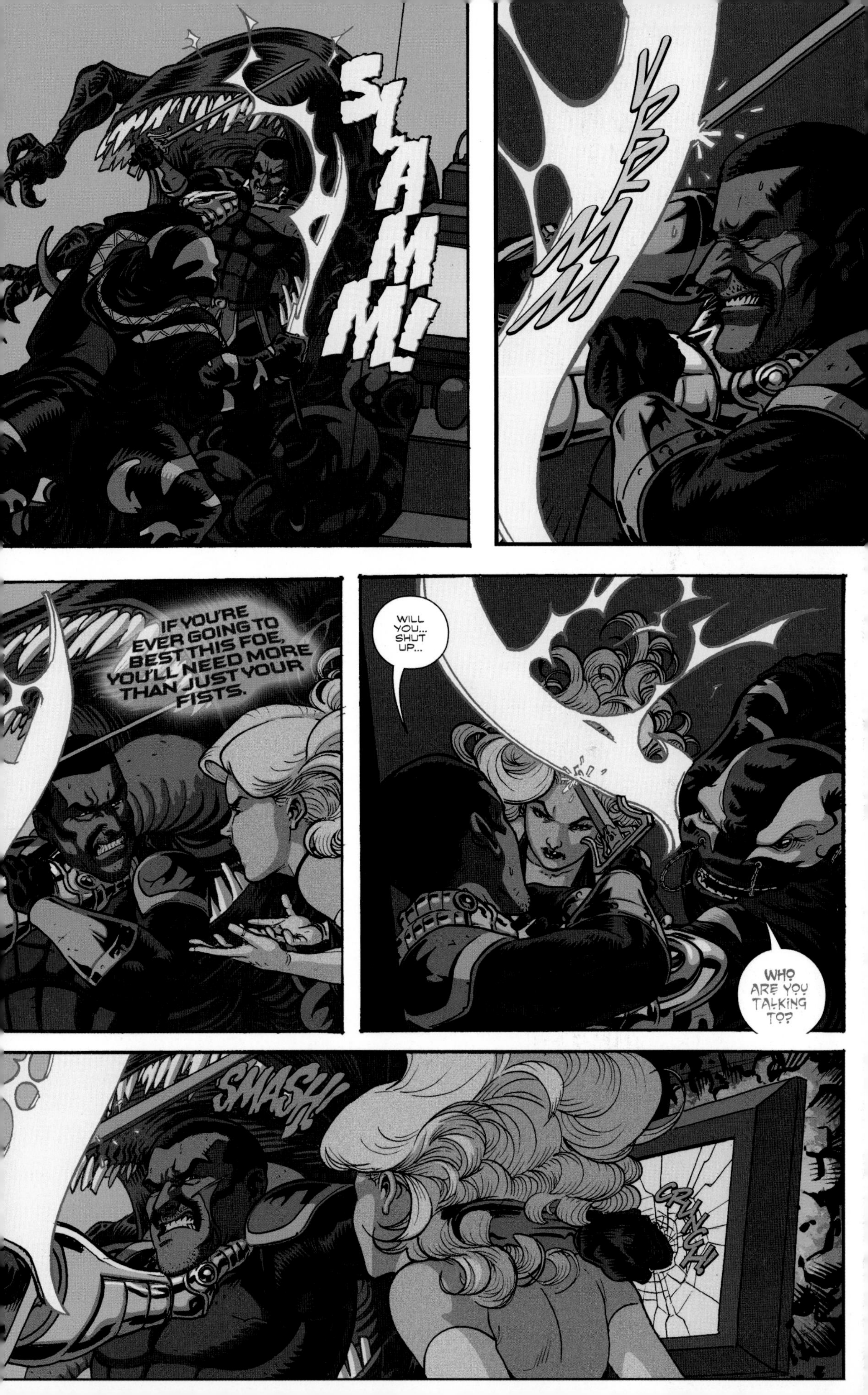

SLAMM!
VREEMMM
IF YOU'RE EVER GOING TO BEST THIS FOE, YOU'LL NEED MORE THAN JUST YOUR FISTS.
WILL YOU... SHUT UP...
WHO ARE YOU TALKING TO?
SMASH!
CRUNCH!

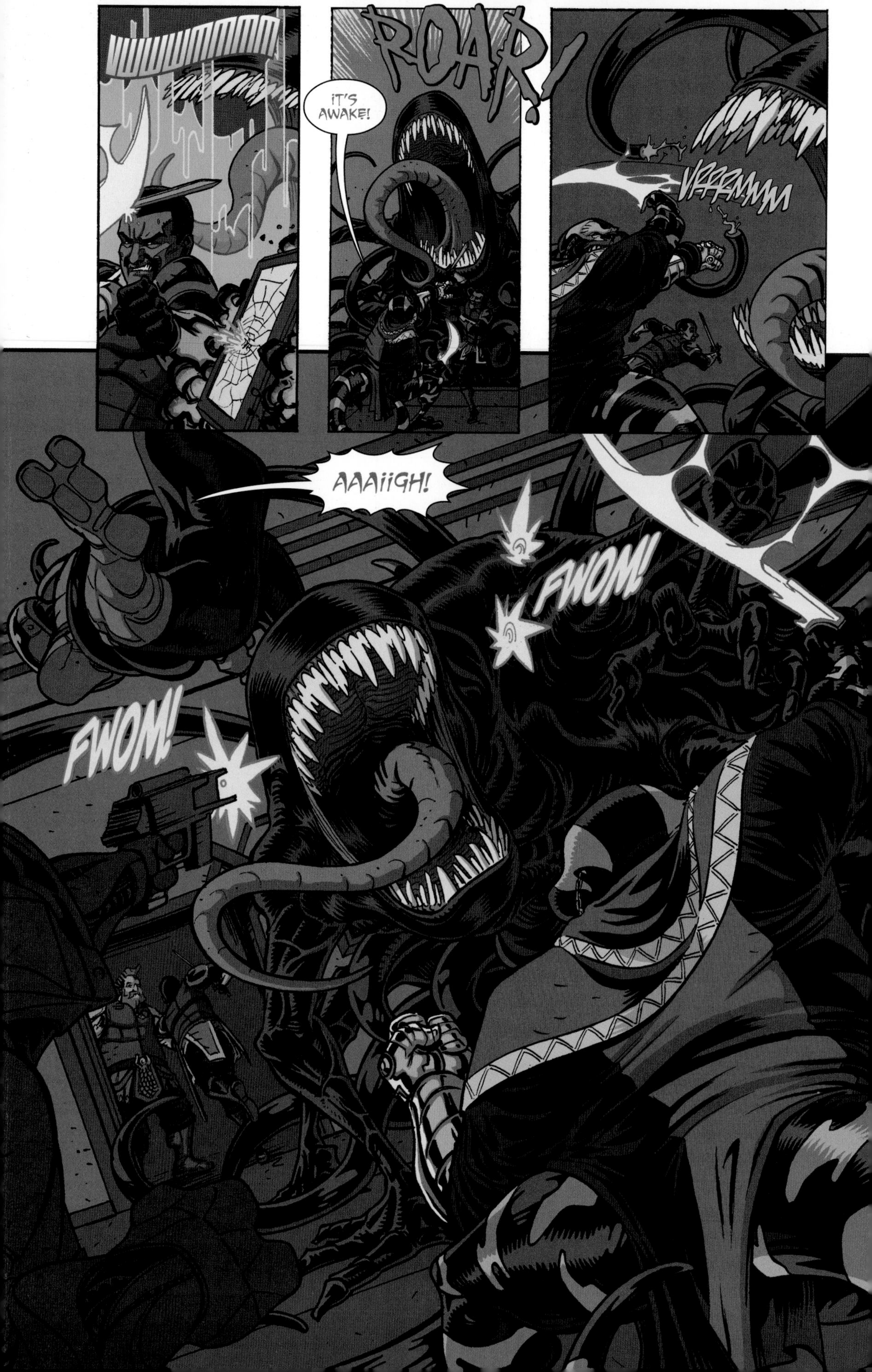
VVVWMMMM
ROAR!
IT'S AWAKE!
VRRRMMMM
AAAIIGH!
FWOM!
FWOM!

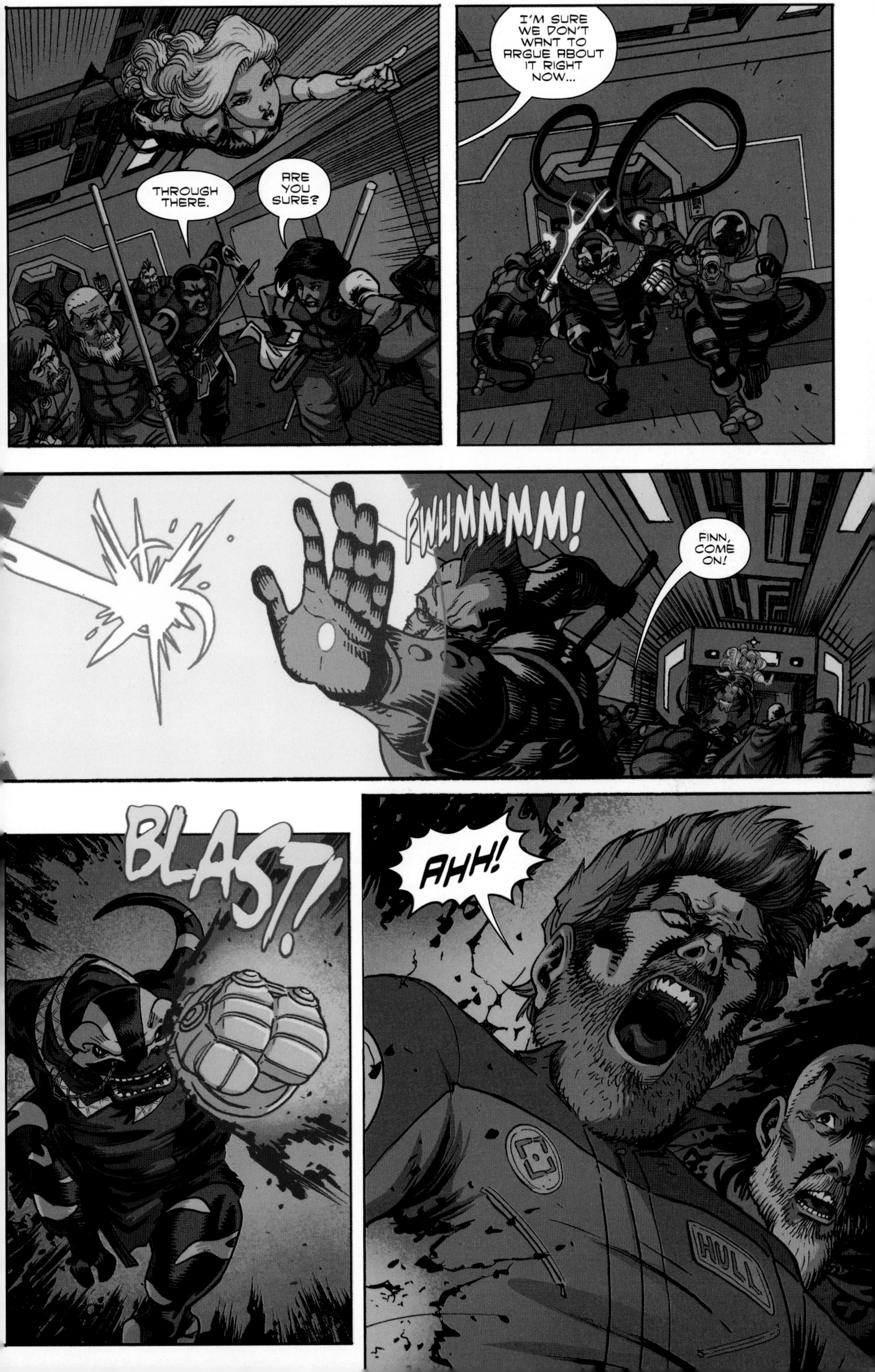
THROUGH THERE.
ARE YOU SURE?
I'M SURE WE DON'T WANT TO ARGUE ABOUT IT RIGHT NOW...
FWUMMMM!
FINN, COME ON!
BLAST!
AHH!
HULL

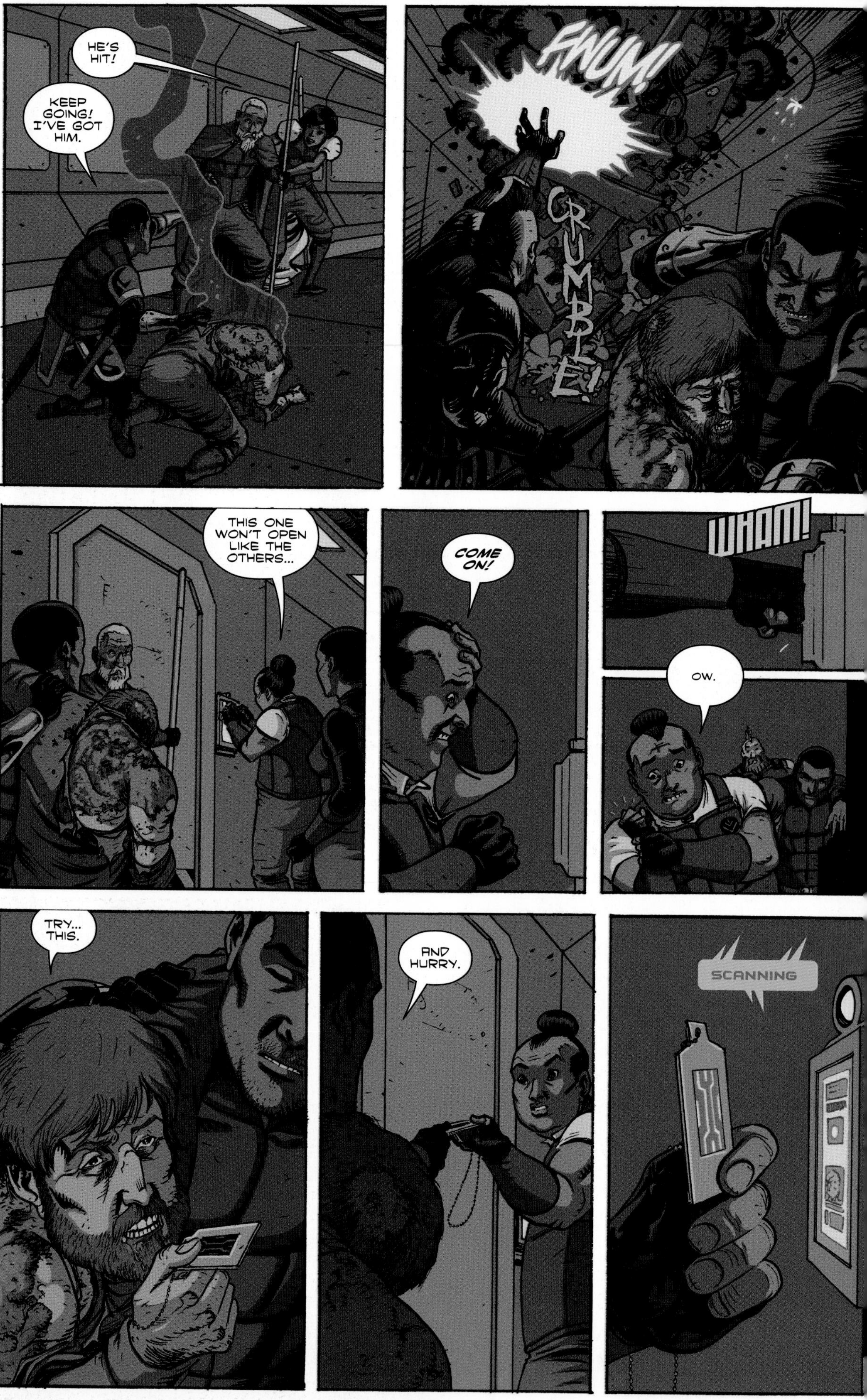
HE'S HIT!
KEEP GOING! I'VE GOT HIM.
FNUM!
CRUMBLE!
THIS ONE WON'T OPEN LIKE THE OTHERS...
COME ON!
WHAM!
OW.
TRY... THIS.
AND HURRY.
SCANNING

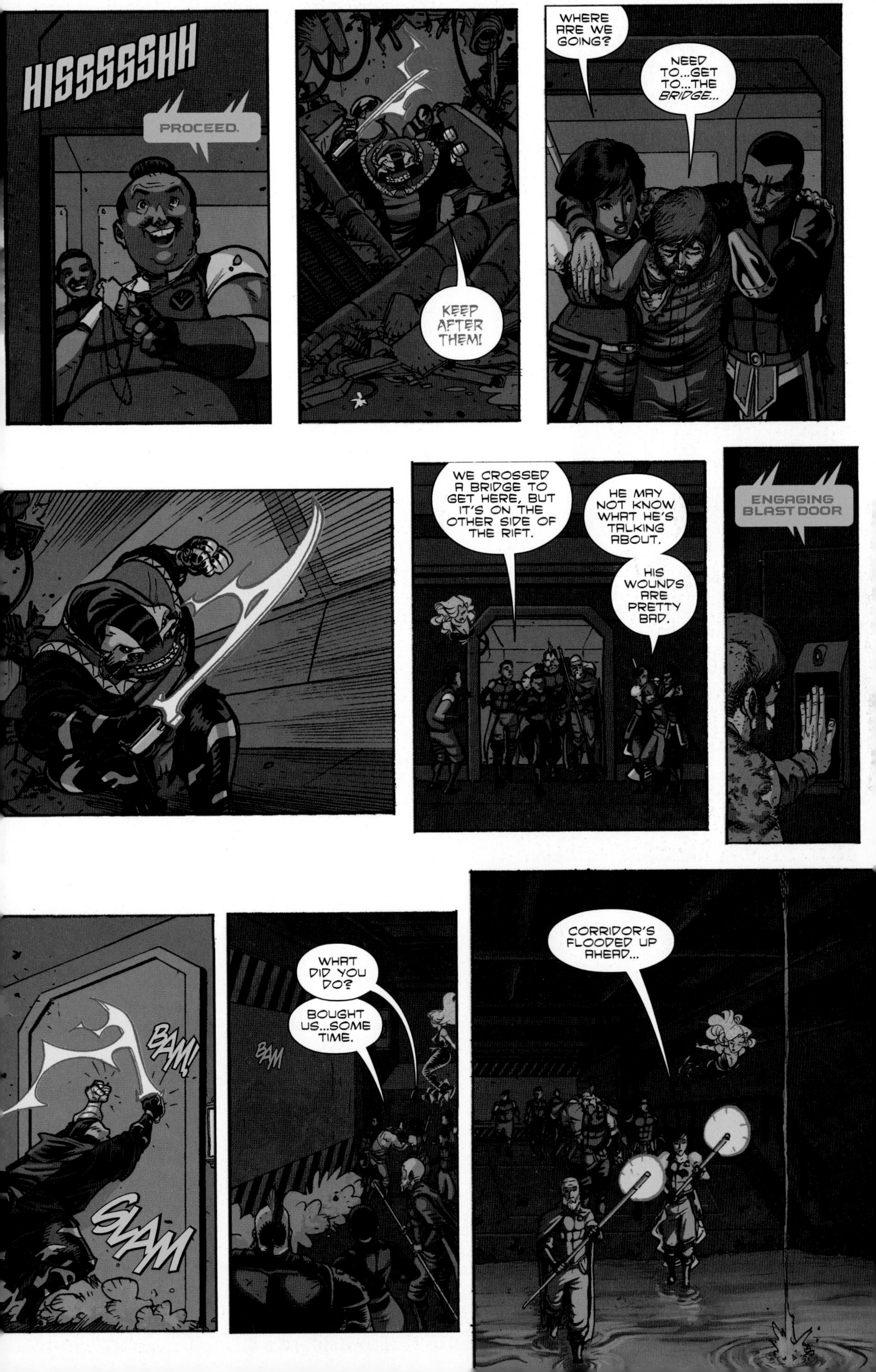
HISSSSSHH
PROCEED.
KEEP AFTER THEM!
WHERE ARE WE GOING?
NEED TO...GET TO...THE BRIDGE...
WE CROSSED A BRIDGE TO GET HERE, BUT IT'S ON THE OTHER SIDE OF THE RIFT.
HE MAY NOT KNOW WHAT HE'S TALKING ABOUT.
HIS WOUNDS ARE PRETTY BAD.
ENGAGING BLAST DOOR
BAM!
SLAM
BAM
WHAT DID YOU DO?
BOUGHT US...SOME TIME.
CORRIDOR'S FLOODED UP AHEAD...

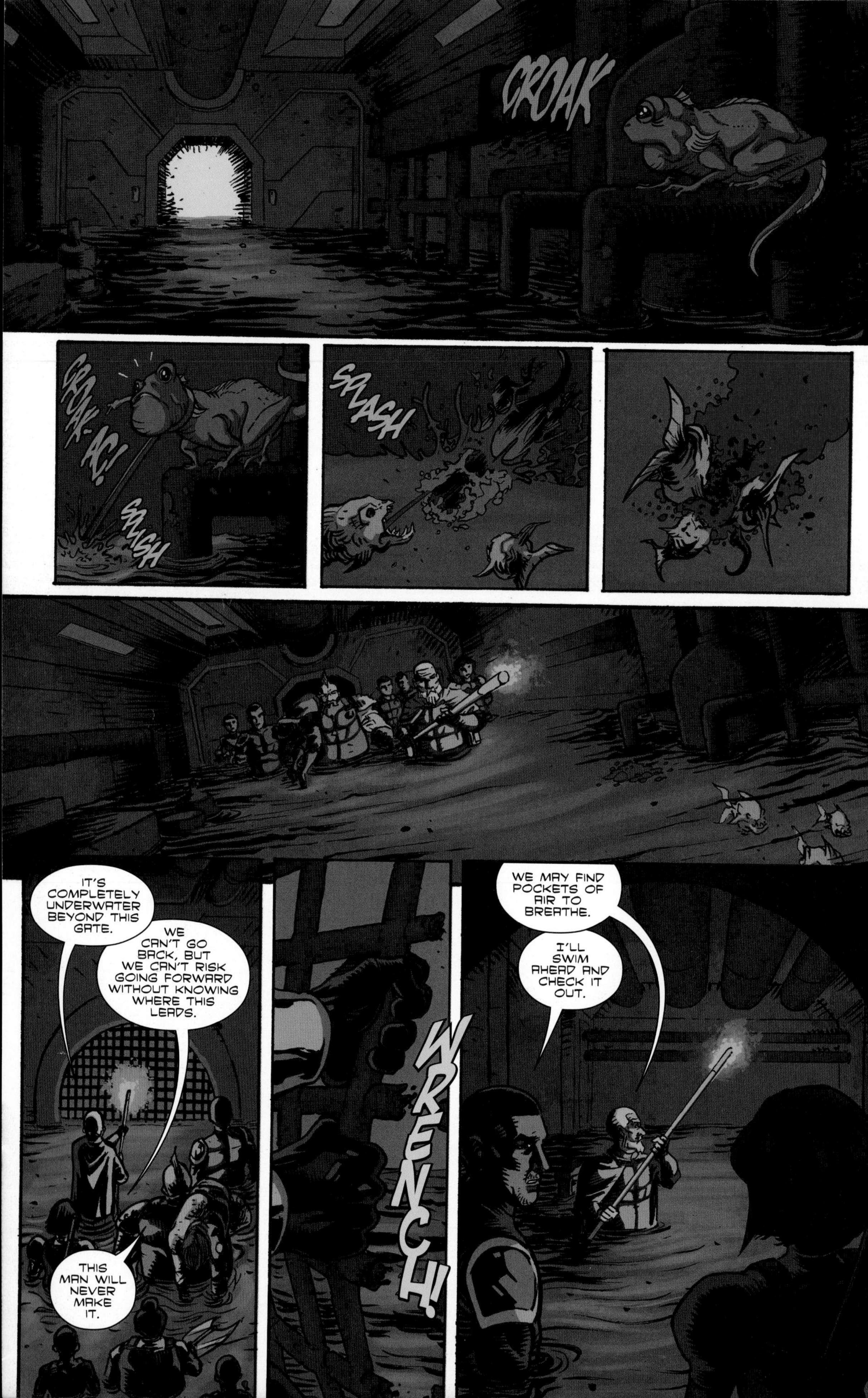
CROAK
CROAK-AC!
SPLISH
SPLASH
IT'S COMPLETELY UNDERWATER BEYOND THIS GATE.
WE CAN'T GO BACK, BUT WE CAN'T RISK GOING FORWARD WITHOUT KNOWING WHERE THIS LEADS.
THIS MAN WILL NEVER MAKE IT.
WRENCH!
WE MAY FIND POCKETS OF AIR TO BREATHE.
I'LL SWIM AHEAD AND CHECK IT OUT.

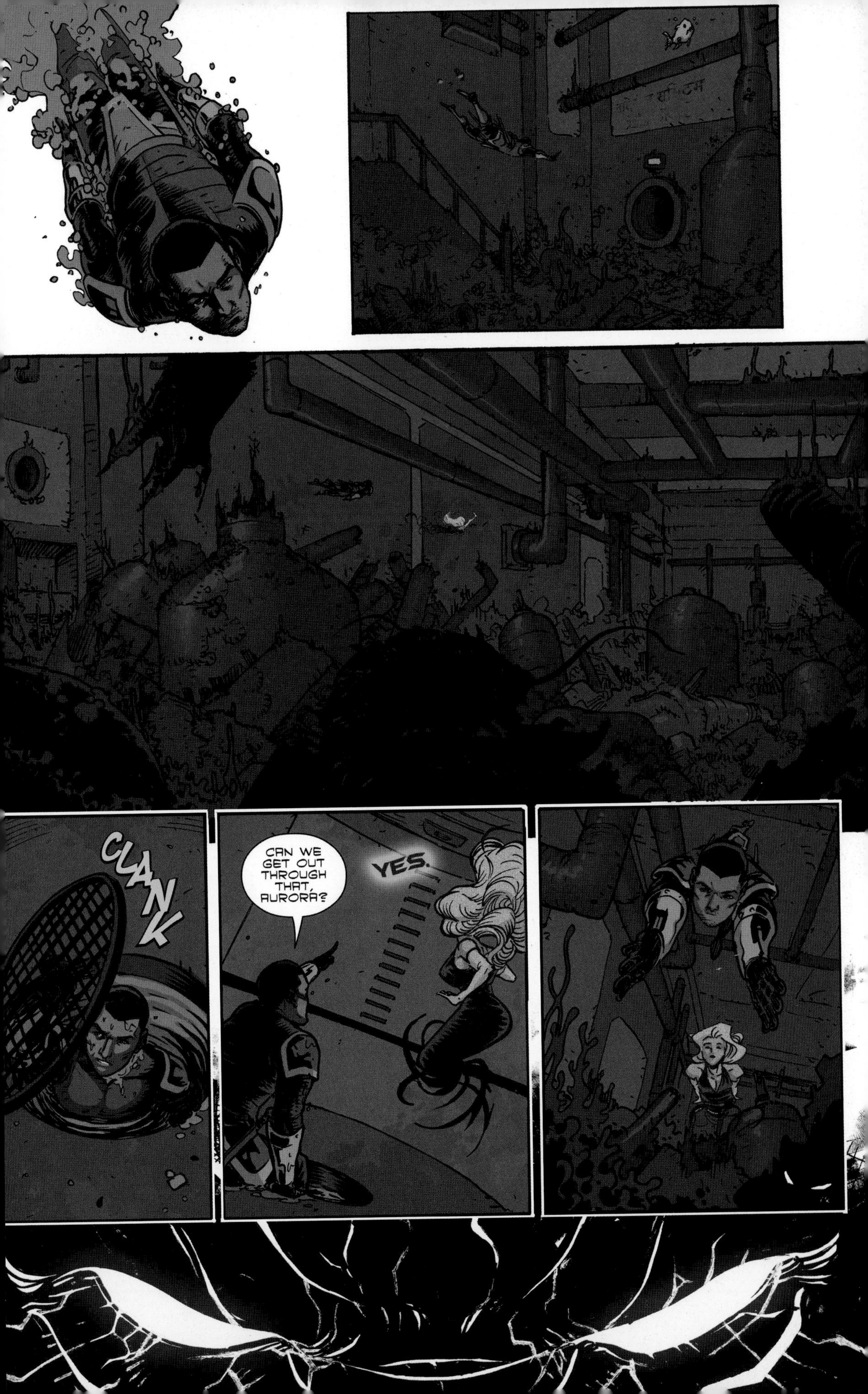
CLANK
CAN WE GET OUT THROUGH THAT, AURORA?
YES.

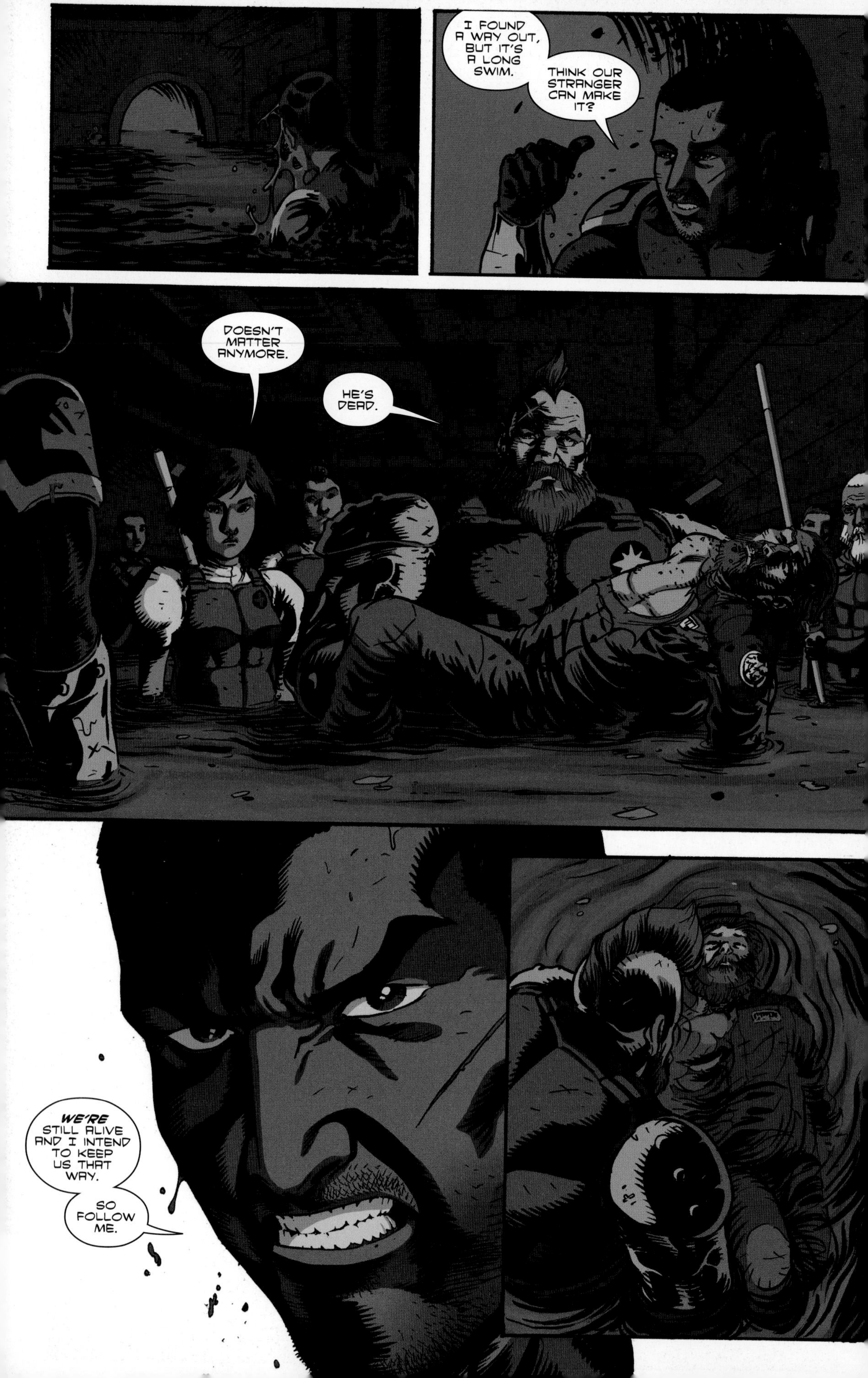
I FOUND A WAY OUT, BUT IT'S A LONG SWIM.
THINK OUR STRANGER CAN MAKE IT?
DOESN'T MATTER ANYMORE.
HE'S DEAD.
WE'RE STILL ALIVE AND I INTEND TO KEEP US THAT WAY.
SO FOLLOW ME.

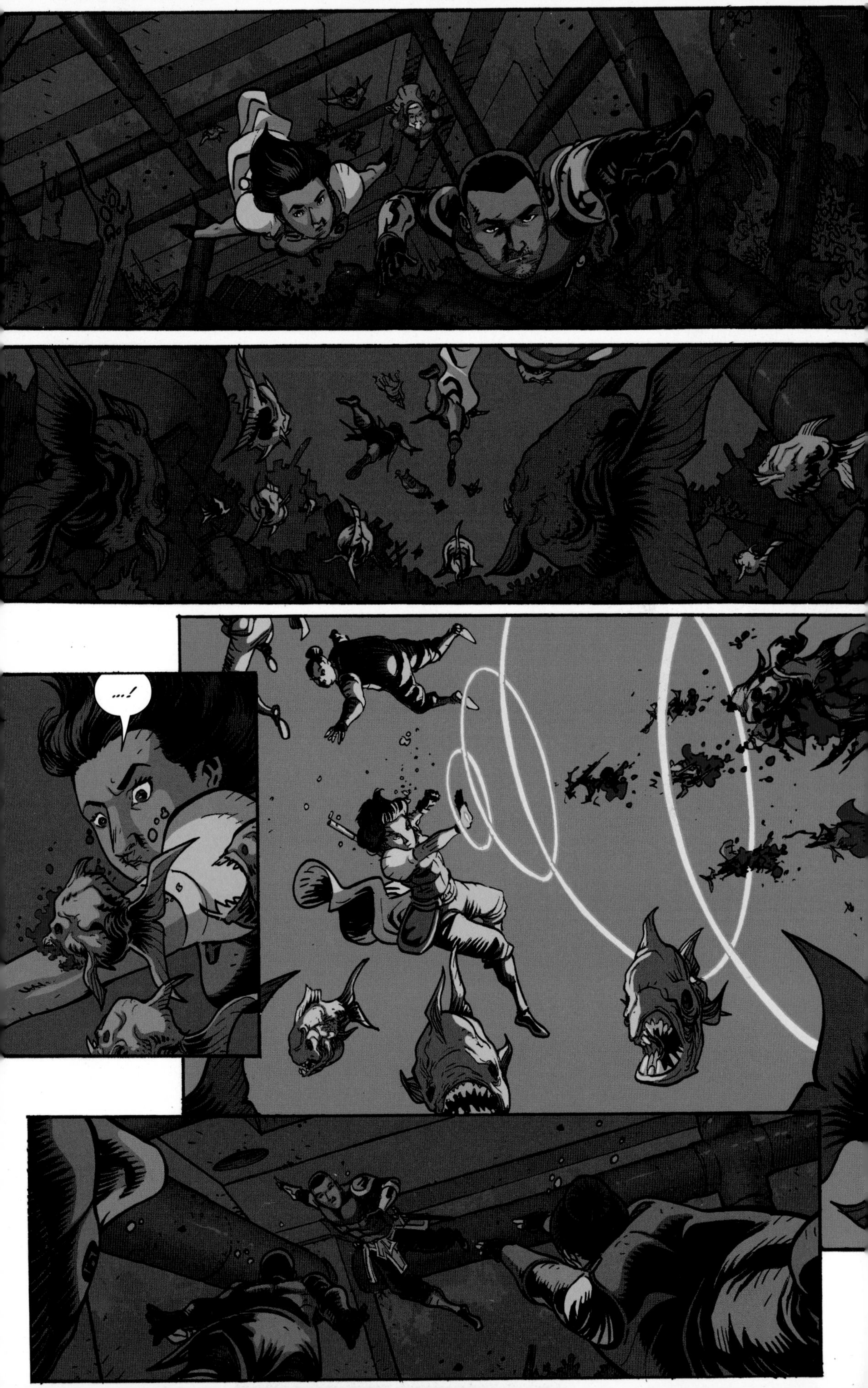
...!

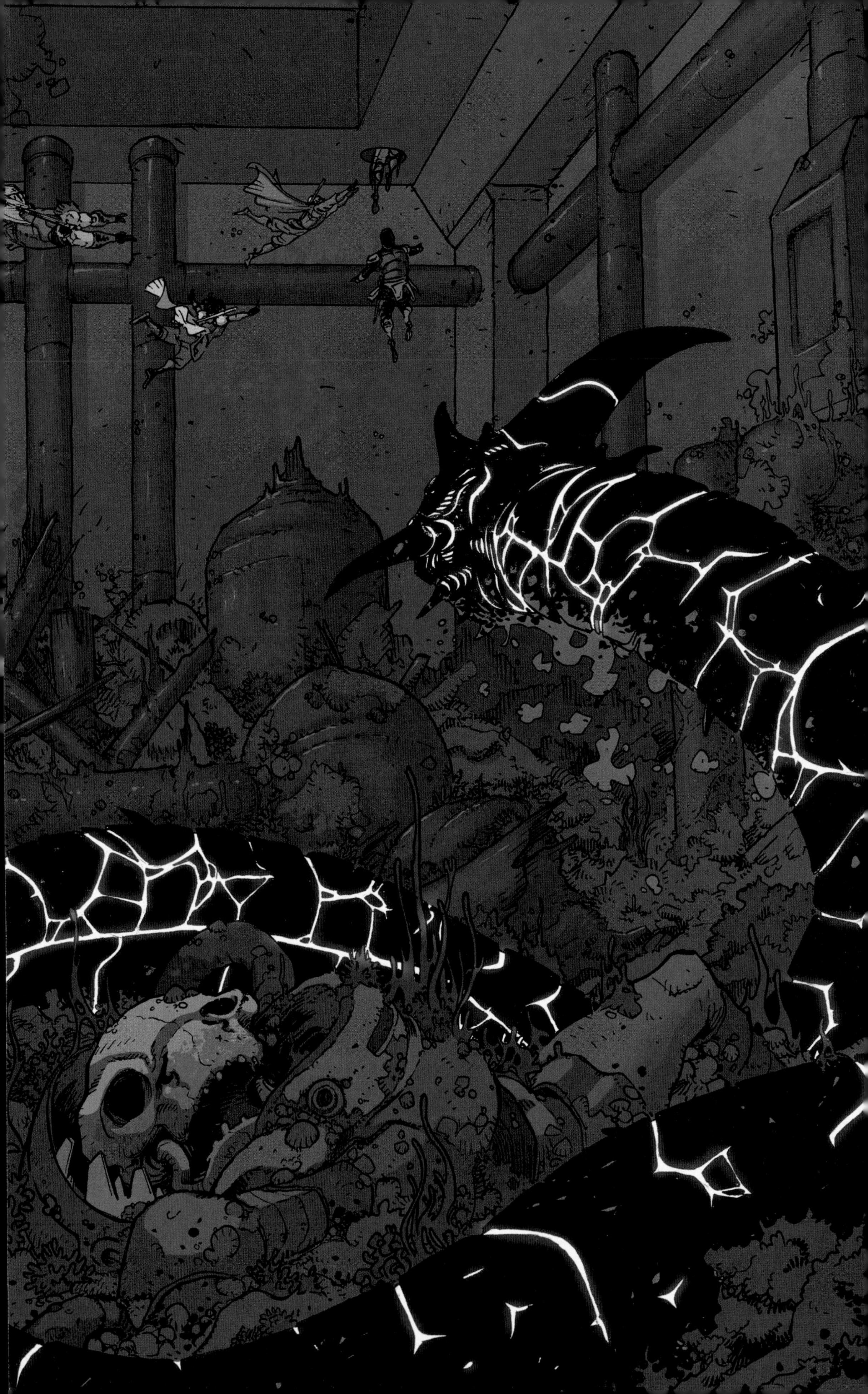

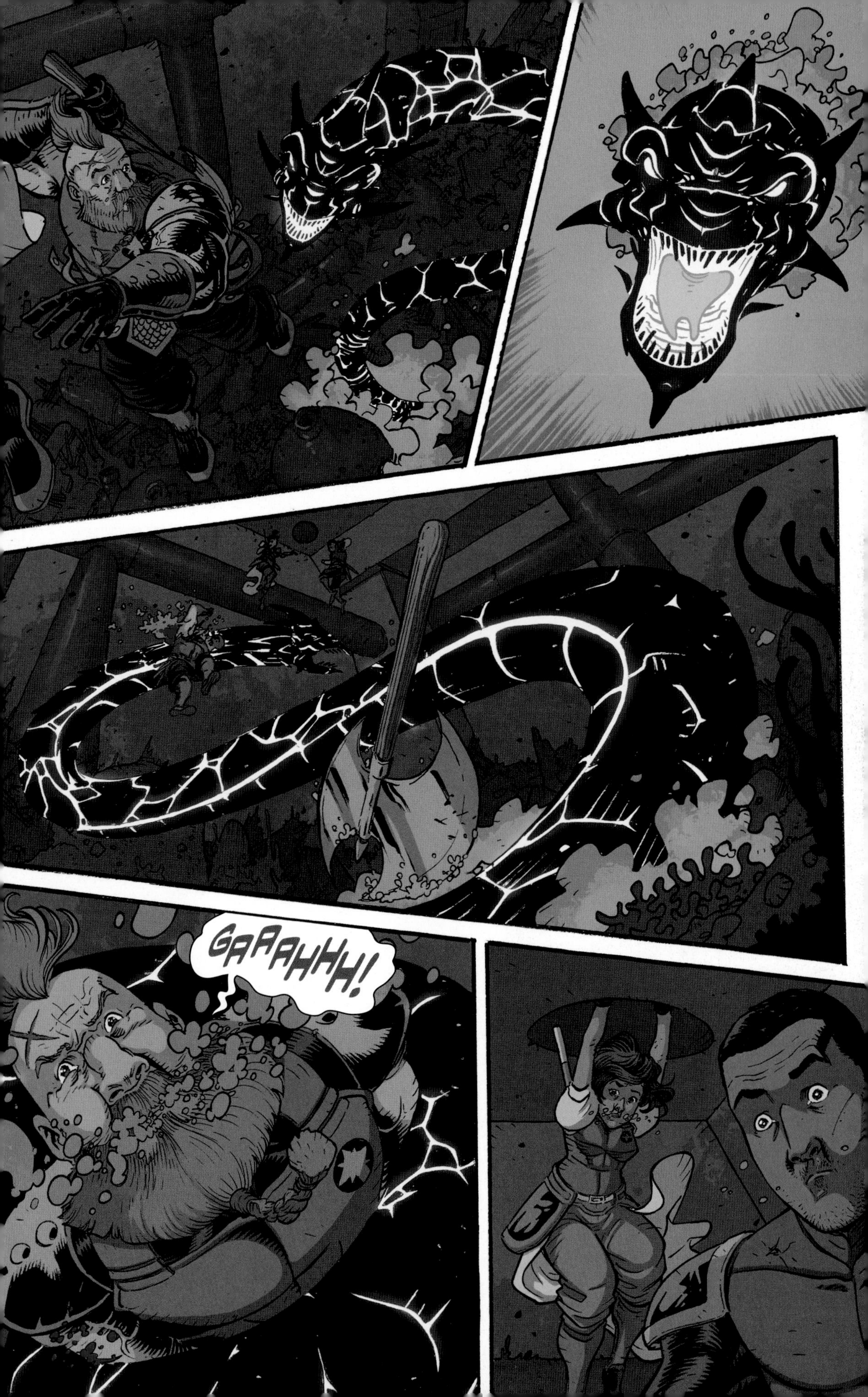
GAAAHHH!

SOMETHING'S GOT HOLD OF FINN!

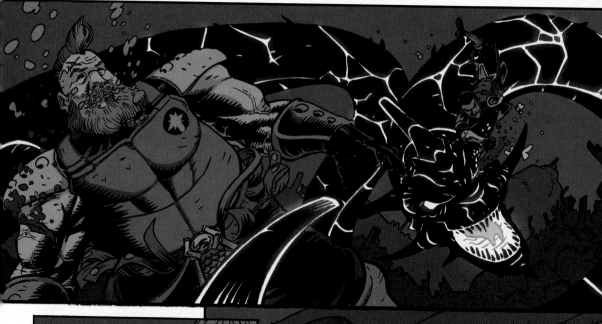

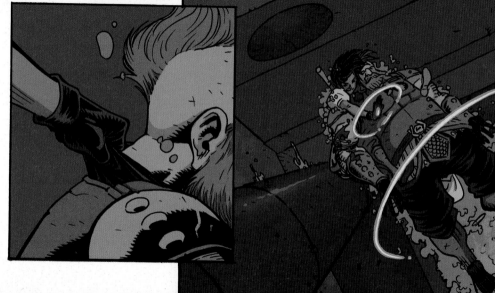

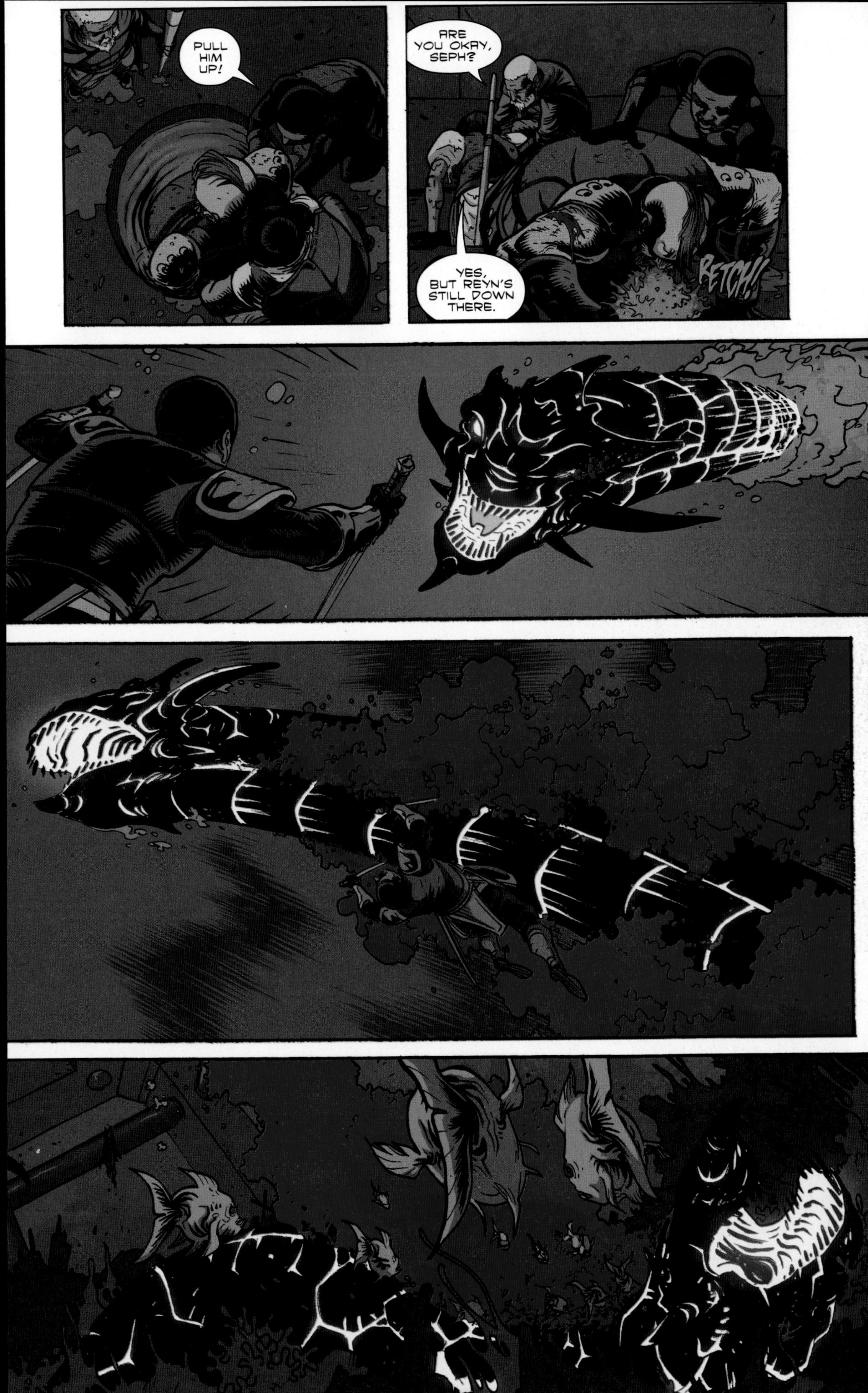
PULL HIM UP!
ARE YOU OKAY, SEPH?
YES, BUT REYN'S STILL DOWN THERE.
RETCH!!

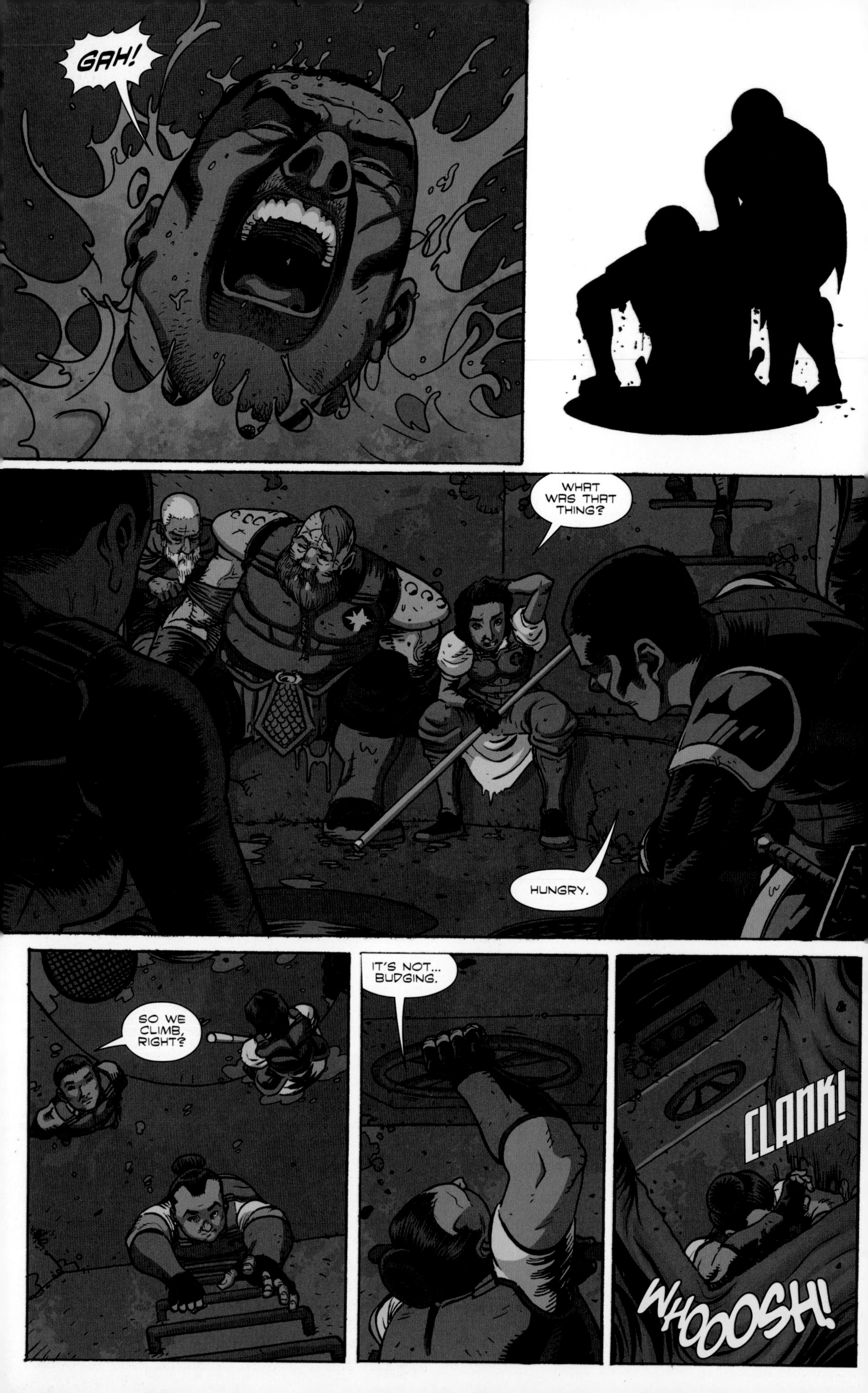
GAH!
WHAT WAS THAT THING?
HUNGRY.
SO WE CLIMB, RIGHT?
IT'S NOT... BUDGING.
CLANK!
WHOOOSH!

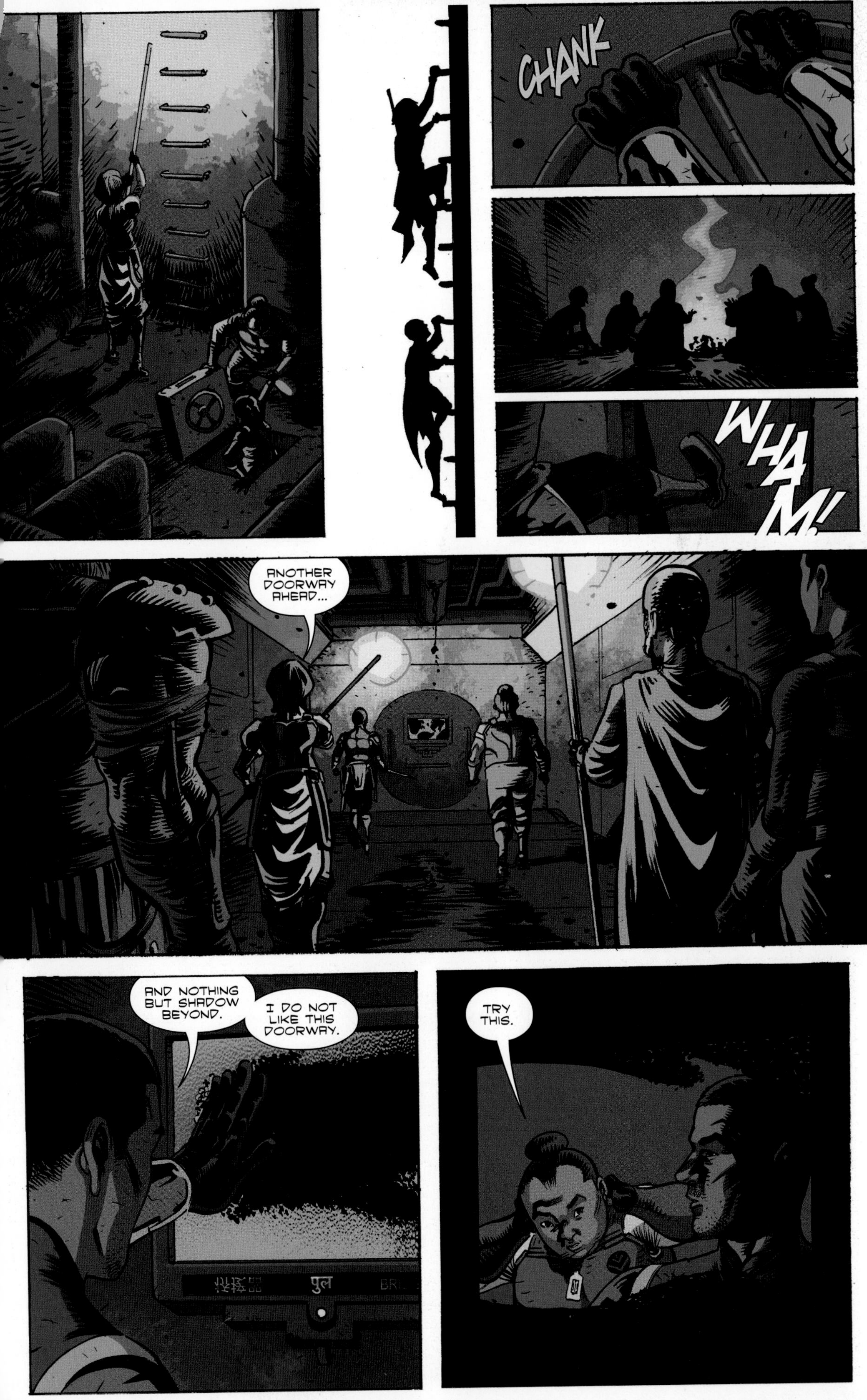
CHANK
WHAM!
ANOTHER DOORWAY AHEAD...
AND NOTHING BUT SHADOW BEYOND.
I DO NOT LIKE THIS DOORWAY.
पुल
TRY THIS.

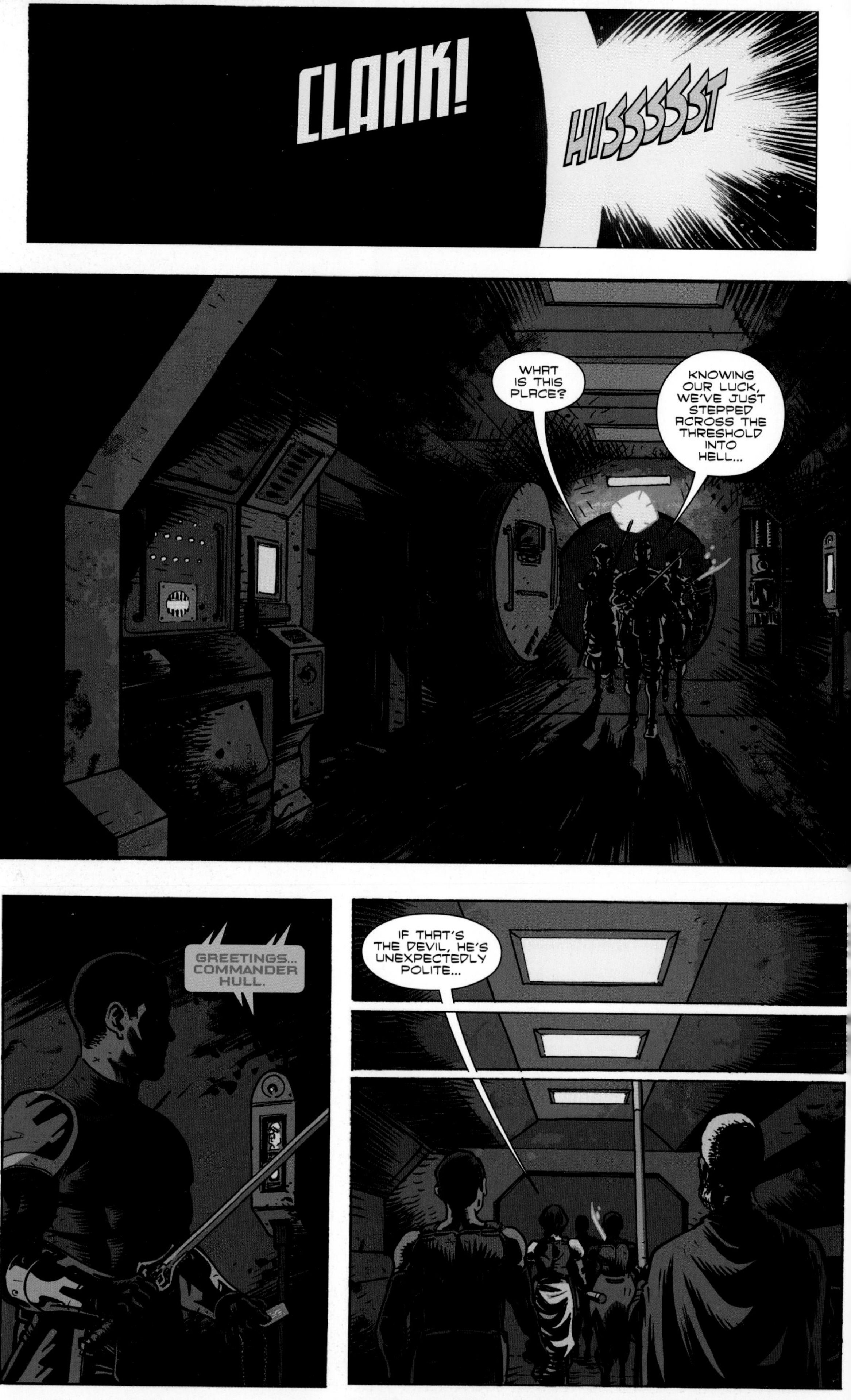
CLANK!
HISSSSST
WHAT IS THIS PLACE?
KNOWING OUR LUCK, WE'VE JUST STEPPED ACROSS THE THRESHOLD INTO HELL...
GREETINGS... COMMANDER HULL.
IF THAT'S THE DEVIL, HE'S UNEXPECTEDLY POLITE...

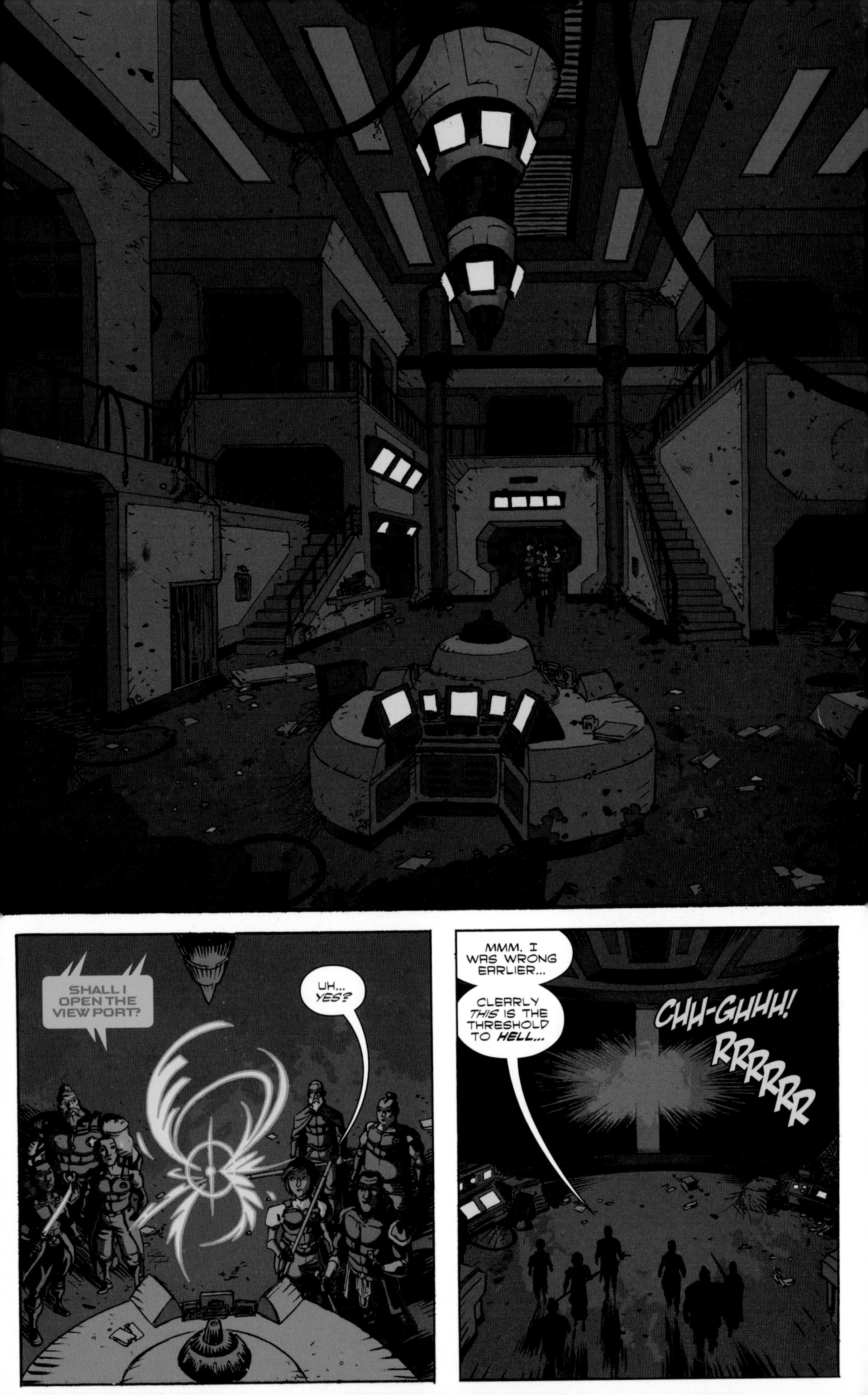
SHALL I OPEN THE VIEW PORT?
UH... *YES?*
MMM. I WAS WRONG EARLIER...
CLEARLY *THIS* IS THE THRESHOLD TO ***HELL...***
CHU-GHHH!
RRRRRR

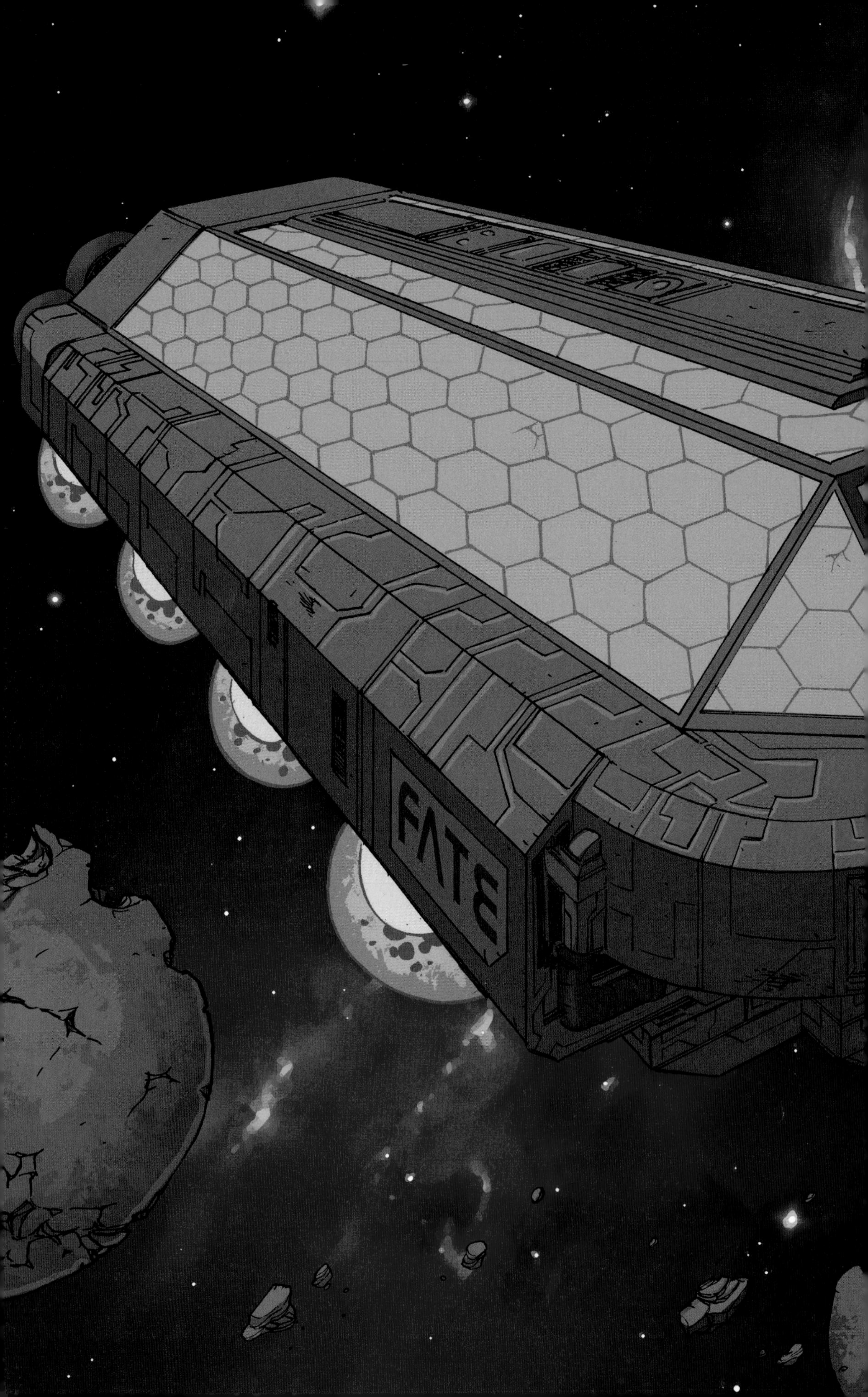
FATE

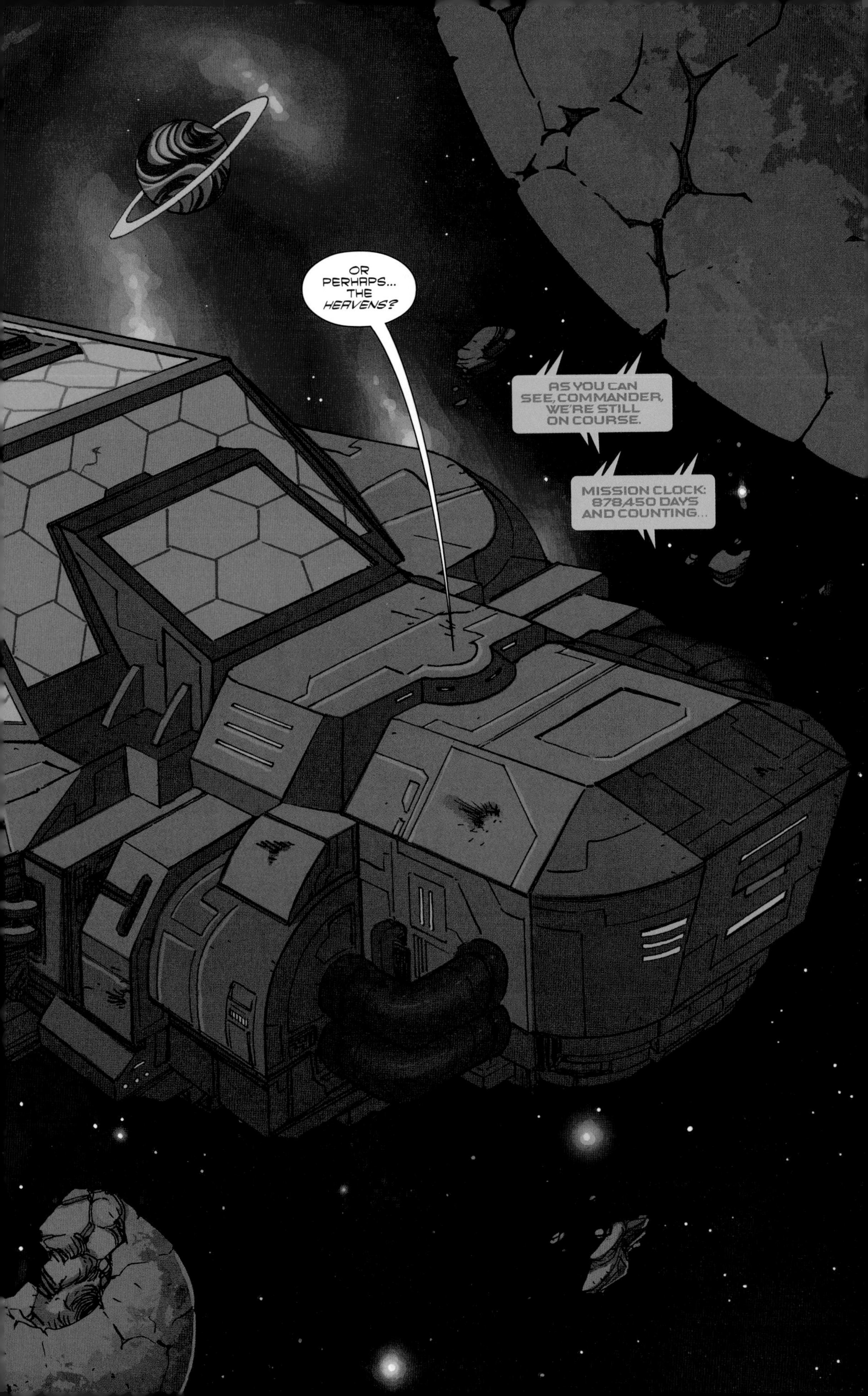
OR PERHAPS... THE *HEAVENS?*
AS YOU CAN SEE, COMMANDER, WE'RE STILL ON COURSE.
MISSION CLOCK: 878,450 DAYS AND COUNTING...

COVER GALLERY

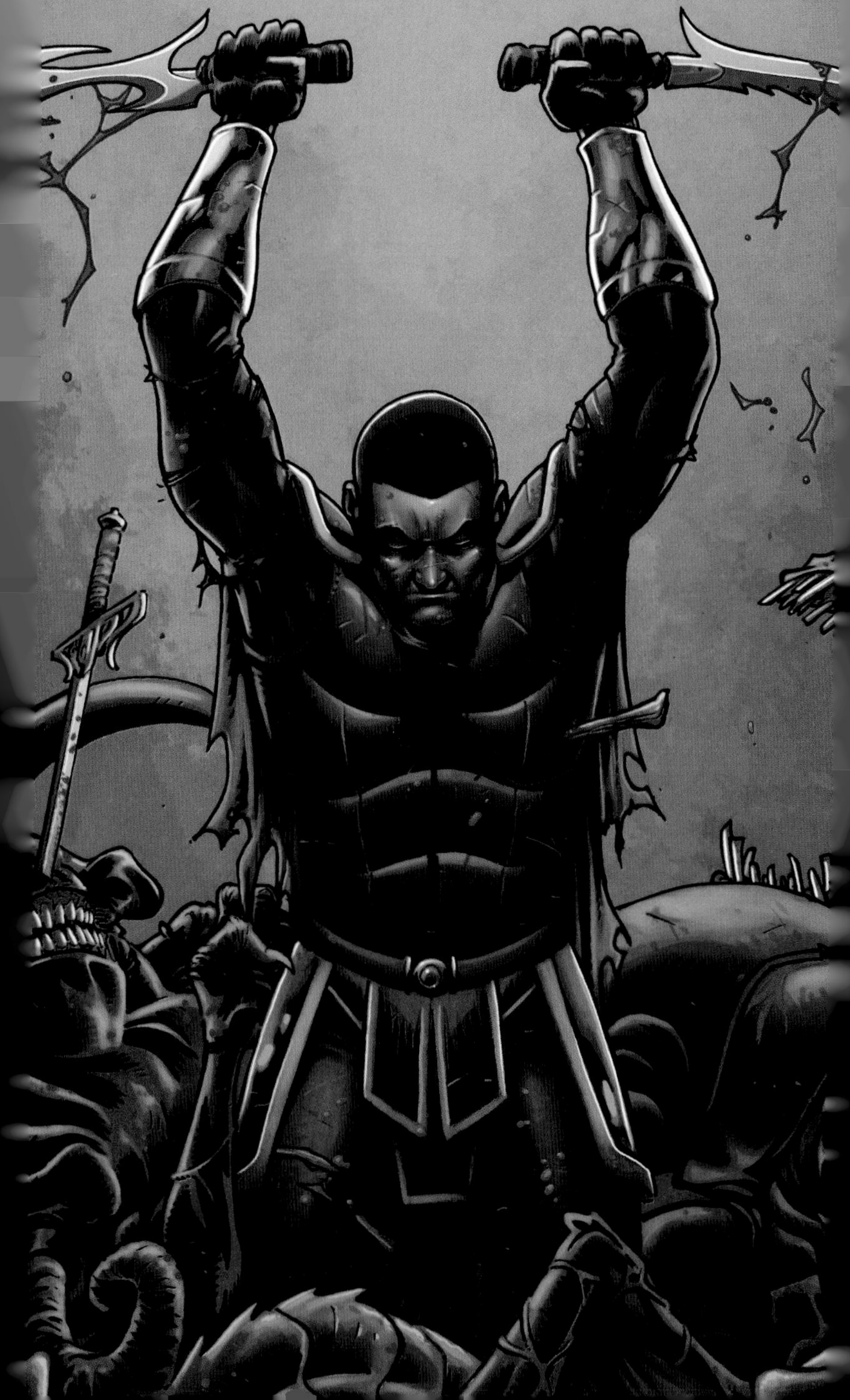

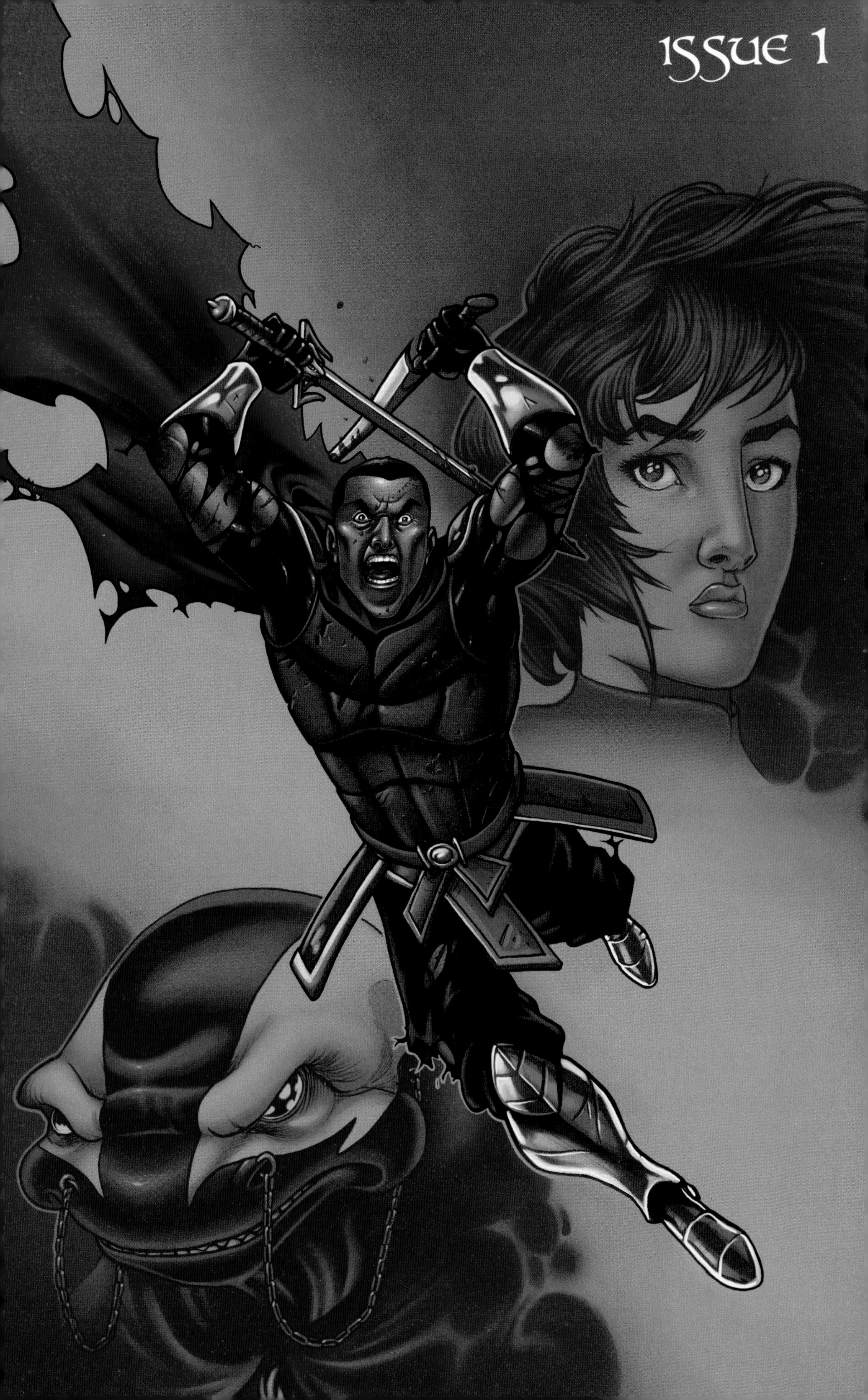
ISSUE 1

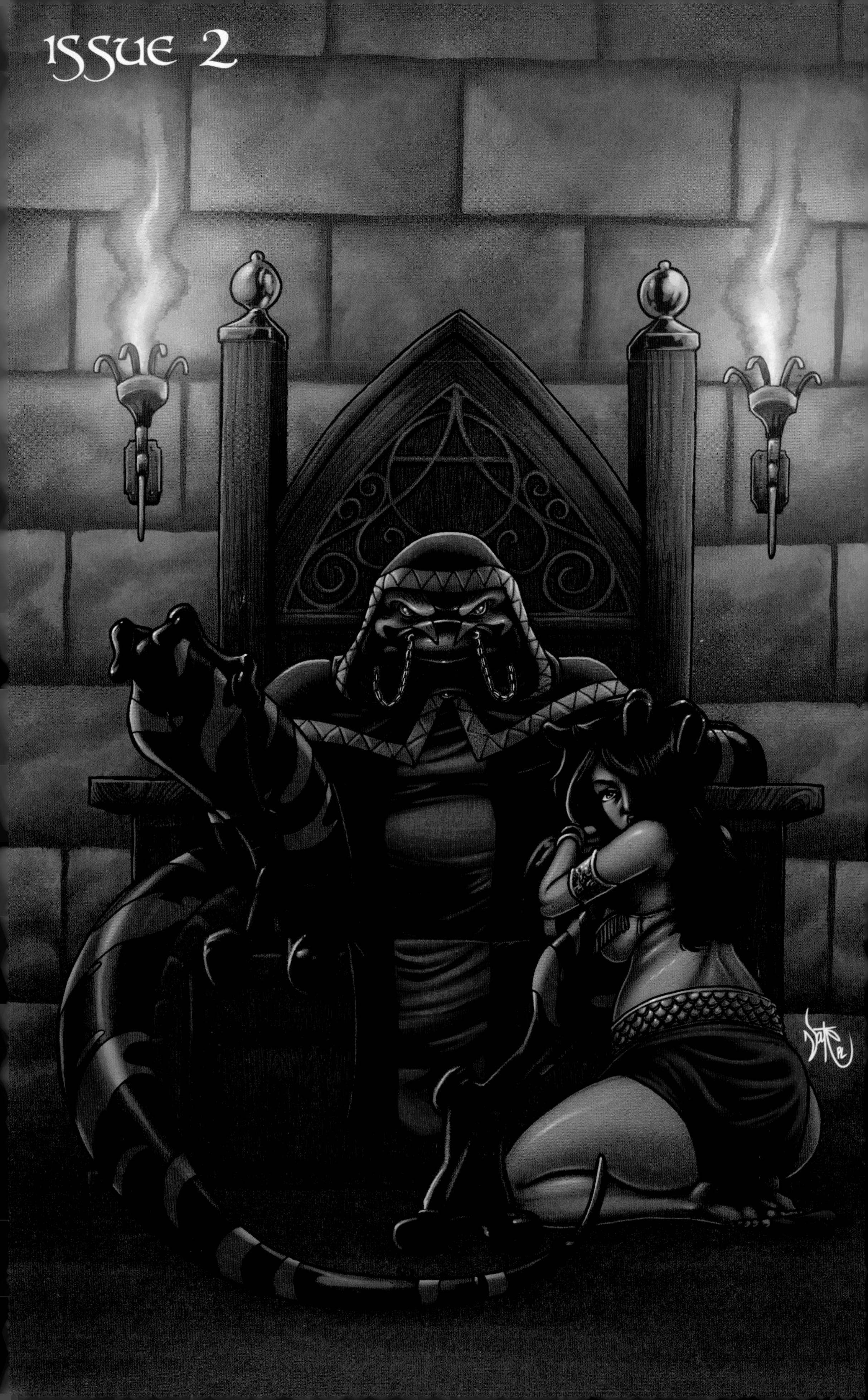
ISSUE 2

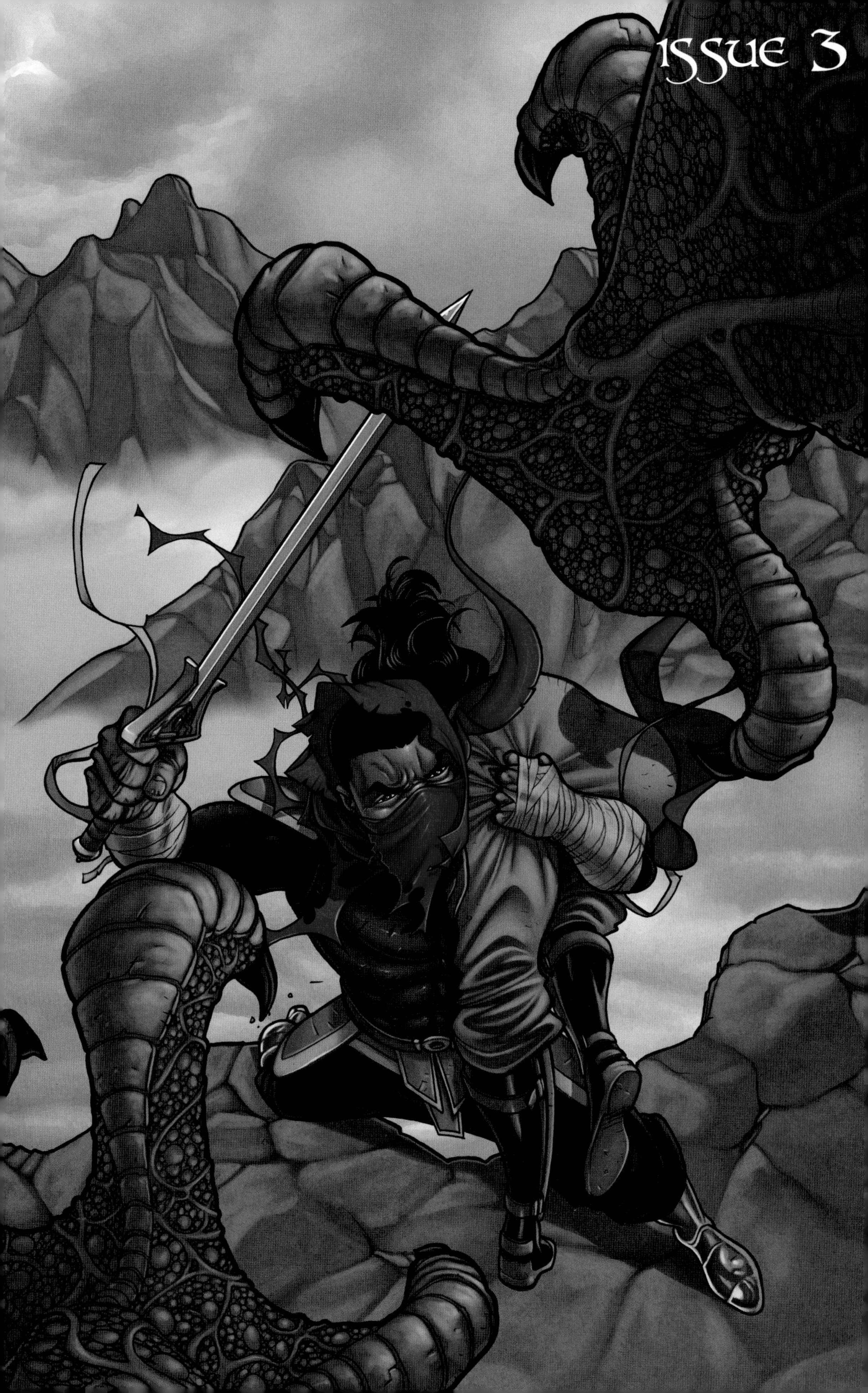
ISSUE 3

ISSUE 4

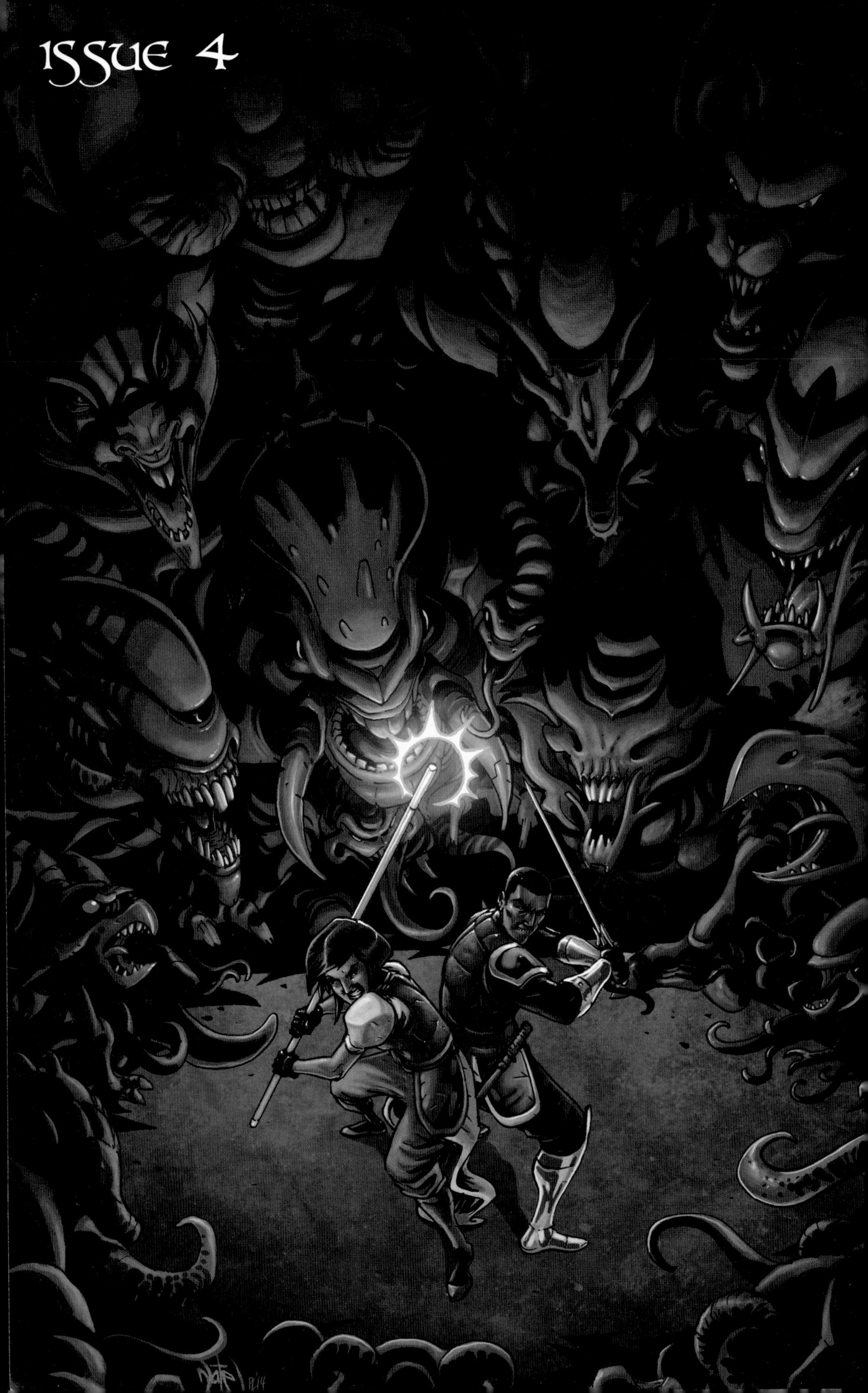

ISSUE 5

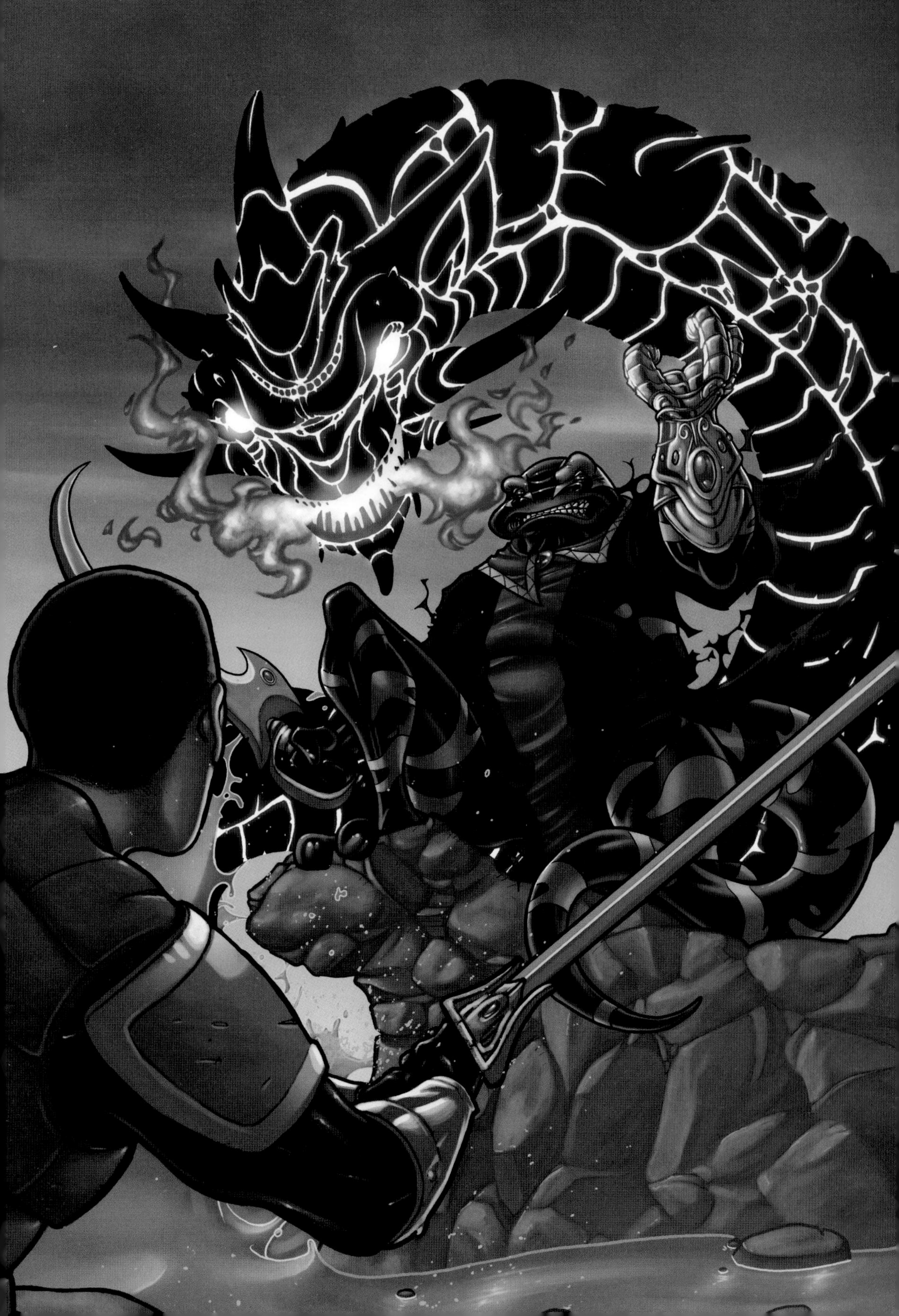

Concept Gallery

With original descriptions from the scripts

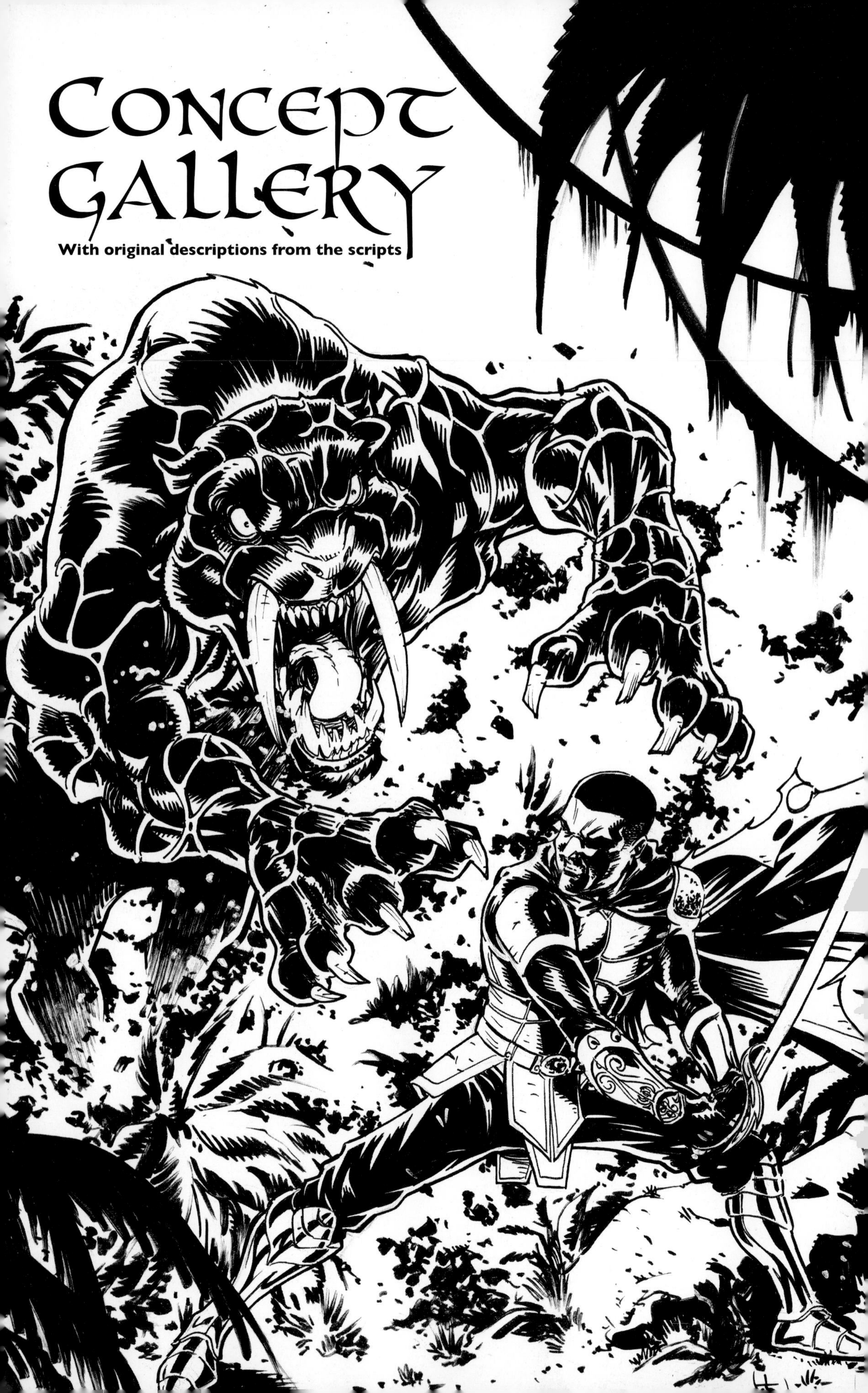

Reyn

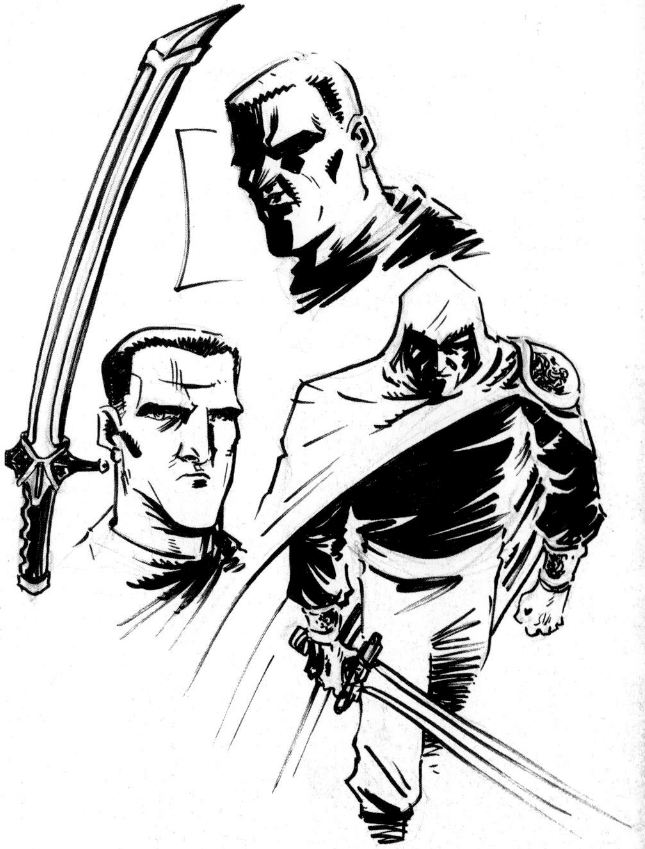

He's tall, his classic warrior architecture betraying countless hours of study, training and conditioning. Handsome and clean shaven, his hair is trim even out here in the middle of nowhere. He shouldn't have the muscle-bound physique of a Conan, or some other steroid-pumped barbarian. Ideally he should have the frame of a Special Forces soldier - compact and muscular, but still sleek and quick. Think a swimmer's physique. Or a panther's.

He wears black leather armor, and as he approaches, there's a definitely retrofitted style to everything, as though Reyn's weapons and equipment may have once had another life, long, long ago.

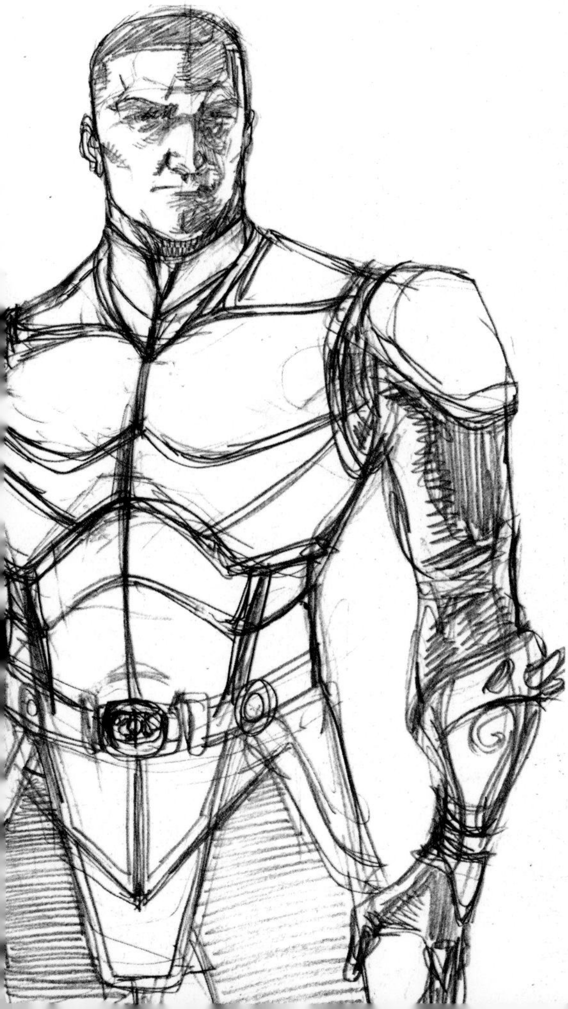

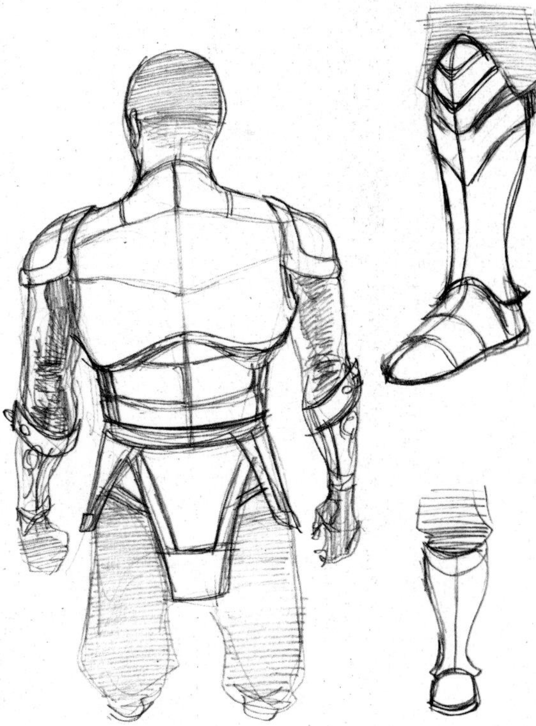

Seph

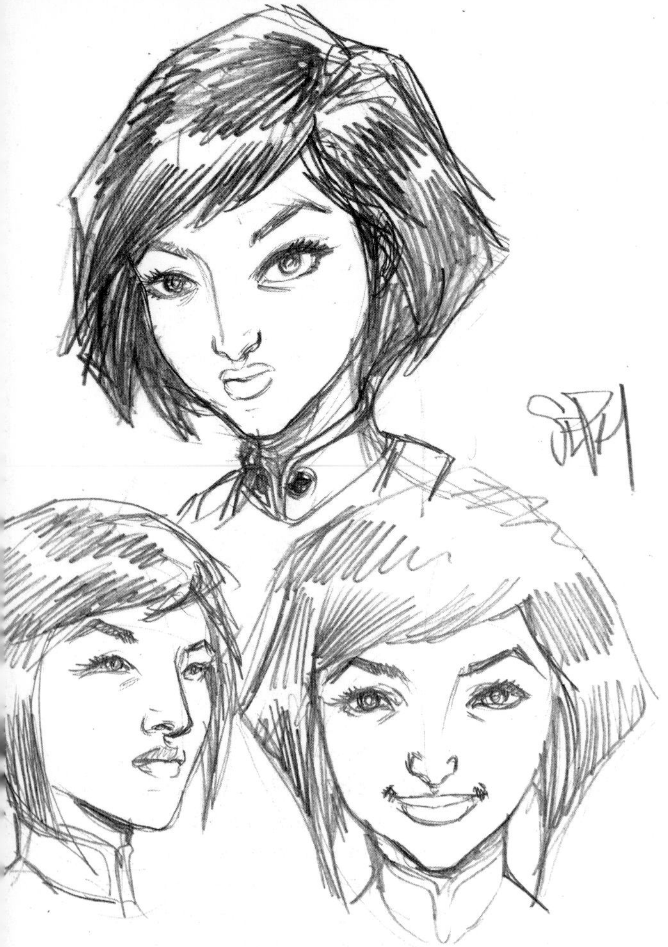
SEPH

A woman in a white hood and cloak watches Reyn pass, bangs from her short haircut hanging in her face. This is Seph, a "sorceress." She wears white armor underneath that cloak with the sigil of a red cross on her breastplate, She's a member of a clandestine order, the Followers of Tek, thought of as heretics for their belief that Fate was once an advanced kingdom. She carries a staff as she stands on a crate or barrel, proselytizing to the few citizens who have come to hear her speak, though we won't hear the sermon.
She's dark complected, with a South Asian ethnicity, though it's hard to identify her as one race or another. In fact, we'll find that many of the citizens of Fate look to be a mix between Asian and Indian descent.

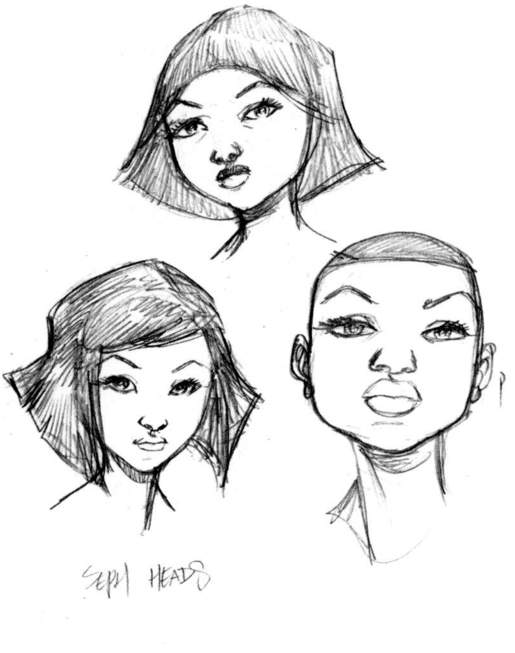
SEPH HEADS

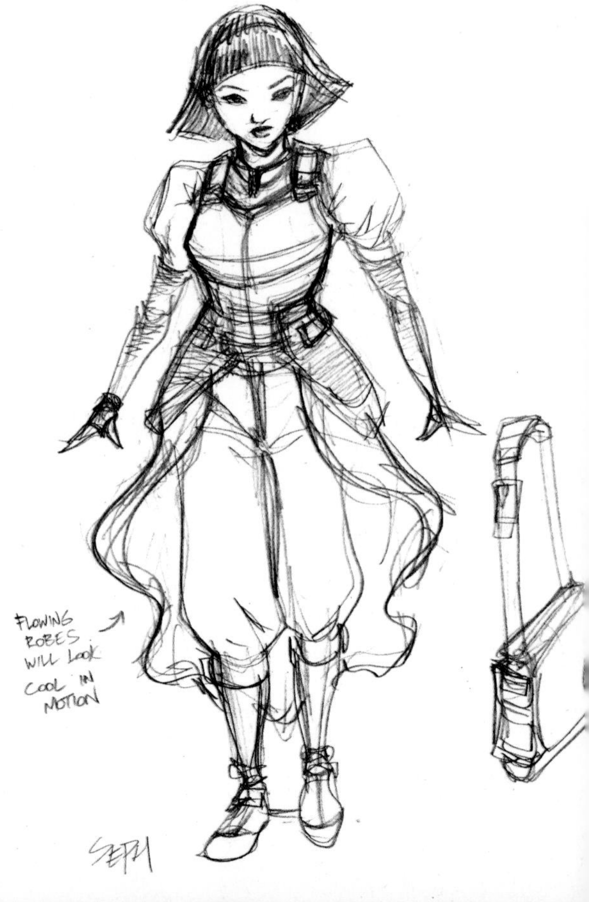
FLOWING ROBES WILL LOOK COOL IN MOTION
SEPH

HEALING   ENGINEERING   NAVIGATION   ENERGY   ARCHIVES

The overall look of the land of "Fate":

If it was to look like some historic era, it might be a cross between the Dark Ages and the Old West frontier (leaning more towards the former). Technology much beyond the wheel or the lever is rare. It's a simple time because its people fear complexity.

Woven into their religion, their scripture and mythology is the belief that technology is the Devil's playground. That if the heretical Followers of Tek were right, and they were once a more advanced civilization, those advances lead to their ultimate downfall.

TEK LOGO

NAVIGATION

ENGINEERING

ENERGY

ARCHIVES

MEDIC

The Followers of Tek believe in a different history for the land. They don't know everything, but they know more than most. They each wear sigils - disciplines they were taught over generations, handed down from mothers and fathers, going back to their ancestors who were the original crew aboard Fate - but this part of their history has been forgotten. They have sigils for agriculture, chemistry, biology, mathematics, etc. All sorts of scientific disciplines. When we finally come aboard the bridge of Fate, we'll see control stations have symbols that correspond to the Tek sigils, too.

Teks

These are our main Teks. Let's give them a diverse mix of looks please, but all wear white armor and cloaks similar to Seph's dress. And each is armed with electrically-charged staves like Seph's.

Fin

Fin is large and looks very Nordic, a giant among men, with flowing red hair and a braided beard. He wears a sigil, like Seph, on his broad breastplate – this one representing "energy."

Haron

a woman, wearing an "engineer" sigil

Britt

wearing a "navigation" sigil

Bram

wears a "computer/archives" sigil.

Adon

(white hair and beard – definite Obi Wan Kenobi vibe), their eldest member and leader, wears the same healing/medical sigil, for he is Seph's father.

FATE

Widest of wide angle shots, from space. Pulling back… way back to reveal "Fate" is merely a giant starship hurtling through the cosmos. Pink and blue gaseous nebula clouds drape across the field of stars – I want this to be a brilliant and Cosmos-worthy starscape.

I don't know how we can show its scale, exactly, but it's massive. Perhaps it hurtles past a moon or other planetoid for comparison. As we discussed, it should be hundreds of miles long… the size of a small continent. Or a big island. I mean, this thing has to be massively big and complex.

The majority of its span is made up of environmental space – that is, the section of the ship dedicated to cultivating and supporting transplanted Earth topography and land. I don't know how you might envision this – but in my head, it's like a massive bubble (though not one single shape – probably cells of a transparent hull spread out geometrically along the x-axis of the ship). Even from this distance, we should see these transparent cells contain mountains, green valleys, plains, deserts, rivers, lakes, streams and ponds, as well as weather and atmosphere. (Okay, we might not be close enough to see weather – but next issue we can get into a lot of details).

Depending on the angle, we might see the thrust of mighty drives (which probably take up almost as much space as the environmental section). Everything should be human in design, and distinctively different from the Venn technology.

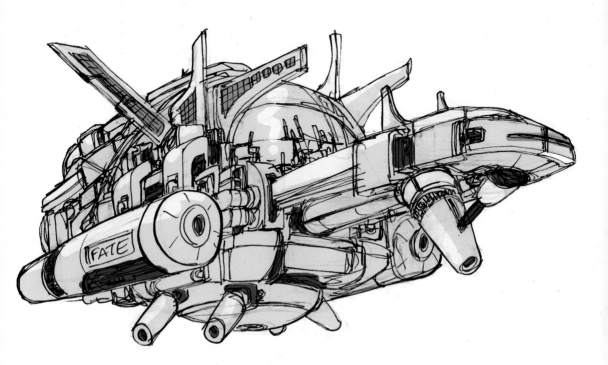

The Venn

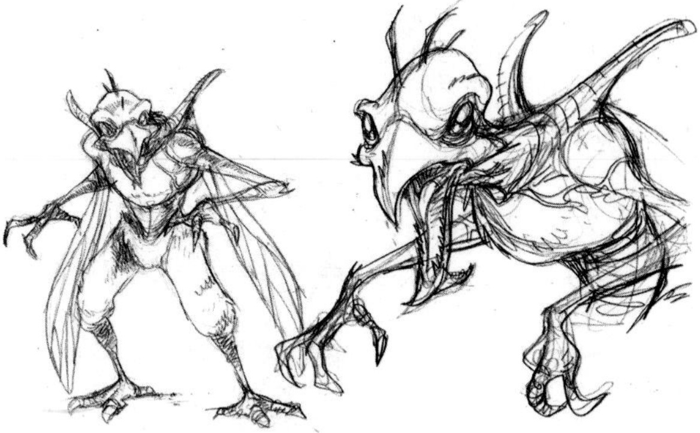

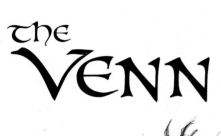

Nathan's original idea for the aliens was to make them avian in appearance, but we settled on the salamander-esque appearance because the colors were exciting and bold.

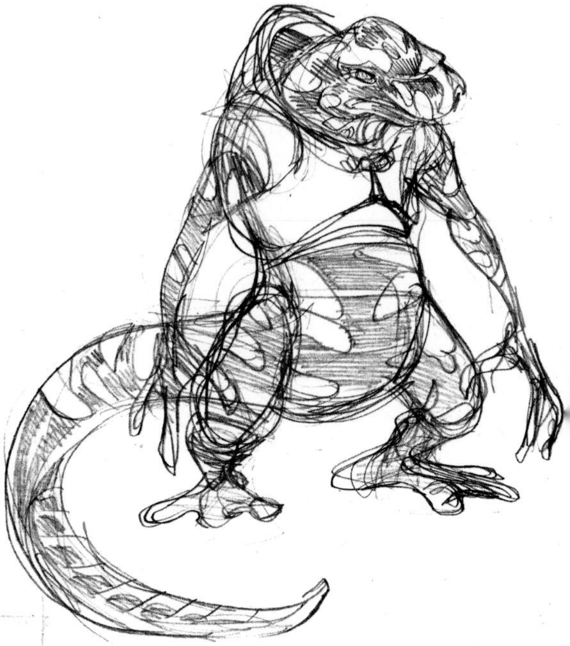

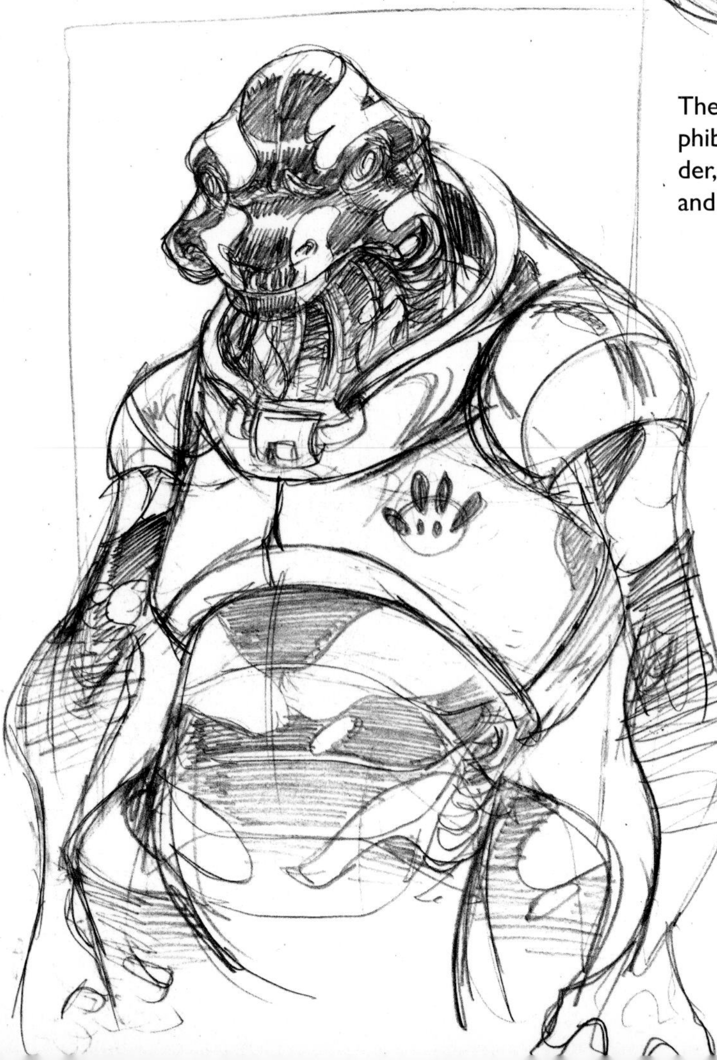

The Venn look somewhat like a humanoid amphibian, somewhat resembling a fire salamander, with patterns of brightly colored stripes and blotches against a deep black skin.